The Whispering Horror

The Whispering Horror

By Eddy C. Bertin

Shadow Publishing

THE WHISPERING HORROR

ISBN: 978-0-9539032-7-6
Shadow Publishing, 194 Station Road, Kings Heath,
Birmingham, B14 7TE, UK
david.sutton986@btinternet.com
http://www.shadowpublishing.webeasysite.co.uk

DEDICATION

Mostly this is done after you're dead and suddenly become a master of great literature. Happily I'm still alive to do it myself. This is dedicated to Yvette, my wife, who has been with me all those bloody long years of writing and writing, and sometimes getting something published.

To my daughter Brenda who fortunately didn't follow in my blood-drenched footsteps of horror but made her own way in theatre and movies. To my son-in-law Bardia who sets his steps into music.

And to my lovely granddaughter Oona Noor who is still too young to hear my horror stories, but she does like my fairy tales of princesses and such stuff.

Last but not least this dedication would be incomplete if it didn't include my old friend David Sutton himself, whose early fanzines gave me inspiration and the push to keep on writing, so David, this is for you for all the good you did for the horror genre, in magazines, books and stories, over forty years or more.

I love you all.

Contents

WHISPERS OF HORROR:
EDDY C. BERTIN
By David A. Sutton

M Y FIRST COMMUNICATION with Eddy Bertin was when he began to submit essays to my small press magazine, *Shadow: Fantasy Literature Review*. His first article appeared in the second issue in 1968, 'Charles Birkin: Master of Cruelty and Horror'. It soon became apparent that Eddy was one of those horror aficionados who could turn his hand to anything—book reviews, articles and fiction. In the following seven years he contributed more than eighty essays, biographies, bibliographies and reviews to the magazine, often providing biographies of the lesser known European writers, such as Maurice Limat and Jean Ray. He contributed many items on H. P. Lovecraft's work, amongst reams of other useful and interesting material. I owe Eddy a great debt of gratitude—*Shadow* was improved immeasurably by his input.

And it was through *Shadow* that I discovered Eddy's fiction, publishing 'A Taste of Rain and Darkness' in my short-lived fiction magazine *Weird Window* in 1970. His first professional sale was to Herbert van Thal's *The Ninth Pan Book of Horror Stories*, 'The Whispering Horror', published in 1968. In the same year 'The City, Dying' appeared in John Carnell's *New Writings in SF* volume 13. A great many genre stories followed, written in Dutch, Flemish and German as well as English. And he has been a genre writer ever since. Collections of his work have been published in Dutch, the first, *De Achtjaarlijkse God* ("The Eight-yearly God"), appeared from Bruna SF in 1971. However, he has never seen a collection of his tales published in English, an oversight that I am delighted to rectify and to be able to introduce many new readers to his distinctive perspective on the horror tale.

Eddy Charly Bertin was born in Hamburg-Altona, West Germany, in December 1944, reportedly in an air raid shelter during a bombing run. His father was Belgian and had been deported to Germany to work there after the collapse of the Belgian army. He met and married

Eddy's mother there, who was German, which led to a not always happy childhood: When the family moved to live in Belgium in the years after the war, everybody in his father's native country hated anything German. Eddy quickly learned to run very fast when the "natives" were after him, as he was, of course, part German. Eddy is proudly Belgian though, and he still lives in Gentbrugge, Flanders, in a dwelling called "Dunwich House".

Ghent at that time, late forties, early fifties, was almost a Victorian city, streets and houses lit by gaslight. Eddy's unhappy situation was amplified when as a child he lived with his parents in an old house, the attic of which he still believes was haunted by an unseen, evil entity whose presence he felt as soon as he entered the dwelling. He says he had one encounter with a dark, hideous, eyeless thing coming down from the attic, which resulted in a loss of consciousness and left him forever with a dread of anything to do with the real occult. Though Eddy has an exhaustive library of occult material which he uses for his stories, he has never wanted at attend a séance or have any direct contact with the supernatural, it still scares him. He had hideous nightmares for years which finally stopped when he began writing them down, finally turning them into his fledgling stories. 'The Whispering Horror' was based on those nightmares, about encounters with the invisible and evil things existing among us. Only years later did he learn that his parents during his early years had been very active with the occult, holding séances!

He started writing at thirteen and sold his first stories, after ten years of trying in Belgium, to British and American anthologies of horror and SF from 1967. He has published over 100 stories in English, several of them featured in *The Year's Best Horror Stories*, and there have been over 1600 appearances worldwide in more than ten languages, including in Poland, Yugoslavia and Japan. In his native language and under his own name he published over twenty-five books: novels, story collections and three poetry collections for adults, all while holding down a nine-to five job as a bank employee. Under various pseudonyms he published over sixty pulp novels and serials, westerns, novels with plenty of sex and horror, thrillers, murder mysteries, comic erotic novels, and so on. He remarks that, "Fortunately, these paid more than my literary work did". During the sixties and seventies he was very active in fan writing, working for some fifty fanzines, and finally publishing his own *SF-Gids* (SF Guide), which ran for 140 issues over eighteen years.

When the boom in horror disappeared in the Netherlands in 1984, rather than switching to writing mystery or historical romances, he continued in the horror field, but now writing for children. However, he grumbles that, "All of my novels have to be cut because they are mostly too gruesome for younger readers!" For young adults he has completed about twenty-seven novels. An example is the *Valentina* series (1993), a projected series of thirteen books which ended up as a series of seven novels about a young witch who comes into contact with all kinds of weird creatures, including some Lovecraftian ones in the trilogy which form the final three books. Most of these have been translated for publication in Sweden, Denmark and Germany. Unfortunately censorship for Young Adult novels in Germany thwarted publication there.

For ten years he was secretary of the "Society of Horror", for younger readers, working for their quarterly magazine and publishing stories in their yearly anthology. Then during an amalgamation a new publisher took over who didn't like horror, so along with six other Dutch fellow writers, Eddy was dropped. He sent in five projects for new novels, but nothing ever came of it. At this time he completed *Anyaka, switchworlds* a dark fantasy YA novel, and also worked on a collection, *Horror Yearbook* also for younger readers. These two are still in the works.

A full time author now, (though the distinction is moot, given that he was even more productive as a writer when he was a bank employee) Eddy intermittently writes for adults (radio plays, short movies, the occasional short story) and in 1999 a new collection of horror & SF stories was published, *Krijsende muren* (Screaming walls). Recent publications in English are 'Dunwich Dreams, Dunwich Screams', a Lovecraftian novella in his "European Mythos" series (in *Tales out of Dunwich*, 2005) and 'When You'll Be Ten', a psychological horror novelette (in *Cemetery Dance*, 2005). 'Belinda's Coming Home' appeared in *Alone on the Darkside: Echoes from Shadows of Horror*, but— and these anecdotes are far from ephemeral—Eddy bought a copy at a bookshop in Dublin, completely unaware that it had appeared; he never received a copy of the book from the publisher or was ever paid for it. 'My Fingers are Eating Me', which was due in *The Cthulhuian Singularity* and which was cancelled, means that you'll read it first in this collection. A new collection of his best science fiction stories is due in Dutch this year, *Sterrensplinters* ("Star Shards").

Eddy married Yvette, a teacher, in 1967, and in 1969 their only daughter Brenda was born. She has had an active career mostly in theatre and musicals (among them the Belgian version of *Jungle Book* followed by an adaption as a TV series), acted in two commercial movies (*Daens* was a nominee for the Oscar in 1992) and lots of guest parts in Belgian and Dutch TV series. Eddy's wife and he are now both retired, have travelled all over the world the last ten years, while they're still in good health. Also, "Lots of babysitting when our granddaughter Oona Noor (almost four now) visits. Unfortunately she isn't old enough to enjoy horror stories yet". He is still writing the occasional story and doing lots of book and DVD reviews for internet sites and the Dutch libraries. Eddy never lacks of anything to read: his personal library takes up four rooms (one and a half floors) and covers some 30,000 books and magazines of horror and SF but he still hasn't read half of them. But he still has time for a few other interests such as music (never writes without it, from classic to pop, rock and soundtracks), theatre and even stand-up comedy, especially if it's dark. And of course, with a library of some thousands of DVDs: "I just enjoy watching Asian horror and ghost movies, and B-movies of things with red eyes and long fangs and claws, all of which my wife hates!"

There's nothing definitive about an Eddy Bertin story. Just take a look through the author's notes at the end of this collection and you will see that, for any given story, he writes, re-writes, translates into more than one language, expands, transforms to another genre and generally is not inclined to leave a story rest on its laurels! 'Behind the White Wall' was written as both a science fiction and a horror story in Dutch in 1964, with the horror version translated into English in the 1970s. It also had the luck to be made into a short film!

Once the preparation for this collection was well underway, Eddy suggested half jokingly that it might be re-titled *Masks of Terror*, due to a running theme in his stories: the masking of personality and intent in his characters. I think readers will readily pick up on this idea in several of the tales, not just the obvious one, 'A Whisper of Leathery Wings'. This revenge story (with its monstrous supernatural creature) also links to others where vengeance is horribly in evidence, such as the elaborate retribution conducted by a slighted student in 'Ten'.

Then there are atmospheric, moody tales that only the Eddy's pen could have created, with their European flavour, such as the sad, tormented lives of the characters in both 'Composed of Cobwebs' and 'A Taste of Rain and Darkness'. I sure you will find these tales hauntingly memorable.

And there's horror of a more ghoulish kind, such as in the title story and in 'Something Small, Something Hungry', with its circus theme and the police investigation into a spate of apparent suicides. And finally, Eddy's interest in H. P. Lovecraft's "Cthulhu Mythos" is expressed in two very powerful novellas: 'Dunwich Dreams, Dunwich Screams' re-locates the legendary New England Dunwich to the very real village in Suffolk, and explores the historical destruction of the place in a fierce storm, but with a gleeful injection of the occult, Mythos trappings and forbidden books. 'My Fingers Are Eating Me' is set in the London Underground and is an extremely dark tale told as a series of reports and diary entries focusing on a Belgian freelance reporter sent to write a piece on "Unknown London". And he discovers that the underbelly of the Underground is much darker and terrifying that he could have imagined.

There are fourteen stories published here, of madness, supernatural terror and gruesome horror and all flavoured with Eddy's fantastic slant on genre fiction. Enjoy!

David A. Sutton
February 2013

COMPOSED OF COBWEBS

A S HE SAT there, resting his head on his hands, two scrawled white spots on the icy steering-wheel, his thoughts seemed to be composed of cobwebs; they drifted in his face as if brought by a playful wind, but before he could touch them to discover what they really were, they dissolved into silken threads, which broke and tore as he reached out to clasp them.

He had just got back inside the car, after having rung the door bell in vain at Radstone's flat. The windows were cold and unlit, and there was no answer to his ringing. He had seen the darkened windows as soon as he arrived, but he had tried anyway, not wanting to face the thought that Radstone wasn't home. Radstone was always home, ready for a drink and a chat, and maybe some TV if there was an interesting programme or a late night film. Where could he have gone to? Well, it hardly mattered, he wasn't home, and that was it. The safe haven he had driven to so gladly was empty and cold.

Spots danced before his eyes, and he closed them for a few seconds, willing the spots to disappear. As soon as he had closed his eyelids, however, the shadows were there too, shrouding the world with their abominable darkness, and he jerked his eyes open again. The shadows were so close already, he couldn't risk them getting any nearer. Even now he spotted them in the driving mirror, a dark grey lingering mist, weaving ghostly fingers at him: The street lights beyond shivered faintly through the shadows.

They had never been as close as now, which was why he had finally driven to Radstone (with whom he wasn't that friendly after all) just to be with someone, anyone. A few strong drinks on his empty stomach and an evening of small talk would have kept them away, at least for tonight. Still his fingers hesitated on the ignition key, not wanting to turn the engine on yet. Why shouldn't he wait a few minutes? Maybe Radstone had just gone out to get cigarettes, or out for a drink, and would be coming home any minute now. But that was ridiculous, Radstone never went out for a drink. Still he decided to wait a few minutes, just in case.

His head was aching again, and he tried to recall how it all had started; he couldn't focus his thoughts, nothing appeared in its proper perspective in the foggy grey blur of his mind. The headaches, that had been the starting point, the headaches which had begun troubling him. He had been working too hard and too late, never getting enough sleep or time for a rest. Every day in a stuffy office, then in the evening hours trying to break into the writing business, sitting up hammering on an old typewriter whose keys always jammed, keeping himself awake with strong coffee, till two, three o'clock in the morning, and then again to the office. He thought of his evenings, coming home to find the rejection slips and returned stories and articles in the mail. It began to get frustrating, spending all that time and money for nothing but he had shut the anger within himself, fed on it, and had continued. Then the spots had begun to appear, coloured spots and circles and dots, dancing before him in the air. He had his eyes tested, but they were all right, there was no reason for him to see spots, except that he needed rest. The office had become more demanding, mountains of paperwork which could be done by any imbecile, and he often wondered if this was why he had spent all those years at school.

He shook his head to make the thoughts go away but they stayed with him. He started the engine again, and drove away. Maybe Lucy and Brett would be home? It wasn't so very far to their place. Looking back, he saw the shadows starting to follow him, keeping the same speed as his car, fat darkish slugs crawling over the pavement stones, along the walls of the houses on both sides of the street.

While driving, the thoughts kept on striking him with black wings. He was always tired, shivering with cold even in the warmth of a summer day. Waking up in the morning was immediately followed by the feeling of not having slept at all, or else by the immense gratitude of being awake, cutting off his nightmarish walks through the haunted dimensions of his mind. He never could remember exactly the face of the terrors that assaulted him during his sleep, they were vague, undefined. Some of the dreams were clear however, so much so that somehow they seemed more real than the car he was driving right now. He remembered sitting in his work room very late, writing or correcting some first-draft manuscripts. Just beside the room was a small stairway, leading upwards to an untenanted room used to store away old junk. He remembered the footsteps coming down those stairs, immensely slow and hollow and threatening, foot-falls coming from somewhere where no one lived. He remembered sitting, shivering with unknown dread, unable to move, only his eyes alive, watching the door which separated him from whatever came downwards. Then the endless moment as the footsteps halted, and something turned the handle of the door, then pushed, and the door opened... and he awoke screaming. Then the nightmare where he was walking along an empty but fully illuminated street, just thinking, and suddenly an icy hand touched the back of his head, freezing him into immobility, during minutes which seemed to stretch into eternity, before he dared turn around, and there was nothing at all behind him. He tried fighting off the nightmares with sleeping pills, but then he began to oversleep too often and got into fights with the superiors at the office, so he had to stop taking them.

That was when the dizzy spells had started. Suddenly his body would seem to feel as rigid as a corpse's, seem to freeze, while his mind began spinning around an uncertain centre somewhere in space. Sometimes he saw his own face and body, while his mind drifted away into an unknown and unknowable darkness. Then the fit passed, and he discovered that his body hadn't stopped moving for even a split second, his movements hadn't faltered one instant. If he had been lighting a cigarette, he was still doing so, and if he had been walking, he still was. No time-lag had happened.

His view cleared and the brakes shrieked loudly as his foot crashed down on the pedal. The screaming car came to stop only a few feet before a bright red traffic light. The idiots, imagine putting lights here where almost no traffic came by. It was like that when the accident with Marciella had happened. No, he didn't want to remem-ber that right now, it was all past and gone, gone, goddamn you idiot, why did you have to think of it? But it was too late, his wandering mind had grasped the scene, and again it flashed through his brain with horrible clarity. He had fallen in love with Marciella two years ago, never thinking himself capable of loving anyone and having proved himself wrong. He had met her at one of those silly parties where everybody knows everybody without really knowing anybody, and made sure to meet her again. When he worked it out for himself, he was surprised to find that though he loved her he hadn't even thought yet of going to bed with her, that had seemed something so far away. Anyway, winning her love didn't turn out as easily as he had expected: she was friendly and kind enough, but she had a steady boyfriend. He had tried to win Marciella without exactly knowing where and how to start, so the results were negligible. They went dancing a few times together when her boyfriend had other things to do, and twice they even slept together, but she made it clear that she had no intention of leaving her boyfriend. It wasn't exactly turning out as he had wanted; he didn't only want her body, he wanted her love, fully and completely.

Then one evening he had seen them leaving her flat, and suddenly he had found his hand on the ignition key of his car, ready to start the engine and crush lover boy against the nearest wall. He checked himself in time, but the hatred had been too real and too deadly, his body had been soaked with sweat, and he had been shaking uncontrollably. He stopped seeing her for some time, but then met them again by accident in a nightclub. They still lived together. They got to chatting about old times, had a drink, and another one, and then a long series of further drinks. He had offered to drive them home, and his head had started spinning as soon as he sat down. The steering-wheel felt unreal in his hands. Marciella got in the back of the car, and her boyfriend sat beside him in the front. He got the engine running at the second try, and with some difficulty got out of the car park. All radio programmes were off the air, and they started singing while he drove. He still heard the tune in his ears, one of those monotonous melodies which keep on returning in the back of one's mind, and he recalled some of the words too, a strange and sad song:

> *"Alone I stand in my ruins,*
> *at home to the wind,*
> *what is left of the walls,*
> *a jagged edge outlined in daylight;*
> *I wonder why my poems*
> *are all composed of cobwebs,*

that shine in the light
of a setting sun..."

A haunting song, whose words he then had noticed for the first time, and had never been able to forget. Long afterwards, he had learned that the song was titled "In Ruins" and had been recorded. He had hunted a long time for the record, and when he had finally found a copy, he hadn't been able to play it. After the first words, he had crashed his fist down on the record, silencing the song forever, hoping that maybe it would also be silenced in his mind.

It had been raining heavily during that afternoon, and the evening was quite cold. There was a slight fog, which was getting thicker, but he never slowed the speed of his car. Feeling her so close to him, and yet further away than ever, had seemed to burn his mind, and he drove like a madman while they sang. When the car skidded, it had almost seemed funny, like sitting on a merry-go-round wheel, going round and round, with flashes of light and darkness, before the crash came, and then silence.

He had stumbled out of the car in a daze, blood running from between his lips, where he felt broken teeth as his mouth had smashed into the steering-wheel. One side of the car had ended up against a concrete pillar, and her lover was sitting straight up, his eyes and face cut to shreds by pieces of glass. Then he slowly toppled sideways, showing what was left of one side of his head. She had been unconscious when the ambulance arrived; he visited her at the hospital, but she hadn't said a word. She had only looked at him with those eyes, and he had left and never returned. Three weeks later she was released from hospital, and the next week she took two dozen sleeping pills. Someone told him when the funeral was, but he didn't go. He had tried to forget it, but it always came back, those staring grey eyes, and the fear of what they might have known about him that he didn't dare to face himself.

He brought the car to a halt at Lucy and Brett's place, and got out. His hands were wet and clammy, and he rubbed them against his jacket as he went up the stairs to their apartment. Silence met him. He knocked a few times on the door. No one answered. He swore, hesitated, then boldly knocked again. Nothing. He turned and bent down. Through the door he could see the shadows, watching him; but they drifted away from him as he left the apartment and went to the car. He had been careless, the lights were still blazing. He switched them off, started the car and just in time remembered to put them on again. He *had* to be with someone this evening, being alone in his rooms would drive him mad. Joey and his wife lived at the far side of the city, but he could just as well drive over to them. It was late already, but they never went to bed early. Besides, they were used to him dropping in at the weirdest hours. They wouldn't mind. He drove carefully now, trying to straighten things out in his mind, which seemed a white mass of moving fog and shadow fragments. His thoughts sped through his brain as a cloud of little black wings, quick and impossible to catch. Then there had been the troubles at the office. Sure, he knew he had been neglecting things a bit, but he had kept up with the new schedules, hadn't he? And he hadn't exactly been working badly, there had been no big mistakes to report, only a few small things which he had been careless about. Surely that couldn't be the real reason for the warning they had given him? The bastards!

Of course he knew they had just been waiting for those small slips to get at him. The fools had always secretly envied him, and probably hated him. They had been after him from the first time he had entered the office, with their blunt jokes he thought vulgar and obscene, and their stupid practical jokes. They enjoyed making him feel small, and how he hated them for it! How often hadn't he felt the insane desire, the *need* to pick up something heavy, just anything as long as it was hard enough to smash their skulls into a bloody pulp. But he kept it all inside, all the choked-up anger, the never-released fury. That's when the fits got stronger, bringing a red patterned web before his eyes, a blood dripping maze from which there was no escape. It changed his vision into a pool of dark red fog, through which he wanted to reach out and burn them with his hatred. But he locked it up inside, there was no one else he could talk to about it, he had forgotten the habit of talking, *really talking* to people who could understand him; or maybe there were just no such people left.

He drove up the big highway, pushing his foot down on the accelerator as on an enemy's face, wanting to lose the shadows, but he knew they were following him at the same speed as his car, drifting over the highway behind him as a palpitating, moving cloud.

He remembered when he had found the diary. A pretty little book, one of those expensive strongly-coloured Japanese imports, bound in silk. It had been hidden in the lowest drawer of his desk, the one where he kept the only picture he had ever had of Marciella, the only drawer which was always locked. He remembered himself smoothing the small book in his hands, wondering where it had come from. He had hesitantly opened it, fearfully seeing the first words, scrawled in an unsteady hand right across the page. "Marciella, I love you", it said, and then another's handwriting over it, stating "Rot in hell, you bitch". The second hand continued through the book, beginning on the next page with "Dear Allan. You won't mind me addressing you, I know. How you must hate me, dear beloved Allan. In fact it must be easy for you to hate me, I who am self-confident and assured, while you are in fact just a self-pitying fool. You always talk so nicely, Allan, a friendly word for everyone, isn't it? Never angry, never a mad gesture, and yet you are burning up, devoured by"...

He had shut the book, standing there shivering, the words addressed to him, Allan, dancing in the air before his eyes. The diary was written to him, and the handwriting was his own, but he couldn't remember writing it. He had burned the book, and taken a week off work. It hadn't helped much, his days had been spent wandering aimlessly in town, or making long pointless drives to places he wasn't interested in seeing at all, and his nights had been horror-filled walks through the empty dark places inside his head. Sometimes the mad desire to pick up something and smash everything around him became almost too much to bear, but he kept clinging on to his precious self-control, always putting on a smiling face.

Then the shadows had come. The first time, he had been looking out of the window and had seen them. He remembered thinking that there was a slight fog coming on, then he had watched more closely and he had seen that the mist had fingers. The mist didn't go away, and two days later it had looked through the window inside. He had looked for the faces to go with the hands and claw-like fingers, but there weren't any.

Startled by the lights of another car passing him, he looked up, and, cursing, he noticed that he had passed the turning to Joey's place. He had to continue for another ten minutes, before he was able to leave the highway on a crossroad. He finally stopped in front of Joey's house, and a deep feeling of warmth and happiness spread over him as he noticed the light spilling through the curtains of their windows. He put out the headlights, closed the car door behind him and walked up to their front door. As he stretched his finger out to push the bell, he heard the TV set blaring loudly inside, some wild pop programme. Fine, this was exactly what he needed to keep the morbid thoughts out of his mind. The lurking shadows behind him were already crawling over his car like fat slugs. A few hours with a loud TV set and overpowering music, a few drinks and afterwards some jokes and small talk, and then he would drive home again; the drinks would hide the shadows. Maybe he could even stay with Joey and his wife, they did have a spare bedroom, and he had slept there before when sometimes it was too late to drive home, or he had had a bit too much to drink. The bell rang, a sharp and angry sound which tore through his naked brain. There was a moment of stunned silence when the sound of the TV set was shut off, as if the house itself was surprised and wondering who the late visitor was. Footsteps came to the door. It was opened, and the face of a young boy with blond hair looked at him with startled eyes. 'Yes, sir?' the face asked.

'I... I... isn't Joey at home?' Allan asked. Already something small and terribly cold began scrambling around in his stomach.

'No, sir, sorry,' replied the boy. 'They're out at a party. Who can I say called?'

'I... No, they weren't expecting me... I just passed by and saw the lights still burning so I... thought... I decided to drop in... Just say a friend called...'

He turned around and almost ran back to his car. As he reached it, he heard the door close, shutting him off from the real world. He fumbled with his keys, dropped them, and had to get down on his knees, soiling his suit, to get them back from under the car, while misty fingers were also groping for them. Finally he was back inside, frantically trying to remember who he was.

As he sat there now, resting his head on his hands, two scrawled

14

white spots on the icy steering-wheel, his thoughts all seemed to be composed of cobwebs; they drifted in his face as if brought in by a playful wind, but before he could touch them to discover what they really were, they dissolved into silken threads, which broke and tore as he reached out to clasp them. There was a horrible feeling of *déjà vu* lurking at the edge of his mind. As the shadows approached again, he started the car and aimlessly drove into the outskirts of the city. He could have gone to a nightclub or a pub, but he knew it would be worse then: he would carry his isolation as a glass cage around him, through which even the music wouldn't be able to reach him.

He finally parked the car and got out, not bothering to lock it behind him. He left the car standing there, both doors wide open, and all lights on, a blazing beacon in a sea of dark silence. He began walking; his shoes making strange empty noises on the pavement. There were many doors, and they were all closed and silent, abnormally silent. Surely no city where thousands of people lived could be as silent as this one? There were many doorbells, and he didn't ring a single one, because if no one came and answered his late call, then he would know with certainty that they were all empty, all those houses, empty and silent. Cobwebbed, with dust covering the carpets and the chairs and the cupboards, with dried-out food in the refrigerator and mould creeping along the walls. Only the street lights were real, and he began counting them as he passed underneath them, but the most he could see at once were two or three, because the shadows were moving with him, obscuring all the others from his sight.

Sometimes they came nearer now, stretching out their fading hands towards him, but they didn't dare touch him yet, not yet; he was still safe from them, if he could only find someone to protect him in this dead city. Memories began to spin through his mind, faces of people he knew or had known, and eyes coldly staring at him, not saying anything, just staring, grey knowing eyes. Hell, how long would he have to walk this city of the dead before the shadows reached him? They were closer, always closer, they took their strength from him, like vampires, they fed on his fears, on his loneliness. "Find someone", his mind shrieked, "you can't be the last one"... But what if he was? What if the world was really dead, and he was the last one alive? No, that couldn't be, he... who was he? He still couldn't recall his name, but he had to, he needed an identity. I am Edgar Allan Poe, he thought, I am walking alone and proud, and then I'm deliriously dying in the gutter of Baltimore, and there's no Virginia Clemm waiting for me. I am Howard Phillips Lovecraft, noting down the symptoms of my sickness, and none of my friends know that I'm dying, but I know. Damn you all, what is my name, who am I? Who am I?

The shadows followed, silently, waiting, always nearer.

He began running, his feet drumming nightmarishly on the pavement. The shadows always kept the same distance, before and after him, shrouding the houses and the street.

They were all dead, he was sure now, the houses were only skulls, empty sentinels, catacombs, pyramids, enormous tombs holding nothing but crumbling and rotting corpses. The shadows had killed them all, and now they would kill him too if they got him. He didn't look where he was running, and stumbled over some spades, where for some reason or another workmen had been opening up the street. Weren't they afraid someone would steal their tools? But no, they were dead too, as all the rest, so who would come and steal them?

Then, as he approached the corner of the street, he stopped. Could it be? Footsteps were nearing, idly walking, closer now, closer. A blackness came from around the corner, and he stood face to face with a surprised policeman. The policeman looked at him with a slight frown of distaste, 'Well, sir, what's the matter? Why are you in such a hurry?'

Allan started to cry, and it all came out, in an unsteady spilling fountain of words, the dead city, the shadows, Marciella, the baby sitter, his night drive, the emptiness of the streets. He was holding the policeman's shoulder, shaking uncontrollably, and it flew out of him as from a deep well which had been opened. 'You're alive,' he shrieked, 'I'll go with you, you're alive, *you're alive!*'

'Now, easy, sir,' the policeman said, 'let's not make such a noise, we wouldn't want to wake people up, would we? After all, it's nearly one o'clock now. Listen, why don't you go home? You'd better leave your car right where you parked it; you can come and get it first thing in the morning. Walking will do you a lot of good, sir, if I may say so.

I have to finish my round, you know.'

'But I... I want to go with you!' Allan screamed. 'You can't send me away. You'll have to lock me up, that's what you'll have to do. You can't leave me alone with the shadows. Please, please take me with you, please!'

The policeman looked with disgust at the wailing man. He had trudged his long beat already, and his feet were aching in his new shoes. He was tired, he only wanted to check in at the station, report that there was nothing to report, and then check out. His feet needed their warm slippers, and his stomach cried out for a steaming cup of coffee. He wasn't going to do poorly paid overtime work for this idiot. If they wanted to get drunk, that was all right with him, but why did they have to make such a nuisance of themselves? He tried again. 'Listen, sir,' he said as calmly but severely as possible, 'why don't you just be a good boy, and go home? Just sleep it off. I can see you're no tramp, and I don't like to run a gentleman in just because he had a bit more than his stomach could take. Listen, there's a phone box on the next corner, I'll phone a cab for you, and you just wait here 'till it arrives and takes you home safely. I'll go and lock your car for you, and then I'll forget I met you and go home also. A good night's sleep, and you'll see, you'll be a new man in the morning. Good night, sir.'

The policeman turned his back, and walked away.

Allan stood there, watching him, the tears running down his cheeks, his hands aimlessly stretched out for help, and help from anybody. The shadows were hovering over him, grinning down on his helplessness. They were long and dark now borne on cloudy dark membranous wings which obscured the night sky, and they had eyes now, glowing eyes which were watching him all the time, sardonically, mercilessly. They would get him, he knew now, they would finally get him as they had been certain to do from the very start. All his running away, all his pleas and trials, they had all been in vain. He had been a fly in a spider's web, trying to escape, and they had let him try, mocking him, making fun of him his whole life through.

And that man walking away, he too was no more than the empty houses and the silent streets. He was just another puppet they had put in his way, for fun, for amusement. The man was an empty walking doll, manipulated on strings by the shadows, he would soon now turn the corner of the street, and then the shadows would loosen the strings, he would drop down and never move again. A puppet, an empty puppet, making fun of him! He took a few shaky steps backwards, again stumbling over the workmen's tools, and fell to his knees. His hands dropped to the earth, and his fingers touched something cold, which he picked up. It was a pick-axe, smooth as ice in his hands, the only reality in this nightmare world of the dead and the shadows. He had to fight them, it was the only escape left. He stood up, taking the heavy axe with him. First a few sneaking steps, and then he broke into a run, bringing the axe up, screaming. It came down on the head of the empty walking doll in the policeman's uniform, and up and down, up and down, the hands of the clock of time, the executioner's sword, up and down, up and down. And see, the man wasn't empty at all, as he had thought, on the contrary, he was full of weak soft flesh and hot red blood. Up and down, slower and slower, as a mechanism running down.

He let the axe fall, and looked down on the empty man at his feet, then at the silent street; lights came on in some houses, there were sounds of voices, and doors opening, and the dead came out, mummified and crumbling rotting corpses as he had known they would be, and some of the older houses fell into ashes, as he began to see through the general illusion.

'You're dead,' he screamed into the darkness which began shrouding him as a heavy muffling cloak of utter silence, 'you're all dead, you're all dead, damn you!'

Then the shadows closed in on him completely, finally.

The lines from the poem quoted in this story are from 'In Ruins' and are reprinted here with the kind permission of the author, Glen E. Symonds, from his poetry collection, Dark Voices, 1971.

TEN

THE BEARDED YOUNG man wore a well-cut but rather worn leather jacket with suede elbow patches. He put down his heavy bag and rang the buzzer on the door. The chimes of some folk tune sounded inside. The blank eye of a small camera top right of the door turned towards him making a soft humming sound. The young man had a quick look at his surroundings while he waited. A respectable and quiet suburb, a small but nice and well kept front garden and an oversized house in the "fermette" style which had become so popular a couple of years ago when every city dweller wanted a house which looked like a colonial mansion. Large tinted windows straight to the ground, above small colonial style upper windows under the grey roofing-tiles, a double garage with closed doors to the left.

The copper nameplate beside the buzzer stated quite soberly "EMMANUEL SCHEERENS-VERSTRATE". The plate didn't mention the various Ph.D. degrees the owner held.

'Yes?' a gritty metallic voice wrung itself out of the small speaker.

'It's the babysitter, sir,' the young man said.

'Come on in.' A dry click as the receiver inside the house was switched off, and the insect like buzzing of the door opener. The young man pushed the door which softly whispered open. The light from inside crashed down on him, placing him in the middle of a beacon. He had to shut his eyes for a second to let them adapt to the sudden change. Then he bent, picked up his bag and carried it inside. The entrance hall was sparingly but tastefully decorated. Expensive carpets in soft colours everywhere, cork with a discreet pattern of gold on the walls; on them three small and delicate paintings, the kind not purchased on the Sunday market. He stepped forward and, as he left the front door behind, the harsh light dimmed and became bearable.

You haven't done so badly, professor, the young man thought grimly. He turned, closed the door behind him, and waited respectfully, as he knew he was supposed to.

Somewhere to the left a door opened with a hush and a tall man entered the hall. The young man hissed slightly between his closed lips. In his mind years crashed down as splintered glass and shattered into weeks and days, as he looked at professor Emmanuel Scheerens.

The face spat venom at his mind. The strong cheek bones with the constant shadows under the eyes, the classic nose as from a Greek statue and the hideous razorblade lips. The years hadn't changed them, neither had they tempered the dumb glare of the somewhat protruding froglike eyes, the colour of cigarette ash. Only the broad forehead had gained in the battle against the now strongly reclining hairline, and the autumn brown now had curly grey fingers twisting in it.

Scheerens' glance swept over the young man's appearance, absorbing it all with one look, the left corner of his mouth rising a little in an almost unnoticeable twitch as he took in the curling black beard and the broad moustache. The young man almost could hear him thinking: Looks like a young Stephen King. He saw the twitch of the lips and remembered the scorn it usually accompanied. Scheerens had been infamous for that twitch, and probably still was.

'So you're from the agency,' Scheerens said. It wasn't a question, who else would he expect?

'Yes sir, I'm from "Sitter". Franklin, Peter Franklin is the name.' He put out his right hand, but Scheerens had already turned his back on him and his hand. 'Follow me,' Scheerens said, not an invitation but an order, given with a voice used to giving orders and implying that he was used to being obeyed immediately. The young man followed Scheerens into a smaller room where several closed doors watched silently, then up a broad staircase of dark stained wood. The carpet on the stairs greedily ate every sound his shoes made.

'There's a widescreen TV with VHS and DVD players upstairs,' Scheerens said with a sneer over his shoulder, without looking back.

The young man, breathing heavily with the bag in his hand, shook his head. Then, as Scheerens wasn't looking at him anyway, he said: 'Very kind of you, sir, but I won't be watching anything. I've some studying to do, so I brought my laptop along. Don't worry, no printer, so I won't me making any noise to keep the little girl from her sleep.'

'Who told you it's a little girl?' Scheerens asked without slowing his steps or turning around.

'The agency, of course, sir. "Sitter" always inquires about the age and sex of the children. Sometimes they're older children who can be a bit difficult when it comes to sleeping hours. So "Sitter" always knows exactly who is suited for which job. But then, you know that. I've been told that Sylvie is three, and a very quiet child.'

'That is correct, Mr. Franklin. Sylvie won't keep you from your... studies. Or your computer games.'

The young man smiled. 'It's not a games computer, sir. I am into IT and have some programs to correct. But don't you worry, I'm here as a baby sitter, not as a computer specialist.'

Well, the young man thought, Scheerens has also kept the habit of getting things immediately in order... his order.

Some years ago.

He closed the door as silently as he could behind him, and of course the bloody thing gave a shrieking protest. He crept to his place and flopped open the writing table over his knees. Professor Scheerens was busy desecrating the writing board with his nearly unreadable hieroglyphs, which none of the students present copied. None of them could read Scheerens' writing, and the full text was in the text books anyway. The writing board was almost full and Scheerens went on reducing the last remaining spaces while reciting with a nasal voice his text for today. He was in fact reciting the text of the book he had written himself almost word by word, and disregarded contemptuously as usual two students trying to catch his attention to ask for some clarification.

'Well, so much for explaining some difficult point today,' a girl sighed. A bit too loud a sigh. The girl shut up, her mouth still open on the last word as Scheerens abruptly stopped talking and her whisper became a bird's wing fluttering over the otherwise silent audience. Scheerens put down the marker and turned around, but his frog eyes didn't focus on the girl.

'Maybe the young gentleman who just came crashing in so embarrassingly loudly can further explain what I've just been saying?' Scheerens asked softly. His lip twitched.

***

Scheerens and the young man entered the living room on the first floor. Here too reigned the same tasteful luxury, not bragging with expensive original art pieces glaring in spotlights, but a subdued quiet luxury which whispered that the people living here had it quite good financially and found this normal. The kind of luxury which tried to be inconspicuous yet subtly advertised its costliness, and finally just proved that the owner had no real personal taste. A room out of the notebook of an interior decorator: plump leather couches, an oversized plasma screen stereo TV, with two identical VCR's, a DVD player and recorder. Well, this looked as if Scheerens liked to copy the movies he liked for his own collection, though he certainly had the money to just buy them. For a moment the young man wondered what kind of movies Scheerens liked. There were no tapes in sight, probably all locked away.

The lady of the house was all set up for an evening out. The kind of trendy dress one saw advertised in the women's magazines as "this is IT now", and with a gold or a platinum card you were dressed as you had to be for a couple of hundreds of dollars. Her hair had a dreary ash blond look as if she wanted the appearance of Debbie Harry in her younger years, but she had a nice, somewhat hesitating smile. Though she was a lot younger than her husband, already the corners of her mouth were deformed, turning down as in defeat.

'I had been expecting that charming girl,' she said. 'I'm sorry, young man, but when I phoned "Sitter" I specifically asked for...'

The young man carefully put down his bag and charmed the most open smile on his face, or what could be seen of that. He had known in advance that the rough beard and heavy moustache, both of which he had been growing for some months now, created suspicion with some people. The agency had even asked him to remove those "werewolf growths" at first but he had refused, and they hesitatingly had taken him on trial. Which had worked out fine for both of them. No way he would've taken off his beard, he had grown it specifically for tonight. He needed the hairy cover here and now, between who he had been and Scheerens.

'You mean Marianne, madam,' he said. 'I know, I'm sorry but she has been taken ill quite suddenly. "Sitter" called me in urgently because I have a good record with very young children. I wasn't expecting a night job, as you can see I brought some work along. Don't you worry a thing, I'm even experienced at changing nappies, but I won't have to worry about that tonight, not with a three year old. If necessary I am even known to have sung lullabies.'

Mrs. Scheerens looked at her husband, the doubtful plea for help from someone who has learned years ago that it is unwise to make even the slightest decision yourself without the approval of His Lordship.

'Of course you can call "Sitter" right away if you want my references,' the young man quickly said. 'Or if you'd rather have someone else, a female, I mean. But I've come this far, and frankly, I doubt if they could find anyone else at this short notice.' He let his shoulders hang down a bit and wrinkled his face into his best cute Big Foot Henderson smile.

'Well, I don't think that we'll have to...' she started.

'Wouldn't make any difference,' Scheerens snarled, his lips barely moving but his voice razor cutting the air, 'you can only reach "Sitter" till seven p.m. Which, as you may have noticed, my dear, is long past. Besides, we don't have any time to spare now.'

How precise as always, the young man thought, not seven o'clock but seven p.m. 'Marianne called to say she thinks she caught the flu so she absolutely didn't want to risk anything with a child,' he continued. 'The agency has all our home numbers so they asked me if I could fill in for her. That's why I brought my laptop along to get the work done I had planned for this evening. Don't want to be unprepared for my class tomorrow.'

That was the kind of answer Scheerens would approve off, the young man knew.

Of course, what happened had been rather different but really quite easy. "Accidently" meeting Marianne this afternoon at her usual junk food restaurant, dropping a pill in her Coke when she had her big mouth stuffed with French fries. Then when she got sick very quickly, helping her back to her flat and offering to take over her sitting job for tonight.

'You've come by car?' Scheerens asked offhand. "Peter Franklin", whose real name was Bart, grinned. What Scheerens really wanted to know of course, was whether he was supposed to drive this bearded troll home in the early morning hours or give him a place to sleep till the first bus came along tomorrow morning. Those were the member rules of "Sitter".

'Don't have a car, sir,' Bart said. 'I came by bicycle, good for my legs. I've padlocked it against the wall of your garage, if that's all right with you.'

'Of course,' Scheerens replied, becoming a bit more compliant. 'You can put it in the garage in case it starts to rain.'

'Don't bother, sir,' Bart answered, 'it's just a rust bucket, not a Harley motorbike. Now if you could inform me about my tasks. Has the girl still to eat, or whatever if special?'

'You take care of those details,' Scheerens said to his wife, again an order not a question. 'I'll get my coat, time's running out.'

The nursery was next to the living room. Pink carpets, rainbow coloured paper flowers crawling up the walls. A collection of expensive-brand toy rabbits, bears and cats carefully set on display on white shelves against the walls, too high for a three year old to reach by herself.

Well, even here reigned His Master's Touch.

The girl, Sylvie, was sleeping soundly on her left side in a wooden bed, quality Swedish wood, made to measure. The girl was blond, her curly hair the luxury of soft melted gold on the blue pillow. Part of the heritage of her mother, that is before she started to flatten her hair to look older and less flattering when seen beside her husband and master.

Bart still wore his jacket; no one had offered to take it. The hard object in his inside pocket scratched against his shirt and chest. He felt the pointed end pressing against his flesh through the protecting leather sheath, a feeling which was strangely erotic, as the sharp nail of a woman's finger stroking him.

Many months before.

'Hello, there "Sitter"? Yes, I've read your ad in the paper, and I'd like to work for you... No, I have a nine to five job, cashier in a supermarket, but I could use some extra cash. Who doesn't, eh? I'm taking evening courses and the books and stuff are quite expensive... Yes, I can deal with all types of children, unless they're

raving maniacs. I grew up in a big family myself, two sisters and three brothers, all younger than me, so I've done my share of babysitting... All right, I'll drop in tomorrow with my references.'

'A sweet little girl,' Bart said in a hushed voice. Play it up a bit, as if awed by the child's beauty. Well, she did look like a cute little thing. Out of the corners of his eyes he saw an abrupt smile flash across Mrs. Scheerens lips. It did her face a lot of good, for that second she was looking her real age, only a few years older than Bart himself. Scheerens had always had a certain reputation when it came to young nubile female students. Bart also knew that Mrs. Scheerens had noticed the subdued tone of his voice, so as not to wake the child. Well, he did have quite a few sitting sessions behind him, he had not lied when he spoke about his past experience.

'And very well behaved too,' Mrs. Scheerens said with a hint of pride. 'In nursery class, she's in the top grade now, they don't have any problems at all with my Sylvie.' Bart noticed the slight emphasis on the word "my". She's only just turned three.'

'I know,' Bart said. Turned three on May thirty-first this year, he thought. "Sitter" kept their files up to date. 'Now if you could just show me where everything is.'

Everything was carefully arranged in a closet: the disposable nappies from a current brand which got a lot of commercial spots on prime TV, the powder, the towels, and all the rest. There was a small changing table, fixed on the wall with two safety grips. The eyes of two wall spots spilled enough light without illuminating the bed itself.

'Usually she sleeps the whole night through, she even remains asleep while she's being changed,' Mrs. Scheerens assured him as they went back to the living room. 'The kitchen is over there, the pink door. You'll find anything you want in the fridge: fruit juice, lemonade, water, Coke, a beer. Nothing stronger than that though.'

Bart noticed the lapse into a more familiar choice of words; madam wasn't from the same class as her stuffy husband.

'Thanks, but I don't drink alcohol. I don't smoke either.'

'Good for you. There are a few sandwiches with cheese and cold cuts, if you get hungry. You can use the TV and there are some comics.'

Bart lifted his eyebrows slightly, Roger Moore playing 007. 'Isn't Sylvie a bit too young for that? I mean, comics.'

Mrs. Scheerens laughed, a little chortle which sounded rather unpleasant. 'Not Sylvie, my husband is a maniacal collector of all kinds of comics,' she explained. 'American and English, but mainly French, Belgian and Spanish stuff for adults. I don't care for that myself, I hate the stories and looking at pictures bores me. You can look through them, but be sure to put them back in their correct places, and don't make a bloody wrinkle in one of them or he'll go absolutely raging mad.

Comics, Bart thought, well, who'd ever have thought Scheerens was collecting comics. Life was indeed full of crazy surprises.

Some years ago.

'That bastard Scheerens has trouble again reading his own text-book' Bart's neighbour whispered in his ear. 'Look at his eyes! I could as well have stayed home and just memorised from the pages of his bloody textbook.'

'Another council meeting yesterday evening, I suppose?'

'Sure, what else did you expect? You should've seen the empty Four Roses and Johnny's they put in the glass recycler this morning. Freddie told me that three of them went home in a cab, couldn't even use their bloody car keys anymore. Well, at least they didn't try to drive, and asshole Scheerens was one of them.'

'How do you know? At least he's standing there.'

'Standing? You mean holding himself steady with the table. I know because his car's in the parking lot, frozen solid. That car hasn't moved since yesterday morning.'

Scheerens was drumming his fingers on the door when they came down. He wore a silk scarf loosely around his thin neck, the colour matching his expensive coat.

'Finally ready to go?' he asked with a vicious snarl.

'Yes, of course,' his wife said quickly, 'I had to tell the boy here to find...'

Scheerens razor-lips cut her off in mid-sentence. 'We are at the

Nightplay Theatre,' he said directly to Bart, treating his wife as if part of the furniture. 'The address and phone number are on the table over there. So is my mobile number but of course that will be turned off during the performance. Just in case something unexpected happens, which I don't expect. Also the number of our house physician. In an emergency you call him right away, no matter what time of the night. Am I making myself clear, young man?'

'Absolutely, sir,' Bart replied. 'I wish everybody was as strict and punctual. But I don't expect any problems. I'll check in on Sylvie every half hour, without waking her.'

'Good, let's go.'

'Have a pleasant evening, sir and madam. Do you have any idea when you'll be back?'

'No, we don't. You're not expecting anyone, are you?'

'Certainly not, sir.'

'Good, I don't want any girlfriends in my house. It's the premiere of *Silent Village* by Doriac Greysun, and afterwards there's a small reception with the critics. I know quite a few people there, so it may be late... or early morning.'

'Don't worry, sir, I'm in no hurry. I've work enough to last me through the night.'

Again Bart was aware of Scheerens' glance, gliding suspiciously over him as a hawk's eye, as if Scheerens was trying to place his face somewhere. But a man can change quite a lot with some wild hair growing on his face, a different haircut and another style of clothing. Maybe Scheerens wouldn't have recognised him anyway, not after those years, probably didn't even remember his real name. Still, Bart hadn't wanted to take any risks, no matter how small.

The sharp fingernail clawed at his chest again. The stainless steel blade was warming up with his body heat, hugged against his heart, and yet it still provided him with a cold searing feeling, the cold innocence of naked steel.

Scheerens turned around. 'Good night then,' he said. His wife nodded at Bart, a smile half forming on her face and immediately washed away again. She followed her master, a well trained house-broken bitch.

* * *

Some time ago.

'Hey Bart, how you're doin' these days?'

'Not so good, man, it's shit finding a job. Been doin' some time in a burger tent, played bartender in a gay club but they kicked me out when they found out I wasn't a fag. How's at High Bullshit?'

'Same shit as when you were there, man. Baghead was pissed out of his mind again because his admired team lost the cup the evening before, and you know how that makes Baghead act. Oh yes, and Asshole Scheerens is getting married.'

'No kidding, you're putting me on, right?'

'No way, bloody truth.'

'Who is the poor sacrificial lamb?'

'One of his ex-students, sweet little thing called Jessie something. Verstrate, Jessie Verstrate, you must remember her. She was one or two classes lower than you before you were thrown out.'

'Let me think, man... Hey, not that broad with the big mouth and the curly hair, the one we always said that with lips like those she could take on an—'

'Yep, that's the one all right. Many years younger than Asshole of course, but that was to be expected. Hell, everybody still talks about the way he still looks up their legs under the tables if they're not wearing jeans. Did you know that he wasn't allowed to take their examinations any more without another teacher sitting by as a watchdog?'

'No, I didn't. I've been out of it for some years now, remember. What happened, he mess around again?'

'He always messed around, but this one redhead chick spilled her guts at home and her parents went straight to the board. They hushed it up, what did you expect of those old farts, but since then they kept a quiet eye on Asshole. And how he hated that. Too bad it was after your time. But then, your case was rather different. Now if you'd been a girl...'

Bart listened to the sound of the front door locking, followed shortly by the loud humming of the electronically opening garage doors and the starting sound of the cold motor. Gravel crunched under wheels on the driveway, and then silence whispered over the house as a smothering blanket.

Bart opened his bag and took out a few books which he opened and distributed across the smoked glass dining room table. He went to the kitchen and inspected the fridge. Mrs. Scheerens hadn't lied, the sandwiches were there, cleanly wrapped up in foil, but Bart wasn't hungry yet. Maybe later. He took a can of Coke and went back to the living room to have a look at Scheerens collection of comics. Well, not exactly the American way. No loose ordinary comics here, no Superman or Batman. A nice set of soft covers, from *Alien*, *Angel* and *Buffy* to *Hellboy*, the *Sandman* and others. But most of them were hardcover albums: Spanish artists Bart had never heard of, French language stuff by guys named Druillet, Comès and Caza, complete bound runs of *Pilote*, *A Suivre* and *Métal Hurlant*. Some wrapped completely in plastic sleeves, with handwritten price stickers on the backs. Bart whistled softly as he looked at some of the prices. Hidden behind were other volumes of less innocent nature, mostly French. Black soft covers with hardcore nudity, *Anita* and other albums by someone named Crépax, bondage and SM. Foreign import, not the kind you'd find in a regular comic store, unless under the counter and at heavy prices.

It was impossible to imagine Scheerens sitting here and reading those albums while his wife was watching some game show or soap on the telly. Somehow this made Scheerens look... almost human. Which was a luxury Bart couldn't afford himself.

When you want to get even with an animal, you want to keep that animal down on its own level and don't start thinking of it as a pet. Such emotions are like social multi-structures or administrative systems, get involved and you drown in them, they suck you in as quicksand. It can lead to understanding and then to pity, and if no one has ever shown any understanding or pity to yourself, then you can better forget them.

Many, many years ago.

TEN is a magic word, a magic number, a magic age. It means a transition and again not. You're no longer a child, but not a teenager yet. Because after TEN come eleven and twelve and only then thirteen. But you feel old and wise as it is, being TEN already, and this is still a kid's party, with strawberry pie and friends—and maybe one or two girls, if they care enough to come—and funny hats and games. With eleven and twelve you'll start desiring the magic thirteen. Then you'll be really tough. Now, at TEN, you're still only a child.

The adults cut the pie for you, the knife is big and shiny, you can see your own eyes glaring back at you from the blade. Then you are allowed to hold the knife, you're already TEN after all. The blade glides through the pie, through the whipped cream, thick and clotty, the strawberries red and glazy below. The tart is like a living being and the knife digs into it, it claws and bites, the knife is a big fang digging into the soft white fur and the red flesh under it, opening it all up, exposing the raw and bleeding innards, and everything inside there is all soft and sloppy and red and red and red...

And as you stumble back it is the cat which is lying there with the blade now sticking out of its open belly as an enormous penis, the big white cat which was crushed under a lorry's wheels last week, your big white cat which had run out of the front door which you had left open, while you weren't looking, just running out and across the street into the heavy traffic, and the brakes were shrieking, the car stopping just in front of you and the one behind it smashing into its rear end so that it performed a short jerk forward, its front bumper touching you oh so lightly, steel caressing your arm but you didn't notice that as you were sitting by your white cat, your dead white cat, with its fur slashed open and everything inside out as an emptied balloon with red cream inside, a white coat with red linings, as the tart into which the knife is now eating, the fang hard and merciless into all which is soft and sticky and red, red, red...

Bart took the knife from his inner pocket, it rose as by itself from its hidden depths, a stretched penis out of its vagina sheath. The stainless steel caught the sharp beam of a wall spotlight and shattered it into searing reflections, dancing on the walls. Ah, the purity of it, he observed silently, the serenity of the blood groove, so straight, so simple, the razor edge and the sharp tip as an immaculately manicured woman's fingernail.

Almost religiously Bart deposited the knife on the table, amidst the opened textbooks, only used as camouflage, just in case. Half an hour had gone by without him noticing it, as he had been lost in his thoughts.

Again he bent over the heavy bag, and extracted the laptop and the connecting cables. He snatched out the input cable from the TV and connected the laptop to the screen.

Bart had all the time he needed. He had taken years to prepare for what he wanted to accomplish, even if the real intent had come only after some time. Before there had been only the mindless rage, the self destroying fury which had been eating his brain because there was no outlet available. He had always been very rational, and at some point the enormity of his caged fury, of this primitive animal anger, had become frightening even to himself. Then, gradually, he had found a way to beam his fury, to direct the hatred, to form it into a shape acceptable to his rational mind, a structure in his mind which satisfied him by its adaptability and rationality. In primal times one could pick up a stick or a stone and simply bash in the head of the hated enemy, but in these times you didn't do that if you were a civilised human being. Not with the prospect of police, a trial and prison grinning broadly in front of you if they caught you. So you imprison the rage and direct it into a logical pattern which won't hurt you... and which will finally deliver you from the absorbing fire.

Some years ago.

'Any idea what you're gonna take?'

'Not yet really. But I think I'd like to take on psychology, seems interesting to me.'

'You gotta be kiddin', man. Don't you know who's teaching psychology? Asshole Scheerens, THE Asshole Scheerens.'

'So what? What's so special about him?'

'Well, you'll get to know him in no time, rest assured. His textbook has twelve-hundred pages, two volumes, small print. Expensive as shit and he sees to it that you annotate the works in the book itself so that you won't be able to sell it later to those who come after you. But he does tell you in advance which chapters he'll choose for the final examination tests.'

Well, ain't that a beauty. So what's the big deal?'

'But of course he'll never ask questions about the two hundred pages of the chapters he made you absorb, he'll pick his choice of questions from the one thousand pages which he explicitly told you not to study by heart. That's why he's called Asshole Scheerens.'

'But that's bloody mean. You don't do things like that, I mean, as a student you can go to the board and...'

'Go to the board and complain about one of their own? Man, Scheerens is the board! Boy, which backward farmyard spawned you?'

The phone rang, once, twice, three times. Bart grinned. Here was the phone call he had known would be coming.

'Hello, this is the Scheerens-Verstrate residence. They aren't at home, this is the sitter. If you care to leave a message for them?'

'This is Mrs. Scheerens. I thought... just a call, to know if every-thing's all right.'

'No problem, madam. Sylvie is sleeping as a rock, I just had a look at her. Are you enjoying the play?'

'Oh, yes... fine. It's the break after the first act right now. I must seem like an overprotective mom. Sorry to have disturbed you.'

'Not at all, madam. Don't you worry. I was just going to have a snack, and the Coke's fine and cold.'

'All right, I'll be going then.'

'Enjoy the rest of the play, madam. You really don't have to hurry back, enjoy your evening. Everything's fine.'

Strange how impersonal it finally becomes, Bart thought, even the hatred. At first it burns you up, makes you want to throw things, break things, crush somebody's skull, but of course you don't do that. And all the time the injustice of it all is shivering inside you with no outlet, so it begins to eat you. It becomes cold, not forgiven neither forgotten, it just keeps on burning slower with a petrifying cold flame, ice burning in your brain. And finally it becomes rationalised into metal and plastic, such as a laptop with its innocent keyboard, and some cables. Into a program on which you've worked very hard and very long to create.

Emotions usually burn themselves up after some time and only the residue remains, the ashes of the hatred caught in the heart of the cremated remains. Dry matter without a personality, the cooled lava of the volcano, the dried crust on a wound which has healed till you pick of the scabs and see the scar.

A white line drawn in raw red meat. You can't stop it, you pick and pick till it starts bleeding again.

A red line in whipped cream.
The white of whipped cream, and the red meat under it.

Some time ago.

'I'd like to order a couple of cakes. Three, in fact.'

'No problem, that's what I bake. What kind of cakes you'd like, sonny?'

'Birthday cakes. For a kid. The kind you put little candles on. With lots of whipped cream. And strawberries inside, and cherries. I'd also like a set of chocolate numbers. Numbers four, five, and so on till ten.'

'Must be some birthday.'

'Want to play some jokes, switching birthdays, ages and such.'

'No problem, sonny. When do you want them?'

'Tomorrow will be fine.'

The wound had closed, hiding the scar below. It had taken a long time, and finally pure coincidence had helped. Him getting a job with "Sitter", just to earn some extra cash to pay for the evening courses, and then finding out that Scheerens himself was a regular customer of theirs. Which had been the beginning of it all.

The last two years (the Scheerens' had used the services of "Sitter" since the little one was one year old, and mostly Marianne had been the regular sitter) had been a waiting period for the exact right time to arrive. When the child had become old enough and when the chance arrived to switch sitters without arousing anyone's suspicions. People could be so bloody nosy, especially when it came to matters which didn't concern them at all.

The rest had been an enormous gamble but Bart had really dug into it. The funny part of it was that Scheerens himself had been a great help. That was the only regret Bart felt: that Scheerens himself would never know, would never understand the beauty of it, just as he had never realised what he had done to others. Now he would never understand what someone else would do to him and why. It was precisely the twelve-hundred page textbook of Scheerens which had been so very helpful.

From Scheerens' textbook:

"The ten billion nerve cells in the human brain contain about forty thousand neurons on each square millimetre of the cortex. As soon as the brain weighs a minimum of seven hundred grams, it is capable of learning a language and storing that information. This is the necessity of having enough neurons to register words and deposit them in the memory circuits. The brain of a human being reaches this stage as early as six months after birth. The real IQ of a human being however stabilises only at the age of four, when the personality becomes fully formed. In the years before, the surroundings have a maximum input on the brain and the memory".

Bart activated the TV and the portable connected to it. The big screen lit up with static, a hissing but featureless demon face. The ON-light on the keyboard winked at him. Small red David and the enormous glass Goliath.

Bart went and got Sylvie. He took the little girl out of her bed and carried her, still half asleep, into the living room. When he put her on the couch, her small face lit by the moving static from the screen, she rubbed her eyes and made confused little sounds. Bart put a cushion against her back so she wouldn't fall. The girl was coming fully awake now, looking around in confusion which had not yet turned into fear.

'Where is Daddy? Mommy?' she asked. 'Who are you?'

'Mommy and Daddy will be back soon,' Bart said. 'I am the baby-sitter, I am here to look after you. You and I are going to be real nice friends, aren't we? We are going to watch TV, you and I together, now won't that be fun?'

'Yes!' Sylvie clapped her small hands. 'I may not watch tel-lie from Mary-ann when she is here. I wanna watch tel-lie. Wanna watch Roger Rab-bit.'

The girl reminded Bart of his younger sister. How often hadn't he had to change her nappies when he was still living at home. His father had been a dock worker, till a careless fork lift driver deposited two tons of steel on his father's left foot, turning his old man into an invalid. Ah, that cursed word: invalid. No longer fit to work. No longer fit for anything. That was when the drinking had started. His father had always liked a pint, and more than one, which wasn't hard to get when your wife runs a harbour-side pub.

"The Gààk" it was called, being the mating cry of some prehistoric flying reptile. Bart never knew where that came from, but a huge evil toothed thing with batwings decorated the windows. The pub always had a clean reputation: a good beer at the right temperature, and though some customers were on the rough side, there was no fighting. A nice place where you could talk without being smothered by canned heavy metal or fuckin' rap at full blast. But once his dad got into the real boozing, it all went down the drain fast.

His mother spent her time chatting up the drunks to make them drink more, since the regulars began to stay away with his father hanging on the bar, his brain pissed to hell and with a temper and mood to match that place. Mostly they were happy the evenings when his dad staggered out and got plastered elsewhere, till they put a stop to his credit at the other pubs.

That was when Bart made his decision, THE decision to get out of the rat hole the pub had become, get away from the daily fights about money between his parents, the constant nagging. There had been a time when he had thought he really could talk to his mom, till he realised that she didn't really listen and only needed a wailing wall to spit her own troubles at. There had been a time when he thought he understood his old man, before that person turned into a complaining and bitching pain in the ass. Bart had to take care of his brothers and sisters, his mom didn't have time for that, she had to keep the pub clean and the customers happy or there'd be no food on the table the next day. Not that it made much of a difference, not the way she started looking after some time. A son should take up his responsibility, his father had said, all the time feeling his crippled foot with a habitual gesture, that's why they let him continue his studies, and didn't he realise what he cost his poor parents?

Bart did realise, oh how he did. The scholarship money he got once a year from the government was ridiculously low (but then, his parents didn't know the right people and channels to get more money) and the prices of textbooks were staggeringly high. Sometimes he got lucky and could buy some leftover books from those who moved up, at second hand prices, but only if there were no handwritten notes or markings in them. If your teacher saw those, you could throw them in the garbage can.

So Bart had continued the first six years, making breakfast for all in the morning and seeing to it that the younger ones got their lunch packages to school, while his parents still slept, the one washed out and the other just plain drunk, or both too tired from another fight.

Some time before:

'Hey, I got your address from the FOR SALE ads. You have a portable for sale, I read? What type..? Could I have a look at it..? No, I'm not interested in software unless it's cheap. I can write my own stuff. I want a set which I can take along wherever I go... Yep, looks fine, not too heavy. What do you want for it..? That's a lot of money for second hand. Now let's see, what do you think of...'

Sylvie was wide awake now. 'Tel-lie, el-lie,' she exclaimed clapping her hands, 'wanna see rab-bit. Or Duckie.'

'Yes, it's coming,' Bart said. He introduced the disc into the jaws of the portable where it was eaten with a hungry click. The screen flashed into electronic life. Bart started typing on the keyboard. The introductory symbols of the program came to life on the screen, quite weird to see them that big. Then came the lines, followed by isolated points connecting into new lines, forming peaks as the graphics of an encephalogram, very short and sharp peaks as knife points stabbing upwards.

'Not fun-ny,' Sylvie protested.

Six months of labour, a short pregnancy, Bart thought, but what a beautiful program as a result. So simple to think it out, so easy to create if you have the right stuff handy and know how to use it.

'Just keep on watching, the rabbit will come,' Bart said.

The lines became waves soundlessly rolling across the wide screen and spilling over the watchers. Sometimes they went faster, then slowed down, swelling and getting fatter, the rhythm following preset sequences. The flowing and crashing waves on the screen lifted and rose, turning over and all the time created something on the screen which always seemed to be just out of the eye's reach. You felt that there was something hidden inside those waves but just couldn't place that impression in the proper perspective.

Bart turned his eyes away from the waves which seemed to want to suck him inside the screen. It was as if they shaped a continuously changing hungry mouth which attracted and yet at the same time evoked an intense feeling of revulsion.

He looked at Sylvie who was stiffly sitting on the couch. Her head moved back and forth as the girl followed the rhythm of the electronic lips on the screen. Her curls were dancing. A beautiful child, Bart thought, how had Scheerens ever managed to procreate something like her? Of course, his wife Jennie had always been a real looker. Whatever had she seen in someone like Scheerens? Love? No way. Must have been the need for security, for a future without the problems they all had been confronted with in their youth. You needed a degree and had to take a government examination just to pick up fallen leaves in the bloody park. You could work yourself to death trying to earn a university degree, and still know that you were as likely to have to stand in line for welfare hand-outs once you got your degree because there were too many candidates and not enough openings.

Scheerens, with his high social status and his steady income represented such a safe future, if he could learn to keep his hands off the young girls. Peter remembered that Jessie never had been very bright so she probably never had gotten her degree. Scheerens wasn't that ugly, so what if he was a much older man with a drinking problem and roaming hands.

Oh hell, Bart thought, look at me, an ex-student analysing the psychology of his former teacher. Maybe someone like Scheerens was exactly what Jessie had been looking for all the time, while marching along in political protests and anti-racism marches.

Bart now took a set of photographs from his pocket and sat down beside Sylvie. He started showing her the pictures, one by one, and when he had finished restarted the set. Always holding the picture for a second in front of the screen, then gone and replaced by the waves and then another picture, gone again, alternating with the rhythm of the waves. Pictures of cakes, big birthday cakes with whipped cream. Pieces had been cut from some of them and they showed the dark-red jelly inside. There were numbers on them, big chocolate ciphers. And "5" and "6"…

Each picture also showed a knife, a big pie cutting knife,

sometimes beside the pie, the steel blade spotted with whipped cream and jelly, sometimes all silver and clean.

From Scheerens' textbook:
'The most interesting changes in consciousness appear when the frequency of the waves produced by the brain activity passes on into those of the theta-waves, which are slower and larger, and count four to seven vibrations each second. This is just a bit faster than the typical sleep rhythm of the delta-waves which dominate sleep with babies and people with brain malfunctions or abnormalities. The brain's activities slow down. By using hypnosis under medical control the storage of specific information can be counteracted so that the patient will remember nothing afterwards.'

Sylvie's eyes were half closed, her pupils enlarged and following the now forked patterns on the screen. The electronic lips were moving slower, sometimes flowing into each other, but the rhythm remained steady.

'Soon you'll be four, Sylvie,' Bart spoke with a low slow voice, stressing every syllable. 'You'll want a birthday party, with a cake, and then...'

The photographs danced through his fingers as magic cards, turning cartwheels in front of Sylvie's eyes, a demonical dance of cakes and knives and ciphers of chocolate.

Then Bart took the doll from his bag, the life-size inflatable rubber doll he had gotten in a sex shop. He had cut away the bumps of the breasts and carefully sealed the holes with rubber, after which he had painted the doll with what could pass for a costume: white shirt, tie, vest, trousers. Bart blew up the doll which took some time. He cursed and for a moment thought he'd better get the air pump from his bike. But he didn't dare leave now.

The soft arms and the legs of the doll were wriggling, almost fighting him as he breathed a mockery of life into it. Its movement looked like those of his father as he had last seen him, staggering out of the pub. To walk in front of a bus two streets farther. The insurance company of the bus hadn't paid a bloody cent as his father had been stoned drunk, and their legal advisor even suggested a suicide.

Fortunately the court ruled that out for a lack of evidence, or the life insurance wouldn't have paid off either.

The doll had a face, an already slightly faded photograph, an enlargement from a picture out of a school yearbook. The picture was a bit grainy due to the enlargement but the face was easily recognisable as that of professor Emmanuel Scheerens.

Years ago:

'What do you mean, you failed? Are you nuts? Is this what we have spent all our money on all those years, you idiot!'

'I can't help it, dad, really, I've studied till my brain threatened to burst.'

'Sure, I can just imagine, having pints at the pub with your no-good friends and trying to get into some chick's pants, and your study books locked away in your closet.'

'I can do the year over, dad, really, it's all the bloody fault of—'

'I don't wanna hear it, Bart, it's nobody's fault except your own, don't try to talk your way out of this with your smart-ass lines. YOU failed, that's all there is to it. And forget about doing the year over, we can't afford that.'

Bart took the broad-bladed knife and showed it to Sylvie.

'Look, Sylvie,' he whispered. 'A knife, big and sharp.' He touched her cheek with it and the girl flinched as the sharp blade stroked her as a cold finger. 'You can do a lot of things with a knife, Sylvie. A lot of good things with a big knife.'

The waves continued to sing silently on the screen, wave and wave and PEAK and wave and wave and PEAK. Crashing on the shores of her mind, eating away the sand, digging at the bare rocks underneath as if exposing a long buried skull.

Bart's words sang and whispered at the same rhythm, softly yet clearly spoken, words forming poisonous pearls creating a string to be stored, not yet understood or fully absorbed but kept in the dark corridors of the mind's caves. The knife moved back and forth, became a part of the pictures of the cakes, and through all this the biorhythms on the screen were dancing their sea ballet.

'A knife is dangerous, Sylvie, but a knife is also beautiful, Sylvie, beautiful and heavenly when there's a tart, Sylvie, a tart with whipped cream and cherries and strawberries inside. When you'll be four, Sylvie, and when you'll be five, and six, and seven and eight and nine. And then you'll be TEN, and when you'll be TEN everything will change, you can cut a cake with a knife, Sylvie, with a knife like this, but you can also cut other things, things which don't look like them but which ARE cake, all weak and red and tasty inside as a strawberry tart, Sylvie, when you'll be TEN...'

Bart's voice was soft and confidential: now he was telling Sylvie little secrets, a confession, and message, the little things you tell a very good friend you trust completely.

From Scheerens' textbook:

"It is a known fact that while under hypnosis the hypnotist cannot enforce something on the medium which is against the moral code of the subject. Let's skip for a moment the fact that in our subconscious we all have kept primary and beastly aspects of our psyche: those are under our control, so much even that we can ignore them... mostly. But is this safety valve correct? Let's suppose that we want our subject to do something which is absolutely against his own moral code. What if we convince the subject that he or she isn't really doing what the subject does, that he is doing something else entirely? What if we tell a young lady under hypnosis that she is now alone in her bathroom. Won't she strip for us? What if we tell a man in a shop that he has already paid for a certain object in the shop, will he not just put it in his pocket and walk out? Our subject will believe what we tell him and even do something illegal because he will not know that what he is doing is wrong. We just give another definition to what he is really doing, a definition which satisfies his own ideas of what is acceptable. We change the environment, the conditions and so we change in the mind's eye the nature of the act itself. Also we must consider that a moral code is an artificial creation pressed upon the subject by his environment during the growing and educating process. Before a certain age there is no question of an intellectual acceptance of moral values. Moral values are those pressing needs which are imposed at that moment."

Bart had the wriggling doll with Scheerens' face in his left hand and made it walk in front of Sylvie so she could see the face clearly. The knife was now in Bart's right hand.

'When you'll be TEN everything will change, Sylvie, you will want another cake and your daddy had a surprise for you, he has changed himself into a cake, he has hidden it inside himself and he wants you to find it. But he won't tell you, he knows how smart you are and he wants you to discover it yourself when you're TEN and then he'll be SO PROUD OF YOU, Sylvie, because you're SO SMART.'

The knife erected itself slowly, the point dug into the belly of the rubber man with the photograph face, pushed and then the blade penetrated. The rubber man farted from his belly. Bart withdrew the blade and stuck it in again and again.

'You must watch carefully and remember, Sylvie, you are TEN now, you WATCH and you REMEMBER and then you DO. You have found the REAL CAKE and your daddy is so PROUD that you have found him out.'

The knife had slit the plastic bags Bart had put inside the doll, and as the rubber man slowly folded the whipped cream and strawberry sauce came oozing out of the slits in the deflating doll. Bart put the knife down, wiped his fingers along the spilled stuff, white as sperm and red as blood. He licked his fingers and then brought them to Sylvie's lips. 'Taste it, Sylvie, taste what is inside the disguised man, see how his face is gone? It is not your daddy, it never was your daddy at all, it is a cake, your daddy had played a joke on you but you have found him out, he had disguised your birthday pie as himself, and now he's laughing and he's SO PROUD of you because you're SO SMART now that you are TEN, SO SMART then you have found him out.'

Sylvie licked her lips and nodded. Slowly Bart put the murdered doll down, carefully so that none of the sauce or cream spilled on the expensive carpet. The timing was perfect, the waves on the screen were slowing down.

'Now you must rest, Sylvie, you are very tired, you have been TEN and now you are NINE and now EIGHT, you will go to sleep now, now you are SEVEN and now SIX and now FIVE, soon you go to sleep and you will awake and feel very rested and you will not remember anything of this now, not until you really will be TEN, because now you are still only four and now you are three, and now you must sleep, sleep. SLEEP.'

The eyes of the girl closed, her breathing became deep and easy. Bart caught her when she slipped sideways. He wiped the cream and sauce from her lips, lifted her and carried her to the nursery. He put her to bed, covered her up to her chin and gave her a goodnight kiss on her check. Then he went to get a sandwich and a Coke from the fridge.

Some years ago:

Bart knocked and opened the door to the examination room. His head felt weird as an empty cave, his thoughts shrieking bats against the bone walls of his skull, no wonder after weeks of trying to absorb the twelve-hundred pages of Scheerens' textbooks. Scheerens was seated at the small metal table, his eyes bloodshot and tired (another meeting yesterday night?) and he was cleaning his nails with a pocket knife. The examination questions were in front of him on the table, a closed grey map, a deposit of Bart's future.

Scheerens put the pocket knife away. 'You haven't knocked,' he said.

'Sorry, but I did, mister Scheerens, I...'

The eyes grew hazy and hateful. One manicured hand moved, the heavy golden ring with the black stone on one finger flashing, a gentle gesture.

'You may leave, young man.'

'Leave? But... mister Scheerens?'

'You may leave, I said!'

Then Bart was standing outside, knowing his cipher, the round zero circling his future and strangling it, hugging in his mind the twelve-hundred pages studied and not a single question asked, and he didn't understand what was happening, didn't understand it at all.

Only later he learned what he had done wrong and realised the total absurdity of it all, the madness and the sheer enjoyment Scheerens got from the use of his total power.

Bart had made two unforgivable mistakes. He had contradicted Scheerens when he had said that he hadn't knocked. And he had said 'mister' and not 'professor' Scheerens...

The Scheerens' came home at half past three in the morning. Scheerens' eyes had the usual dull glare but he wasn't swaying though clearly he had had his fill. Probably experience had taught him to coordinate his movements, no matter in what condition he was.

Bart's bag stood ready, the books and the laptop, the dummy and the knife all inside. He was sitting on the couch, the TV turned off, reading one of Scheerens' adult comics.

'You have an admirable collection, sir,' Bart said.

'I know,' Scheerens said. 'No problems, no phone calls?'

'Nothing at all, sir,' Bart said, carefully putting the comic back in its place. 'Sylvie is soundly asleep. I took a look at her every half hour, but she never woke.'

'Good, good,' Scheerens murmured. He took his wallet, and tipped Bart quite generously. 'Should I drive you home? It's late and it's raining, you can pick up your bike tomorrow.'

Bart shook his head and picked up his bag. 'Very kind of you, sir, but it isn't necessary. I'm used to these hours. Have a good night sir, and madam. You have charming daughter.'

The year after, Sylvie Scheerens developed a, to her parents, quite incomprehensible but almost fanatical taste for strawberry and cherry tart with whipped cream.

A TASTE OF RAIN AND DARKNESS

NIGHT HAD CRAWLED over the city, as a slug over a small fish. In thick layers, she had drowned the evening sounds, until now there was only the silence of darkness and the rain. Night was a mother for her children, protecting them, smoothing them in her black cloak, Soft and tender and terrifying.

The street was empty now, the throbbing of its life-blood ebbed away with the going of its inhabitants. The dim light of a few lanterns created false twilights in the deep portals and corners of the old houses, and gave a wet glitter to the pavement. It transformed the downpouring November rain into a silver-threaded spiderweb, with downgliding pearls.

He was an unmoving statue, a part of the darkness and the rain. The wetness seeped ice-fingers through his drenched coat. He waited, with his closed hands protecting the spark of fire in his cupped palms, a half-finished cigarette. He waited, as he had waited ten years ago, and nine years ago, and every night between the seventh and the eighth of November. It rained, as it always rained that night, every damned year.

He hated the waiting.

At last the fire burned the palms of his hands, and he threw the rest of the cigarette away, knowing with a sick certainty that it was exactly the same fraction of a second he had thrown his cigarette away ten years ago, and nine years ago, and seven years ago...

A church bell started chiming in the distance, the echoes of its strokes shattering through his ears and brain. Eleven strokes.

Eleven strokes of horror, creating false images in the rain curtain in his brain. Lightning flashed, drawing with an electric pencil a short nightmare vision out of a surrealist painting, the houses as waiting sentinels with dead eyes and hungry mouths, the pavement stones upturned faces under his feet in the unreal light, just before the shadows closed again their eager tentacles around him.

It was like a short awakening from the climax of a nightmare, a moment of petrified time, the exact face of terror unremembered, but the fear running on and on through his veins.

It would be soon now. The waiting was almost finished.

Footfalls. Light steps from high-heeled shoes, sharply ticking sounds like a lonely clock. They came through the curtain of rain and darkness, walking through the still echoing sound of the church bells, through the empty street. Footsteps, where a few seconds before there had been nothing but silence. She must have come from one of the many small side streets, suddenly taking a corner. That was why he heard her approaching suddenly so clearly. Not that it mattered, he'd known they were coming. The footsteps were what he'd been waiting for.

They came nearer, their sounds gliding through the separating layers of rain, now almost beside him. A second bolt of lightning cut the sky, dimmed through the downpour, and he saw her face.

The white pastel face, wetness glittering as sparks on the colour-less cheeks, and the half-open, red painted mouth. Water pearls on her black hair, falling in her eyes, a mass of dripping wetness; the classical straight nose with the quick-moving nostrils; the blue coloured cosmetic of the eyelids and the far-away looking eyes, seeing in a distance which she alone could perceive. She passed by, uncon-scious of his presence. The lightning had gone, and the rain kept on falling from the open skies. Her high-heeled shoes clattered against the silence, as she went, the darkness closing after her passage.

He started to follow her. He knew the way very well now, every street, every damn corner, as seconds submerged in the eternity of ten years of torture. He lit a new cigarette, and had to throw it away because it was wet immediately, and crumbled into a brown mass of pulp between his fingers.

The light invited him, the only beacon before him in the darkness, changed and slightly pulsating through the rain fog. He stumbled from the three small steps and then was inside the cafe. Cold damp-ness welled out of the cellar, but it was still better than the wetness outside. At first there was only the thick blue-grey tobacco smoke cloud, slowly crawling through the low, veiled room. Then his tearful eyes accustomed themselves to the moving fog, and he started to see. The ceiling was very low indeed, and rested on heavy wooden pillars.

There was a poor-looking bar at the other end and besides it a juke-box, cold and dead with a big, crudely lettered sign *"Out of Use".*

The left and right sides contained about five wooden tables each, and posters decorated the walls, their colours faded and their corners wrinkled and brown. A few would-be artists, bearded, in ragged trousers and heavy pullovers, were seated at the extreme left, the origin of the tobacco fog.

The man entering received a short nod from the barkeeper, who was wrestling with his towel and dusty glasses, as if he was trying to scrub his emptiness off on them.

She was seated at the third table on the right, the same place as before. Oh God, if only *one* small detail would be different this year. But then, it never was, and the nightmare continued, carrying him along, unresisting, while each small detail of the night fitted into the other ones, as a clock's cogs. She was just sitting on her chair, with the neutral grey bag in her hand, and the untouched cup of coffee before her on the round table, losing its warmth in steady curls of smoke, slowly crawling up to the ceiling.

He went over to her and sat down in the chair opposite her. There was no sign of recognition from her, she didn't even acknowledge his presence; he was a ghost among the living. He observed her carefully, the patterns of ten years superimposing like paintings on glass plates, placed one upon the other. She was pretty and well built, with just the right proportions where they belonged. On her, even the formless raincoat looked like something very feminine.

Her hands were lying across her handbag. She didn't wear gloves, and he saw she had no rings on her fingers. Her hands were long and small, and very white—the hands of a secretary or a typist.

Her eyes were focused on the faded wall posters, but she saw through them, almost as if she studied the cracks and spiderwebs of the naked wall beyond them. He didn't try to start a conversation; it would be completely useless. She wouldn't react in any way, not even when he would touch her. To her, he didn't exist; he could just as well be another wall poster, to be neglected and stared through, just like the others whose discoloured smiles were grinning down on him. He was just a player in the dark game, a toy without a life of his own.

The proprietor came over to him, and he ordered a glass of cheap red wine. After being paid his fifteen francs, the barman returned to the bar and continued whipping imaginary dust from his beer glasses.

The man took a sip from his glass, and put it down again. He waited for her to turn, which she did exactly at seventeen minutes past twelve. Slowly she revolved in her chair, and he saw the gliding movement; of her hands, as coiled snakes over her well formed legs. Her skirt had crawled up, and he had a short glimpse of the softness of her leg above her stockings. As a statue on a moving turntable, her profile turned, and the cold grey knowing eyes met his for a split second—a dip into a deep fog, which left him shivering.

At exactly half past twelve, when the chimes sounded, she checked the time on her wrist watch, then stood up and left. The night closed after her, as if she'd never been there.

He called the bartender, and asked him the question he had asked over and over again in those ten years, the question whose answer was engraved with letters of ice in his shrieking mind.

'Do you know the woman who was sitting here with me?'

The bartender looked surprised and suspicious. 'Woman? What woman? Excuse me, but you have been sitting here alone for over twenty minutes. All by yourself.' He returned to his bar; his hands crawled like two enormous fat white-bellied spiders over the glasses and bottles, and he shot half angry glances at the man who asked such questions.

The man had known it all the time, and his beating heart was transformed into a giant freezing vault, from which ice water was pumped through his veins. The coldness was all over his stomach. He was slowly preparing himself for hell. He left, too, and the night engulfed him, suspicious, hostile. He had walked that night ten years, had tasted every bitter drop of rain and darkness and fear, and yet still he was an outsider, someone beyond even the laws of darkness.

He followed the street, the sound of his nailed shoes following him... tik... tik... tik... tik... If he could only stop them; but he couldn't, and the sound went on and on, echoing through his mind. The dead eyes of the houses he passed looked down on him. Go away, they shrieked, go away from us, you don't belong. Their mouth doors were closed to him, as to all unwanted night creatures. And his feet walked on, carrying him with them, like their own private zombie. How he wanted to stop them. But just as he hadn't stopped them ten years ago, so he couldn't now. Tik, tik, tik, the sounds crawling up the house walls, and falling down on him, burying him, petrifying his brain, like an insect caught in wax, fossilized. His mind didn't react now; it cowered inside his skull, screaming soundlessly, and his body, the frozen flesh and blood machine, went along the empty street, following the girl before him.

Now he had seen her, quickly stepping. When he had approached her to within ten metres distance, he knew that she had heard him. This was where and when she always heard him coming nearer, the hunter closing in on the game. She looked over her shoulder, puzzled, then frightened. She hurried her steps, tik, tik, tik, meaningless echoes in a night for fear. Now five metres, now four, now three, his own steps smothering hers. Two metres, it all went so quickly now, she started running, too late, much too late—damn you why didn't you run earlier when there was still time? Now there's no time left, now, now, not ever! He stretched out his hands across ten years.

He wished he could cry out the horror cupped inside him. If he could only stop this time circle and end the game, but he couldn't, he never could. His feet ran, and his arms went out like striking snakes; his hands very young, and very white, the veins as cords running under his skin, blood pumping through them at the speeded up rhythm of his heartbeat. He felt the excitement crawling like an uneasy animal in his belly, beating in his brain, drowning everything else except the horror. Then she turned and opened her mouth to scream, and his hands closed around her throat.

Her mouth stayed open, her teeth flashing as she curled up her lips like a snarling cat. He pushed her against the wall of a house, the light of a nearby lantern spilling over her face, like a faded close-up. He was almost one with her squirming body, feeling every movement of it against his own. She tried to kick, but his legs were between hers and stopped the frantic movements. She made small sounds, krrh, ahrrg, and her nails made bloody patterns on his iron hands. They felt the softness of her throat, the pulsing power of her aorta, as they pressed and pressed; the convulsive movements of her esophagus; her gasping mouth open to the night and the rain; the excitement was all over his body now, and he fell, his legs trembling, with red waves pulsing.

Her face grew dark, as her eyes grew wide and the tongue came out of her mouth, dark and swollen between her teeth, lolling out of her gasping mouth. Spittle dripped on his hands. Her body made short shaking movements, a small animal running crazy in a trap, slowly dying. Only his brain kept screaming, *stop it, goddamnyou stopitstopitstopit,* but it didn't stop. He felt the corners of his mouth draw up, forming the insane grin his face had worn that time, his breath coming in groaning gasps. She suddenly made a last gurgling sound and stiffened, her eyes bulging as those of a frog, her legs making one last convulsive movement.

His hands loosened their grip, and her shawl stayed between his fingers. She stayed upright against the wall, her eyes staring doors into emptiness, her lolling tongue a dark piece of paper placed against her blue lips. He leaned against the wall, wishing desperately to be sick, but again he couldn't. Time restarted running, and as he looked, her left eye became fluid and ran across her cheek, leaving a wet slimy trail like a snail's. Her right eye followed, and blood started streaming from the holes, then dried up and left dusty trails. Her body sagged slowly, while the flesh of her face decayed, first the cheeks falling inwards in her mouth, then crumbling into rotting flesh. Yellow bones came splintering through, as the face fell further into ashes, the teeth making small rattling sounds as they clattered upon the street. The disintegrating body fell upon its knees, then slowly keeled backwards, to the sound of cracking bones and tearing rotted flesh and muscles.

Then he turned and began to run through the horror-ridden streets of night, the slightest sound of high heeled footsteps following him and meeting him from every corner, her death rattle echoing from every black window. At last, when he couldn't run any more, he fell flat on his face, his hands beating the stones until the blood ran from them and stained his clothes. Then he was very sick, and when his insides stopped turning inside out, and he stopped panting, he looked up at the rain shrouded stars and prayed, 'My God, please *PLEASE LET IT BE THE LAST TIME, LET IT BE FINISHED NOW.'* A senseless prayer, because he *knew.*

He knew that next year, the night of November seventh, he would

again stand in the lonely street, smoking a cigarette in the downpouring rain, tasting the rain and the darkness, waiting for the sound of
her high heels. He looked at his hands. They were old and tired,
without any strength left; but next year again, they would become
the claws of the other, waiting one, deep inside him, while he again
would be no more than a watching, tormented machine. He felt the
shawl he still held in his hand, and kneaded it into a silken mass over
his hot face, the last straw before the opening edge of definite
madness, so near and yet never near enough for him. How senseless,
his prayer. If there was a God, it was the God from the Old
Testament, who wanted an eye for an eye. Because she had not really
been there. He knew that for sure, like the fact that the shawl
between his clasped fingers would turn into dust, mixing with the
mud on his shoes, as soon as he entered the threshold of his home.

I WONDER WHAT HE WANTED...

SELECTED FRAGMENTS FROM the diary of Miss Francie Denvar former teacher at Cornoudghe College, found among the possessions of the late inhabitant of Number Nine, Nowhill Street.

June 2nd:
Wonderful! The rest, the peace! At last I'm finished with the school turmoil, the endless mountains and mountains of examination papers to be checked, the exhausting interrogations of uninteresting and uninterested youngsters who really couldn't care less, the reports in "X" duplicates to be made, and all the rest! College has fallen from my shoulders like a badly-smelling, dusty cloak, and I feel as if I'm arisen like a phoenix. The restfulness is like a soft wine, it reanimates me, thrills through my whole body. A real pity Georges couldn't be here with me now for the whole vacation. But it was impossible, he said. Within the next week he has to leave for France, for some special article or other which he has to do for his paper. He thinks he'll be away for at least three weeks, or maybe even more. Well, I'll manage by myself, I suppose.

June 3rd:
Poor diary, I'm sorry but I'm much too happy to spend much time in writing today! It is now half past eleven, and Georges has just left. I'm dreaming on my old, worn seat, and I'd rather go on doing nothing, but it would be unfair to you, my old companion, not to record this evening for the future. Georges has just asked me to marry him. Oh, the way he did it, so simple and straightforward, like everything he does, in fact not so very romantic. He just put his arm around me, and said, 'Darling, when do we get married?' It seems so awfully down-to-earth and practical, when I see it written down; he should have done it with a kiss and a bunch of flowers (he knows I love roses—every young girl does... but that's just not *his* way of doing things). He caught me completely off guard, I didn't know what to

say. I just nodded. He'll buy me an engagement ring tomorrow, first thing he'll do in the morning before he goes to the office, he said. A very pretty one in platinum gold, with a sparkling diamond in its heart. But only a small one, he added as an afterthought. A small diamond, but a big heart. Georges *can* be romantic, if he wants to. As soon as he gets back from his Parisian assignment, we'll announce our engagement officially. The wedding will be in October, we can't make it sooner. Georges has too many things to do, and he won't be able to get a vacation from the paper until that time. It doesn't matter. I'm so happy, so happy!

June 8th:

I have taken Georges to the train. He kissed me and said, 'I'll be back soon darling. Don't run too far.' I cried a bit, after the train had left, but I still feel so happy I could sing the whole day through. I'll be married in October! Of course I knew he'd ask me one day but he waited so long...

June 10th:

I've found a marvel of a little house with a pretty though neglected garden, just what I've wanted all my life. It all came about accidentally. I was lonely and took a bus out of town, and then started walking... and I stumbled upon it. A very small villa house, a bit old and really isolated, but I'm sure it will be beautiful once I've finished with it. It's almost the only house left in an old street, all the others on both sides have been torn down a long time ago. I liked it at first sight—what a cliché—and out of curiosity went into the garden to have a good look at it. Imagine, it was for rent! I immediately went to the address mentioned on the sign (you know how impulsive I am) and see! Now I already have the keys and the signed contract in my purse. Maybe I have been rather rushed with it, but after all I only rented it for one year to start with. I must phone the removal company, so that they can bring my few bits of furniture from the studio—I already phoned my landlord, Miss Esphalton, and she's probably only too glad to be rid of me, though she didn't say it in so many words. She never liked me anyway, and she has already got several people on her waiting list. I must send the great news to

Georges immediately, and give him my new address.

June 13th:

Today they have brought the furniture. The fools broke the legs of one of my best chairs, and I didn't tip them. That'll show them, though they said that I will be refunded by their insurance company. I doubt that, but it hasn't spoilt my good humour. The house simply is a jewel. Dusty and in need of painting, but a gem all the same. It has a kitchen, a living room and a library room downstairs, two big bedrooms and a work-room upstairs, and a big attic above. I brought someone to fix a few small holes in the walls, and one broken window. I'll need other windows attended to, though, as the glass is murky and soiled. There are no cellars, and even in the attic there is hardly a trace of real decay. No holes in the roof either, I checked that but I didn't stay long. I don't like attics. In the living-room there is a big fireplace with antique Flemish brickwork, and beside it a colossal mirror, with only a few small spots. I think I'll go into town and choose a suitable wallpaper. I must pick up some of my savings from the bank too, after having paid a guarantee deposit and two months' rent in advance.

June 14th:

Georges just wrote me a long and lovely letter. He's doing fine, and hopes to finish his "reportage du coeur de Paris" much sooner than he thought. He's very excited about our house, and can't wait to see it, though he writes that he would have preferred to inspect it himself first before I moved in. I should really start giving the house a good cleaning now, but I don't feel like it. That's not like me, but I think it's the heat which makes me feel so listless and tired. These last days, the sun seems almost to have burned a blazing hole in the cloudless sky, and the heat is lying over the house and me like some enormous suffocating hand. I hope it'll rain soon. It usually does in this country. Just try taking a really long walk when the sun is so hot, and you're very likely to return completely soaked by the rain.

June 19th:

I took a short walk this morning to get some supplies from the grocer. When I got back, I thought at first there was somebody there, waiting for me. But I was wrong, there was nobody. Still, the whole day I have had the impression that somebody is in the house, somebody always watching me, spying on me. I couldn't shake that impression off, and I'm usually *not* a nervous woman. I've taken the big mirror away from beside the fireplace because it frightened me nearly to death this morning. I had just got up, and went downstairs, and somebody else came suddenly walking up to me. Of course I was still partly asleep, like I always am before I've had my first cup of coffee, but I should have known that it was only my reflection in that mirror. Well I *do* feel better, more at ease now that it's gone, though the place where it hung shows clearly now against the discoloured wallpaper.

June 20th:
    I can't write much, I'm nervous, the slightest sound outside makes me jump as if the earth is opening under me. I can't get rid of that weird feeling that somebody or something is looking over my shoulder, following me wherever I go. Another letter came from Georges this morning, a short hurried note. Something unforeseen happened, and he won't be back till the end of August.

June 22nd:
    I made a horrible discovery today. There must be rats in the house. I heard them, scrambling around in the attic. I went up, and when I threw the door open, something small and dark ran away. I stood there for a while, all the time feeling its eyes fixed on me, watching, waiting for me to do something. I locked the door, and tomorrow I'm going to buy a dose of rat poison and a big cat.

June 23rd:
    I put the cat in the attic, and I left the door ajar, so she could come and go whenever she felt like it. Later in the evening, I heard the door of the attic creak. I went upstairs with a strong flashlight, and something small hurried away from the beacon. When I came down, the cat was at the front door, frantically trying to get out. Every one of

my attempts to catch her failed, and she acted as if she'd gone mad. The only result of my chase are some severe scratches on my hands from her claws.

June 24th:

This morning as I came down, I found the blasted cat in the living-room. The beast was dead, but there were no marks on her body. The eyes were bulging horribly, and the jaws wide open. Saliva and a bit of blood had dripped on to the floor. The cat must have been sick when I bought her. At first I wanted to go and complain to the pet shop where I got her, but I decided to leave it at that. I went upstairs again and searched the whole attic, but I found nothing living there, and no holes in the walls either. I have re-locked the attic. I don't think I'll bother buying another cat, though it is getting rather lonely in the house.

Late afternoon. Another discovery, and a creepy one this time. While I was walking through the garden, I suddenly stumbled over something. When I pushed the tall grass away, I found a stone under it, the biggest part buried under the ground. Then when I looked closely I spotted the marks on it. They turned out to be letters, forming a name, which I could decipher after cleaning the stone a bit: Francesca Denverra. There were dates too, but I couldn't make them out. I was only able to discover that they were sometime in the late 19th Century. It must be an old tombstone. I don't want that thing lying around in my garden. First thing tomorrow morning I'll complain to the landlord to get it taken away.

June 25th:

The landlord wasn't home, so I left a note, and I'll see him tomorrow. I want a garden with my house, not a miniature graveyard. Every day seems to bring new discoveries. As I had again heard the scurrying in the attic, I decided to try the rat poison. While I was laying it down, I found heaps of yellowed paper and old writing material in one of the cabinets. There were several notebooks, full of a spidery handwriting, definitely female, all notes for novels or short stories, apparently. I took them down with me to have a good look at them. They seem strange stories for a woman to write: fictional notes on witchcraft, the occult, ghostly appearances, vampirism, lycanthropy, Satanism, and other weird things. The titles alone seem sufficient: *The Creature from the Tomb*, *Hands of Decay*, *The Whispering Thing*, *A Taste of Rain and Darkness*... Once I started reading them, I had to finish them, though their contents often disgusted me. The horribly realistic way she wrote about those things, as if she really believed in them herself, had even experienced them! But then, once there was an eighteen-year-old girl who wrote *Frankenstein*, and many other female writers have gone in for horror stories. I'll ask the landlord also about these things tomorrow. Maybe the manuscripts, even if many seem unfinished, might have a certain bibliographical value. Who knows, I might even make some money out of them!

June 26th:
I had a long talk with the proprietor this morning. I was dead right—what a choice of words! The thing in the garden is indeed a gravestone. Fortunately there's nothing under it. Miss Denverra, born in 1834 died in 1917 seems to have had a certain reputation as an author. The landlord said that she had written several novels, but that of course was before his time, he hadn't read them, but probably they were in the local library. When she died, he had bought the house from a distant cousin who had inherited it. In her will, she had requested that her grave in the garden shouldn't be disturbed. The queer woman had bought the tombstone several years before her death, and had it placed where I'd seen it, but of course she was buried in the cemetery—though the landlord had kept the stone in the garden.

'Rather picturesque,' he said, 'it makes the house something a bit special you know.' He refused to remove the stone—'It doesn't hurt you, does it?' he said—and as I don't want to give up my lovely house, I'll have to put up with it, at least till Georges arrives and finds a solution.

I still have that idea of someone watching over my shoulder. It gives me the creeps.

June 27th:
I went to the library and borrowed a few books by Francesca

Denverra. They didn't have all her works the librarian said, but they did have all her best and most important novels. He told me that she died at the peak of her creative power. He seemed quite an expert in the field, and told me many details he knew about Denverra, how she sometimes worked for several years on one book, refusing to use a typewriter, living only on her savings and the irregular income her books brought her. He gave me *Scream from the Cellar*, *All the Shadows of Fear* and *Eye of the Vampire*, and said that if I wanted some others he had many by Machen, James and Poe, and even a few scarce titles by Lovecraft and Hodgson. But I have enough with Denverra. Besides, I never liked horror stories, and these only interest me because the woman has lived in the house. I leafed through some of the books. Horrible. How could a woman in her sane mind ever write those accursed blasphemous things? The books themselves seem filled with their evil, overflowing with decay and corruption. They disgust me... and yet, in a strange way, they fascinate by their horror.

June 29th:
    I still feel listless. The heat keeps on, the earth feels dry and hot, the air stale and strangling, trees give almost no shade. The world outside seems dead, burned, and only the house gives peace and shadow. The damned tombstone is giving me nightmares now. To-night I dreamed that I saw Francesca Denverra, sitting in one of my chairs, now in the attic, with the notes of her novel *The Smell of Blood* in her lap. She was making corrections in the notebook, and I could read everything she wrote, and it made me feel sick. When I awoke I was soaked in sweat.

July 3rd:
    At last another letter from dear Georges. Good news this time! He thinks he'll be back very soon now, no date fixed but much earlier than expected. Thank God! I just can't wait till he gets here, though the feeling of being watched has gone away now. I sleep much better too, untroubled by the weird nightmares I was having up till a few nights ago. It's almost as if finally I've been accepted by this house as its new inhabitant, and now it gives me peace.

July 4th:

I have read *Scream from the Cellar* a second time through. I had wanted to go to the library to pick up some love stories and historical romances, but the heat was just too much; it engulfed me in a suffocating grip as soon as I left the house. When will it ever rain? So there's nothing left in the house but Denverra's books. It doesn't seem so horrible any more upon a second reading, mainly I guess because now I know in advance what is going to happen. The shock elements have lost their power, and now I can spend more time on the literary qualities, and ignore the plot. In a way there is a weird beauty in her books, a beauty which is evil and yet absorbing. It is like the night-marish quality of a Bosch painting, or a Dali, or the shrieking yet hilarious madness of a Topor or a Gahan Wilson cartoon, and sometimes even the weird and unreal fascination of a Matisse.

July 6th:

This afternoon, I slept a bit in a chair in the garden. When I walked back into the house I felt strange, as if something had been very subtly changed while I was away; as if something was really out of place. Only after a while did I realize what it was. It's my furniture, my own modern furniture, which doesn't fit the rooms. I had thought at first to change the rooms completely into something modern, but you can't do that with these old houses and their high ceilings and their building structure. But I must do something about it, maybe rearranging the furniture will make it look better, more homely.

July 7th:

I re-read Denverra's notes, her unfinished manuscripts. The librarian was right, the manuscripts are grotesque, horrible, almost the work of a deranged mind, and yet they are powerful, much better written than any of the published books, much more meaningful in content and researched details. Literature really lost something with her. There were even a few parts I must have skipped over the first time, they seem to have been added later, all in her small spidery handwriting.

July 8th:

Today I had all the modern furniture removed. I tried to make it look better, but it kept on degrading the atmosphere of the rooms. Now it looks much better. I only kept some chairs, and brought down the old cabinets from the attic and dusted them off. It looks now like it must have looked before, so easy, solemn, and peaceful. I even put the big mirror back in its place. I couldn't stand looking at the awful mark on the wallpaper where it had hung.

July 9th:
The weather is beautiful. I have been sitting idly in the garden through the whole day, without bothering to do anything. A lot of sun is good for me, the doctor once said, and I have always kept that in mind. Come to think of it, it's really been a long time since I saw him. Not that I need him for anything, I feel better than I have ever felt before, perfectly healthy.

July 12th:
I think I'll have to start working again one of these days. No doubt my publisher will be severely angry with me yet again, though he should know my habits by now! I'm very surprised he hasn't written already, asking for my first draft, or at least for some working notes on my latest novel. I have re-read my draft notes for the plot structure, and they're good. A complete synopsis already, with detailed notes on all the central characters. Now only a few researches on the background, and I can begin writing in earnest. *Metempsychosis* will be my best novel so far.

July 14th:
Something very strange happened this morning. A young man called, a certain Georges Vaarberg, who had come direct from Paris. He was very surprised when I opened the door, and mumbled something about a probable mistake. He asked me if I knew a young teacher, a certain Miss Frances Denvar, who used to live here. I answered him that no-one lived here except me. He excused himself, and went away. At the entrance he turned and looked back, a baffled expression on his face. I didn't see him again.

I wonder what he wanted from an old woman like me?

A WHISPER OF LEATHERY WINGS

SLOWLY COLIN BARKER approached the old shack, gratefully making use of every shadow, every tree to obscure his nearness. Soft grass whispered beneath his tennis shoes, still wet from the evening rain. The woodland night felt refreshed after that rain, breathing again after a long period of drought. Now and then there was the scattering of small animals through the dark, the swiftly moving shadow-shape of a weasel on the hunt through the low bushes, the almost unnoticed insect sounds, the short spidery flutter of wings, as a bat darted into the full face of the moon, and then away again into the shrouding darkness, borne on silent stretched wings. The wood seemed fully awake, bursting with dark and venomous life, as small things died and other things fed. The house, on the contrary, seemed dead. Very old and very dead. Colin wiped the sweat from his hands on his trousers. He had put on the dark brown jeans, and the black pullover. Even his shoes had been turned dark in the mud, so that now only his face was a pale echo of his body.

The house of Old Woman Spidernose loomed up in front of him, at the end of the small clearing along the road through the wood. Well, road wasn't exactly the correct word to describe it, a foot-trodden path traced at random through the wilderness, running through the wood at stupid angles, and passing two clearings, on the first of which Joe J. Harker had built his house. That had been long before Colin's time, of course and J. J. Harker was long dead and gone now, his bones rotting in peace in Denwire's churchyard. After his death, once in a week, one of the Millar women had gone to his place to keep it more or less in clean shape, and hunt out the small animals which would dearly have loved making it their continuous living space. Not that anyone really cared much for it, but well, old Harker had left no relatives that anyone knew of at that time, so that made his house more or less public property till someone came along to claim it, and Denwire was a clean community. Then Old Woman Spidernose had moved in with her daughter Myriam. Spidernose wasn't her real name of course, she was called Duveuille or Dovaila or some similar weird unpronounceable name. She wasn't that ugly either, though old she certainly was, but she had no hunchback or nose with warts. Her nose was small yet very sharp, as the beak of a hawk, and her eyes were of a strange tint of grey, and seemed very alive and very sharp for someone her age. Her hair was very long, and darkish grey, it wasn't exactly unkempt, but hung down in long strands which always fell over her face from both sides, so that one always had the impression of being stared at just by a pair of eyes and a nose, lurking behind a spider's web of grey hair. Which immediately procured the nickname "Spidernose" for her.

It had all been rather funny, the sudden way in which the old woman appeared in the village, nodding curtly to passersby and heading straight to the notary's office, and then with him to the burgomaster. Before anyone really realized it, a van arrived with some furniture and luggage, and Old Woman Spidernose and Myriam moved into the old Harker house. It had become the local gossip for the next week, but Colin had heard in the inn that it had all been very legal. The old woman had some valid documents proving her to be some distant relative of the Harker's, and she had even offered to pay for the way the house had been kept clean and intact. This the burgomaster had kindly refused to accept, to the annoyance of the Millar woman who had done the job.

A twig snapped suddenly under Colin's feet, and he froze, cursing inwardly. He should keep his mind on the matter at hand, and not be thinking back to the time Old Spidernose and her daughter had arrived. Was it his imagination or did the wood really freeze with him, as if the trees held their breath, petrified their branches which no longer seemed to move softly in the wind? Did that bat hesitate in its flight? A few clouds passed before the moon's surface, and an alien darkness settled over the silent wood. Colin didn't move, though he felt the sweat dripping along his back, and his armpits itched horribly. He should have known better than to put on that pullover, but it had been the only dark garment he had been able to find. It wouldn't do to get caught now. He shivered lightly, rolling the muscles of his shoulders, hoping to stop the itching. Of course he could always try to find some excuse, say that he had come to say hello to Myriam or something like that. But then what? How could he explain his strange attire, his muddy shoes, and the way he had been sneaking up on the house? Well, they shouldn't be in. It was a full moon night, and the two women would be out now. He had watched them leave on other moon nights, their heads covered by the black shawls with the cryptic marks on them, when they thought nobody was there to notice them, carefully making their way into the depths of the night wood. He hadn't followed them.

Myriam would believe what he said, she would believe anything he told, but old Woman Spidernose wouldn't, oh no, she wouldn't! She must have noticed him hanging around Myriam a bit, but certainly she wouldn't know how far his relationship with the girl had gone already. And of that she surely wouldn't approve either. He had no intention of having the old bitch after his skin. He knew now what she could do, and he had pried enough out of Myriam to know more or less how she did it. Ah, Myriam, sweet little Myriam. She wasn't that pretty in fact, exactly as her mother she had hollow cheeks with big burning eyes, and a mouth which was a bit too large to make her face beautiful. Her long uncombed black hair mostly covered part of her face anyway, except when she was lying down, then it spread as a dark shawl under her head, seeming to twist with a strange life of its own. She was so young that Colin sometimes had wondered if the old woman was really her mother, there seemed to be too much difference in age to accept that. But she always spoke of Old Spidernose as "Mother", maybe she meant grandmother.

Not that it really made a difference, mother or grandmother, no respectable witch would be glad to learn that her daughter had been initiated in the age-old rites of love by some village lad. Myriam's breasts were too small for Colin's taste, but the girl was a damned good lay, and she seemed to have no feelings of shame at all, at anything. She had proved much better in fact than fat butcher Blonk's heavy-breasted daughter, or even thin-lipped sensual Katie from the inn, and THAT girl had been doing it with every guy above sixteen from the village, including a few seasonal workers it was rumoured. But Myriam had a special way of working with her hips, something really extraordinary, which was as well as it meant combining fun with business. Strange that such a young chick should be so good at it, when she still had been a virgin when he had her the first time. The two women had been living for more than one year in the Harker house by then, and he'd been playing it up to Myriam for several weeks, accidently walking across her path as she walked in the woods, chatting a bit and so on, the regular routine, before the first kisses. She had managed to slip out of the back door of the house when the old woman was asleep. In fact neither of them had expected to go all the way that first time, but they had gotten carried away, as one says. The next time Colin was smart enough to take his precautions, having the girl was all well and good, but he didn't want any trouble, and certainly not getting Old Woman Spidernose's daughter pregnant.

The night sounds had started again, and nothing moved in the house. It just stood there, as some vast and hideous prey animal, seemingly asleep, yet giving the impression of waiting for the oncoming intruder, its empty eyes half closed, its white fangs waiting just behind the door, ready to strike.

Nonsense, Colin thought, I have to get rid of this morbid imagination if I want to play it through to the end. I'll need my nerves more than that once I'm inside, once I have... IT. It's just a goddamn bloody old house, and there's no one inside now, but what I want is inside. So if I want it badly enough, I have to get it, so I'd better get my feet moving now.

His feet refused, they seemed caught in driftsand, sinking down in the wet grass and the mud, as if his toes had been rooted into the ground, fixing him in his place as a young rebellious tree, fighting the damp earth. Damn, he thought, I won't give up, not now I'm so close.

Then he thought of Ludo, and the sudden surge of hate rose as red spit in his mouth. He bit his lips, so hard that he suddenly tasted the sweetness of his own blood. He spat it out, and licked his sore lip with the tip of his tongue. Ludo, that accursed whore's son, that bastard! This was his only chance to get even with Ludo, maybe the only chance he'd ever get in his life. Automatically his hands went up and touched the painfully swollen flesh around his blackened eye, the results of yesterday's meeting with Ludo after their argument in the inn. He had known Ludo would be waiting for him outside, and had left through the back door, but Ludo was smart, and he was fast.

Colin hadn't run far, before Ludo caught up with him. Thinking, hating, Colin's fingers carefully traced the deep scar on his left cheek... another one of Ludo's presents. Fear and hatred formed a strong mixture, warming his heart, burning in his veins. If only he could have Ludo at his mercy, only once, so he could kick his teeth, wipe the flashing toothpaste smile from his mocking face. But Ludo, the grocer's son, stood twenty-eight centimetres taller than Colin, his shadow hid Colin completely, and he had some odd ten kilos more weight, all distributed in the correct places. In short, he could knock Colin around as much as he liked, which he regularly did, and had been doing just for fun for a few years, which was not quite Colin's idea of amusement.

Hate comes and goes easily with young children, sometimes it just fades away while growing up, when one starts to know people better, and sometimes it goes the other way and just keeps on growing, till a skull is too small a place to hide the hatred. Then it spreads through the body, a slow and deadly poison, it lives on in hands and feet and belly, a continuous fire of hate, sometimes shrinking down to a small spark which then again flowers open at the slightest occasion. Colin had been nursing his particular hate-fire for years, watching it grow with a strange fascination, breeding it, nursing it till now it was an essential part of his mind and body. He had been dreaming of once getting even with Ludo, humiliating him in front of the whole village, making him lick his feet, crawl into the dirt before him, and yet knowing that it would never come true. Ludo was a born dominator, and he, Colin, was a born underdog. That had been till he had learned about Old Woman Spidernose.

Now he was able to move again, the hatred had burned the roots holding his feet prisoner, and slowly he advanced again. Nothing to be afraid of, they were away, gathering the weird herbs they needed for... well, for whatever it was witches and their breed needed them. Or maybe they were holding some hidden alien ceremony in the darkness of the woods, of which he rather wanted no part or even knowledge. A stupid word, witchcraft, and one he would have laughed at heartily some months ago, but not now, not after he had SEEN.

The Duveuilles had been accepted by the town after the initial gossip had died down. They did their usual shopping, talked with the shop keepers, sometimes gossiped a bit themselves, but mostly they seemed rather uninterested in local matters and kept pretty much to themselves. They caused nobody any trouble, so in fact those who did learn of their... powers, brought it on their own heads. Blonk, the fat sweating butcher with his plump red hands, had been the first to learn that. Well, it was true that he sometimes dared to overcharge on his steaks, that his chickens weren't always as fresh as he said they were, and everybody knew that they had to check their change while still inside the shop. But well, everyone has some bad habits, and those were Blonk's; some villagers even made a game out of it, trying to cheat Blonk or get cheated by him. Old Woman Spidernose didn't know about Blonk's habits of course, so it wasn't really nice of him to cheat on her, and then commence a big laughing party when she went back to complain that he had given her ten francs short. She seemed baffled by his reaction, just stood there staring at him with the change money loose in her hand. Her nose moved as if she smelled something awful, and with someone else it would have been hilarious, but seeing it from her it wasn't even funny, rather disquieting. Her cruel grey eyes were fixed on Blonk's face, and the mirth just seemed to be drained out of him. He cursed her, and said that if she thought that she'd just have to go to another butcher. Which she did, she suddenly turned around and walked out of the shop. In fact she didn't show up in the village for a whole week, and during the week Blonk walked around cursing and with a hideous black eye. 'Ran smack into an open door,' he explained when someone made a joke about it, suggesting that it was the final result of a difference of opinion with Blonk's wife. Well, it just wasn't like Blonk, and certainly not the odd nervousness he began displaying after that week, the strange habit he got of looking over his shoulder, and jumping up when you spoke to him suddenly. Even weirder, however, was his attack of rage when a customer once asked him how he could manage to sleep in the heat of summer with his bed-room windows closed. Then of course people started noticing that he DID close his bedroom windows at night.

Colin knew, of course, he was one of the four or five people who knew because they had SEEN... and sometimes FELT. Bucket Bernie had been next, who had tripped Old Woman Spidernose while drunk, as usual. There was no need for strangers in town to wonder where Bucket Bernie had picked up his name, one only had to look at his eyes and pose to understand that it certainly was not from drinking a bucket of water. Maybe Bernie hadn't quite meant it that way as he stretched out his long legs just as she walked by with her shopping bag, but that was the way it worked out nevertheless. She landed right on her nose in the middle of the road, in front of him, making it such a nice landing that for a few days the village kids yelled about "Falling Woman Spidernose" before her old name fell back into use. Well, Bucket Bernie was just too drunk to apologize, and probably he wouldn't have anyway, not even while sober, so the best he could do, and did, was sit there laughing his head off. He almost lost his head the next evening when he ran shrieking into the inn, yelling for help against something which was out there trying to get him. Well, Bucket Bernie sometimes had this thing about things which were out to get him, but this time something HAD got him. A couple of his front teeth had been knocked out, and there were long bleeding scratches showing on both sides of his face. He could have stumbled against a tree knocking out his own teeth, and he could have scared some woodland animal and frightened it, or maybe even low tree branches could have been responsible for the scratches, though they were rather deep and bleeding like hell. However, he was sober that evening, though not for long. After a while he calmed down, and started gulping down more than his usual quota of cognac. He refused to say anything more, but we all had heard what he had been screaming when he arrived, something about a golden faced beast after him, which had long talons and which flew on leathery wings, as an enormous bat. Of course he became the joking matter of the evening, but he only got more sullen, just not his usual self, and when the inn was closing he refused to go out. Not that he was still really able to WALK, but he made such a fuss anyway that the landlord finally let him sleep on a chair. Again Old Woman Spidernose didn't show her nose, or anything else, in the village for two weeks. During those two weeks, Bucket Bernie got more and more nervous, and one evening he drank himself to death, beating his own drinking record.

The hatred was subsiding now, and again Colin felt very cold. He was now walking straight towards the house, crossing the open space in front of it. Why did that blasted thing really SEEM to stare at him? He refused to blame it all on his imagination, and after all, he had heard, and he had seen... IT. Now he was at the door, still hesitating. He stretched out his hands and touched the wood, which was wet and very cold to his fingertips. No normal wood should be so cold, and no normal house should be that silent; it was draining his courage. Yet he had nothing to fear as much as his own fear. The two weren't inside, but what he wanted was. The thing which would give him power, enough power to strike back at Ludo. Maybe once he had it, he could even fend off the two women, because it was what she used for her power. Once he had it, just let her try to get it away from him!

The wood around the house was stirring softly, yet nothing moved close to the house, no insects crawled on the walls, no small animals ran through the open space, no bird's shadow crossed it, as if even they preferred to stay away from the house. There was a faint rustling behind him, and he whirled around, his eyes bulging, his hands rising in an automatic defense, protecting his face. But the thing with the golden face wasn't there, there was nothing there, it must have been in his imagination, that whisper of leathery wings, or else the wind moving carefully through the trees' branches. Yet it brought exactly those memories back which he shunned, because they turned his knees weak.

It had happened about two months before he had decided to start chatting Myriam up. He had been drifting idly along one of the side-paths of the wood, having spent a nice evening with some friends at the inn at a card game, and fortunately Ludo hadn't come that evening as at that time he had been having his affair with the Saunders girl from Tuckdown, some three miles from Denwire. Colin hadn't drunk much, no more than a pint or three, but he felt at ease with the world and himself. Then he heard the sound, and the screams. He hadn't hesitated, but thrown himself straight into a dry ditch along the path. He preferred not to get involved in anything which had screams in it. Then the two Cochran boys had run by, shrieking and stumbling over their own feet. He had noticed it then for the first time, the flapping of two mighty wings, yet no wings as a bird has, more the silent movements of bat wings, but something in between, a rustling of featherless leathery wings. He had looked up, just in time to see what passed overhead, a hideous dark floating shape, almost as big as a man, something which was a bird and yet not, because it sprouted arms and feet, very long and tentacle-like, ending in thin claws with long sharp talons, glittering in the full moonlight. But the most hideous sight had been the face, of which he had caught only a passing glimpse, a twisted golden mask with red burning eyes and a mouth with fangs he rather didn't want to think of right now. He had buried his face in the dirt, clasping his hands over his ears, wishing that he was dead drunk and having hallucinations, and after he had been lying there for what he thought had been hours, he had dared to get up and run home. The next day he had assured himself that he had been drunk, but then he learned by careful inquiries that the two Cochran boys were both in bed with a strange heavy fever, one of them was delirious and screaming continuously about a bat-thing with a golden face which was trying to get into his bedroom at night. The Cochran family moved to another town. Later Colin had overheard a conversation between the burgomaster and one of the notables, and so learned that Old Woman Spidernose had complained against the two Cochran boys who had lured Myriam into the woods and there tried to rape her. Fortunately for her, and also for them, they hadn't succeeded, as Colin had indeed found out a few months later.

Things added up very nicely, and then he had taken up his interest in Myriam. He had no real fixed idea, just hoped that his luck would bring him to what he wanted. He could talk nicely, and he wasn't that bad looking at all. He didn't have the muscles of Ludo, but he did possess what he liked to think of as a special charm of his own. Myriam fell readily for his kind words, or maybe it was really just that he was the first one who tried to be nice and friendly to her. He learned very much from her, though not directly of course. Yes, her mother had many old books, and she had tried to read some, and no, she hadn't understood them, but they were about this and that. And no, they couldn't meet tonight, because it was a full moon and they had to get out and gather some herbs that should only be picked at that time of the month. Yes, they always did that on full moon nights. And many more, much more interesting things, he learned from his conversations with Myriam.

Slowly he pressed against the door, fighting back the cold fear which ran pricks of ice along his back. No turning back now. The door creaked lightly but was locked of course. He had expected it, and went around the house to the kitchen window next to the back door. Carefully he inserted the blade of his knife under the window, then started moving it till he found the handle. The wood was rotten, as he had hoped it would be. Luck seemed to be with him this night of all nights. He pushed, and the wooden handle broke with a short snap. He pushed the window up and slithered inside. He let his eyes adjust to the deeper darkness inside, while he slowly lowered the window back into its original position. There was a musky odour, mingling with the smells of food, old wood, and some spicy aromas from the assorted herbs and leaves that were lying in bowls scattered over the table. He felt his way through the kitchen, easily avoiding the chairs. Luckily the old witch had no familiar; in stories they always had some black cat or raven in the house, spitting or shrieking at intruders. But then, Old Woman Spidernose didn't fit the descrip- tion of a witch, and maybe in the strictest sense of the word she wasn't. Or maybe she was, after all—the golden faced thing could be a familiar of sorts, and she possessed a terrifying alien power, which Colin wanted. Nothing would stop him getting his hands on it. He had spied on the house on former occasions, and went straight towards the small windowless room in the back. He felt as if he was walking into the stomach of a waiting and very hungry beast, which would suddenly close its mouth and smack its lips. The fear was leaving him however, being replaced by expectancy now that he was so close to his goal. He opened the small door.

The stupid woman hadn't even locked it! The smell of strong spice and a sweet nauseating odour rushed out to embrace him, and instinctively he did one step back. Then he flashed on his light, and a yellow sun burst open before his eyes. There IT was, just as he had once spotted it as a golden glitter on the wall, seen through one of the windows from which he had been observing the old woman going about her tasks, with the door partly open.

IT was half lying, half standing against the wall, resting on a small three-legged table of ancient black wood, carved in weird designs. A glitter of gold, or something like gold, with a wide, partly opened mouth displaying needlelike fangs, and which was staring at him with hollow dark eyes. The demon mask.

Its nose was blunt, almost non-existent, overshadowed by the three enormous nostrils. The cheeks were hollow, the eyes two dark pits of nothingness. It seemed so damned alive, that he really had to force his hands forwards to touch it. The fangs seemed ready to strike, and nail his fingers down into the wood of the black table.

The horrible thing was warm to his touch, as no metal should be. He put the flashlight on the table, so that the light spilled on the evil mask. It wasn't gold, streaks of a strange greenish metal ran as veins through its surface. There were dark dried spots on the mask, near the mouth, and he shivered when he realized what they were. A small bowl stood before the mask, filled to the rim with small leaves of some unknown plant, sprinkled with a dry brown-red powder. He looked around. The room was fully curtained in black cloth, covering all the wooden walls, even the low ceiling. There didn't seem to be any light in the place. A low bookcase stood lonely in one corner, loaded with heavy volumes, some of them seemingly ready to fall apart when touched. He took a few of the more recent looking ones and read a few sentences here and there without understanding much of it. Some of it was written in Latin or Greek, or something like that, then there were others in old French, and even some filled with dots and lines which could only be Arabic or something similar. Disgusted, he put them back. He couldn't do anything with those, and they weren't what he had comic to find.

Carefully he took up the mask, shivering uncontrollably at its alien warm touch, as if he was feeling living flesh in his hands. He would have to hurry, he couldn't be certain that the old woman would stay away the whole night. Fortunately he had gotten enough out of Myriam to know what he had to do, without having to use the old books: He would never have figured those out on his own. He took his matches and lit the mixture in the bowl. A few sparks shot out, and it hissed as a snake, before it began smoking and then burning lowly, with a strong heavy odour. Then Colin turned the mask around, facing its dark interior for a short hesitating moment, and put it on his face. He almost dropped it as the stench hit his face, a sickening smell of oldness and dried blood. It fit his face, as if the demon mask adapted itself to the shape of his head; it was all sticky inside, as if covered with slimy mold, clinging to his face as a spider's web. Then he opened his eyes, looking through the eyes of the mask, and no longer into the house.

He was seeing trees and bushes, and straight up into the white moon. He stretched his hands, watching the needle talons glitter in the pale night. He saw his muscled arms, not those of a human being, but ebony black, and strangely rubberlike. He rose into the air moving the alien wings as if they always had been part of his body. Part of his mind realized that this was so in fact, he was not really flying himself, but watching from inside the skull of the... thing which he had called and controlled through the mask. Colin didn't care what the thing really was, or where it came from. It was some-thing to be used for his own means, and if it was some spawn of hell, he couldn't care less. The wood fell away below him, and a night bird scattered away in panic. The wood turned strange and alien, as seen from the sky, and he had some difficulty orientating himself. Soon, however, he found out where he was, and immediately started towards the village. He flew around the outskirts, passing the former Cochran farm and the main houses themselves, with their scattering of light. Carefully he lowered himself on the roof of the inn, and began the waiting. Several people left, but he stayed hidden in the shadows, biding his... or rather, ITS time. His wings made faint rustling sounds in the wind, but no one noticed, there was noise enough in the inn. Then below him again the front doors opened, and a tall broad shouldered shadow made his way out. Ludo at last, on his way home, and staggering slightly. Colin let him go, knowing by heart the way he'd take. Then, after a short lapse of time, he unfolded his mighty wings and began the hunt.

The darkness was no problem; he seemed to possess night vision with the demon mask, as a cat or a night bird. He flew close to the road now, slowly approaching the walking form of Ludo from behind. When he was about twenty metres from him, Ludo must have heard him. He turned around, mumbling something, and then he just stared, his eyes bulging, his mouth working frantically on a scream which wouldn't come. He didn't move, as if unable to, just looked at the moving nightmare which was coming down on him.

All the buried anger, all the hidden fury unleashed themselves in Colin's mind at the sight of his enemy's fear. He dived down, stretching his claws, and hit. The talon blow took Ludo straight in the face, tearing open his right cheek and gashing upwards across his one eye. There was nothing human in his scream, as he brought his hands up to where blood mingled with the parts of his torn eye, hanging from the socket by a few muscles and nerves. Colin turned with one flapping of his wings, and then fell down on Ludo, biting and clawing. Ludo fought as if insane, shrieking in madness, but he was no match for the demon being Colin had become, and maybe Colin himself was no longer quite sane at this moment. His left claw hooked deep into Ludo's wrist, and when he brought it up, the joint snapped, splitting bones, perforating the skin, tearing the flesh and muscles. A gush of dark warm blood spattered his body. Frantically Ludo tried to hit the abomination on top of him with his good hand but Colin didn't even feel the weak blows. He buried his fangs in Ludo's shoulder, tearing his jacket, and then ripping strips of vibrating flesh loose. Ludo's face was a wrecked mess of blood and gibbering fear, his body twisting in his vain attempts to ward off his attacker. Colin rose, and Ludo stumbled upright. He made a few shaking steps, holding his crushed arm to his body, and leaving a dark trail, which was greedily sucked up by the ground and the leaves. he fell again, tried to squirm away as a thick, fat bleeding worm. 'Nononono,' he gibbered, 'go away please, go, god go away nonono...' Colin walked towards him, the talons of his feet drawing deep trails in the earth. The insane hatred was a red-glowing ball in his brain, an icily cold spot, shutting out all human emotions, banning all rational thoughts. Ludo had crawled with his back against a tree, he was cradling his arm, slowly rocking back and forward, hitting the tree with his head with every movement. His mouth was working silently, but no sounds came from his lips, only spit and foam. Colin bent over him, and his shadow fell over Ludo as an enormous hideous toad. With one slow deliberate movement he stretched out his right claw, pushed his talons deep in Ludo's throat, enjoying the spasmodic movement the body made, and then ripped his throat out. There was only a short gurgling sound, and blood from the torn central vein hit Colin's face, blinding him as he stepped back from the convulsively jerking body.

He closed his eyes, feeling the warm stickiness dripping down along his brows and cheeks, then holding them closed, he lifted his talons, feeling the wet face of the demon thing, and took off the mask.

He was back in the small dark-clothed room, holding the dripping demon mask in his hands. It dropped from his hands, as he doubled up and vomited on the floor, falling on his knees as if in prayer to the grinning blood-spattered golden mask. The world was turning around him, and it seemed an eternity before his stomach stopped heaving. His legs still shaking, he stood up, wiping his mouth. The leaves and the powder were still burning, but the strong smell couldn't camouflage the thick stench of blood and vomit. He felt empty, drained of all power, as if he was awakening from a particularly ghoulish nightmare. He felt sick, and steadied himself against the wall. He had to get out, into the open clean air. All the hatred, all the insane fury, they were gone, and only a sick nauseating emptiness remained. He hadn't wanted that, only to teach him a lesson, he hadn't intended to kill him... to slaughter him. It couldn't have been *him*, could it, that thing which slashed and clawed and bit... that demon thing, that hadn't been he himself, it had been the mask, the power of the demon mask which he had breathed into fearful life. It hadn't been he...

'Oh yes, boy, it was you all right,' a cold voice said behind him.

He whirled, his head spinning, his heart missing a few beats. They were standing behind him, blocking the door, the old woman and Myriam; looking at him with their alien eyes boring through his skull. He couldn't say anything, just stare at them. There were tears in Myriam's eyes. The old woman pushed him out of her way, bent and took up the demon mask from the floor. Reverently she put it back on the table, making no attempts to wipe away the bloodstains. It sat there, grinning at him with its red fangs and its hollow eyes.

'Oh yes, it was you all right,' the old woman repeated, 'the demon mask is only a balance, a projector. Don't try to hide it from yourself, boy, it all came out of yourself, all the hatred, all the evil, all the slaughter. It was all inside you before you took the mask...'

He watched them. The old crone was standing behind him now, and only Myriam stood in the doorway. He was assembling his strength, inwardly cursing that he had left his knife in the kitchen. He would have to make a sprint for it, they couldn't hold him back, those two. Just jump, push her away, and run. He tensed his muscles, tried to move his weak legs.

'You don't have to try, Colin,' Myriam said. She left the doorway and went to stand beside her mother. 'We won't hold you. You can go, the way is free...' Then she suddenly broke down, tears streaming freely from her face, 'Colin oh Colin, why? WHY? I thought you really cared for me, if you had only said what... there would have been other ways... I could have warned you then...'

'Warned about what?' he snapped. His courage was coming back now that the escape route was free. They were only two weak women, and without... With a sudden rush he pushed them to the wall and grasped the mask, clasping it to his chest. Slowly he backed away, keeping his eyes on them, and still they made no move to stop him. 'I'll keep this,' he hissed, 'maybe I won't use it anymore, and maybe I will. But I'll keep it anyway, and you won't be able to use it against me.'

'Oh no, you won't use it again, boy,' the old woman said. 'The way you used it tonight, you could only use it once. Maybe you'd better leave it right here. It will give you a few extra minutes to run.'

'To run?' He laughed wildly. What were those two fools talking about? They were helpless, and he had the mask, the seat of power.

Then she laughed, a high shrieking sound, splitting his ears with her unearthly mirth. Myriam turned away, burying her face against the wall. 'Don't you listen, boy?' the old woman continued, 'don't you understand what I said? The mask is a projector, it brings your own evil into focus, spits it out and puts it into a form you can use. But you have to KNOW how to use it. See my mouth? See those two missing teeth in front?' She took her hair in her hands, and pushed it away from her face. 'See those scars on my cheeks? Teeth I wanted to kick out, scars I wanted to give someone. Evil bounces back, and the mask is its balance. Your own evil will return to you, exactly as you created it. And you realize now, don't you, what will bring your evil back to you?'

Then he did understand, but his mind rebelled, refused to accept it. No familiar, he thought stupidly, of course, who needed a familiar? The mask slipped from his fingers, fell to the ground and turned over. Its face was looking up at him, still illuminated by the weak flashlight. He saw the blunt nose, the hollow cheekbones, the long thin mouth, and then he looked at Myriam, who had turned around and was now staring straight at him. Her eyes had contracted into two pinpoints of red light. Her face seemed to be flowing with a strange inner light, while the room seemed to darken around her, as if darkness formed a cloak which was sinking into her body. 'No, Myriam,' he stammered, 'it isn't true, it can't be true!' She didn't answer. She licked her lips with the tip of her tongue. The red needle-points had spread over the whole of her eyes, glowing coals, yet unable to light the dark shadows of her hollow cheeks. 'Run, boy,' the old woman chuckled.

He turned and ran, and they didn't stop him. He burst out of the house, wrecking the door lock, and into the clearing. The moon grinned down on him, cold and merciless, the eye of an alien god. He began running, branches hitting his face and drawing patterns of blood, bushes tearing at his pullover and trousers with long taloned fingers.

Behind him, there was a whisper of leathery wings...

THE TASTE OF YOUR LOVE

THAT NIGHT HE decided to pick one up in Riccione. The last one he had had been in Bellariva, three weeks ago, and he'd had a hell of a job getting rid of the body. A pretty one, that girl had been, a small blonde German tourist with well-formed legs. Of course, she had been only a small parcel of selected items, after he'd finished making love to her, in his own way. It was not quite what he had expected. She was so soft, she had already fainted the first time, and she had been dead before he had been able to make five cuts; but he'd enjoyed it all the same. The night had been beautiful afterwards, after he had disposed of the parcel in the sea, and he had walked on the beach for a long time. He had looked up at the sky, and almost felt himself crushed by the coldness and depth of the eternity above him. He had felt very small and thankful for the joys life and love had brought him.

He had been very careful, and though he needed love very badly, he had kept away from it for three weeks. Then the hunger, the desperate need for love became too much to bear alone any longer. He was a man who needed people, as much as food and drink. He liked to walk among people, masses of people, unnoticed; a man in the crowd, wondering about the others, who they really were deep inside, the very insides of their narrow minds. Each one had another face; another world from which he was excluded. Sometimes he wished to be able to read their faces as if they were so many open books, not out of an unhealthy curiosity to pry into their tiny secrets, but to really feel like them, understand them.

After those three weeks, he couldn't wait any longer. That after-noon he had been lying on the beach; the sand scratching his back, his mind a kaleidoscope of tumbling memories, like the first time he had caught an alley cat and cut its belly open with a piece of a broken bottle. He remembered the first girl he had, a tiny built brunette, who lived two blocks away. It had been a very fumbling attempt, but they both liked it very much, till she suddenly became frightened and tried to get away from him. He had been mad, and his hands were around her throat of their own accord. Orgasm came just as her eyes turned upwards and her swollen tongue came lolling out between her purple lips. He still heard the gurgling sounds she had made in his ears. Then somebody had come up behind him, just in time they later said, and he had been kept in another place for several years before they set him free again.

He was of legal age then, his mind cured, and with some pocket money on him. With the money he bought a long butcher's knife, went to a brothel, and strangled the prostitute in her room. He possessed her, then hung her body on a strong hook in the wall and made a work of art out of her body. He had to cut away several parts before she was the shape he desired. Then he painted a landscape on the walls with the red stickiness which was everywhere by the time he had finished, cleaned himself and left the country. He had been travelling all over Europe ever since, working here and there a bit. He had also perfected his love-making techniques during those years, and discovered quite a number of unusual enjoyments.

He had been dozing on the sand, and when he opened his eyes, the sun burned deep into them. Through the coloured dots and circles he saw a pair of shapely legs walking by, and the burning hunger in his insides told him that he needed a woman's love, and badly.

He rented a new room in Rimini, and took the bus to Riccione. The driver took his one hundred lira, and he found a place for himself among the packed mass of humanity. It was only a short drive, in fact he could have walked the distance in less than half an hour, but he just didn't feel like walking. It was an evening for driving, with the sound of the big motor a steady roar, the ground drumming under his feet like the membrane of a heavy drum, a strong beating heart. In fact there were too many people, and he could hardly see the numbers of the stops, very inconveniently placed between trees beside the road. He went too far, and had to return one stop on foot.

After walking through some of the small streets, he decided on one of the lesser known clubs. He paid his entrance fee, and stepped from the lamp-lit darkness outside into the soft red-and-blue miniature world inside. The loud music bombarded him at the entrance, deafening his ears for a few seconds. The dancing floor was small and filled with a mass of humanity, slowly moving like a lazy dinosaur, to the sound of hard rock. Funny, he thought, how Italians dance slowly to every damn kind of music; it was in strange contrast with their hurried movements and speech to see them dancing, never leaving the square of floor on which they're standing.

He found a table beside the dancing area and ordered a bottle of cheap white wine, experience having taught him the horrible prices they considered normal for a glass of beer. Slowly he adjusted to the music, letting the rhythm build up inside his blood, together with the crawling need in him. He adapted his senses to the hard electronic sounds and tried without success to hear the voice of the singer amid the music. He liked discotheques, they had a special atmosphere of intimacy. They were apart from the outside world, small worlds by themselves in which people and love affairs are born and die, in the space of one evening. They were also ideal hunting grounds.

He danced a few times, but didn't find what he was looking for. Most Italians girls were with their steady boyfriends, and most of the foreign girls were with tourist groups or holiday lovers. He danced with a young French girl with a delicious accent and long legs, and then with a smaller German woman whose breasts were too large for her figure and too hard to be real. But both left him cold. They were not his type.

Then he noticed her. He couldn't have seen her before, because she was like a painting on the wall. One sees it but somehow doesn't really notice it. She moved shadowlike, slowly, observing yet unobserved herself. He first noticed her hair, long and dark, neither brown nor black, which lay flat against her shoulders. Then she passed under one of the few lights, her face turning into a black and white ink sketch, finely drawn features and dark lonely eyes.

She attracted him immediately, there was something in her way of walking, something in her whole posture, not exciting or inviting but rather the opposite, a coldness. He knew that he needed that girl tonight. He took note of where she sat down, then simply went over and asked her for the next dance.

She accepted without words. She had a very small waist, his arms almost completely circling her. He said a few things, unimportant small talk one says to a stranger. When she didn't answer, he tried a few other languages. Finally she responded in a weird combination of broken English and a few snatches of an unknown language. It could have been Greek, but he wasn't sure. He tried to find out where she was from, but she only answered with a slight smile, more a lifting of her lips, half sad and half mocking. He was strongly aware of her apartness, which surrounded her like a cloak. The dancing couples around them formed a fog of chaotic lights, swimming among colour waves, their heads and shoulders submerged in the flowing waves of music and movement.

They were dancing apart at first, his one arm around her shoulders. There was the faintest touch of her hair against his face, and a soft smell of perfume, sweet and unoffending. He felt the desire, the burning need for her love growing in him. Deliberately he pulled her closer, and they danced cheek to cheek, her flesh a warm and soothing softness next to his face. They had exactly the same time-sense and rhythm. They rode the music, something which rarely happens, two complete strangers adapting fully to each other's way of dancing.

After the dance, he brought her back to her table and joined her. She didn't protest, but there was not much to talk about except senseless small things. He noticed the way her hair fell half over her left cheek, and saw to his surprise that her hair was fastened to her dress, so it always covered that cheek. She had hollows under her eyes, he also noticed, as if she'd been awake for a long time. Maybe he wouldn't use the scalpel right away this time. Why not start with the pins? It was years since he had used them.

She took a sip of her drink, and he noticed with pleasure that she wore no ornaments, no rings, no watch, only a very small silver brace-let which seemed very old. It was best that way. Once he had made love to an older Belgian woman who had refused to part with her ornaments, and he had broken one of his best knives on her wrist watch during love play. He drank in the dark wine of her presence, fondly making comparisons with his earlier loves. Her breasts would be small and pointed, he thought. Yes, he would start with the breasts and use a small scalpel after all, the one he had used for detailed work. He would have to truss her up well, of course, and gag her strongly, so that she would only be able to make the little throaty sounds which excited him so strongly. He would start at the nipples, slowly working in circles around her breasts, going downwards, drawing red patterns towards her navel. Only then he would start using the pins, the wooden ones which he could drive into her sides, slowly.

They danced again and again, sometimes staying on the dance floor for many minutes, pressing closer to each other, her hair against his hot cheek. He nibbled her ear and tried to kiss the corners of her mouth, but she turned away. 'Not here, not now,' she said. 'Later.'

'Why not?' he asked mockingly. 'I want you. I need your love.'

She smiled, that half-mocking drawing of her lips. 'I will taste your love tonight,' she answered.

Indeed you will, my dear, he thought, you'll never forget how my love tastes. Not in the short time you have left in this world. Maybe he could mix pleasures tonight? First the knives and the pins, and then conclude with the cord? If she was weak enough after his love making, and there was a hook in the wall strong enough to hold her, he could even watch her dangling, her body arching itself, in spasmodic movements, her legs jerking like a spider's. Yes, he would have a wonderful night. He felt sure of that.

The band broke up at closing time, and he got her coat from the cloakroom. She wanted to wait for one of the late buses at first, but he convinced her that it was only a short walk. She followed him into his room without question, and he locked the door carefully behind him.

'Please wait here,' she whispered, and went into the bathroom. He put on the bedside lamp, and put his love instruments into the pockets of his pajamas, and the strong cord to tie her with. Then the bathroom door opened and she came out.

The soft light played as a lover's hands over her youthful body, well-built and yet fragile looking, with slightly sagging breasts and a dark-shadowed navel. Her long hair hung loose now, still covering half of her face. She came over to him hurriedly, and pressed her body strongly against his. There was a look of fierce hunger in her eyes as their tongues met, and he felt desire rising in him, pumping in his blood. He tried to bring his left hand up along her spine, while the other searched for the cord, and suddenly found that he couldn't. Her arms were like steel, pinning down his own against his sides, unable to move. Her eyes smiled at him, and for the first time he noticed their glow. 'Now, my dear,' she whispered, 'I will taste your love', and with a sharp movement of her head, she tossed her hair away and uncovered the left part of her face. A scream bubbled up in his throat, but was never voiced, because her tongue erupted like a burning volcano in his mouth. Unable to move, unable to shriek, he saw the slimy, dark-haired, proboscis-like thing which covered half of her face uncoil itself as a tentacle, the many toothless mouths on it opening and closing. It moved along her lips, and then it was in his mouth, wet, slimy and sickly, moving and sucking, while blood-red pain tore his mind apart into a million silently screaming shards.

The landlady had seen the girl leaving the room in the middle of the night, and she had decided to throw her lodger out. After all, this was a respectable house, and she wanted nothing to do with things like that happening under her roof. She was very surprised that she didn't find her tenant in his apartment. The only things she saw were his clothes, lying in disorder on the floor, and a big plastic bag on the bed. Angrily she picked up the bag, and it felt wet and sticky and had red spots on it. The bag rattled, and she peered more closely and saw the bones through the plastic. But she definitely started to scream when she saw that part of the bag had the flattened form of a man's face.

THE WHISPERING HORROR

I HAD KNOWN Harvey Denver since we were both four years old. We went together to the kindergarten, and thereafter to the same small village school. We shared the same friends, the same enemies and a dislike for the same teacher. We enjoyed the same games and hobbies, almost as two brothers.

To his memory, I will now write the real facts, as much as I know them or WANT TO KNOW THEM, about that summer day, many years back now, when I ran screaming from the graveyard where Harvey was buried. Maybe you'll think them part of a boy's nightmare, something which doesn't or *can't* happen in this nice, safe little world of ours, where there is no place for the unknown, the impossible. I know otherwise, and I don't care if you believe me or not. There is no proof, not any more. The only proof is in my brain, where it has been haunting me ever since, always returning in horrible nightmares, in a fear of dark places. But maybe this is the way to whip it all out of my mind, where every detail is engraved, our walks together, the ruins... and the whispering...

It started the summer when we were both nine years old. We were born the same year, Harvey in April and I in June, which made him the natural leader for our two-man expeditions, the more as he was bigger and stronger than myself. After school time, we enjoyed taking long walks so that we could play in the forest which was about a kilometre from our village.

The wood was nothing exceptional, a bunch of trees and bushes, thrown together by playful nature, but to us it was paradise. Usually, we didn't go deep into the wood; we had felt once (on our bottoms) the troubles which arose when we had stayed out too late. Also, the forest soon became much thicker and darker, and we still feared we would get lost some day. We no longer believed in witches and gnomes, but we were still afraid of the dark, even if we would never confess it. Still, on a free afternoon, with time to spare, we penetrated much deeper than usual.

It was then that we found the house, or what was still left of it. That wasn't much, just the entrance to a cellar, a mass of stones and part of one crumbling side wall, miraculously still standing, like a lonely sentinel. It must have been a very small house, most of which was built of timber, that later on had been used for other purposes. Only the cellar seemed to be intact. Curious, we went and looked into the black hole, waiting each for the other to go in first. It would have to be Harvey, of course. But he didn't seem very anxious to lead the way. He descended two steps, bent and looked once again.

'Can't see a thing,' he whispered.

'Of course not, how could you?' I answered, whispering too. 'There isn't a single window anywhere. Must be dark like hell, down there.'

I don't know why we whispered. Maybe it was the loneliness of the ruins of the house, the dampness which welled up out of the dark cave in gulps of foul air. I shivered, although it wasn't cold, but somehow the warmth couldn't quite reach me.

'Could there be anyone there?' Harvey asked. His voice, soft as he spoke, seemed to bounce back against the spiderwebbed cellar walls and return to us in a hollow whispering, like some lost voice, drifting off on far-away winds.

'Are you crazy?' I hushed him. 'Who could live in a hole like this? There's nothing there. Come on, let's go and play somewhere else.'

Our voices answered out of the dark entrance. The lonely, crumbling wall, bitten through by time, the damp steps, leading down into the abyss of shadows, almost seemed to radiate a feeling of... there's no right word for it. Something old, unholy, something evil. Evil, especially to us, intruders in its domain.

'Come on, Harvey,' I whispered. 'I don't like this at all. Let's get out of here.'

But he didn't hear me. His head bent, he was listening very sharply. Suddenly he looked up at me.

'Did you hear that?' he asked.

'I didn't hear anything,' I answered. I tried to laugh, but it sounded so strange and out of place that I stopped immediately. The only thing I heard was the echo of my own voice.

'I thought... I thought I heard someone breathing,' he whispered.

My ears had received no sound, and I didn't like it at all. Whatever could breathe in a dark cave like this? But then, it couldn't, he must have heard wrong. There was nothing down there. There couldn't be.

I took Harvey's arm. 'Come on, let's get away!'

'No, wait.' He shook himself free and listened intently, holding his breath, scanning the darkness with his ears, almost eager to capture a sound.

'It sounds... like a dog panting...'

'A dog?' I said. 'Why should a dog be down there? Could be anything, even a wild animal!'

'Maybe he fell,' Harvey said. 'Maybe he slipped on the stairs and broke a leg. Maybe his owner got tired of him and just chained him in there to let him die of starvation. Some people would just do a thing like that.'

He had stopped whispering. 'You wouldn't let a dog die down there, all alone in the darkness, hurt and wanting company, would you?'

I didn't answer.

'Listen,' he said, 'it's almost like moaning. Now I'm sure, there's something down there, something alive and hurt. I'm going to see what it is.'

Suddenly, I was deadly afraid to be left alone. I grasped Harvey. 'No, please, don't go down. It is bad, I feel it!'

'Now don't start acting like a sissy,' he snapped. 'The poor thing's probably just hungry. You stay here if you're scared.'

Slowly, taking care not to slip on the stone steps, covered with lichens and dirt, he descended. It smelled dusty and damp. Small creatures hurried away over the steps. Of course, I couldn't stay behind now, which would have proved me a coward. So I followed him, the fear throbbing in my throat. Down there the absolute darkness filled my eyes the first seconds with coloured lights and stripes and circles, dancing on my irises. Then, after a while, I made out the dark shapes of old furniture, the walls of the cave, and... something dark, in a corner of the cellar, something slowly moving. It seemed almost to flow, an indefinable black form, laying flat on the floor.

'There is the poor animal,' Harvey said. With a courage I would never have believed him capable of—or maybe it now seems recklessness—he stretched his hand to touch it.

And then... the thing WHISPERED. Not a moan or a groan, not a recognizable sound, but a thick, slimy whisper, which seemed to go on and on between the slippery walls. The whisper of something old and feeble, something slimy and swollen, which seemed dead and yet alive, as if it had just awakened from a long sleep. Something petrified and timeless, suddenly coming to itself.

I turned and ran, my only thoughts for free air and light. I slipped on the stairs and hurt my knee, but then I was out of the darkness and away from the horrible whispering.

Outside I got my breath and courage back, but not enough of the last to go back inside. I cursed my own cowardliness, but I didn't return. I just sat down and waited, then got up and started to walk around the ruins. Twice I called, but got no response of any kind. Not a sound came from the cellar. Harvey was alone down there, with the whispering thing. I waited. There was nothing else to do. Then, after a quarter of an hour, Harvey came out of the infernal darkness. He was pale, and so I knew that he too had been scared, even if he was laughing now.

'Coward,' he teased, 'whatever did you run away from? There's nothing horrible down there, just a poor sick old dog, feeling lonesome.'

I didn't say anything. I knew Harvey had lied to me. Whatever had whispered down there in the slimy darkness, hadn't been a dog or any other animal I knew.

We went home and got our second spanking for being late for supper. The next days and weeks, I saw less and less of Harvey. He almost seemed to evade me. Whenever he spoke to me, he was short and unfriendly, not at all his usual self. Sometimes, on free days, I saw him leave the village, as soon as he could get away, to go to the cellar in the forest. Twice I accompanied him, but I didn't follow him down into the darkness, although he asked me to. He told me the dog was better now, and wanted to play with me also. It was a very old and friendly dog, Harvey said, he was so long and thin. Harvey nicknamed him "Stake" for that.

Sometimes he told Harvey stories, and that's how I cornered Harvey. Outside a circus, I had never heard a dog speak, and everyone knew in a circus it was just a trick. So Harvey had to admit, it wasn't a dog that whispered to him. Stake was a man, he said at last, a friend. He was old, very old. More than two hundred years, he had told Harvey, and he had come a long way. He had been very sick, and he had been so long in the dark that the sun hurt his eyes. He never came out, not even at night. So if I wanted to meet Stake, I should go to him.

One day, I almost did. I followed Harvey down the slithery stone steps, leading downward into a hungry stomach of waiting shadows. My back felt hot and cold at the same time, and I was deadly afraid. Nevertheless, I followed. Then I was down, and groping my way, trying to see the thing. Then it whispered. A soft, throaty whisper, slimy and unspeakably evil.

'Don,' it whispered my name, an almost unrecognizable word, as if it spoke with a tongue not meant to utter human words.

I cried out, I couldn't hold it back. I panicked, stumbling out of the nauseating cave in a mad flight, and then I ran, away from the forest and the cave with its hellish horror. I never went near it again.

Harvey stopped playing with me altogether from that day on. In fact, he avoided all the other boys and girls of the village, too, and always went out to play alone. Once I overheard a conversation between our parents, and I heard them say that Harvey always stayed out much too late. They said he even one night leaped from his window, thinking them asleep, and went out to the forest. Then they started suspecting things about Harvey and girls, which I didn't understand completely, but his father finished the argument, saying that Harvey was still much too young for that. It was just the boy's wild nature, he thought.

But after a while, people began to notice how pale and sick he looked. I had seen it already for a long time, and I knew it to be the bad influence of the thick, stale air in the cellar, and the fact that he was always down there in the dark and never played any more in the sunlight. But I didn't tell on him, and maybe that's my big guilt.

Then he fell sick. The doctor said he had never seen a boy of his age looking so pale. His whole face was thin, almost fallen-in flesh around his skull bones. You could see his cheekbones sticking out. He had lost much weight too. The doc couldn't exactly say what was the matter with him, and that was strange too. Harvey had never been sick before, except the usual children's diseases. The doc ordered plenty of fresh air, wholesome food and some vitamin pills, and if that didn't help, his parents should go and see a specialist in the city. And Harvey had always been so strong and healthy looking!

The second week of his sickness, I'll never forget. It was the next time I came unwillingly in contact with Harvey's "friend" Stake.

It was a cloudy, moonless night. The weather was fine, warm and windless, but just not too hot. I had left the window of my room open. I wasn't asleep yet, which was lucky for me. Otherwise I'd never have heard it before it would have been too late.

It came from the woods, towards the village. Maybe it was bored. Maybe it wanted some company, or just wanted to find Harvey. They were my thoughts then; now I know the much more important and much more horrible reason it had to come out of its cellar.

I heard the slow, dragging steps on the path, and then the crunching of the gravel. Don't ask me how, I just *knew*, with an unsettling clearness, what it was that walked stealthily towards our house through the protecting darkness outside, hidden even from the moonlight. In one movement, I was out of bed and smashed the window shut. The very next second, something whispered very softly outside. There was a rubbing sound against the window, as if some soft body pressed against the cold wall, trying to get in, always whispering. There was nothing to be seen in the darkness outside.

Then the moon came through the clouds for a few fleeting moments, an eye of ice looking downwards that gave me the first glimpse ever of the unknown which is always at our side. The whispering went on and something clawed against the glass, etching sharp lines in it, as for some eternal-seeming seconds moonlight flooded the scene outside. AND THERE WAS NOTHING THERE.

Real fear runs through your veins like ice, it crawls upwards under your skin to your neck. It feels like suddenly standing on the brink of an abominably deep pit with crawling emptiness. Something was there and yet wasn't. I don't know how I managed to move, but somehow I shrunk backwards, never letting the window out of my sight. I couldn't breathe, unseen claws seemed to grope in my stomach and lungs. I'll never know which reflex or instinct made me reach for the chair. I was very young then, and I had never had any experience with the unseen. I had reached in those few seconds a breaking point. I cried out and threw the chair towards the thing beyond the window. The glass splintered, as I ran to the door. It wasn't necessary, it moved outside very quickly, away from the house.

I got a spanking for having broken the window, and then they had to call the doctor to give me a sedative. Nobody paid attention to the glass splinters, which all lay inside the room. I had seen how the glass cracked and broke, just before the chair reached it!

Then Harvey died. Very suddenly, in the middle of the night.

The doctor said his heart unexpectedly gave up, for no special reason at all. He had grown very weak and thin, almost just skin over his bones. He just simply passed away, from this world into another. I hope it was into a better one.

Two days later, he was buried. Everyone I knew from the neighbourhood was there. Serious-looking people everywhere.

Many people wept. I don't know if I cried. When you're nine years old, there's no real understanding of the word "death". I only felt Harvey was far, far away from me now, and he would never come back. Yes, maybe I did cry.

The next day, a free afternoon, I went alone to the churchyard to look at Harvey's tombstone and all the pretty flowers on it. Then I heard it again. Now it wasn't sneaking, covered by the dark of night and a moonless sky. It came as an angry thunder-storm, angry, mad, towards Harvey's grave. I jumped away, ran a few steps and let myself roll behind a large tombstone, where I stayed hidden, shivering with uncontrollable fear, while the raving terror came nearer and nearer, until it was so close I could hear it, the loathsome, angry whispering.

Much, much later, I came home, to break down in my mother's arms, raving and crying, trying to escape from every shadow in the room. They didn't believe anything I said, until my father, to calm me, went to the graveyard and saw what somebody or something had done to the fresh grave and the stone, to the dug-up, broken coffin and to what was now still left of Harvey's little body. I was delirious for two days before I could speak coherently of the cellar in the wood, and Harvey's friend who lived there. They didn't believe it at first, but they went nevertheless, to find out what was true of my story. They went in a crowd, armed with shovels, pickaxes, guns and electric lamps. They came back, late in the night, looking very tired and somehow scared. None of them said anything. The next day, my father told me I must have dreamed everything. They had only found a dead dog in the cave.

Only now, many years later, my father, too, has passed away, and before me I have his diary on that day. In his fine and yet strong hand-writing, at last I know what they really found down there.

It was something which could have been human once, but I can't be sure. Neither can any one of us. It was a skeleton, smaller than a normal man, and crouching as if it wasn't meant to walk upright. But on those yellow bones, NEW FLESH, NEW MUSCLES AND FRESH, SOFT SKIN WERE GROWING. Weak ones, nevertheless, the muscles and flesh of a young boy. They could hardly keep the heavy thing moving. It tried to strike us, and it whispered to us, as Don had told us. When Frank and then Wilfrid hit it with their shovels, it whimpered. We crushed it with our spades, split the bones of the unspeakable thing, and all the time it kept on whispering to us and trying to fight us. It couldn't get past us out of the cellar, and we kept it in the white burning circles of our lights. God forgive me, if it was something which had the right to live, but I don't think it had. The life which moved it was stolen, as was the flesh which grew on it. A foul stench of decay came in gulps out of it, when we broke the bones and split the soft skin. There was blood too, thick and spreading a foul stench of something very old and very dead. Harold cut an arm with a blow of his shovel, and the arm and the hand kept on moving, crawling over the floor, Then Frank heard something outside. He and Peter went to look, and they swear there was nothing to be seen, yet suddenly trees were pushed aside and something struck them away from the entrance with a formidable strength. We all heard something come down the stairs, and at that exact moment I split the skull of the moaning horror with my pick-axe. There was a loud shriek, suddenly cut off and then there was nothing beside us in the cellar. The whispering had stopped, and the loathsome parts of flesh, bones and muscles lay silent.

I can't think of that moment, without shuddering. What could the thing have done to us, if by pure luck, I hadn't hit the skull at the exact moment before the invisible projection (I can't think of a better suited word for it) reached us? We burned everything which was on the floor of the cave, and then we made the cellar collapse over the ashes so that now there is nothing there but a heap of crumbling stones.

They never knew what it had been exactly. Neither did they make much effort to find out. There are some things which don't belong to this world. It is best to leave them alone completely.

But I can't forget what is burned in my memory by such a petrifying fear as I had never known, and hope will never know again. It is that day, when I lay alone behind the shadow of a tomb, shivering madly in the full sunlight, while something unseen crushed Harvey's tombstone and broke open his grave, always whispering, whispering...

THE MAN WHO COLLECTED EYES

CLAES PERQUOI HAD always been extremely interested in eyes. Already in his youth, when he used to live in the house next to my parents', he could spend hours just standing before a mirror, or outside bent over a small stream, making silly faces to his own reflection, watching, no, *studying* his own eyes.

This mania—because I can hardly name it otherwise, was created very early in his life by his parents, not withstanding their good intentions. Parents *all* have only the best of intentions concerning their offspring. Being very Catholic, they had decorated the children's room in the best possible way to their rather narrow minds. On the wall, opposite the little child's bed, they had hung one of those prints, still often encountered in older farm houses, featuring in burning colours a large triangle surrounding an enormous eye, looking down on anyone unfortunate enough to be in the room. Above the eye, which was supposed to have a kind and benevolent look, in red letters of flame, the painting said *"God Sees You"*. One could not escape the eye; it saw everything, and especially the young occupant of the room.

It can be called typical for the young Claes' character, that the eye had exactly the opposite reaction on him than it would have had on any normal human being. Instead of beginning to fear the omnipresent eye, he got rather attached to and interested in it. Instead of starting to hate its influence, he started to love it. After that, one thing led to another, and I could rightfully say "One eye led to the others" in this case. His own eyes were the first to receive his fullest attention. Before the mirror, he turned his eyeballs in all directions, an art he mastered very quickly, so that soon only the white and the small red veins stayed visible, like a blank piece of paper with smears of red ink on it. Sometimes when he was rolling his eyes, I was afraid that one day they'd escape from their orbits and roll over the floor like large bloody marbles, or just burst open like fallen eggs.

At the age of fourteen, Claes started studying girls' eyes with an even more fixed attention that before. This time not before mirrors, but on small shaded benches in parks, and on the back seats of theatres and other quiet places, where it was in fact a bit too dark to see really much of their *eyes*. He didn't find what he was looking for anyway, because ten years later, he was still a bachelor. Maybe the girls he dated just wanted something more besides a monologue about the qualities, faults or purity of their eyes.

It was after those first ten years that he started his collection. He hated it when somebody called his innocent hobby "horrible" or "morbid". 'The eye,' he preferred to reply to accusations of that kind, 'is the most beautiful thing of creation. One should look at the iris as upon a diamond, full of sparkling life, a moving black expression with coloured dots around it like a crown of pearls. The pupil is a star, a heart, the brain of the eye, the inner mirror of the soul. The white should be approached like a lake of pure milk, an anti-galaxy of snow purity, in which the pupil drifts like an island in space, a miniature planetoid. The little, almost invisible strings of slime are small clouds, the little arteries as undersea volcanoes, full or burning fire, veins of pulsating life force, blood!'

He started indeed rather innocently with eyes of dead birds, dogs, cats and even fish, all of which he kept as a real treasure. Big and small eyes, in all colours, which he cut out of the bodies of dead animals, and treated with a special recipe—a magical recipe, he used to joke—so they didn't go slimy and rot away. His living room began to fill, with the results of his collection. Eyes in glass cases, like flowers on the cupboards; other eyes swimming in aquariums like lazy fish, trailing their nerves slowly behind tails; eyes in hermetically closed terrariums, sunning themselves as tortoises. He had a pair of sparkling lizard eyes made into a pair of cuff-links, and a parrot's eye fixed into a tie-pin.

Great details of reproductions of famous paintings decorated the walls of his house; one eye of the Mona Lisa, a distorted eye from a blue Picasso creation, the eye of the *Head with Lizard* from Paul Klee, a few demonical eyes from the works of Hieronymus Bosch.

One day, he took me secretly to his study room, and opened a hidden safe. He took a small glass case from it, treating it as he would the Crown Jewels, and showed the two black points in it to me. Two very' small eyes, black as ink, locked forever in a solution which one could see through, although it had hardened as stone to the touch. They looked like two fossilized insects in a block of resin. 'A snake's eyes,' he whispered almost reverently, 'from a cobra. Notice their expression? The cruel pain, the blind hatred? They were cut out while the beast was still alive, just after they had skinned her.'

I had to stop myself from retching. Casually, I had gotten used to his abominable collection of horrors, so far even that they didn't touch me at all. But vivisection, cold-blooded sadism perpetrated on a helpless animal, which was more than my stomach could stand.

I gave it straight to him. He seemed hurt. 'But I didn't know,' he defended himself rather weakly. 'They only told me afterwards, after I had bought and paid them, almost like a kind of picturesque detail. Surely, you don't believe *me* being able to really cut a living beast apart, do you? No, you know me better than that. But wait, there's something you just *have* to see. Something *really* special, and they arrived only this very morning.'

He reached deeper into the safe, and I heard the clicking sounds of a second lock being opened by the blind touch of his fingers. He took a second box out of it, also locked. Like tentacles, his fingers crawled into his pockets, from which he took a bunch of small keys. He had to use two different ones to open the box, almost making a ceremony of it. With eyes, small with greedy expectation, he looked up at me, and then pushed the contents of the small box under my nose.

Eternally staring into unseeing emptiness, a pair of light blue human eyes looked up at me.

'Paid for very expensively,' he whispered, 'straight from the morgue. Aren't they beautiful?'

That was the last time I entered his house, before... but let me tell the story chronologically. I simply had enough of his mania. We didn't become enemies; there was just a coolness between us and we didn't meet each other regularly any more, except in clubs or as passersby on the street. But never again did I accompany him to his house, or invite him in for a glass of cognac at my apartment.

Just because I didn't see him so often any more, I noticed the change in him sooner than most people who knew him. Something was plaguing him, and it wasn't very difficult to find out what was the exact cause of his unrest. It was completeness, the death stroke to every fanatical collector. Collecting becomes a mania by itself, and when there's nothing any more to collect, interest fails. Claes had arrived at a dead point, and couldn't even hope to add another curious and rare specimen to his treasury. What indeed could be more rare and costly than a pair of human eyes? He became moody, was irritated by the slightest remark; he retired into his shell like a snail, hiding himself and his weird collection from the world.

And then, suddenly, a new metamorphosis came over him, changing him back to his old usual self. He started searching out company again, reappeared at private parties, started coming back on club evenings. He was like a reborn man, but the origin of that mysterious rebirth stayed hidden in secrecy. He never mentioned it openly, except the few times when he would whisper half jokingly about an enormous experiment in black magic, but he refused to give any details.

From a friend, an antiquarian, I learned that he spent masses of money on old and expensive volumes on magic and sorcery. During his vacations he went to London and Paris, visiting specialist dealers in the very rare and sought-after books of the occult. He sought out well-known genuine mediums and serious students of the "old sciences"; he even attended a few séances. A few times he got me so curious that I asked him straight away what he had in mind. He just laughed, and 'One day *you* will know, and *I* will see,' became his stock answer on such occasions.

Then complaints started filtering in. His neighbours didn't appreciate the odd smells which sometimes came drifting from the cellar of his house. They also didn't like being kept awake by his weird chanting at the unluckiest hours of the night. Stray dogs and alley cats mysteriously started disappearing in the neighbourhood.

But that period didn't last very long, because one night, early in autumn, he burst screaming from his house and ran through the empty streets, tried to climb a tree; and when he didn't succeed, he tried to dig himself into the very paving stones. He screamed the whole neighbourhood awake, crawled on his belly like a large black reptile. This impression was mainly due to the black coat he wore, covered in strange and weirdly woven designs of astrological origin, and some others I've never seen before. A hospital car came, with four strong men in white jackets, but they also needed the help of two policemen to get him inside.

After a month, in which they analysed and psychically vivisected him, they gave up and sent him to a state asylum, where he still is confined. He is very inoffensive, in fact, and he likes nothing better than just sitting in his easy chair. He eats, drinks, goes to the toilet and sleeps; sometimes he is even capable of a few simple words.

But wherever he goes, in the garden in summer, or in the white corridors of the home in winter, by day or by night, always he carries his dark glasses. At first they tried to take them away, but he became so violent they had to let him keep them. But they have replaced the original ones with plastic ones, so he is unable to hurt himself by breaking them.

Now I know what destroyed his mind, what sent him screaming up the road like a lunatic. At first I assumed that he had brought madness upon himself (his mind was never very stable, and his dabbling in the occult sciences and magic formulas certainly didn't help), until quite accidentally I found out the truth. God knows, sometimes I wish I had never known. My nights would be more peaceful. Now, whenever I stare into a mirror, I sometimes seem like an alien creature from another world to myself. When I look up to the night sky, the stars look down upon me like a thousand hostile eyes. We are so small, so incredibly small and unimportant in this universe, a dust particle, a microbe, which can be crushed under one fingernail... and there is so very much we don't know. Maybe there *are* worlds besides ours, only separated by a small layer of reality, worlds peopled like ours, only not with human beings.

However Claes succeeded in completing his collection with the missing item, that's something we'll never know. I found out when they emptied his house, and burned his macabre collection on the authority's orders. As I was still looked upon as his best (and practically only, I found out) personal friend, and he had no relatives left, I had agreed to be present at the burning; in fact, I threw some ingredients, which I'd rather not mention in detail, into the purifying fire, after we had taken them from the locked safe.

It was then that I found the painting, and the hole in it, the circular hole into nothing. A dark emptiness in which I thought I saw stars sparkle, and in which enormous shadow-forms seemed to move and approach. At that moment, I understood which eye Claes had wanted to add to his collection. As soon as I touched the picture, I felt the weird suction from the hole, a slimy tearing movement, and I felt the almost irresistible compulsion—I *had* to look down into the hole, down in its depths and upon the face of whatever lurked down there.

Then I hurled the cursed thing into the flames. There was an enormous rain of fire sparks, a mass of green-blue fire curling in fat tongues upwards, accompanied by a hissing and crackling sound and a strange far-away wailing sound. The flames lowered and a disgusting soft-sweet smell began spreading. I ran away, still unable to understand fully what I had witnessed and almost seen, only knowing with dead certainty that I had destroyed something which didn't belong to this world, something which should never have existed in it.

It had been the big painting which had hung above his bed in his youth, the print with the triangle and the eye inside it, and the letters of flame. *"God Sees You"*.

But only the triangle and the letters were still there; the rest had been empty, the enormous black hole into nothing; as if there had never been anything there which had looked down on the world.

BELINDA'S COMING HOME!

WEDNESDAY.
  Dear Diary. I hope you're not mad at me. It's been so very long since I told you anything. But you know, Mom says that diaries are silly. That only little stupid girls write stupid things in silly diaries. That's really dumb. Sometimes I think I really hate Mom when she says things like that. It's just to hurt me, I know. She knows she hurts me. But she says it anyway. Why? I love Mom and I love Daddy. And I love you, dear Diary. Maybe most of all. I can tell you everything. Everything!

That's why I have hidden you, dear Diary. I know Mom has been snooping, she's been reading you. Reading the very secret things I've told only to you. You know I am not a little dumb stupid silly girl. I've hidden you very safely. Mom won't find you. I hope she thinks I threw you away. Then she'll stop looking for you. I don't want Mom to read what I only told to you. Those are OUR secrets. Mom has no business with them. None at all.

So you don't have to be mad at me. I've hidden you very safely. In the back of my closet. Under those old books of Belinda and me. To make sure I put a mountain of dolls on top of them. No way Mom's gonna search there.

The light is out in my room. I'm under the blankets, as in a tent. I use my *Star Wars* lamp. Mom can't see the light under the bedroom door. She thinks I'm fast asleep. Now I can talk freely to you.

I think Mom hates you so much because Daddy once gave you to me. Mom always hates things I got from Daddy. Like Teddy. I never told you about Teddy. I was too sad at that time. He was such a lovely puppy. I loved him very much. Daddy gave him to me last year on my birthday. Teddy was so small and all black with curly hair. So sweet. I bought a little collar for him with his name on. From my own pocket money, I did. Two weeks later he was gone. Mom said he had run away. But I know better. Teddy would never run away from me. He knew our house was his house. Jenny saw it all. Jenny is the girl next door. She's a bit older than me. Daddy was at his office. I was at a matinee at the movies. Jenny said there came a white car to our house. And a man in uniform who rang the bell. Mom gave Teddy to that man and I never saw my puppy again. When I told Mom she got very upset. She said I was a liar and a bad girl. She said Jenny was lying too, and she would speak with her parents. Jenny never spoke to me again after that.

Then there was that beautiful music *Swan Lake*. Daddy gave it to me, long ago when I still went to ballet class. I know Mom broke it. It was no accident, as she claims. It was a record, you know. One of those old big discs which I had to play on that ancient thing, a grammo-something. Daddy sometimes uses it to play very old jazz music. He calls it vinyl records. One day it was partly melted. Mom said I had left it lying in the sun. That isn't true. Mom bought me a CD with that music. I have never put it in my player. It's lying in a drawer. With the melted vinyl disc.

I never told Daddy about *Swan Lake*. Maybe he would get very angry at Mom. It happens. Then they have a very loud argument. So loud that it scares me. After a time Mom always begins to cry. Then Daddy says he's sorry. That makes Mom cry even harder. She's an expert in crying whenever she wants to. And she always gets her way. Sometimes Daddy thinks it's my fault that he got mad at Mom. Then he gets mad at me. And so it's always my fault.

Everything is always my fault. Always. I think I should've never been born. Then they could only get mad at each other. That's why I never dared to tell everything, that time with Belinda. It would've been my fault again. I couldn't stand them both being mad at me.

If Mom would find you, dear Diary, she would destroy you. Tear you apart or burn you. I know. That's why I only get you out of hiding now and then. To tell you something really important. When Teddy was gone, that was important too. But I was so sad then. I couldn't tell you. But now, dear Diary, surprise!

BELINDA'S COMING HOME!

Yes, it's true. They haven't really told me yet. I overheard them talking in the kitchen. They didn't know I was there.

Belinda's coming home. This very Saturday evening! Maybe they want it to be a surprise for me. So I pretend I know nothing. I do love

Belinda so very much. Now she's finally coming home. She's been at that school so long. I know I won't be able to sleep tonight. But I will not give away anything. I have reread what I told you in the past about Belinda, dear Diary. I won't betray anything.

I'm so happy. I could dance!

THURSDAY.

I have not hidden you after last night, dear Diary. Well, not far away anyway. I need you close now. I know I will have much to tell you now that Belinda's coming home. Important things.

But right now I feel sad. You can't help me, dear Diary, you only listen to what I tell you. You understand what I'm writing down. As if I was really speaking to you. My writing is my speaking. Words have trouble coming out of my mouth. But writing is like speaking. It goes slower. I have a very good memory. I can remember very long sentences. And difficult words. But when I try to really say them, it goes all wrong. My tongue objects. My lips close. I start mumbling. My writing speaks only to you. But of course you never answer.

The teacher comes three times a week. He once said something very beautiful. I always remembered it: Not eyes but words are the mirror of the soul. There, I said it with my pen. In one sentence! Now tell me again that I'm dumb!

You, dear Diary, are my speech, my words. So that makes you my soul, right? You know that I'm really very smart. Mom doesn't know. Daddy doesn't know. He always says I'm his lovely smart daughter. But he doesn't mean it. He loves me, but he lies to me. Why else won't he let me go to a normal school? Why do I need a teacher at home? Because Daddy has a lot of money?

But that's not why I feel sad. They had another fight. Mom and Daddy. Mom sent me away, to my room. But I sneaked down the stairs. Listened at the door. I know that's bad. I couldn't help it. Because it was about me and Belinda. So I had to know.

They still haven't told me she's coming home. Daddy was very angry. He spoke with that quiet and hard voice. Hard and cold as a knife. He always uses that voice when he's very very angry. Mom was crying again. I hate it when she cries because she wants to get her way. They said horrible words to each other. I was afraid they might really hit each other!

I don't understand grown-ups. Yesterday I was so happy. Mom was happy too then. Now they're fighting again. Why? They should both be so happy that Belinda's coming home. Away from that awful school. But that was what they were fighting about. About Belinda. I couldn't understand it all, dear Diary. Sometimes they spoke very quietly, then they were yelling. But I have a very good memory, as you know. I'll tell you what I understood.

Daddy said: I don't want her here in this house do you hear me I don't care what the doctor said I don't want your goddamn freak in this house with Karen not now not ever.

Mom cried and yelled: But I want her back you fucking asshole I want her back she's my child.

Then Daddy yelled so hard I couldn't even hear Mom crying. So loud that surely even the neighbours must have heard it: I should've kicked you out years ago you slut you and your fucking freak I should've thrown you down the stairs you and your lover boy, should've broken his neck when I caught you then all of this never would've happened.

And then Mom got ice angry. I call it that. When she stops crying and her voice changes. It gets cold and sharp. As if she thinks about every word before she says it. She no longer yells. Every word is cold and clear and smells of hatred: But you didn't you didn't dare shorty with your soft dick you were so glad to brag with your snotty friends that you could do it you were fucking happy that I got pregnant and it didn't matter that she wasn't yours you only started hating Belinda after Karen was born then it was all Karen here and Karen there and my Belinda could go fuck herself.

Then I stopped listening, dear Diary. I'm making spots on your pages. I'm sorry. I'm crying. I can't help myself. I told you all I heard. As I heard it. But I don't understand it. I can't ask anybody. Then I would have to tell about you. I can't do that. They would laugh at me. They would say I'm dumb. Maybe I am. Why else don't I understand what they mean?

Because when I sneaked away from that door below, Daddy said something else. I didn't get it all. He spoke very soft then: ... retard...

needs all the love of her parents. That wasn't about Belinda. Daddy said that. And it was about me, me, ME!

Then Mom said: you know who the retard is. With that cold voice of hers. And Daddy hit her. I heard the smacking loud sound as I rushed up the stairs.

I'm scared. I'm alone. Teddy is gone. Belinda is gone. Mom and Daddy hit each other! Do they still love me? I love them. Even Mom.

Maybe it'll be better when Belinda gets here.

FRIDAY.

At last they have told me, dear Diary. They really told me Belinda's coming home tomorrow evening! Finally we'll be together again. It seems like ages since we saw each other. Mom never let me go with her. When she went to that school to visit Belinda. She'll be taller now, I think. She was always taller than me. She already had a bra when she left. But now I have one too! Yep. Mom said I had to wear one. I find it rather stupid. My titties aren't that big. Not much more than oranges.

Of course Belinda is two years older than me. Years ago hers were already bigger than mine now. Her nipples also, so very pink and pointed. Always jiggling loose under her sweater. Till she began to wear that bra.

I'm so happy she'll be back. We love each other so very much. Now we will play together again. As in those days. I have put all our dolls in rows, as then. In front of our big dollhouse. Daddy made that himself in the shed in the back of the garden. Where we never were allowed to enter. Daddy keeps his gardening tools there. He always said we might hurt ourselves there. I've put all our favourite books and comics in neat stacks. Belinda will be so glad. It will be as if she never left.

I don't understand why Mom is still mad at Daddy. She wears her angry face all day. Daddy isn't happy either. Mom says he's tired from his job at the office. But I know that isn't the reason. It's about Belinda. Daddy said to Mom that Belinda's a freak. They often use such difficult words when they fight. I looked it up in the dictionary when Mom was upstairs. It says that a freak is an abnormal person. Like the vendor at the corner shop. He has a strange growth on his hand. It looks like a sixth finger. Or like people with three legs. Or the Elephant Man. I saw him in a movie on the telly one night. He was a nice man but so horrible to look at. Or like two children who are grown together. With their heads. Sometimes they have only one head and two bodies.

But Belinda is not like that at all! She is so very normal. Two eyes, two hands, two legs, two titties. One nose and one mouth. I don't understand why Daddy would call her a freak. Sometimes grown-ups use weird words when they mean something else. Maybe I have misunderstood. I am smart. But sometimes even smart people misunderstand things. When they know that it proves that they are smart. I could ask Daddy to explain it to me. But I don't dare. I never get any answers when I ask about Belinda. Daddy might understand that I had listened at the door. Then he would be very cross with me. He would tell Mom and she would be mad too. She is always very quickly mad at me. She never got mad at Belinda. Why can't she love us both? I think she blames me for Belinda being away. At that school. But why? Is it because she already had Belinda before she met Daddy?

That is no reason to hate me as she does. I know what she says to Daddy. I know what retard means. But I am not! No matter what she says. I cannot speak very well. But I can read and write. I can write very well. You know, dear Diary. Sometimes it's difficult when they're long words. Then I write very slowly and carefully. And I do get them right. I am a good pupil, the teacher once said so to me. He said I am doing very well. So you see! He is a teacher, he knows.

I don't like playing outside with the other children. They aren't nice, not at all like Belinda. Sometimes they are really nasty. Sometimes they laugh at me. They tear at my hair, my clothes. Last time there was that boy, pimpleface Tom. He lives two streets further. He grabbed my titties under my sweater and pinched my nipples. Then he tried to kiss me, imagine. He was slobbering like a dog, his mouth all wet. And they all just laughed. Till I hit him on his nose. When I came home with blood on my sweater I told Daddy. He went and had a talk with Tom's dad. Tom never bothered me again. The kids broke one of my prettiest dolls too. One Belinda loved very much. I hope she won't miss that doll when she gets here. I buried the doll behind the shed. And said a little prayer for it.

I had a very bad dream last night, dear Diary. About that dead doll. It was all smashed into little pieces. The doll was bleeding everywhere, also between its legs. There was a hand with big scissors carving between those legs. Till there was a big hole there and more blood kept on pumping out. I got sick. I thought I was going to vomit. Then I woke up. I couldn't go back to sleep. I kept on seeing that doll. Only now it had Tom's face who had been at my titties. I started sweating, I felt very strange. I felt very hot as if I had a fever. And I got all wet down there. I was tossing and turning in bed. I kept on seeing Tom and that lump in his trousers. I went to the toilet and dried myself. When I touched myself down there, it got all tingly. As that time when my fingers touched an electric plug. But different. It felt weird but nice. As with Belinda when we slept together. Very close together, all cuddly and warm. Just the two of us.

Maybe she won't miss that one doll. There are so many of them left. And it's been years since then. I have been thinking about that. I can't remember how long it's been. And I wonder. Do Daddy and Mom think it's my fault Belinda was sent away? Is that why Mom hates me? Why Daddy sometimes is mad at me? But I haven't done anything. I haven't told. Well, not everything. It was Belinda. She always dared more than me. When Dan said he would show it to us it was Belinda who laughed. Who said he didn't dare. But he did. And he let us play with it. Then when it began to rise and grow we laughed. It was so funny. But then Belinda began to act weird, she got all red in her face. Then Dan grabbed under her skirt and they made me turn away. But I looked anyway and I saw it all, what they did. Everything! That's what I told, I had to. Daddy was very angry and Mom got all white. I thought she was going to faint right there. When they took Dan away on that stretcher. He didn't say anything, he was more pale even than Mom. I felt so scared then. I tried to tell it all but the words wouldn't come. Then they took Belinda away to that school. I haven't done anything wrong. I only told what Belinda had done, nothing more, nothing more! My mouth refused to tell the rest. It wasn't my fault at all!

Daddy and Mom told me very quietly. As if they thought I wouldn't be glad for Belinda to come home. Of course I'm glad. I'm very happy, and so excited!

SATURDAY MORNING.

They have left, to get Belinda. Finally, finally! I know she won't be mad at me because I told some of the things she did with Dan. Besides, everybody could see it at her face. And it's been years ago.

I've done some checking. It wasn't easy. I'm not very good with numbers and years. But I have kept all my birthday cards. In a big paper box under my bed. I am not seventeen years old. I looked through all the cards I got through the years. From Daddy and Mom and Belinda. Tell me again I'm a stupid retard! I can SEE which ones are true and which are false. I just compare the ones Belinda gave to me before she left. I know her handwriting so well. Then I look at the cards Daddy and Mom signed with Belinda's name. The ones they said she had sent me from that school. I know she never sent me a card from there! But I acted as if I believed them. The last real card from Belinda she gave to me when I was twelve. Then she was fourteen. Five cards with fake handwriting. So she has been at that school for five years. That long! Why did she never send me a card herself? Or answered one of my letters? I wrote so many to her but I never got one back. Why did they never take me with them when they went to visit her?

Because they didn't want me to! That's why! Mom hates me because what I said about Belinda. And Daddy always gives Mom her way. He always says I'm his daughter. But he never really protects me against Mom. Mom always talks about Belinda. Only Belinda counts. As if I don't exist. As if I'm not her daughter. Still, I love Belinda. That scares me. What if she doesn't love me after that time?

Dan's gone too. His parents moved away shortly after... that.

I wonder what kind of school Belinda went to. They were talking about it when they left this morning. Very softly so I didn't get much of it. I just heard Daddy say something like: fully normal progress, and: no more problems.

Normal? What problems? Why can't grown-ups say it like it is? Why don't they tell me? I want to understand, dear Diary, but they make such a big secret out of it. They act as if I don't understand anything. As if I do everything wrong. Why normal? Belinda's always been normal. Or does he mean she can talk again? Would that be it, Diary? That would be wonderful.

It will be so marvellous when they get here with Belinda. My sweet sister, my sweet Belinda. I've put all our dolls in the bath. Dried their hair and brushed it. Put all new clothes on them. They look lovely. Belinda will be delighted. We'll reread our favourite books. I wonder if they had books like ours at that school. We'll have fun together. Then together in bed we'll whisper in the dark. Just as if nothing happened. We'll be nice to each other and play those little games Belinda taught me. Those games which make me feel tingly and good.

Belinda will understand. Why I had to tell things about her and Dan. I hope they taught her to speak again. Not like that time with Dan. Sitting there screaming with her mouth wide open. But making no sound at all. Her lips moving but no words came out. Moving her hands like butterfly wings. But she couldn't say anything, so I had to take care of that.

I do hope she can do better now. Does it take five years to learn to speak again? Belinda is older but maybe she's not really as smart as I am. Maybe she needed so much time.

Anyway, I'm sure she still loves me. Maybe she never got my letters. Or maybe Mom and Daddy never gave me her letters. It doesn't matter now. Soon she'll be with me again. So happy. So happy!

SATURDAY AFTERNOON.

I read what I wrote this morning, dear Diary. I'm crying again. I can't help it. I feel so miserable. Belinda's home but she doesn't love me. She hates me. She hates me! I was so glad when she came in. I almost didn't recognise her. She's grown so much. She looks so much older. That dress she wears, that make-up. It makes her look like Mom. She acts absent. I heard Daddy use that word. As if she isn't all here. As if part of her is somewhere else. She speaks but only a few words. In very short sentences. As if it gives her trouble. I would think after five years she'd do better than that.

I showed her our room. Our dolls. All dolls said hello when she came in. But it was as if she didn't hear. I'd gone to all that trouble. Washing the dolls and dressing them up. Making them pretty for Belinda. She didn't look at them at all. She didn't even notice that one of her favourites was missing. I told her about our books and how much fun we would have together. She didn't smile once. It was so weird. The way she didn't seem to hear what I was saying. The way she looked at things. Her head making shaky little movements, as a bird does. She kept her hands clasped together. All fingers intertwining each other. When she looked at me she got a fine wrinkle between her eyes. As if she was trying to remember me. She doesn't speak to me. When I kissed her she was standing there as stiff as a doll. In that silly grown-up dress. I think it's supposed to look joyful. All flowers in strong colours melting together. But it makes her look so old fashioned. She is not the Belinda I remember. She is a strange grown-up woman. She's gotten huge tits. She wears panties.

When I touched her arm she really shivered and drew back. I thought that's the homecoming. After five years in that school everything here is strange, as new. When we were alone, in the circle of our dolls. I told her about before. How sweet and nice we were to each other. Our whispers in the bed. What we did together in the dark. How we slept afterwards, huddled together, so warm and soft. How much we loved each other. I really begged her to say something to me. To know she still loved me.

And then she said those things to me. With that weird cold voice of hers. A voice like Mom's. Not loud but so very cold. Words I can't write down, dear Diary. Mean, filthy words. Each word cut me as an ice pick. So mean, so cruel! Then she just turned and left me with our dolls. My dolls.

I don't understand, dear Diary. Why would she say that I was mean and nasty? What's wrong with her? She hates me as Mom hates me. Then Daddy came up and he wasn't nice either. He asked what I had said or done. But I had done nothing! He'll start to hate me too as all the others. You must help me, dear Diary. I feel so alone. I'm scared. All our dolls are in the corner now. All their heads are with me, in bed. They keep me company. They weep with me.

SATURDAY NIGHT.

Everything's fine now, dear Diary. Oh, I'm so glad it all worked out right. Belinda's not here with me. She sleeps in the spare bedroom. Where Mom sometimes sleeps after a fight with Daddy. Belinda didn't want to sleep with me. That hurts very much. But I understand. It's been so long. She has to adapt. That's what Daddy said when Belinda was out of the room. She has to get used to us again. After five years. Maybe she couldn't love me after that thing with Dan. But it was for her, wasn't it? Because I loved her so much. My sweet Belinda. I'd do anything for her. Then and now.

I'm smart. I've been thinking about it after I stopped crying. At that time I thought maybe it's like a hunger. Belinda used to bite me. When we were playing in bed, you know, in the dark. It was fun. Her small sharp teeth biting in my neck and shoulders. Never hard, you know, just for fun. Sometimes she began panting very hard then.

As she did with Dan. When he showed his thing and then grabbed under her skirt. Then, when Dan was lying on top of her and they were moving and shaking. She bit him too, in his ears and lips. Making funny gasping noises. When they stopped and he rolled away on the grass. Just lying there with his eyes closed. Breathing very hard and his thing in the open. Wet and still stiff. I thought she'd like to have it forever. Maybe we could use it to have fun together.

So I went into the shed and got the scissors Daddy used for cutting the flowers. And I cut it off. Gave it to Belinda. She liked to bite what she loved. So I put it in her open mouth. It went so easy, so quick. Then Dan sat up and started screaming. Belinda started screaming too but her mouth was full. There was blood everywhere. I never thought there would be so much blood! She started waving with her hands as if mad. Grasping at my hands and so I put the scissors in her hand. The way she acted made me scared and I ran away.

Then all those people came. Dan was very white and very still. I don't know if he was dead. And Belinda was choking on Dan's thing in her mouth. The red dripping from her mouth as spaghetti sauce. When they took it out of her mouth, she kept on screaming without making any sound. That scared me even more. They asked all those questions. I just shook my head. But they persisted, specially that nice lady in uniform. Finally I told them a few things about what Belinda and Dan had been doing. I said that scared me and I ran away. They asked me where Belinda had gotten the scissors. I didn't know. Had she been fighting with Dan? I didn't know. So finally they let me alone.

Now Belinda can talk again. But mostly she keeps silent. The only thing she said was that I was sick. When I mentioned Dan she started shaking her head. She put both hands to her ears. She didn't want to hear. And she looked real funny as if she was trying to remember something. Then she just walked away from me.

Is it possible that she doesn't know? That she has forgotten it? Maybe at that school they taught her to forget everything. Then she doesn't remember that I did it because I loved her so much. That I only wanted to do her a favour. That hurts.

I think she's just an egoist. No more. She just thinks of herself. She doesn't care about me. She refuses to touch me. She won't even look straight at me. Maybe she thinks I'm silly too, as the others. It's Mom and Daddy's fault. They sent Belinda to that school. They made her hate me.

Only Belinda was really nice to me. Belinda was mine till Dan came along. I only wanted her to love me more. Even when she and Dan were doing it. They saw me watching and they laughed. But I wasn't hurt. I wasn't ashamed. I was happy for Belinda because she liked it. I thought if that is what she wants from Dan, I'll give it to her. As a present.

I know now that I made a mistake. I don't know what I did wrong, but I did something wrong. I'll fix it. I'll make her love me again. She kicked at our dolls, she didn't look at our books. She didn't notice all our birthday cards. But I don't care. She can't have changed that much.

Once she understands how much I need her, she'll come back to me. Mom and Daddy did this to her. They had sent her away. They never took me along to visit her. No wonder she's angry with me. She thinks I have forgotten her all those years. That isn't true. I have always been thinking about her. I'll make her understand that.

SUNDAY EARLY MORNING.

Mom and Daddy were fast asleep. They had been talking for a long time before they slept. It all went so easy. I used a chair to get to the knife rack in the kitchen. I just took the biggest one. It's almost as long as my forearm. Then I took it upstairs.

I was very quiet and careful. I had to be very fast too. Didn't want to wake them. But they slept so deeply. First Mom, then Daddy. After I had done Mom I had to wrench the knife because it stuck. But I got it out without waking Daddy. He just snored and turned over in his sleep. It was a messy job, all wet and sticky afterwards. It was hard work and it took some time. But I think I managed it quite well. Now Belinda will know how much I love her. I took a shower first before I went to Belinda's room.

She was sound asleep. She looks so restful and lovely. I arranged all the heads of our dolls on her bed, around her. Very quiet, very careful. But she didn't wake up. She's snoring softly. Then I put those of Mom and Daddy between the doll heads. In the place of honour so she will see those first when she wakes up. It wasn't easy, they kept falling over. I had to use a spare pillow to support them.

Now I'm sitting in a chair besides Belinda. It's hard writing in the dark, dear Diary, but I manage. Soon it'll be light. I wait for Belinda to wake up. For the big surprise.

I have Daddy's here. It looks like Dan's but a bit bigger. I've cleaned it under the tap. When Belinda wakes up I'll put it in her mouth. So she can bite on it as with Dan. I can't wait to see her happy shining face!

LIKE TWO WHITE SPIDERS

COME IN, COME in, Father. Yes, please close the door, there's a bit of a cold draft in here. You have brought the tape recorder with you? Oh yes, I see it's running already. Fine, that's exactly what I wanted. I want everybody to know the truth, you, the doctors, the whole world. I'm very glad you came.

Yes, I did ask for you myself. No, thanks, I don't smoke. I used to, you know, too much. My fingertips were always stained with those tell-tale yellow-brown stains of nicotine. Now you don't have to look at me like that! Oh yes, yes, I understand now.

No, it doesn't disturb me at all to speak frankly about it. Not at all! I am already used to being without them. Sometimes I even forget that once... it seems incredible, doesn't it? But yet it is like that; after all, near the end I didn't really consider them as parts of me anymore. They weren't really mine. But please, why don't you sit down, yes, there on the bed. I'll keep on standing, after all I've been sitting here for weeks, and there's not enough space for two people to sit down. Now isn't that a good joke, "I've been sitting here"... literally and symbolically! What do you say? It's been only about one week? But it seems like weeks to me! Oh, but you forgot, Father, I've been in the prison hospital for a long time, before they finally made up their minds and put me in this madhouse.

But why shouldn't I call it by its real name? After all this IS a nut house, and I AM a dangerous lunatic! Else I wouldn't be here, would I? Aren't YOU afraid of me? But there, you see? I forgot it again! I COULDN'T hurt you. I could always try to bite you, but why should I? You don't have to cast those looks at the door, there's no need to be afraid. Didn't I ask you myself to come here because I wanted to have a long talk with you?

No, not about your God, nor about Heaven and Hell, nor anything like that. Please don't bother, I don't believe in them. I really don't, you'll just be wasting your own time, and mine too. Even supposing that there is such a thing as an afterlife, well, my conscience is at rest... I'm sure of that. No, I'm not being vain; it's just that I personally haven't done anything, you hear? I haven't killed a human being! Maybe in a way I am to blame for his death, and maybe I should feel slightly guilty about that, but I didn't kill Howard Bretner. THEY did. But everything was blamed on me, as was to be expected. Well, I can understand it. Tell me, have you ever met another case like mine? I don't mean absolutely identical, but just a similar case which proved... strange, inexplicable. The impossible isn't accepted nowadays, and once you end up with an impossibility, you're classified as a madman. Simple things such as cars, aeroplanes, atomic energy, spaceships: in earlier centuries they too would have been called "impossible" and "mad nonsense". Maybe one day they'll be able to give a name to what happened to me also. Parapsychology, neurosis, psychosis, metaphysics, telekinesis... they're always learning more about the borderline sciences, and they put nice little labels on them with a long Latin name, and then they store them carefully away somewhere where they can't hurt anybody's feelings. In such a set of files, there's still no place open for the supernatural, the demoniacal. But your Church, Father, doesn't it know about white and black magic, about the powers of witches and warlocks? Isn't there even an exorcism ritual from some Pope Gregorius the... whichever it was? The Fourteenth? I don't know, and it doesn't really matter now. But maybe something like that could have saved me. Do you believe in EVIL, Father?

No, that's not what I mean. I do mean EVIL spelled in capital letters, evil, as a personification, as an existing and influencing force, naked purified evil, which needs no motives for its deeds. No, thanks again, I never smoke now, not even to calm down, it is too difficult in my condition. But you can smoke, if you want to. Did you hear my story, Father? No, I don't mean the nonsense they wrote in the news-papers, and I don't mean the things my lawyer said at the trial either. I mean what I told my lawyer, the truth which he refused to believe, so he had to make up a story of his own to save my neck. But you, Father, your mental constitution is better tuned to things about the mind, the soul if you want to call it that. So listen, and I will tell you the truth.

Let me remind you first of what are known as "the facts in the case"; I suppose you've read those on my personal files before you came, but if I repeat them it will be easier for you to make the comparison. I did hate Howard Bretner; no use denying it: the whole neighbourhood knew it. He had humiliated, ridiculed and even struck me. That evening, someone knocked on his front door. Bretner went to open it, then his wife heard a muffled scream, a short rattle, and the sound of a heavy body falling down. The rest you know: they found him strangled, his neck broken even, and me a few metres farther on, nearly dead myself from loss of blood.

Now listen to how it all really happened.

I think I'll have to journey back into the past, to my early youth, because that's where it started. I used to be a very frightened little boy, you know. Not just the usual children's fears, but always about things that just weren't there to the others. I saw and felt things that weren't seen by other people, including my parents, who thought they existed solely in my feverish imagination. I didn't dare walk through an empty street, not even when my parents were at my side. Being alone brought me into a condition of complete, utter panic. Finally, after a time, my friends began evading me. No wonder, considering how I must have looked to them! A slender gypsy-like boy with slick black hair and haunted eyes, staring eyes which saw things no one ever saw or understood. Nyctophobia, they call it, a nervous sickly fear of the dark, and anything which goes with it.

But it became worse than I could imagine. If you live with something long enough for it to become familiar, finally you stop noticing it. The dark world, which had frightened me so much, finally became something very ordinary; I stopped being afraid of it, and I even had the impression that... the darkness felt friendly towards me. Maybe that was the real reason why the other boys ran away from me. The dark atmosphere surrounding me went unnoticed to ME, but instinctively they must have sensed its ever-near presence, and it scared THEM.

I must have been about six years old, when I discovered the first mild traces of lunacy: the fact that I sleep-walked on the nights of the full moon. I discovered this quite by accident: that night, it suddenly started raining, and I woke up with a start. I was in the garden behind our house, on my naked feet and dressed only in my pyjamas. I can assure you that it gave me quite a shock! Now I have been reading up the symptoms of all those little eccentricities of mine, and I have put labels on them myself; but at that time it all seemed as alien as possible. Another and later discovery was my being a nyctalops. Just like a cat, I could see in the dark. Quite strange, you know, it is more the use of an unsuspected organ of sense, than a really clear "sight".

Then I started noticing my hands. Have you seen my hands? No? Not even after all the pictures they put in that cheap sensational paper? They got them from a blow-up of an old school picture. Heaven knows where they managed to find that one! You see, I had beautiful hands. I can still see them as they were at that age. Slender and very white, a bit too thin perhaps, almost bony even, with very narrow wrists. But what they had were muscles as strong as steel! My fingers too were long and slender, nearly claw-like. No, not eerie or hairy or dirty! Pretty claws, if I may say so myself. I always kept them absolutely clean, but the nails were too long, they used to break all the time, but I took good care of them. I loved my hands. Sometimes when they were lying on top of the table in front of me, I made the fingers move, and my hands crawled across the table like two big white spiders. It amused me, and once I got so absorbed in that innocent pastime that I didn't hear my mother coming in. It scared her, I could see that, and after that I stopped playing with my hands when someone was near me and could watch them. I used to go and hide in a nearby wood or in some meadow, or else I locked myself in my room. There it was that they acted DIFFERENTLY for the first time.

It was one of those hot, suffocating summer afternoons. My parents had gone shopping, so there was no one around likely to disturb my game. I was sitting on a chair at the big table in the living room. The sun made a burning white spot in the centre of the polished table -leaf, and sparkled on the metal of the big bird cage. My hands were enjoying themselves in the warmth of the sun's rays; they moved lazily across the table, with slow movements of my fingers, which kept them balanced with short thrusts of my thumbs. The forefingers and middle fingers were the real organs of motion, while the little fingers and the ring-fingers constituted the balance with the thumbs, at the same time giving the wanted direction to the movements. I had been playing for some time already, and it began boring me, so I decided to stop it. AND I COULDN'T!

My hands didn't obey, my brain was emitting the order to stop, but the muscles of the hands refused to accept the impulse and stop. They kept on crawling, as if they were acting of their own free will.

The horror didn't come immediatcly. At first there was a feeling of astonishment, of alienation. I would have felt the same if a tree had bent over to me, or if a chair suddenly had started talking to me. These hands, they were MINE, so why didn't they obey me? Then there came a feeling of independence. When I saw them moving like that, with short sneaky movements like two pale scorpions, like two fat-bellied white spiders, I suddenly saw them not as my hands, but as two living entities, separated from me and yet connected.

The two things were bad, my whole being felt it. The hands had always been my willing slaves and servants, and now they felt out of place, almost as if my whole body rebelled against them, wanted to reject them as something unwanted. I KNEW they were evil now, because they were possessed by... yes, by what? Even now I don't know for sure. Some demoniacal power from outside our world, something which had crashed through a barrier and had taken possession of them.

Only THEN came the horror, at what happened next. The hands crawled towards the bird's cage, in which a solitary canary-bird was sitting. I had always disliked it because it was so scared of people, and never came to sit on my finger or sing for me. While I was watching with terrified eyes, the left hand opened the door of the cage with sure movements, and the right hand crawled inside. Like an enormous insect, it erected itself to its full length, leaning on the wrist to attach itself to the bars of the cage with three fingers, and drew itself up along the bars inside the cage. The muscles of my arms seemed completely benumbed, will-less they were carried along with the hands. The hand inside the cage was now moving sidewards, like a hunter approaching his prey. Then suddenly the hand JUMPED, and small feathers were thrown around as the bird made a last desperate bid to escape. I closed my eyes so I wouldn't have to watch the terrible thing which was happening, but to my horror I could still FEEL everything the hand did. The little heart of the caught bird was pumping insanely in the palm of the hand, and with rapid movements the thumb and index-finger took the little head between them, and squeezed. It made a sickening cracking noise, and tepid moisture ran between the fingers of the monstrous hand, but still it wasn't satisfied. Quickly it crawled outside with its victim, and together the two hands now tore the small body in pieces, using their nails, and covering the table with pieces of quivering flesh and shattered feathers, in the midst of insane patterns of fresh blood and innards. The nightmare continued for more than half an hour, before suddenly the hands became lifeless, and lay down. The evil power had withdrawn itself, and now they were mine again.

The rest of the nightmare was nauseating. I had to hide what was left scattered on the table, and then clean everything up so no one would notice anything. Later I told my parents that I had left the cage door open, and the bird had flown away, and no one ever suspected anything close to the truth. For weeks I was living in continuous dread of the hands. When would they again come alive, and do things with their own power which I despised, but was unable to stop? I was forced to be a powerless spectator. But years passed, and nothing happened, the demoniacal power didn't manifest itself again. So finally I stopped believing myself that it had ever really happened. I made myself think that I had fallen asleep that afternoon, that the bird really had escaped, and I had made up the whole thing. Until the night when the terror came back...

I was already in my twenties then, and was living alone, my parents both having died in a car crash. It was very late, and I was strolling house-wards after a little private party with some friends. I admit it, I wasn't exactly sober, but neither was I really drunk. I had absorbed enough gin to find everything bathed in a rosy glow. Then I saw the girl coming, a child of some eight years old or so, dressed in a heavy winter coat and carrying a shopping bag. I remember thinking that it was really irresponsible of her parents, to send a little girl alone out into the night at such an hour. I knew the girl too, a real brat without the slightest manners or respect, whose family lived not very far from my own house. Then unexpectedly the hands PUSHED me backwards into a dark doorway, where I waited till the child had passed. Before I really understood what was happening, the hands flew away from me, they pulled themselves against my body, crooking the fingers like springs, and then they were around the throat of the child, attacking her from behind so she couldn't see me. The bag fell on the ground, the girl didn't even get the slightest chance to scream, because already the hands were pushing into the flesh of her throat, choking her silent scream. I felt the silken flesh shrink under their pressure, the little throat made spasmodic movements, as she gasped for breath which didn't come. The hands lifted the struggling body from the ground, it seemed just a doll, desperately kicking with its wooden legs. I then understood that the hands too had grown, and just like my body they also needed food, but an entirely different kind. Death fed them, and as life was flying away from the spasmodic shaking body of the child, the power and insane blood lust of the hands increased. Then my brain, numbed by terror, awoke and I tried to resist the alien power. I ordered the hands to loosen their grip, I ordered them with all my willpower, but it was useless. No matter how I fought them, the strangling satanic claws were stronger. Sweat dripped from my forehead into my eyes, and I had the feeling that any second now my skull would burst open and spatter my brains against the house wall. Then, with courage born of desperation, I threw myself down, knocking the little victim and the hands against the wall. Their grip loosened, and then slowly I could force my own will upon them. I fought and fought, silently and bitterly, and as suddenly as it had come, the monstrous power left them. Groaning, I leaned against the cold wall, waiting till I had regained complete possession over my whole body. Then I bent over the child. She was unconscious, the breath came squeaking and groaning out of the open mouth with the swollen tongue and blue lips, and there was a nasty bump on her forehead where it had hit the wall. But thank God, she was alive! I put the girl on the doorstep of the nearby house, where light was still burning inside, then I rang the bell and hurried away. The next day, I read in the papers that the police were looking for her attacker. Fortunately the child survived, and the policemen never found out anything about me.

That same day, I made a big fire at the end of my garden, using some old rags and petrol. When the licking flames were high enough, I put my hands in them. The suffering was intolerable for that one second before I became unconscious. I woke up in a hospital. My hands had been horribly burned and they stayed disfigured and marked, but the monsters were still alive, and they healed. A few months later I tried pushing them into a circular saw, but they had been warned now, and they didn't let me.

Still, the evil power stayed away till last year, apart from the fact that I couldn't harm the hands. But then Howard Bretner came to live in the neighbourhood. It wasn't exactly hate at first sight, though I did consider him a bit repulsive and ugly. He was fat, an extravagant, thick man with a three-lobed chin and real bags of fat surrounding his slightly sunken pig like eyes. His hands were always moist and had a weak touch, and his lips were thick and always trembling. He seemed hostile, sneaking... but the hate only came later.

It all started with those typical little difficulties between neighbours, the kind that happen all the time. Just little things, you know, small happenings without any real importance, but they left a lasting bad taste. Then he began visiting the same pubs I used to go to, and that's where the real troubles started. Bretner was one of that breed of people who are only happy when they are able to make themselves feel important by humiliating others. That's what he did to me, making scornful remarks, practical (and stupid) jokes, and things like that. I tried to stay out of his way as much as possible but it was inevitable that we would run into each other now and then. So one evening, the long-expected eruption came. I had drunk a few pints of beer, and again he started making insulting and sarcastic remarks: if I remember right it was about my hair-cut or my shoes or something stupid like that. I let him go on for some time enjoying himself, trying not to notice him, and then quite suddenly it was too much. I turned round and hit him straight in his face. He stood up, and looked at the blood running out of his mouth onto his shirt, surprised, and almost as if he didn't know what had happened. Then suddenly he grabbed his glass of beer, and threw its contents in my eyes. While I was still wiping the stuff out of my eyes, two of his friends grabbed my arms from behind, and then the coward hit me in the stomach, again and again while I was unable to defend myself. And all those good friends of mine just stood around, and only after the fourth or fifth hit, they interfered and tore the brute away from me. They had to half carry me to my house, and I felt sick and miserable.

Of course I wanted to pay him back, but the opportunity never came. I didn't meet him alone, always his friends were with him, as if the rotten coward didn't dare walk alone in the street. For more than three months the hatred mounted in me, accumulated in me... and in my hands. And the evil in them, as horrible and distorted as themselves, fed on my hatred, and grew with it.

Then that fatal evening, they moved again. I was going to the shed at the back of my yard, to get something or other, when the hands stopped my movement. The now well-known numbness came over my arms, and the hands took hold of the door of the shed, and started crawling down towards the ground. I resisted them with all my power, propping my knees against the wall, but without results. The hands continued their macabre crawling walk over the ground, with long clawing movements of the fingers, burying themselves in the earth and leaving deep grooves in it. They carried my struggling body with them like a piece of ballast. Then I understood what they were going to do. All those years they had been quiet, during all that time I had been able to impose my own volition on them, but now my accumulated hatred against Bretner had given them sufficient power to break their chains. They were two malignant "Hounds of Tindalos", nightmare creatures, possessed by an unnatural and evil life force. They would kill Bretner, and I couldn't stop them. Don't get me wrong, I hated Bretner as only a human being can hate another, and knowing him dead would only have given me a feeling of immense satisfaction. It was absolutely not for HIM that I wanted to stop the monsters, but I knew that once they had killed again, there would be no more stopping them. Again and again they would be free, and I would be the powerless tool of their horrible deeds. I am no murderer, no psychopath. I would have desired Bretner's death, but NOT through the hands, because they were the personification of absolute evil. I was being drawn forwards through the darkness, seeing the hands as two white spots in front of me. Then they moved into the light of the street lamp a bit further away, two quickly crawling horrors, which had now reached the hedge separating Bretner's garden from mine.

That's when I saw the scythe. It was standing against Bretner's hedge, where he had probably forgotten it. An old, rusty scythe, which balanced there precariously. The horrible murderous hands were crawling just underneath it, on their way to Bretner's house. I don't know what impulse made me do it, it was an idea born and executed in a fraction of a second. If I had let the hands have their way, how many others would die, strangled or torn to ribbons of flesh by the hands without my control? How was I to foresee that the amount of blood still in them would have been sufficient to...

I made a desperate movement with my whole body, throwing my right leg forward. It was one chance out of a hundred... but it succeeded.

My feet barely touched the scythe, it swayed... and fell.

The rusty but still razor-sharp edge of the blade crashed down on my wrists. I still believe that I must have shrieked in agony, but nobody seems to have heard me. Crouching and nearly unconscious from pain, I lay there. What happened then, they have distorted. Some things are too horrible to be true, so it feels better not to speak of them, but rather adapt them to our world and the way we like to think it is.

They say I killed Bretner first, and afterwards amputated my own hands, just as if they don't see themselves that this would clearly have been impossible. I haven't seen Bretner's body with the torn eyes and broken neck, and neither did I see the two bloodless things they found with him. But from a friend whose name I won't mention here, but who was at the inquest and who has some relations here and there, I know some of the things they have kept from the papers and even from me. In each one of the hands, they found... a complete set of miniature organs, a complete nervous system, strongly developed muscles, a heart and lungs feeding on my own body, and very primitive brains. The things disintegrated into a fluid mass after only a few hours, but I KNOW that there must exist pictures of them, somewhere safely filed away in the files of some doctor. But even without that, I knew in advance what would happen afterwards.

You see, after the falling of the scythe but before my awakening in the jail hospital, I regained consciousness for a very short time, probably caused by the horrible pain. Very briefly only, but it was enough. I saw the two trails of blood, leading from the hedge where I was lying, towards Bretner's door. Even before the police, I knew what they would later find on Bretner's throat.

DUNWICH DREAMS, DUNWICH SCREAMS

In den Tiefen des Meeres fanden Sie Geburt,
nicht die Meere unsrer Erde
sondern in die Abgründe Jenseits,
und das Licht ferner schwarze Sonnen
hat Sie hierher gebracht, unter Uns,
in die Tiefen unsrer eigenen Meere,
die Abgründe in unser eigenes Herz,
die schwarze Leere in jeder von Uns.
Da warten Sie. Da fressen Sie.
Die Bestien des Meeres, und die dunkelste
Gedanken unseres Gehirn.
Städte, Länder under Völker gehen,
und die Zeit is weniger dan eine Sekunde für Sie.
Sie warten. Sie haben alle Zeit.

- from the rewritten version of *Von denen Verdammten, oder: Eine Verhandlung über die unheimlichen Kulten der Alten*, by Edith Brendall, 1907, based on the original and suppressed, untitled book by Kazaj Heinz Vogel.

(In the depths of the seas they were given birth,
not the seas of our world
but the abysses beyond,
and the light of far dark suns
brought them here, among us,
in the depths of our own seas,
the dark emptiness in each of us.
There they wait. There they feed.
The beasts in the seas, and the darkest
thoughts in our brain.
Cities, countries and nations pass on,
and time is less than a second to them.
They wait. They have all the time.)

Die Kehle war übergeschnitten, mit eine Kraft die genügend war sodasz der Kopf beinahe loskam von den Körper wenn man ihm aus dem Wasser holte. Die Augen waren ausgebrennt mit ein Zeug dat die Form hat von ein Stern mit fünf Spitzen, mit eine Spitz scharf nach Unten gerichtet. Met dasselbde Folterzeug waren Märke gemacht über ganz den Körper, der nackt war wenn gefunden. Alle Zähne waren mit Gewalt ausgezogen und mit irsinniger Wut in den Schädel von die Frau geslagen.

(The throat was cut with such force that the head almost came loose from the body when it was recovered from the water. The eyes had been burned out with an instrument in the shape of a five-pointed star, with one point in the downward direction of the body. The body was covered with marks created by the same torture instrument. All teeth had been forcibly removed and had then been hammered with insane force into the skull of the woman.)

- from the official report of Dorich Grauswalt from the German Police Department of Bonn, on the recovery of the body of Edith Brendall from the Rhine on April the 6th, 1910. The German student had been missing from the cheap hotel where she stayed since the night of March 27th, when other guests complained about the noises in her room. When the concierge arrived he found the door open, the room overturned and his guest missing, which he informed the police about.

PROLOGUE: ARRIVAL

IT HAD BEEN a traditional British day, as any European visitor such as myself should have expected in the month of April, and of course hopes for the better and is disappointed as he should have known. I didn't enjoy the cloudy grey skies and the few short showers of bitter cold rain they showered down every now and then, almost as if to say: Go home, bloody foreigner, who wants you down here? I couldn't say I liked the driving either, cursing their bloody left-hand driving; at every corner of the road, always having to be careful to stay on the far left lane while British maniacs shrieked past me to the right with speeds which certainly were not regular, not even over here. But then, the British had many years ago accepted the decimal system for their currency which didn't mean they had to be logical in all the rest. Why couldn't they become civilised like everybody else in the world and drive to the right. And use kilometres instead of those bloody miles. And put explicit road signs up! Not to mention comprehensible road maps...

I blessed myself for having brought my own car instead of renting a local car here; I hated to think what having to sit on the right hand driving seat would have done to my nerves.

From bloody boring Ramsgate on, I had driven steadily to the north, following the A253 and continuing the A28 past Canterbury and Rochester, then skipping the heavy traffic around London itself. After noon I had made a stop at a local pub where I tried a pint of one their bitters called "Speckled Goose". I discovered that it was quite tasty though not as foamy as their Guinness, but much better than the tasteless lager beers which all taste the same for someone used to the endless variety of European beers. I also could imagine that after three or four of those pints (44 centilitres instead of the usual European 25 centilitres.) one was likely to see speckled geese instead of pink elephants. Less agreeable was when I asked for a piece of cake to go with it and heard that the kitchen was closed, after all it was after two o'clock. I'll never figure their habits out, why have to pass by the kitchen to order a bloody piece of cake which is lying ready to eat in front of you in a cabinet? I stopped at a shop and bought some rolls only to find out that I needed a microwave for them. Well, I swallowed some of it dry and threw the rest away.

But finally, after what seemed an eternity of rather mindless and directionless driving, I began to see the indicators to Yarmouth, and after two false turns I drove along a small asphalt road, on both sides shadowed by heavy greenery and trees, now and then interrupted by the sight of a small cottage hiding behind the bushes, looking like some big toy stacked away. Then the road took a left turn and to my right I saw a big irregular wall of obviously hand-cut stones rising out of the grass and weeds. There was a more or less arched open gateway with a stone table to its right with a display board and printed information set behind plastic.

I stopped the car and got out, and took my first look at the abbey, or what was left of it after all those centuries. I didn't need to look at the plan to know what this place was. I had almost arrived at my destination. I debated with myself whether I would take a look at the ruins first since I was now here anyway, but then decided against it. I had the whole afternoon to check things out, and I wanted to have a general look at the place first. So I drove on along the winding road, turned right and then abruptly to the left where the road ended in a crude parking lot, no more than an open asphalted place at the end of which was the side view of an inn and a large sign.

"The Dunwich Inn".

"When a traveller in north central Massachusetts takes the wrong fork at the junction of the Aylesbury pike just beyond Dean's Corners he comes upon a lonely and curious country. The ground gets higher, and the brier-bordered stone walls press closer and closer against the ruts of the dusty, curving road. The trees of the frequent forest belts seem too large, and the wild weeds, brambles, and grasses attain a luxuriance not often found in settled regions..."

I shook my head in wonder. I still know the first lines by heart with which Lovecraft introduced his readers to Dunwich, his own version of Dunwich, made in the U.S.A. A story very dear to me, as it was the very first one I read when I bought a second-hand hardcover copy of *The Best Supernatural Stories of H. P. Lovecraft*, in a third reprint of the Tower Books edition, with browning and sometimes crumbling pages on cheap paper, back when I was fourteen or fifteen years old. I had never heard of the author and I bought the book for a couple of cents because I had just started to read English and I always liked horror stories. Which was why I read *The Dunwich Horror* first of all, and I never forgot the story. Much later I found out about the real Dunwich, in a Belgian newspaper—which printed a picture of the ruins of the abbey I had just passed—and titled it "Dunwich - the British Atlantis". Later I checked up on Lovecraft, discovered Arkham House and though I liked his stories very much, I dismissed them as the fiction they were supposed to be. It always remained a mystery to me why he had chosen to create a completely different Dunwich in America, as with his knowledge of British history I felt certain that he must have known about the real Dunwich, but I never bothered further with it. That is, until I developed an interest in the history of the occult and during some research in Hamburg met a man who had access to a copy of *Von denen Verdammten*, the old study of ancient cults in America, written by Kazaj Heinz Vogel, a German immigrant who, on returning to his home country wrote his book. Vogel's book was immediately seized and forbidden, all known copies were supposed to be destroyed. Vogel himself disappeared from the scene, probably murdered or if he was smart enough, started a new life in a far country under a completely new identity. A young German student, Edith Brendall got, quite by accident, her hands on a surviving copy of the book in a library, and possessing a photographic memory, rewrote most of the book. Though she knew of its history, foolhardily she published it herself, and took the consequences. Hunted by people she wouldn't or couldn't name, she tried to get away but they—whoever they were—finally caught up with her. Her naked body was found floating in the Rhine, and it wasn't pretty after what her murderers had done to her.

I was delighted having the chance to take a look at that famous forbidden book, but unfortunately as it turned out, it was a photo-copy and consisted only of parts of the book. The copy was old and some of the cheap copy was already fading, but it did give me some startling insights. There were references to the domain Steinhaus near a place Brendall called Grauhaus. I immediately recognised the names; typically Brendall had translated the names themselves into her German "adaption". So I knew that this had to be the domain of "Steenveld" somewhere in the Netherlands near the eerie village of "Greyhuysen". This had a history of ancient evil going back to the 14th century and the reign of Ebbelbuez Greys who was executed by the members of a white coven, his body being cut into twelve parts and buried at secret places, separate from his heart which was the thirteenth part. I had been in Greyhuysen, in the old cemetery, looking for the grave of Greys but without finding it. There were other parts in *Von denen Verdammten*, and the most difficult part of it all was trying to find out what had been in the original book by Vogel, and what was maybe wrongly interpreted by Brendall. But there were references to Salem, to Innsmouth and to Dunwich. Not the Dunwich I knew from Lovecraft's story, but another place entirely. At first I thought about an elaborate hoax, Salem was real all right, but I knew that Innsmouth was a strictly fictional place. Or was it? I knew that Vogel wasn't a phantast, he was a methodical researcher, and whatever Brendall may have missed in accurateness, she was devoted too and not likely to mix fiction with truth. Then I remembered when Lovecraft's stories had been published. Brendall wrote her "adaption" in 1907, before the first world war. How in hell could she have known of a fictional Innsmouth? Unless the place was *not* a fiction, but erased from the geography of the nation. Lovecraft with his erudition could have found out things about Innsmouth and made his story around the name or place... or maybe he found out things which had been real. He didn't like Germans but maybe he did get a smattering of the language? Was it possible that he, at one time or another—snooper in old books as he was—could have had access to maybe translated parts of *Von denen Verdammten*? Could it have been possible that he found what was in that book so atrocious that he did use parts of it, disguised as fiction, but—maybe knowing what had happened to its translator— never even mentioned it in his own fiction? Maybe disguised it under other titles of fictitious books, such as *The Necronomicon*, and others? I suppose I'll never know, and neither will all the scholars who have been researching his stories for clues, or the historians of the occult, some of whom are claiming that he wrote fact disguised as fiction. I only know about the mentions Brendall gave about Dunwich and things which happened there, though *Von denen Verdammten* doesn't offer straight clues. It's second hand: what happened in Dunwich, the real Dunwich, happened along the east coast of England, not in a fictitious town in Massachusetts. And Brendall is vague, only referring to the happenings at Dunwich to other things which are supposed to have happened in the States.

My colleague in Hamburg had talked to me about the fabled five Vaeyens, the strange statues, and referred to strange occurrences—in Germany or Austria, he was reluctant to talk about it—where the Vaeyens had been crucial in closing of a site which no one has ever been able to enter since without being in the possession of a far more ancient knowledge than what I posses. Besides I didn't have the money to go the States and continue my research there. But I could go to England and find out what was there. Which was what I did. Which was why I was here now. In the real Dunwich, the new

Dunwich.

Or was I? I gazed at the cheap looking sign, at the few cars parked rather randomly, at the small road to the right going down between trees to where I supposed the sea was. At the beginning of the road was a lonely bus stop, but no welcoming bench below it to sit upon. I parked the car and got out. The bus timetable told me that there was a bus three times a day, on weekdays, not on Sundays or holidays. Looking at the facade of the nearby pub, The Ship, it was as any other British pub I'd seen so far. The road going down was, according to my map, the only street here. I entered the pub. Quite nice looking, with wooden benches, an open fire but no logs burning. Well, it wasn't that cold. Scattered empty glasses and coffee cups on the tables.

'Sorry, we're closed,' the man behind the counter said.

'You mean I can't get even a drink?'

'No. It's after three o'clock.'

I smiled. 'But that's all in the past, I mean in London I can get a...'

'We're not in London here,' the man said, smiling gently. 'We stick to the original licensing rules. We open again at five o'clock. Till then, no drinks. No, not even soft drinks or coffee.'

'Can I at least book a room?'

'That's no problem. It's not exactly the season, so rooms aplenty. How long you're thinking of staying?'

'Let's say just for tonight.'

'Ghost hunting, aye? All Hallow's Night.'

'Well, not exactly. Or maybe, yes.'

'Well, whatever you want.'

I booked the room and dropped my luggage in it, and then went out again. I walked down the road to where I was told the museum was. It was indeed, but not quite what I had expected. A small cottage, with a cannon in front and an old anchor. I bought some souvenirs, some small brochures about the history of the place. I must say it was worth the visit, giving a detailed history in pictures of what had happened to Dunwich. Or should I say, what history claims had happened to Dunwich. I learned about how there were still archaeological dives going on, bringing up old tombs and coins and stuff like that. The caretaker was an old gentleman, very nice and quiet and very eager to talk since I was the only visitor. But nothing of what he told me was really what I had come to hear. I knew the whole history of Dunwich, as I had found in the history books. I knew that it had once been a prosperous harbour, with gates of bronze, with six churches and chapels, two abbeys, a palace, windmills and several cemeteries. I knew that now there were less than 120 inhabitants, and that it now was only a small village, thriving on its history.

I made the Sign with my fingers, twice, so he must have seen it but the man didn't give any indication of recognising what I did. I dropped a few names, but got no reaction. Maybe he really didn't know anything, or else he refused to acknowledge my knowledge. So I left and strolled back up the street, and down to the sea.

I was as disappointed as I should have been. No sand beach but stones, and several abandoned small fishing boats. There was some kind of modern structure, more looking like a hangar than anything else, which proclaimed that it was a cafe, with a sign "Closed, open at 10 am". Looking inside I spotted plastic tables and chairs. On one wall of the awful building was another history chart of Dunwich. It seems, I thought, that the few local businesses are trying to make the most of their dubious history.

I sat down close to the sea on the stones and gazed about. So this is Dunwich, I thought, watching the leaden, ugly water below the grey clouds. What did I come here to find? It seemed so foolish at that moment, seeing the slowly rotting fishing boats which couldn't carry more than half a dozen men and remembering the big fishing ships which once went out from Dunwich Bay into the sea, sometimes going up to Great Yarmouth. A time when the city and harbour went out at least another mile into the sea, a big city high on the cliffs, completely protected by a sea wall. The cobbly stones, grey white and mostly rounded by the sea tide, felt hard and cold under me, and just stretched out on all sides and into the sea. To the left the beach was flat, only rising slightly further on. To my right were the cliffs, sand and stone rising up out of the beach and eaten at by the tides so that the top hung over the beach. They weren't very high, maybe three or four metres, a charade of what they once had been, centuries ago. Just this boring place, the "new" Dunwich seemed a mockery of what it had been once. An elderly couple was strolling along the beach, close to the water, looking very British and slowly making their way to the cafeteria. I looked behind me and saw the frown on their faces when they noticed the closed sign. No afternoon tea here, I thought.

Finally I got up and walked the way back to my car and beyond, toward the ruins of the abbey. The wall and gate were remarkably well preserved for their age, but inside it was one big open space with grass and shrubbery, and three shire horses grazing freely. Only two small parts of the original building were still standing. I searched, but the signs of the fire were of course long gone. It was fortunate that the abbey was standing this far inland, which had saved it from the sea. Two young girls entered the gate, a guidebook in their hand which they consulted while looking at probably every bloody stone still standing. Suddenly they started giggling. At first I thought this was about me, until I noticed that their interest was in the horses. One of them was chasing another, with an enormous erection. I crossed the open space and found a small path leading upward to the dunes. From there on it was fighting against the wild growths, and I discovered that a small metal fence closed off the precipice downwards to the sea. A pitiful sight, this view of the leaden sea and knowing what was below it, less than half a mile out. I looked further but didn't find what I was searching for. By that time it was after five o'clock, I felt chilly and went back to the inn.

This was rapidly filling now. The elderly couple were there, as well as one or two others who were obviously tourists, but all the rest were locals, chatting behind pints of dark ale and clouds of cigarette and pipe smoke. There was music from a radio tuned to a station of pop muzak, but playing so soft that it was all but drowned out by the constant chatter. I sat down at the bar, looked at the brands of the bitters and, not recognising any of them, just ordered a pint of his best bitter, and some fish and chips to go with it. I had long learned not to try the abominable things they sell as "meat pies" in pubs. Then I asked where I could find the tombstone and from his directions learned that I probably had been standing almost on top of it up there.

'Aye, a bad day to go looking for the stone,' said an elderly woman sitting at a table behind me. I looked around. She must have been in her sixties, a spidery lady sporting an enormous abomination on her head which was supposed to be a hat with plastic fruit. 'And why is that?'

'All Hallow's Eve,' she said, and made a small movement with her fingers. 'Ding dong.'

'Ding dong?'

'The bells,' she said, and then fell silent. I looked at the bartender who gave me a slow grin. 'Go on, ask her,' he said, 'ol' Mabel will tell ya anyway.'

I took my pint and sat down at her table, inquiring first if she didn't mind. She didn't. She was a very nice lady; though I doubt if she even took everything seriously which she told me.

'The bells under the water,' she said, 'sometimes you can hear them on this night of all nights. 'Tis the night when the gates of Hell are opened and all doomed souls are free to roam the earth for one night. 'Is a bad night to be out there then, looking for trouble. I heard them several times, the bells o' the ol' Dun'ich.' This was the first time I heard the name spoken by a local, they dropped the "w", making it 'Dun'ich'.

'You're hearing the bells of our own church, Mabel,' said the bartender, 'don't go spooking my customers away unless they are here for the ghost stories.'

'I *know* the sound of the bells,' Mabel said, 'one of them has a tone missing, you can't confuse the sound with the normal bells.'

'I must say your country is rich in ghost stories,' I said encouragingly.

'Oh , there's the ghost of the well,' she said, 'closer to Yarmouth. And the ghosts in the ol' abbey.'

'The tourists have long scared those away,' the bartender grinned, 'even the horses there aren't afraid of the ghosts.'

'The ghosts don't harm anyone,' Mabel said, 'not animals and not people, they just are. It's when the bells toll that it's dangerous.'

Later the bartender told me, over my third pint: 'Don't bother about them bells; it's a nice legend, a spooky tale which you'll find mentioned in several books of ghost tales they sell at the museum. But the bells she's taking about were taken out of the last tower before it went down in the sea. And the bells from the older towers, which went down first, have long since been recovered by the diving teams.'

The pub filled with more people, games of darts were started and somehow it seemed as if everybody was trying to down as many pints as possible in as short a time as possible. The reason, which I came to understand, as at ten thirty the barman rang a big gong. 'Last orders, please,' he called, which started a rush towards the bar. Of course, the old habits. Warning half an hour in advance so you could get your orders filled, and finish them off, and at eleven the front door was opened wide and everybody filtered out. I said I was going for an evening walk and pocketed the key to the front door.

The evening was clear, with a full moon and most of the clouds gone. The rain kept away too for which I was grateful. I had brought a torch but didn't really need it. I went back to the abbey, which loomed dark and forbidding in front of me, but there was no feeling of menace. They were just old crumbling stones and no ghosts glared at me from the open spaces. Even the horses were gone now. I repeated my late afternoon walk, remembering the directions the bartender had given me, and this time I did find it.

Hidden behind some bushes, almost totally overgrown by fungus so green it almost looked black, with weeds embracing the lower parts. A thick brownish gravestone, less than a metre high, standing there lopsided, as an old and ugly deformed tooth rising out of the dead earth. I shone my light on the stone but the inscription was now all but illegible. This was the last tombstone, the only thing remaining of the original Dunwich. Within a few years, when the sea would have further hollowed out and eaten the earth below it, one day it too would go down into the sea. And join the rest of the original Dunwich, the once proud medieval city which was now resting a mile out below the waves.

I sat down beside the stone, feeling its oldness under my touch, trying to sense something, but nothing came. It's all useless, I thought, they're just legends, no matter what Brendall wrote in her book, no matter what she probably misinterpreted when rewriting the book of Vogel. This here is just an old stone, nothing more, a memorial to what maybe once has been but is no more. Even the sea had lost some of its dirty aspect now that the silver of the moon was spilling over the lazy waves. It was hard to believe that this calm leaden sea once had created natural waves high enough to tumble over these dunes and bring a complete city crashing down into its depths. Natural waves, that was the point of course, where the writings of Brendall (and maybe the original ones of Vogel?) differed from recorded history.

'It's a quite nice view, isn't it?' a voice suddenly said beside me. I jumped up, my heart beating wildly at the abrupt interruption of my solitary thoughts. An old man was standing there at my right side as if he had appeared out of nowhere, leaning on a thick walking cane with a silver handle. Of course, lost in thoughts as I had been, I couldn't have heard him approaching through the undergrowth and weeds. His face was drawn and withered, his features shrivelled and hollowed, marked with sharp lines, and he looked white in the moonlight, the lower part of his face hidden behind a wild grey and unkempt beard. He wasn't looking at me however, but at the sea down below us.

'Yes, it is nice, nicer than by daylight,' I said. 'It is peaceful now. Not as it once used to be when the old Dunwich still existed.'

''Tis always peaceful now with the ol' Dun'ich gone. 'Tis a strange place for a tourist to be on this night of all nights,' he said.

'I like the quiet,' I said, 'and the ghost stories.' I laughed but it sounded false and out of place. 'Who knows, maybe I'll hear the ghost bells tonight.'

The old man grinned, exposing his scarce brown teeth rising out of his gums as blunt daggers. 'Could be,' he said, 'who knows. One never knows at this night of all nights, though I woul' think i's better not to 'ear them. It's just one of the tales they tell, mind you. They have so many fairy tales now about Dunwich, the biggest one being what they tell you as being the truth.'

'Truth is truth,' I said, 'history is truth.'

'History is often the biggest lie,' the old man said. He put his cane aside and sat down. 'They look at old charts and papers, they dive under the waves and swim between the ruins and dig up old coins and stones, and they think they can piece together the truth from those. Then they write books about it and everybody believes those. Specially now, with all the older folks gone after the last bell tower went down. Now they're all new folks in their modern cottages, with radio and television, their kids go to the school on the bus, and the tourism people try to make money out of faked history.'

'You're from around here?' I asked.

'My folks were,' he said, 'a long time ago. They have told the real stories for generations, kept the truth alive. Or what they believed to be the truth, because as you know, it's been so long ago. Tales have the habit of being changed with every generation. My ancestors were fishermen from here, from the old Dun'ich but after the disaster they became scared, went inland and became farmers and horse keepers. You know how it is, my children and grandchildren are all gone now, to the universities and the big cities, away from their heritage. No one cares, so what the hell. It's all gone anyway. At least, I hope it's all gone, but how can one ever be certain? The kids wanted to put me in a home for elderly people, imagine that. I said, no way I'm going to die in a wheelchair among drooling emptyheads. So I sold my place and bought a small house, not far from here. I like to come here at nights like this, look out over the waters and remember the old tales.'

'I would like to hear them,' I said.

'That's not so hard at all,' he said smiling. 'You just have to remember what happened here, back in 1537 when it all began. I suppose you've been to the museum, and have read about the slow disintegration of Dun'ich. That's true, mind you, specially about the last century when the last remaining parts of Dun'ich went down. The last tower kept its place till 1909 or was it 1919, I forget, and it really doesn't matter. Everything which mattered in Dun'ich went down long before that, and what was left on top of the dunes was not important to them down there. So they let them stand, these parts of walls and a single church tower and this bloody single unimportant gravestone, and let the sea to its work. But those brochures will not tell you what happened at the start. Oh, I remember those stories so vividly, as if I heard them only yesterday. Just get the feeling of this place. Look out over that silver sea, those slow lazy waves. You would never know what waves that sweet sea can create. Or better, what something in the sea created. Less than a quarter mile in the sea, about eleven metres deep, that is where the recent parts lie. The rest is farther out, with the currents now maybe about a mile out I would say, the really old parts. Over four hundred years ago the banshee of Dunwich shrieked her anger, and hundreds of people died, maybe even thousand, because in those days no one counted them, and most of them were totally innocent victims. But isn't it always the innocent who die first? Sometimes, at nights like this, I think I can hear her screaming, out there, the banshee, full of anger and hatred and the all absorbing need for revenge. But then, the wind makes strange noises at night.'

'I would like to hear that story,' I said again.

And this is what the old stranger told me, as we were sitting each beside the only surviving gravestone of the ol' Dun'ich...

I
THE BURNING ABBEY

Christopher was standing on top of the sea wall which spread all around Dunwich. Deep below him the sea moved sluggishly in the bay, which swept further around inwards, toward the inner harbour, where most of the fisherman's boats were moored. Christopher, young and tall with sea-browned face and golden curly hair, was a fisherman's son. His father's boat often went up to Great Yarmouth, where the big harbour was, several miles up north, and where they often paid much more for the fresh fish than at the smaller Dunwich market. Christopher was only twelve, but was eagerly looking forward to the next year when he would be thirteen and be allowed to go seawards with his father "taming the waves" as he thought of it, but which his father called "just catchin' bloody fish and tryin' to sell 'em".

'Hey, Christopher, quick, come quick!'

Christopher turned around and faced his friend Darrel. Darrel was the son of a blacksmith, a slightly smaller boy than Christopher, and he limped on his left leg, the result of an angry horse's kick while he was helping his father out at the forge. Now his freckled face was red, and he was pumping for breath.

'Wha's the matter, Darrel?'

Darrel was still trying to catch his breath, he shook his head and pointed behind him. Christopher turned around and looked at

Dunwich, with its many church towers and windmills, and saw, behind the landside wall a cloud of thick black smoke rising up as the breath of an unseen beast.

'The abbey's burning,' Darrel gasped, 'c'mon, let's go looking.'

Christopher jumped down from the sea wall and joined Darrel. They went through the bronze gate and the small streets of stamped earth and dirt, with its small wooden storehouses and glassless windows. Now and then Christopher had to wait for Darrel to catch up with him. They crossed the market which was almost deserted, only the shopkeepers were standing by their stalls, afraid to leave them, knowing that they would find them looted empty when left unattended. They left the centre through the last back gate, and found most of Dunwich's population gathered there to watch whatever was going on.

'It's the Greyfriar's Priory!'

The Greyfriar's Priory had been inside the city walls many years ago, but when the sea started taking the sand from under the protecting rocks one night over a hundred houses fell into the sea during a particularly heavy storm, including part of the abbey. The monks moved out and rebuilt the abbey outside the city's wall further inland. And now the abbey was on fire, tongues of flame leaping up at the sky and spitting angry dark clouds of raw smoke.

Soldiers in harness were running around, carrying halberds, axes and swords.

'Hey, what're they doing? Why isn't nobody trying to put out the fire?' Christopher asked.

Darrel's father was among the watching crowd, and turned around quickly as he caught Christopher's words. 'Watch up, lad,' he said, 'it's them soldiers that put fire to the abbey.'

The monks were all gathered in small groups outside the abbey, and now Christopher saw that they had been chained together, and were guarded by soldiers.

'Why are they in chains, pa? What've they done?' Darrel asked.

'Look, there's Sir Lewis himself!' Christopher said. 'This must be really important for him to come out 'ere.'

Sir Lewis was walking around, constantly accompanied by two armed guards with swords drawn, giving orders to the soldiers.

'It's by order of our King, Henry the Eighth,' the blacksmith said under his breath so only the two boys could understand him. 'They've read the new orders from the King out in the market place th's morning. Our King has forbidden all forms o'religion.'

'What? I'dun' understand', pa.'

'The power o' the church had to be lessened. Priests an' monks have no longer any power in Britain, lad. Henry is now also King of the Church. Whatever belonged to the churches, now belongs to our King.'

Soldiers were carrying wooden statues and oil paintings of saints outside, thrashing them on the bare earth and then wrecking them with hammers and axes before putting fire to them. Paintings, heavily and painstakingly illustrated books, ancient scrolls of parchment, it was all put to the axe and the fire.

'What a pity,' Christopher murmured, 'all those beautiful things.' He remembered the beautiful paintings in the churches of the saints in pain and torture, and the heavenly look on the faces of the saints as they were taken up to heaven.

A nearby soldier turned. 'D'ya have any comments, lad?'

Christopher shook his head. 'No, sir soldier.'

'Then better shut up,' the soldier said, his hand on his sword. 'It's by the word of Sir Lewis, which is by law the word of our King. The word of the Law of Britain.'

There were some murmurings in the crowd, but none interfered or made loud comments when the soldiers led the chained monks away.

The abbey burned the whole night.

That evening, as Christopher and his parents were sitting in their cabin, eating baked fish and hard brown bread, and drinking milk thinned with water, Christopher said angrily: 'The monks never hurt anybody. There was no reason to treat them as if they were some kind of criminals.'

His father shook his head. 'It's no good talking about it, laddy. It happened, thats'e way it goes. The word of our King is the Law.'

'But the monks were good people, they helped so many people when there was sickness,' Christopher's mother said. 'They taught us in church to love another, to love Christopher. They ain't bad people.'

His father's fist crashed down hard on the wooden table, rattling it.

'Why don'ya all shut up about it? What do you think we can do about it? I know, everybody in Dun'ich, we all know Sir Lewis is a filthy crook and a thief, who has a wife and a mistress, but he's the may'r of Dun'ich. As long as he follows the orders of the King, as 'e does now, his word is the law here. So you better remember that or you might end up in prison just as the monks. I talk'd with John, the shoemaker, who has heard the reading of the King's letter. The monks were officially ordered to leave the abbey by order of the King, and they refused. Can'ya imagine that, they refused, said theirs was God's place and God was above the King. That's when the soldiers got them all out and chained them, and then put the fire to the abbey.'

II

THE WITCH CHILD

The next morning Christopher's father left very early, to get an early catch up north. Christopher helped his mother as usual, cleaning a basket of fish his father had brought in yesterday, then taking their single lean cow to the pasture inland. They lived in a small fisherman's cabin on Hen Hills, close to the harbour sideways from the city. The cabin had one single room, their beds were sacks of dry hay. After his daily chores, Christopher was allowed to go. He went looking for Darrel, but Darrel had to help his father who was very busy at the forge. So Christopher continued his way alone and caught up with Laurie. Laurie was already sixteen, big and slender, the son of a King's soldier, but not very bright at all. He should've been a full soldier by now, but he had caught the sickness when he was young. He had recovered, but the sickness had eaten part of his brain and now Laurie just loafed around, mostly annoying other people with his bragging that he would be a soldier one day, just as his pa. As always he was childishly happy when someone asked him along, as Christopher did. The two of them went to the market, where something always was to be seen or happening.

A new parchment was nailed to the message pole, but of course no one could read it. They waited for the town crier to come along, announcing his arrival with the sound of a bell, afterwards to read the message aloud for everybody in Dunwich to hear.

'The Grey Friars have been banned by orders of our King, passed on to Sir Lewis, and the abbey has been burned according to those instructions forbidding all religious things which are now part of the reign of our King and Sir Lewis, in His Name. All religious things have been destroyed. The other things of value from the abbey now belong to our King, and Sir Lewis will guard these treasuries for him.'

Christopher pushed Laurie in the back. 'D'ya know what have they done with the monks, Laurie? They're good people, y'a know that.'

Laurie winced. 'Don' push so hard, Christopher, m'back hurts when ya do that. The monks don' wanna lis'en to the words of Sir Lewis, my pa told me so. Next week Sir Lewis will be sending them to London, where they'll be put in prison or set to work for the King. C'mon, there's nothing to be done 'ere, let's go.'

Laurie grabbed an apple out of a basket and put his teeth into it. 'Hey you, put that down,' the vendor snapped and tried to grab the apple from between Laurie's teeth.

Then he recognised Laurie, and smiled sourly. 'All right, son, take it. You've had ya're bit in it anyway. But next time ya pay, as anybody else.' Being a soldier's son had its advantages.

The market was quite full now and busy. Farmers selling vegetables and fruits, the butchers with their joints of meat and sheep. The fisherwomen came with baskets full of herring, mackerel and eel, and big crabs, crawling frantically in their baskets. Everywhere was the incense of fresh bread, dough and paste, spices and sour wine, but also of shit and piss. Whoever had to relieve himself just did it on the street.

Laurie bit the apple and offered a piece to Christopher, who declined. He had seen something else.

A couple of Dunwich city boys were teasing a small girl. They had caught her in a circle and were throwing her from one to another. The girl was very small and slender, dressed in long grey shredded rags. She had curly hair which was as red as the falling sun, a wild crown around her head.

'Witch child, witch child,' the boys were singing. The girl was frantically trying to escape from the locked circle of greedy boys' hands which were grabbing and pushing wherever they could but usually wouldn't dare to grab in public. The boys were pushing her roughly but the girl didn't cry out. She fought the greedy hands while clenching her teeth and baring them as a trapped animal, hissing and spitting but otherwise making no sounds.

'Hey, that's Lizzy,' Christopher said, 'those bastards got her cornered, we gotta help her.'

'Don't fuss,' Laurie grinned, sucking on his apple, 'it's only mad Sarah's bastard breed. Let 'em have some fun, 's no concern o'ours.'

'Sarah healed my ol' man when he was sick, ya fishhead, ya don' wanna be in it, stay out'a it,' Christopher said. He took a few steps forward, using his broad arms to push two of the grabbing boys away and get into the circle. 'That's enough,' he said, grabbing the girl by the arm.

'Wha'ya think you're doing, fisherboy?' They closed the circle again, their faces eager and looking for trouble. Christopher looked them over. Six of them, most of them taller than he was, but typical city buggers, lots 'o snot an' no muscles on them arms. Sure, they had mean faces but they were just city boys, he knew their type. One of them took out a knife, the clean blade sparkling as silver, cleaned very well but never used for anything except for show.

'Go play with your fish, seaboy, you smell o'them,' the boy said, 'the crazy girl's ours, so jus' walk 'way 'n let us be 'n you won' get hurt.'

Lizzy hid behind Christopher, now whimpering softly. Laurie stood outside the circle, his hands on his hips, smiling. Christopher wondered if he would help him if it came to a real fight. Not that he cared very much, Laurie was just a pussy. The leader of the pack was throwing his small blade from one hand to the other, enjoying the feel of power it gave him, imagining himself bein' one o'those bloody Lond'n street thugs who'd cut y'r neck with their blade.

'You wanna play, boy?' Christopher said sneering. He put his right hand behind his back and brought out his fish-hook from his belt, weighing the stained rusty blade in his hand. 'This nice one goes into your mouth and out through your nose, in one simple move. Or into y'ar guts and gets th'm out so I c'n shovel y'r stinking entrails into y'r puking mouth.'

The boy hesitated, looked around at his friends. They all saw something very interesting to look at, to the left and right or above in the air above. None of them looked at Christopher and the rusty hook in his hand. The leader of the pack slowly put his knife away with as much dignity as he could. 'G't lost, fisherboy,' he said, 'we'll get even another time.' He snapped his fingers, and the pack turned and left, following him as geese follow their mother. Laurie grinned. 'I knew they weren't going to take on the hook,' he said.

Lizzie looked up at Christopher, she hardly came to his chest. Her left eyelid was constantly half closed over the empty socket. Some city boys had done that with stones, some years ago. The one who had taken her eye out with his stone had gotten very sick afterwards, and had died from the sickness. Since then they usually left her alone, whither the influence of older tales, when a new generation of young bastards starts to roam the streets.

'Well, that's it, off you go, go home,' Christopher said, putting his hook away.

Lizzie murmured something, then just turned and ran away on her naked feet, the rags fluttering around her frail body as grey wings.

'Well, she said somethin', could've been thanks,' Christopher said.

'Just let her be,' Laurie said, 'we don't mix with witches' breed. It's safer not to.'

III

THE MONK DRESSED IN BLOOD

Laurie looked up at the sun. 'Aye, 's getting late, gotta go back. I have to take care o' the horses. You're coming, Christopher?'

'I was planning to catch some crabs, but aye, why not?' Christopher liked the horses, those fine strong animals. He was pretty jealous of the soldiers, when he saw them on horseback, all glittering harness and helmets and swords. One day Laurie would be one of them, even if Christopher was a lot smarter than he was. But you didn't have to be smart to be a soldier. Fisherman's sons didn't become soldiers. Only sons of soldiers became soldiers even if they were as empty headed as Laurie.

He followed Laurie to the pastures, behind the city walls where it was safe. The cliffs on which Dunwich stood were high but brittle, under continuous attack by the sea. Now and then another piece of rock was lost to the sea, sometimes a couple of houses. The city was moving slowly over the years, reaching seawards.

'Later I will ride one of those horses,' Laurie said, 'and wear a sword like my pa.'

Sure, thought Christopher, and hit people with it, people like me. Nobody in Dunwich liked the soldiers, but they were part of everyday life. They collected the taxes for the sheriff, Sir Lewis. If you couldn't pay them, they took your animals, sometimes the women, and then just burned your place down for the fun of it.

Darrel joined them, sweating heavily and smelling of sweat. "s been a heavy day,' he said, 'three horses needed re-shoeing.'

Then they heard the noise.

'What's that?' Laurie said.

'Came from behind those bushes,' Darrel said, 'let's have a look. Might be a horse thief.'

Darrel grabbed the iron stick he always carried, Christopher felt his hook. They went behind the bushes and found the monk dressed in blood.

On his face, his hands, his clothes. He was lying on his belly, his clothes showing burn marks. Christopher turned the man over. The monk groaned and felt his side, blood dripping between his fingers.

'He's been stabbed,' Laurie said.

'Seems so,' Darrel agreed, 'probably by a soldier's sword.'

The monk opened his eyes, looking at the sky seemingly without seeing the boys, and murmured something.

'He has something in his hand,' Darrel said. He tried to grab it but the monk held on to it.

'It's a cross,' Christopher said, looking careful. 'Weird, it has six arms. And look, it has all kinds of marks on it, looking like fish.'

Laurie straightened. 'It's some kind of religious thing,' he said. 'That's now forbidden by the King.'

'And by Sir Lewis,' Darrel remarked grinning. 'Don't piss your pants, Laurie.'

Christopher shook his head. 'I've never heard of a god of fishes,' he said.

Laurie said: 'It doesn't matter. This is one who got away from the abbey. We gotta tell Sir Lewis of it.'

'Sod off,' Darrel said, 'this man is wounded, what he needs is help.'

The monk seemed to hear them. 'No soldiers,' he begged, pointing with a shaking finger to a place a bit farther.

The boys went to look. A big hole had been dug there. Stiff bloody fingers were sticking out of the hole.

IV

THE BETRAYAL

The boys went closer, as if beckoned by the petrified fingers. They came to the edge of the pit, and looked at what was inside. Darrel quickly turned away and threw up his lunch. Laurie went all pale and took a few steps backwards. Christopher took his arm, and they went back to the monk.

'They're all dead,' Christopher said. 'Who? Why?'

'Dead?' Darrel managed. 'They're not just dead, they've been hacked to bloody pieces. Dear Jesus, the blood, the blood, they're swimming in their own blood!' He turned and started throwing up again. Laurie coughed, then joined him.

'The soldiers,' the monk said, gritting his teeth, 'they did it tonight, when everybody was gone. We didn't know what would happen, they just made us dig that grave and then... they just started striking with their swords, their axes, their spears. They just kept on and on and on...'

He coughed and spat wads of blood and slime. 'They said we were just prisoners, they were... going to take us to London... and then...'

'I don't believe this,' Laurie said, 'the soldiers, they are honourable men, my pa's a man of honour, they wouldn't...'

'They did, child,' the monk said. 'Believe me, they did, and some of them even enjoyed it. They had orders to kill us all. No mercy.'

'But how did you get away?'

'I was one of the first struck, I just didn't know what hit me. A sharp pain in my side, then I fell, and immediately Brother Theodore fell on top of me, he and his head, separately. I was numb and shocked, at first I didn't even feel the pain, only a fierce fire in my side. I opened my eyes and I looked in the dead eyes of brother Theodore, saw that it was only his head. I heard the cries, the begging for mercy, and the laughter. Then came the pain, but I kept silent. I prayed, and the pain burned through me but I kept silent. Maybe I fell unconscious at some time. When I woke up, I crawled from under the bodies. The soldiers were gone, but they will be back to fill the grave. Then you found me.'

Laurie shook his head. 'I don't understand,' he said, 'why? Why would they do a thing like that? My pa said they would send you all to London.'

'That would have been expensive,' the monk said, 'but that's not why they did it. I can tell you no more.'

'We gotta get him away from here,' Christopher said, 'before the soldiers return to finish their bloody work. C'mon Darrel, gimme a hand.' The two of them got hold of the monk's arms and got him up. 'We'll bring you to Sarah,' Christopher said, 'she can give you something for the pain and your wound.'

'I will have no part of this,' Laurie said, 'do you know what you're doing? This is against the law.'

'Is it the law who did this to innocent monks?' Christopher asked between clashed teeth. 'Your father did this, the soldiers did this, and why? What have the monks ever done to us except teach us kindness?'

'The soldiers burned the books,' Darrel said, 'they crushed the lovely statues with their axes and hammers. Did the law say this?'

'I don't care, I will have no part of this,' Laurie repeated. He turned and walked away from them.

'He's trouble,' Darrel said.

'I know,' Christopher replied, 'but there's nothing we can do about him. Let's get this man some help first.'

They got the monk to the small hut of Sarah Lovecraft, which was on the seaward side of Dunwich. It was as if the place of the cottage marked its otherness. The cottage was very small, made from driftwood, with a small orchard nearby. But the trees in that were bare and deformed, their branches resembling claws reaching upwards to the skies. Sarah's husband had died at sea during a heavy storm. At least, that was what the townsfolk said. There were other tales, which the sailors told among themselves, away from their wives and offspring. They said her husband had been strange all along, making no friends, always keeping to himself, taking long walks at night along the beach, swimming in the sea at night. These tales, told in the local inns, said that he had jumped overboard, his eyes those of a madman, shrieking words in a language no one understood, while some tried to restrain him. No one ever said what it was he wanted in jumping into the sea.

Now Sarah earned her living by making healing potions from herbs, exchanging those for bread, meat, fish and milk.

Lizzie was playing in front of the cottage when the two boys arrived with their bleeding burden. Sarah came out. She was a small, slender woman, with a strangely puffed moonface and staring fishy eyes, and red marks on her neck, made by several strokes of a short bladed knife. No one knew where the marks came from, but they were always deep red.

The monk tore himself from the hands of Christopher and Darrel and stumbled forwards, then fell on his knees. He raised up the strange six-armed cross with the fish symbols at Sarah as a beacon.

'In the name of Dagon, sister,' he whimpered. 'They're dead, they're all dead.'

Sarah looked at him, then she bent and kissed the strange cross. 'In the name of Dagon, brother,' she said. 'What happened? I heard they burned the abbey. What else did they burn?'

The monk lowered the cross. 'There were three of us,' he whispered. 'Brother Hayshan and brother Kendar went down to destroy the altar and seal the door to the sea when the soldiers invaded the abbey. I think they managed, but as they came out the soldiers got them too. They are all dead. The soldiers didn't ask questions, they killed them all, even the innocent who didn't know anything.'

Sarah beckoned the boys. 'Get this man inside, and quick,' she said, 'he's losing much blood. I'll take care of him.'

They dropped the monk on a bed of straw, and helped Sarah

remove his bloodied habit. The wound on his side was deep, a bad cut which was bleeding heavily.

The blood, Christopher thought, my God, it is red and green, mixed together!

Sarah took a cup and smeared a badly smelling potion from it on the wound. The monk shrieked.

'Shut up,' Sarah said, 'It isn't a mortal wound, you were lucky. It'll heal. It would've killed a human, but not one of ours. You should've been more careful, I warned you all.'

The monk shook his head. 'No one knew, no one suspected,' he said, 'I don't know if it was an act against the order or against all religion. Sir Lewis' soldiers didn't differentiate, they killed them all, I don't think they knew anything about the order of Dagon. No one of the other brothers knew.'

'What is the order of Dagon?' Darrel asked Lizzie, who was standing and watching.

'Dagon is the Lord of...' Lizzie started.

Sarah turned around, and Lizzie shut up immediately.

Outside there was the muffled sound of horseshoes on grass, and the whinnying of a horse.

'The soldiers,' the monk murmured, 'they're coming.'

'Laurie did this, he betrayed us, the bastard,' Darrel said.

V

DAGON, LORD OF THE FISHES

Sarah's eyes swirled around. 'Get out, all of you,' she said, 'fast!'

Christopher and Darrel ran out, followed by Lizzie. A group of mounted soldiers were approaching the cottage, the spears they carried glittering in the sun. The boys ran out the back, and down the slopes towards the sea where they hid between the dunes. Lizzie followed them down, then ran further down and away from them.

The soldiers dismounted in front of the building, eight of them, only the captain staying on horseback. They entered the cottage, then came out some time later. They had Sarah with them, her hands tied behind her back. They threw her on the back of a horse, and rode away. Black smoke began swirling behind them.

Christopher and Darrel waited till the soldiers were out of sight, then ran back up the slope to the cottage. The six-armed cross had been nailed to the front door. They pushed the door open and went inside. Already the small room was filling with smoke, tongues of fire licking the walls and the humble furniture. The smoke created a black fog. Christopher banged his head against something, then slipped on the floor and went down on his behind, his fingers grasping something wet and slimy on the floor. He looked up.

The monk was hanging from the ceiling, a rope around his neck, his tongue cut bloody by his own teeth and now protruding blackly from his open mouth. The potion hadn't had the time to heal him, his belly had been slashed open wide down to his naked crotch, his genitals and innards hanging down loosely from the body and dripping wetly on the floor.

This time Christopher threw up. Darrel carried him outside, where he wiped the red and green stuff from his hands while the house burned.

When Christopher told his parents, his father shook his head. 'You had no business being there,' he said grimly, 'the law is the law, you can't fight the law of the King and Sir Lewis. If them soldiers had caught you, you'd both be in prison also, or they just could've cut y'ar bloody heads off right there. The monks knew that they'd been outlawed. They'd been warned, they just should 'ave left the abbey.'

'But Sir Lewis cannot order his soldiers just to murder people,' Christopher said.

'Sir Lewis represents our King here,' his father said sternly, 'he can do whatever he likes. The monks stuck to their religion, an' they died for that. But if what you tell me is true, some of them did much worse than jus' their religion.'

'They were of the order of Dagon,' his mother whispered. She crossed herself.

'Who is Dagon?' Christopher asked. 'And what was that strange cross with six arms the monk carried? Sarah recognised it, she kissed it.'

'The King forbids all religion,' his father said, 'but the order of Dagon is much older than our religion. Dagon is the Lord of the

Fishes. He is the God of all what lives in the sea. It is a very ancient religion, which some of the older people here still cling to though the religion of the monks denies it. They came and preached their religion, but it seems some held on to the ol' habits. It is told that in the old times, before the monks came, our people wed the people of the sea. People who were neither men nor fish, but both and more. Weddings which gave birth to children with fishy eyes and gills, children who lived in the sea as well as on land.'

Christopher thought about the red marks on the neck of Sarah Lovecraft. And her eyes. Eyes like a fish, marks like what once had been gills.

'They sacrificed humans to the sea,' his father continued. 'Mind you, this was long ago, and I thought the order of Dagon was long dead and forgotten, except in the old tales. When the monks came, people turned to the new religion they taught, no more sacrifices to the sea, no more human blood shed to the things out there. The church outlawed the order of Dagon, and the monks of the Greyfriars build their abbey, first the one which went down in the sea. That's when the rumours started, that the abbey shouldn't have been there, not that close to the sea, not that close to Dagon and his people. Then, after the first disaster from the sea, the first attack maybe, they built the second abbey, further inland where it was safe from the sea and what is inside it.'

'The order never died,' Christopher's mother said, 'we all knew it, that some survived, and mixed with the brothers of the abbey. We always knew the order couldn't die.'

'The King isn't afraid of Dagon. Neither is Sir Lewis, as we have seen,' Christopher's father said. 'He has killed them all, just to get those few who belonged to the order. Or maybe he just doesn't know, he's a townie, maybe he never heard the old tales.'

VI
THE EXECUTION

The next morning they heard the sound of the drums, the messenger of Sir Lewis doing his rounds in Dunwich. Everybody should be there at noon, on the cliffs outside the sea wall. The boats didn't sail out that morning, the farmers didn't go to their fields. The word of Sir Lewis had been heard, and his word was the law of the King.

At noon the cliffs were crowded. On the edge a wooden cross had been built, surrounded by piles of wood and brushwood. When the soldiers arrived, they were pulling an open cart. Sarah Lovecraft stood upright in it, her arms chained, and a wooden board on her chest with the single word: WITCH.

The old woman was bound to the cross, at the moment Sir Lewis himself arrived, wearing his red ceremonial cape and his sheriff's hat topped with glittering jewels. The drums rapped again as he descended and went to the cross on the cliffs. His messenger opened a scroll and read aloud:

'Sarah Lovecraft is a member of the forbidden order of Dagon, a religion long condemned even before the orders of our King forbade every religion. Sarah Lovecraft is a witch, an evil to all decent men and women, a blasphemy to the King himself. For this, Sir Lewis and the Council of the City of Dunwich, pronounce herewith her sentence to death by fire, in the name of our King.'

The crowd murmured but went silent quickly as the soldiers drew their swords and formed a barrier between the cross and the people.

Suddenly there came a wild shriek. A huge white seagull was flying above them, and suddenly swooped down, dropping dead as a stone in front of Sir Lewis. It's wings were spread white and wide open, its beak spilling green blood on the sand.

Sir Lewis took a step backward, looking in horror at the thing lying at his feet.

'An omen,' a woman in the crowd whispered, 'an evil omen.'

A farmer's woman nodded. 'The cow's milk turned sour this morning,' she said.

'My apple tree was in full bloom,' another woman said, 'and it isn't the season yet.'

'All bad signs,' the blacksmith said, 'this means no good for any of us.'

Sir Lewis kicked the dead bird aside and took a step forward.

'Sarah Lovecraft,' he said,' you have heard the verdict pronounced on you. Have you anything to say in your defence? Do you freely admit that you are truly a witch? If you have to say anything, say it now.'

Sarah lifted her head. There were bloody marks on her face, one of her eyes was swollen shut. Slowly her head turned as she looked at the people in front of her, searching them out.

'John, I healed you from the fever,' she said. 'You know I'm no witch.'

John, in the crowd, looked away and said nothing.

'Marian, I helped you when your foot swelled up and got all blue, I gave you an ointment and cured you. Would a witch do this, help people and cure them? Tell them, Marian. For the sake of God, for the sake of your God, tell them.'

But Marian shut her eyes and kept her tongue, when the soldiers looked at her.

Slowly Sarah's head turned the other way, searching the silent mouths, the empty faces, looking for someone, someone.

'Erwin, I cured your daughter when you thought she was dying. That was not witchcraft, it was just the right herbs and the right potion.'

Erwin tucked his head lower into his shoulders, and tried to hide behind other onlookers.

'She hasn't done anything wrong,' Christopher said, 'she's just an old woman who has helped people of Dun'ich all her life. Everybody knows that.'

A heavy hand fell on Christopher's shoulders and pulled him back. 'Will ya shut up,' his father said, 'you wan' get yourself burned as well?'

Sir Lewis looked around at the silent crowd, and smiled. 'This will be enough,' he said, 'no more ravings. No one has spoken out in favour of Sarah Lovecraft. Besides, we found a six-armed cross in her possession, and she sheltered a monk. Execute the sentence, as ordered by our King. A witch is an evil in the eye of man. Burn the witch.'

The executioner stepped forward, wearing a black mask so no one would know who he was. That would bring bad luck. He put fire to the stacks of wood around the cross. The fire was slow to start burning, but then got hold, and soon the flames were soaring high, spreading the smoke and smell of dry wood and wet leaves.

Sarah Lovecraft laughed. She tilted her head sideways, her toothless mouth opening wide. 'You fools, you stupid fools,' she said.

The sky darkened as out of nowhere, dense clouds appeared and obscured the heavens, setting the place to night on full day. Only the blazing fire lighted the cliffs, the skies changed into a turmoil of swirling clouds the colour of the blackest night.

'Your fire is a joke to the power of Dagon,' Sarah shrieked out loud. 'Your King, even your religion is a joke in the face of eternity. You want to burn me in the name of your idiot King, who thinks he is God now. You stupid fools of Dun'ich, I cared for you, I cared about you, I kept you safe, all those years. I was your shelter, I was your safeguard, I prayed to Dagon and saved you bloody lives, all those years. And now, what do you offer me now? Fire! Death by fire!'

Rain fell down, not slowly but in heavy showers, wetting everybody and putting out the fire in a hiss of white smoke and fog swirling around Sarah as loving arms, embracing her and the cross she was chained to.

Sir Lewis took another step forward, and drew the ceremonial sword he kept at his side, the sword marked with the sign of our King. 'Thou shalt not suffer a witch to live,' he pronounced, 'I will destroy you myself, in the name of our King.'

Sarah laughed again, a shrill weird laugh, as she shook her arms and the chains loosened, rattled down on the smoking wood. The marks on her neck opened on both sides, showing red raw inside, opening and closing in rhythmic movements as lips and toothless mouths.

'I spit on you, Sir Lewis, sheriff of Dun'ich,' Sarah said, softly yet everybody in the crowd heard her words, as if he spoke them aloud also inside their heads. 'I spit on your King and his crown, I spit on the stupid religions you have forbidden. For you all I feel only anger.'

She pointed at the crowd with her stretched finger. 'All of you,' she said, 'all of you of Dun'ich, which I have helped and healed and cured, and saved all that time. You have rejected me, and I curse you for your cowardliness. For that I curse all of Dun'ich. Dun'ich will become the first real city of Dagon. I see the future, I see the shapes that will rise from the depths and walk on the land, I see Innsmouth and Arkham, cities where Dagon will rise and bring great Cthulhu with him. Dun'ich will be the first, and you will all suffer for what you have done to me.'

Sir Lewis stood motionless, his sword loosely in his hand. The crowd was silent. Sarah came down from the cross, stepping on the smoking wood, then walking backwards to the edge of the cliffs.

'The banshee curses you, curses you all forever,' she said.

Something rose behind her, and as the rain stopped and the black clouds parted and disappeared in thin air, an enormous grey wave, shaped as a hand, rose up out of the sea behind the cliffs and came tumbling over the edge, taking Sarah Lovecraft with it. The cross crashed down, and then the wave retreated and portions of the cliffs were gone, as was Sarah Lovecraft.

VII
THE BELL, THE BELL!

The crowd dispersed, the merchants going back to open their stalls on the market, the farmers passing through Dunwich to leave it at the west gate to their farmland. There was a lot of small talk, but mostly in whispers. The soldiers had drawn together around Sir Lewis but it was evident that he had nothing to fear from Dunwich's cowering citizens.

When Christopher and his parents reached home, the door of their cottage stood wide open. His father drew his big carving knife, and Christopher took out his fishhook. 'Who's there? Show yourself or feel the consequences.' No answer came out of the silent dwelling, but as they went inside a small shadow suddenly moved and tried to dart out of the door between them. Christopher's hand flashed and got hold of the small shape.

'Lizzie!'

The girl was shaking, her one good eye darting from left to right, spit dripping from the corners of her mouth. Christopher's mother took over and took the girl from Christopher. 'It's all right, girl,' she said, 'stop shaking, no one will hurt you here.'

'What's she doing here?' Christopher's father asked.

'The poor thing, she's no place to go now. C'm inside, girl, I'll fetch you something to eat.'

Christopher father scratched his beard. 'O yeah? And what will that be, woman? There's hardly enough for the three of us.'

'Where there's food for three, there's for four. The poor thing has no home left now.'

Outside was the muffled sound of hooves approaching. 'I'll hide her,' Christopher's mother said, 'go and look who's that coming.

Christopher and his father went out as Laurie dismounted. Christopher jumped at him and hit him in the face. 'Dirty bastard,' Christopher yelled, and kicked Laurie in his ribs. Laurie rolled on his back and protected his face, but he didn't fight back. He was crying.

'I had to do it,' he sobbed, 'I had no idea that they would kill the monk and Sarah.'

Suddenly Christopher felt ashamed of what he was doing. Laurie knew no better, he was so much older but just plain stupid. Christopher helped him get up. Laurie wiped the blood from his jaw.

'I'm sorry,' Christopher said, 'it wasn't your fault. But you can do something to make it right. Lizzie is with us now. You can get her some food, we don't have enough. And maybe some decent clothes.'

'That's all right,' Laurie said, 'they don't want Lizzie. They don't even know she exists.'

Later that evening they were sitting by the fire, with the cold lurking around about. Lizzie had eaten a little, but she said nothing. She just looked at them with her one staring eye. None of them felt hungry, they all were thinking about the stake, and the hand-like wave which had come out of the sea. Was Sarah really a witch? None of them broached the subject with Lizzie, but it was foremost in all their thoughts.

'Well, 's about time to get some rest,' Christopher's father said. 'With no fishing done today, I gotta take an early start tomorrow to catch up. And the sea looked real bad this afternoon, crashing against the cliffs all day. Let's hope there's no big storm tomorrow.'

Suddenly Lizzie stood up and tilted her head sideways. She closed her good eye and opened her dead eye, the empty hole staring at them as a small pit of darkness. 'Not many days,' Lizzie said, 'listen, listen...' She opened the door, letting the cold of night inside, and something else.

Coming as from very far away, a weird hollow sound.

'The bells,' Lizzie whispered, 'the bells... they call...'

Louder now, coming not from Dunwich but from beyond the cliffs, from the open sea, dark and hollow and muffled, yet unmistakably the sound of bells. Among them one which missed a single stroke.

They stood up and went to the door, as Christopher's mother crossed herself. 'The bell of the old chapel,' she said, 'no other has that distinct sound, with that missing note.'

From the door they could see the sea wall of Dunwich. A white vapour was crawling over the sea wall, clinging to it with sticky, ghostly fingers, a white light-giving fog which crawled inland, then retreated.

They went back inside and closed the door, but they kept on hearing the bells.

'What does it mean?' Christopher asked.

'Just old wives' tales,' his father said softly.

'You know better,' his wife said, 'they are the bells of the old chapel, the one from the first Greyfriars Abbey, the one which once stood beyond the sea wall. The sea claimed that chapel three hundred year ago. It had one bell which always missed a single stroke. Everybody in Dun'ich knows the tale of that bell, it started ringing by itself the night the chapel fell into the sea.'

'The bloody thing is out there in the sea, deep under water.'

'Then who's ringing the bells?'

'It's them folks of Dagon,' Christopher's father said, speaking more honestly. 'The dead, the drowned, and the others... the changed ones who are neither man nor sea-creature. The people of Dagon are ringing the bells.'

'Don't say that aloud, don't speak of the changed ones,' Christopher's mother said, 'that brings bad luck.'

'It's already here,' he replied. 'Why else would the bells be ringing? Tomorrow some will not return from the sea, the waves will claim them.'

Then they heard it, above the muffled sound of the bells. Something which sounded like a voice yet wasn't, which shrieked as the wind but was no wind, something which sang a song which begged and pleaded, then shrieked as a knife cutting through one's head, full of anger.

Lizzie sat down and put her hands to her ears. 'Ma,' she whimpered, 'ma.'

'That's not your mother, child,' Christopher's mother said and put her arms around the shivering child. 'It's the wind, only the wind, and nothing more.' But she knew better, as did her husband, who crossed himself while cold sweat broke out on his forehead. They all knew what that sound was, though they had never heard it themselves until now. Only one being cried like that, full of sadness and pity while at the same time shrieking with insane rage. But none of them could bring themselves to utter the name of the dreaded being they were listening to. It was the child who spoke the name aloud.

Lizzie stood up, her blind eye blazing darkness as she gritted her teeth and balled her little fingers into fists. Her uncut nails drew blood from her palms which she smeared on her face, as if fulfilling a weird ritual she alone understood.

'Banshee o' the sea,' she said, 'ma's become the banshee, the ghost of death. Not many days now for Dun'ich. The banshee will come for Dun'ich.'

VIII
GREY SHADOWS

The next morning was grey and cloudy. Christopher's mother tried to stop her husband from going out, but he handled her roughly and went anyway. 'We need the catch, and the money,' he said. Christopher was busy repairing fishing nets, while his mother made her way to the market to exchange their last fish for bread and milk.

Lizzie was sitting on the edge of the cliff, looking at the sea wall farther away. She had said no more last evening, and even now she was silent, just sitting there, her hands grasping her knees, a small statue. None had gotten much sleep, the bells had kept on ringing, and in between they had constantly heard the wailing sound from that thing out there somewhere.

Darrel joined them. 'Did ya hear her last night, Christopher?'

'Hear who?'

'The banshee. Everybody in town has heard her, some say she was wailing right in front of their door, others heard her in the ruins of the abbey. All of Dun'ich is speaking of the banshee, and the haunted bells. But there's more.'

'Tell me.'

Darrel shook his head. 'No, better come with me, I'll show you.'

Christopher followed him to the entrance of the harbour, past the sea wall and down, to the pebbly beach, where a lot of people had gathered, pointing and murmuring to each other.

The beach was covered with bones. Human bones, arms, pieces of ribs, shattered skulls with empty eye sockets and missing teeth.

'So what? They're from the cemetery of the ancient abbey,' Christopher said, 'I find them bones now and then on the beach when the sea has been very wild, the waves just throw them on the beach.'

Laurie joined them. 'But not that many in one night, eh?' he said, 'Not after a night when the banshee has howled. And look at their shape, look how they are lying there, them bones.'

Now Christopher understood why no one approached them. They were lying on the pebbles, forming a yellow-brownish cross with six arms.

'There's more,' Laurie said, 'but I'm not supposed to tell anybody.'

'Don't be a sissy,' Christopher said, 'or you wanna another poke in y'r mouth?'

'Hold on, Christopher. I deserved what I got yesterday, but I am stronger than you, don't forget that.'

'All right, why don't you just tell us? You're dying to tell us anyway.'

'Tonight my pa had to go to the abbey,' Laurie said, 'with the other soldiers.'

'To hide the murdered monks,' Darrel said.

'To bury them,' Laurie agreed. 'But the bodies were gone. All of them. There were marks, and lots of blood. Something had come out of the abbey and carried the bodies away.'

'So they went into the ruins...'

'No, they didn't. There were lights in the ruins, green dancing lights, and grey shadows which walked there among the lights. They got scared and returned.'

Darrel laughed. 'I suppose Sir Lewis wasn't very nice about that,' he said.

'They didn't tell him. They said they'd buried the dead in the ruins. And that's where they are now.'

'C'mon.'

'I mean it. The abbey is haunted. I think the dead have risen by themselves and have returned to their home, the abbey. Now at night they walk there.'

'The banshee,' Darrel said, 'that's what my father said. The banshee brings death to the living, and life to the dead. Her song has awakened the slaughtered monks and led them back to the abbey.'

Above their heads there was a loud shrieking. A crowd of black ravens passed over them.

'Another omen,' he said, 'the ravens. They never come out here, this close to the sea where they can get into fights with the gulls. But now everything is different, the banshee o' the sea has changed everything. Them ravens are here to take the souls of the dead to their resting places.'

'Shut up with your old wives' tales,' Christopher said.

Lizzie laughed behind them, a rattling cackle which sounded more as if it came out of the throat of an old woman than out of the mouth of a small child. Silently she had followed them, and looked down at the bones on the stones of the beach. Her hands moved, her fingers pointing as she made six movements, mimicking the arms of the sea cross.

'Not many days left for Dun'ich,' she said. 'First the dead. Then the living. The banshee will come for them all.'

IX
MORE EVIL OMENS

That evening Christopher's father was in a very bad mood. The sea had been rough but not really dangerous, and notwithstanding their fears, fortunately no lives had been lost. No fish had been caught either: all the boats had returned with empty nets and buckets, apart from the usual crabs and cuttlefish. 'Bad omens everywhere,'

Christopher's father muttered, chewing on a piece of salted mackerel, which he always did when he felt very bad. 'The fish are going away from Dun'ich. We met a boat from Great Yarmouth, which had strayed a bit from its usual grounds, and they had a full catch.' He shook his head when he heard from Christopher what had been found on the stone beach that morning.

'We can't eat no bloody bones,' he said. 'We are suffering the sea's revenge for what Sir Lewis and his men did, in the name of our bloody King, to the monks, to Sarah. It's all his bloody fault. He should've left the Grey friars alone, specially if he knew that some at least were of the Order. But Sir Lewis is safe, and we pay the price.'

'What do you think happened to the bodies of the monks?' Christopher asked.

'Dunno, but there's been talk. There's always been talk about hidden rooms, deep below the cellars of the abbey, rooms which opened to the sea caves. Maybe some monks escaped the massacre, and came out at night to give their dead brothers a decent sea burial.'

'Maybe something other came out o' those caves and got them,' Christopher's mother said. 'We all saw what happened to Sarah, what came out of the—'

'Shut up, woman, I'll have no more of this. What came out of the sea was just one bloody wave.'

'Certainly a very big wave, and it didn't look like a wave, it looked like a—'

Christopher's father hit her in the face with his fist, and she shut up and huddled in a corner of the cottage, away from his wild anger which he just had to direct at anyone close enough to be hit. 'What happened to Sarah Lovecraft was she was condemned as a witch, and she was of the Order. We all saw the marks on her throat, the open red mouths, the gills. Doesn't matter if she burned or drowned.' Then his arms dropped. 'I'm sorry,' he said, 'I shouldn've hit ya.'

'But somebody should've defended Sarah,' Christopher said. 'She helped a lot of people. Maybe she was of the Order, she certainly recognised the sign the monk had. But so what? We've never had any trouble from the Order, the townsfolk should've stood up for her. We should've.'

His father laughed grimly. 'C'mon Christopher, who would've

dared to confront the soldiers? With their harnesses, their swords and axes and spears. The Dun'ich people are townies, some of them carry knives and sticks, and that's it, mos' o' these bloody fools dunno how to use a knife in fight. Besides, ya can't fight a sword with that. Ya can't fight the law or y'll end up in prison or with your feet dancing in the air and a noose around y'r neck on the gallows.'

'There was a new message in town this afternoon,' Christopher said, 'Sir Lewis has raised the taxes again.'

'The bastard is killing us all,' his father exclaimed, 'we've hardly enough left to live. He's sucking us dry as a leech.'

Lizzie, who had sat silently in a corner, suddenly stood up and grabbed Christopher's father's hand.

'Go away,' she said, 'go away from Dun'ich. Now still time, to go away.'

Christopher's father grabbed her small little fingers tightly. 'Maybe you're right, lass,' he said, 'but we can't. I am a man of the sea, a fisherman, the boat I rent, this house I built myself, this Dun'ich is our home, the only home we have.'

Lizzie shook her head. 'You don' believe,' she said, 'soon you'll believe. Then maybe too late.' She went out and Christopher followed her, as she walked to the sea wall. Lizzie crawled up, getting hold of the stone edges, and Christopher followed her. Together they stood on the wall, looking out over the sea, which was very calm, its waves rolling lazily. Looking at this peaceful sight, with the moon reflecting as a pupil-less eye moving over the waves and no clouds in sight, it was hard to believe that this sea could become such a destructive monster when it stormed.

'We are all sorry about Sarah, about your ma', Christopher said. 'You must miss her very much.'

Lizzie shook her head. 'I don't,' she said. 'She's not dead. I know. I feel it.'

Christopher dismissed this. If the lass wanted to believe that, let her, he thought. In a few days the body of Sarah Lovecraft would be washed ashore by the waves, swollen as a fat slug, her eyes, nose and lips eaten away by the crabs and parts of her face picked clean by the seagulls, unless the waves had taken it further out into the open sea, in which case it would turn up at Yarmouth, or maybe never.

'There was nothing anybody could've done to save her,' he said. 'No one can fight the power of the law, and Sir Lewis is a stinking bastard, but he is the power, he represents the King.'

Lizzie turned to him. She was so frail, in the long dress of crude cotton, falling down to her naked feet, yet somehow, the way she stood there, her small fingers clasped into fists, her long dirty hair blowing backward from the sea wind, carrying its aroma of salt, suddenly Christopher got an impression of strength which no one would have suspected in so fragile a body. She opened her dead eye, and in the dark hollow something white and sparkling glittered, as a pearl, a sudden flash of something very white and very cold.

'Not much longer,' Lizzie said. 'Ma, she told me how to look, she taught me how to see.' She stretched out her arms and opened her fists, spreading her fingers, then putting her hands over each other, the open palms towards the sea, her fingers intermingling so that only her two thumbs stood out, and six digits were turned toward the sea.

'Listen,' Lizzie said, 'the sea is crying.'

Then Christopher heard it too, hidden in the sound of the wind, a faraway almost unrecognisable sobbing sound which was anything but human. A big, slow wave rolled closer to the pebbles beneath the sea wall, disturbing the pale reflection of the moon. The wave rose, and rose, not falling over but carrying its crest of foam as if it was white hair on top, and then just before the sea wall it halted, remaining motionless. The wave opened two red wet glittering eyes which looked at Christopher and Lizzie, staring straight into their faces. Not human eyes but lizard eyes, with vertical pupils. Then the crest of the wave spilled over and closed the eyes; the wave went down and crashed with shuddering force against the cliffs beyond the sea wall.

But the crying continued, became louder and turned to a shrieking, wailing sound which was carried landwards by the sea wind to spread its cries above the city of Dunwich.

Lizzie pointed.

'Mam,' she said, 'banshee o' the sea. The spirit of death, the spirit of revenge. It'll come for Dun'ich. It'll get us all if we don't go away.'

X
WANDERING GHOSTS

Pa and ma slept in a corner of the cottage, hidden behind a cotton curtain. Lizzie slept in another corner, on a bed of straw. Christopher slept beside her, or tried to. As soon as they had gotten back, Lizzie had curled up as a kitten and went to sleep, but Christopher couldn't. He kept on hearing the shrieking of the banshee, and wondered how his parents and Lizzie could sleep through this noise. Finally he got up and walked outside. The cold sea wind blew all traces of sleep he might have felt away, and he breathed deeply in and out, enjoying the salt taste on his lips and tongue, the prickling on his face. He didn't want to ask himself what he had seen while standing with Lizzie on the sea wall. Surely he must have imagined it, the wave, the red eyes. Whatever he might have seen, Lizzie hadn't been afraid of it, and somehow Christopher felt that he too was safe. Whatever the thing was which howled and shrieked in the sea, it meant him no harm. And if Sarah was indeed now the banshee, then Lizzie was safe too.

He walked along the sea wall, and past the Dunwich gates which were locked now for the night, no one being able to get in or out. Christopher went around, a long walk, in the direction of what was left of the abbey. The soldiers hadn't only burned it from the inside, with their horses and carriages they had torn down most of the walls also. The ruins of the walls were like big black teeth rising out of the earth; the smell of burning and blood was still present everywhere as a bad breath hovering over the place. There was no sound, only the wind and the shrieking of the banshee far away. Christopher wondered who was sleeping inside the closed walls of Dunwich, and who was listening to that wailing, praying to the gods they believed in to protect them from the anger of the banshee.

Then he saw the lights. Small, flickering lights, moving amidst the ruins of the abbey. Now here, now there, suddenly appearing, then gone.

Christopher went closer, very slowly, very carefully.

A hand clamped on his shoulder. His breath and heart stopped for an instant, his mouth open to voice a scream which just wouldn't come out of his constricted throat.

'Now do you believe me?' Darrel asked softly in his ear. Christopher tore himself loose. 'You bastard, ya scared the hell outa me,' he said. 'What's this all about?'

'Look 't them,' Darrel whispered. 'You didn't believe me, but now you see it for y'rself. I slipp'd out of the gates before nightfall so I could see. They're there. The ghosts. The ghosts of the monks, walking in the ruins.'

Christopher looked closer. 'Oh yeah?' he said. 'Ghosts wearing a harness, ever seen some of those? Carrying torches? They're soldiers. They're treasure hunting, trying to find anything left in the ruins worth stealing. I bet Laurie will not believe this either when we tell him.'

Then the first scream came. Then another. There was yelling in the ruins, torches moving fast from here to there. Faintly there was a sound of metal striking stone. The flickering lights were leaving the abbey. A man came running away from the ruins, and something followed him. It all went so fast neither of the boys could get a good sight of it, of what it was. It came swirling like a loop, like a piece of rope but a rope has no claws, and it grabbed the running man and lifted him, his booted feet treading air, his right hand still clutching a bared sword which then came clattering down as whatever it was that held him lifted him higher and tore him in two pieces, wet glistening things falling out of both parts, then the whole was dropped to the ground and the thing retreated to the abbey where shrieking grew louder, an insane wail from human throats. As more lights went out, the screaming subsided, but not before they saw something hovering above the abbey, something which had its roots inside the ruins, something shapeless, with many arms and claws, reaching out to all sides, grabbing, cutting. No eyes, no face, no arms or hands, but things spreading out as from an enormous leech, thick wet glimmering things which grabbed and tore, soundlessly, the only sound being the human screams, abruptly cut short as the last scream ended and the last torchlight went out. Now only the moon lit the abbey in a soft silver glow, reflecting on the dark oily mass which was above the abbey, which then slowly descended, disappearing inside the ruins, and then was gone.

'I wanna see,' Christopher said.

'You're sick, let's get outta here,' Darrel sobbed, 'Christopher, that thing, that thing, it can come out and get us too.'

'No,' Christopher said, 'it won't. It's gone back, to those secret chambers from where it came. The chambers of the Order. There are no ghosts. This is something else. And I wanna see what it did.'

He stood up and walked towards the abbey. Shivering, Darrel followed him.

They found the running man, a quarter mile before the abbey, he really had made a run for it, but it hadn't saved him. They found his upper part, ending just above the stomach, and what had been inside that part scattered in the grass around him, glittering wetly.

They halted and looked at the silent ruins. Only darkness stared back at them. There were no more screams, only a weird wet sucking and slithering sound coming from within the ruins.

'I think... we've seen enough,' Christopher said. 'We better get back before it comes out again. Whatever it is.'

As if in answer from the abbey came a clanging hollow sound, as of enormous stones being smashed together, or heavy doors being pulled shut.

The two boys retreated. 'Can I stay at your place for the night?' Darrel shivered. 'I can't get back in the city, them doors being closed, and I don't feel like sleeping in the open right now.'

'O' course,' Christopher answered, 'though I doubt any of us will close an eye this night.'

Answering him the triumphant howling of the banshee was carried to them by the wind passing over the sleeping roofs of Dunwich. They walked around the city walls, coming to the gate, and Christopher suddenly halted.

'What's that? The west gates are open.'

As they looked, a man walked out, on his naked feet, wearing only his ankle-long nightgown. A small shape walked beside him and held him by the hand, leading him as a blind man needs guiding.

Darrel gripped Christopher's arm. 'That's... that's Sir Lewis,' he whispered.

'And the girl is Lizzie,' Christopher nodded. 'What the hell is going on here?'

Sir Lewis and the girl seemed unaware of their presence. The little girl led the man away from the gate, to the sea wall.

Christopher and Darrel followed them, passing the open gate. It hadn't been opened, it had been smashed from the inside, forcing the metal plates outwards in spidery threads, and splintering the inches-thick wood. Christopher looked inside. All was dark in Dunwich, only the gate's guardsman was sitting with his back against the wall, his sword in its sheath, his halberd on his knees. Christopher nudged him. The man bent forwards and his head rolled away over the trampled earth, a helmed ball leaving a darker smear on the earth, which greedily sucked in the blood.

'C'mon, or we'll lose them,' Darrel whispered.

Lizzie was standing on the sea wall, her face turned towards Sir Lewis. He was climbing up the sharp stones, using hands and naked feet, shaking all over his body. His movements were strange, abrupt, as if he was a marionette and somebody was dragging him up on the strings. Two white eyes, pupil-less, were glaring at him: Lizzie's one hand was pointing something towards him, the six-armed cross from the centre of which a single white eye stared. The second eye was Lizzie's dead eye, wide open and white. As Sir Lewis reached the top of the sea wall, his shoulders shook and he turned his head, looking back to the city. They saw his face, his wide open eyes, his mouth working, forming soundless words, his tongue lolling between his teeth which had grazed his tongue, drawing blood.

Then slowly his left hand rose and touched the cross which Lizzie held. The white eye formed a misty finger circling the cross, and the hands of Lizzie and Sir Lewis.

They both turned to face toward the sea, the white fog moving around their bodies. Then they jumped, the cross linking them. Sir Lewis shrieked once, a mindless insane shriek which mingled with the howling of the banshee.

Christopher and Darrel ran to the sea wall, and up. There was nothing to be seen. The silent sea lapped at the rocks.

'I'm going back in, the gate's open anyway,' Darrel said. 'I haven't seen this. I am dreaming all this. I'm going to bed and wake up tomorrow and nothing will have happened.'

'Just be careful inside the gate,' Christopher said. 'There's something lying there which you'd better not take a good look at.'

Returning home, he shook his head. He didn't understand any of this. What was happening? What had the killing of the monks and Sarah released? What would tomorrow bring? Sir Lewis disappeared, and dead of course, but Christopher and Darrel were the only ones who knew that. The crushed gate, the beheaded soldier, the others at the abbey, probably slaughtered as well as the running man by whatever had come out of the abbey. Lizzie dead too. She was linked... had been linked to the mystery, but what that mystery was, Christopher didn't want to think too much of it.

He entered the cottage, and stopped dead in his tracks. Lizzie was lying on her sack of straw, in the corner, sleeping peacefully.

Christopher shook his head. Maybe Darrel is right, he thought, I've been dreaming all of this.

Something icy cold passed him, a small white shape entering the cabin and gliding soundlessly past him. The shape was Lizzie, and Christopher could see right through her. The glasslike shape went to the corner, bent over Lizzie and just glided into her. Lizzie turned over in her sleep, and slept on.

Christopher slept outside.

XI
BANSHEE O' THE SEA

Christopher heard the news from Laurie the next afternoon. Sir Lewis was not missing, he was dead, he had died in his sleep, in his bed in the city hall of Dunwich. The six-armed cross had been hammered in his skull, but that was not what had killed him. His body was swollen, dripping salt seawater from his nostrils, and his open mouth was full of water, as was his body. He had drowned in his own bed, which was soaked with seawater.

A whole garrison of soldiers was missing too, until a farmer found the upper half of one near the abbey. The others were found inside, smeared all over the walls. None of them was left whole, some had their innards taken from them and draped around their heads, others had been dismembered and stripped of the flesh down to the bare bones. Body parts had been torn out by brute force and the parts introduced into various unspeakable orifices of the bodies.

None of the fishing boats went out that day. 'The wind is bad,' his father said, 'and some of us have been summoned to the abbey to clean up the... pieces.'

Rumours of what could have happened were all over town, but three words returned always, whispered: "banshee", "ghosts" and "Dagon". The beach was again littered with whitewashed bones, forming strange patterns on the stones. The city council sent a messenger to London to apply for a new sheriff, who had to be appointed by the King.

The sea was angry the whole day, the clashing sound of the waves mixing with the distant howling of the banshee.

It got dark very early, strangely shaped clouds closing above the sea and the city, not moving with the wind as clouds should do, but swirling around each other as tentacles swirling around a vortex. The waves of the sea became higher, their foam crowns spilling against the sea wall and then over it. All the churches in Dunwich started to ring their bells at the same time, but they couldn't drown out the sound of the other bells, coming from the sea. The bells of which one missed a single stroke.

Lizzie grabbed Christopher's hand. 'Go away, now,' she begged, 'away from Dun'ich. The banshee's coming.'

Christopher's father went outside. A huge wave crashed against the sea wall, spilling over it, roaring loudly.

'She's right,' he said, 'we're too close.' He grabbed a sack and put some dried fish, cheese, bread and a jar of milk in it. Christopher's mother gathered most of their clothes and humble possessions. "'S gonna be a big one,' she said, 'we'll sit it out in Dun'ich.'

'No,' Christopher said. 'Lizzie is right. We must go farther inland. This is not just another storm. We'll warn the townies.'

But in Dunwich business was as usual. Those they talked to on their way through the market, laughed their worries away as fisherman's superstitions. All right, so Sir Lewis had died a strange death, but that was the work of an assassin from the old Order. Some must have survived and slaughtered the soldiers too. The song of the banshee? Well, yes, the seawind sounded strange, and the sea was wild, but Dunwich had known other storms. The sea wall was strong, and so were the city walls themselves.

The last clouds closed in on themselves as Christopher and his family left through the inland gate of Dunwich, where all torches were now lit. They were joined by other fisher families, all with sacks and packages, holding their meagre belongings. Some of the older townsfolk joined them too, those who still believed the old stories about the big storms. They went beyond the abbey, making a wide circle around its dark ruins, though nothing moved there anymore.

'It's not there any longer,' Darrel said, who had joined them also. He was alone, his father hadn't wanted to come and had laughed with his story.

'No,' Christopher said, 'it's gone down.'

'Through the Black Doors,' Lizzie said, 'it rose from there and it went down again and closed them. Now it's out there, with the banshee.'

In the sea the banshee was shrieking loudly now, the waves rolling higher and higher, crashing and roaring against the cliffs and the sea wall. They were standing on a slope, and could see the sea wall beyond Dunwich, and the greenish glow which came from the sea. Onslaught upon onslaught, the waves soaring above the sea wall, crashing against it, tearing at it, loosening stones, making cracks. Then came a deep rumbling sound and as the bells from the sea shrieked in unholy glee as the lower part of the cliffs collapsed, the shattered sea wall going down along with the deserted fisherman's homes. Then followed the sea-facing city wall which was smashed inwards and then torn outwards as the earth gave way under it, the rocks under it hollowed out, the caves caving in and dropping the first row of houses into the screaming sea. The alarm bells started ringing, too late, much too late. The inland gates opened as a tidal wave spilled over and drowned the marketplace, crashing the city hall. Masses of townies spilled out of the gates, most in nightclothes, some naked, all running in panic. Their screams were subdued by the roaring of the sea and the banshee, mixing with the insane tolling of the cursed sea-bells.

Then, beyond what was left of the cliffs, a wave was rising out of the sea, a wall of water going up and up as a green-shrouded cloud reaching up into the skies. The wave came on, and opened a face with staring white eyes, and a wide open watery mouth, sending its shriek over Dunwich. The wave thrust out swirling tentacles which glittered as oil, which were water yet had claws and small hideous faces with inhuman mouths.

The banshee o' the sea was coming, for the first time showing not only her own face but also the face of the being she was part of.

The wave rolled over the cliffs, absorbing them and then crashed down over Dunwich, extinguishing its torches, crushing its houses and churches, then cracking the earth itself as Dunwich was lifted up into the sky, parts of it flying in all directions, and then it all went down into the howling sea, which received Dunwich with greedy claws and tentacles, and many many waiting mouths, ready to feed on the flesh and brains of its inhabitants.

As the wave retreated only the inland wall was still standing.

The bells stopped. The banshee became silent.

Dunwich was no more.

EPILOGUE:
THE TOMBSTONE AND THE SILENT SEA

'Well, that's quite a story,' I said breathlessly. 'It isn't exactly what's written down in the history books though.'

'The banshee o' the sea, and that... other thing... came for Dun'ich in the year of our lord 1537. What do you think any sane man would write down of what I told you? Most true stories aren't in them books,' the old man said. 'So many dead that night, for months afterwards their bodies would wash ashore on the beaches and farther away, as if that which came for Dunwich had enjoyed distributing their bodies... mostly parts of them... miles and miles away from Dun'ich itself.'

'And Christopher, Lizzie, and the others?'

The old man sighed. 'Life went on. Life always goes on, even after disasters such as this. Christopher's father stayed. He helped rebuild Dun'ich, but he remained a fisherman. They built a new Dun'ich farther away, but it never became a big city after that. The sand kept on coming, finally destroyed the harbour, and the sea kept on attacking and eating the dunes from below, though never again with the force of that infamous night of 1537. The banshee o' the sea had gotten what she wanted: the total destruction of the ol' Dun'ich. Mind you, she took her time, after her first onslaught but then, with that attack she got all those she wanted. The destruction of what remained was more kind of a... traditional ceremony, ya might say. For centuries she was still called the banshee o' the sea, though most of those who survived by then knew that the being which had destroyed Dun'ich was something much more powerful, more ancient. The traditional banshee was a ghostly being predicting disaster and death, not provoking it. What came for Dun'ich that night... well, does it matter what it was? From which closed ancient sea caves it came, what name it carried? No one ever tried to find out what the "Black Doors" were which were supposed to have been down in the abbey, below sea level, or what being was worshipped there. Maybe it was Dagon, maybe it was something even older, the being Dagon and his kinship worshipped and which came to their help. No one will ever know, and it's best so. The last wall and tower of the old city fell into the sea in 1919. All of the old Dun'ich is down there now, below the waves, except for this single gravestone. Christopher went away, with Lizzie. He married her later when she was older, and they became farmers. They had three children. Lizzie died when she was eighty-three, and Christopher died a few years later. He had become a happy grandfather by then.'

'And so you come here, just look at the sea, and remember the old story.'

'Remember is not quite the word,' the man said. His voice sounded different, and I looked up. A tall young boy was sitting next to me, smiling softly. 'I relive what happened every time,' he said. 'I am part of the old and part of the new. The old Order never died, Lizzie taught me, and we taught others. Sometimes we pass on what we know to those we feel that want to know. As you. You came here to find some proof. I can give you no proof, only what I told you what I know is true because I was there. Your quest will go on until you find all you need to know. You came here for knowledge, carrying with you knowledge of the Vaeyens and the Signs. The Order is not dead, it is just sleeping as Great Cthulhu in R'lyehh, waiting, waiting.

I told you what I know. You must go on, find the others, in due time, when you're ready. Or maybe they'll find you by that time. This is beyond me, I am of the past, only a small link to the present, and to those like you who search and know.'

His shape was shimmering, changing, becoming an old man again.

'This is... your grave?' I asked.

'No, no,' he said, 'I was buried inland, where I lived and died. This stone is meaningless, just an old reminder. All the rest is there, down there and below, where the Black Door still is, waiting for someone to find her, and what's beyond her. Maybe waiting for someone like you, who knows. When the time comes, you'll know. You'll find them. Or they'll find you. Be ready then.'

He rose slowly, putting his hands together, fingers above each other with the two thumbs sticking out, forming a six-armed cross.

Then he was gone, and I was alone with the tombstone and the silent sea.

BEHIND THE WHITE WALL

W HEN HE SAW his own hand crawling across the table to the telephone, its fingers lazily moving like the feet of a fat fleshy spider, and forming a number he didn't recognize, he knew that something was very, very wrong.

He hadn't ordered his hand to dial a number.

A good ordinary hand didn't do such things, except upon the specific instructions of its owner. And his hand *had* to be a good hand, because he, the owner, knew himself to be a good person. So it *had* to be wrong that a good hand, owned by a good man, dialled a telephone number all by itself. Now wasn't that very logically reasoned? Notice how logical he thought, stating the facts, and then drawing the correct conclusions from them. If he could only *reason* with *them* like this, they would have to believe that he was sane, and let him out. Only he never could, whenever they were near, it was as if unseen clamps shut his mouth, and he couldn't bring a word out which made sense.

Still full of angry surprise, he kept on staring at the moving fingers. It *was* his own hand, wasn't it? Of course it was; not only was the hand attached to his own arm, and he himself to that arm (how logical! How reasonably thought through!), but the left little finger wore his own signet-ring with his initials engraved in it. Now the rebelling hand took up the receiver, which it had deposited on the table, and raised it to his ear. Now he couldn't see the hand any more, as it was beside his eyes. He became rigid, with the receiver very cold against his ear and cheek.

'Hello,' the voice on the other end of the line said, 'who's speaking, please?'

It was a woman's voice, soft, friendly. But it wasn't that which had shocked him so much. His throat felt very dry, and he wetted his lips with the tip of his tongue. He desperately tried to speak, but his tongue wouldn't form the words, and his mouth refused to utter them.

'Hello?' the voice repeated, 'hello? Who's there?' Then came the clicking sound, which cut the connection. He stood there for five full long minutes, time slowly ticking by, but his eyes stayed fixed on the empty air, staring into nothingness. It had been the voice of his wife, speaking on the other end of the telephone. But something wasn't right with *that* statement, it couldn't be. Because his wife had been dead and buried for four years.

The shrill sound of the dinner bell disturbed his racing thoughts, and he had to leave the room and the telephone. He could hardly wait till dinner was over. Even the white walls couldn't calm him. He was so nervous and on edge that he spilled part of his soup and even the male nurse of his wing noticed it and asked him if something was wrong. Nothing was wrong; of course, he had just been a bit clumsy. Afterwards there was an annoying hour of mutual recreation and intermingling with the other patients in the sports hall, an hour which seemed to go on for an eternity. But it was over at last, and he could return to his own room.

Hurriedly he closed the door after him and ran to the table with the telephone, but once his hand (now acting upon his orders) rested upon the receiver, he hesitated. His lips felt dry again and grainy. He tried his voice, and it was hoarse and faint. Ice water seemed to drip through his veins, instead of warm blood. There was something... something at the back of his mind, behind the white wall that was there, something which he should remember, but couldn't. It was something very important, he felt that, but it stayed safely hidden behind the white wall in his mind, and wouldn't come out. Then, slowly, deliberately, he took up the receiver, and his hand crawled to the dial and began to form a number.

'Hello? Who's speaking?' the voice said at his ear. A quiver ran uncontrollably through his body, and suddenly he felt very weak and vulnerable and had to sit down, before his knees changed into protoplasm under him. There couldn't be the slightest doubt now, he knew his wife's voice too well. That special intonation on the first tones, that slight accent, understandable even through the telephone. She was the one, all right!

'*Hello?*' the voice asked again, impatient, slightly angered.

'Martha?' His voice sounded strange even in his own ears, as he hesitatingly spoke her name.

'Who is this?' she asked, 'Who's speaking?'

'Martha love, it's me,' he said.

'I'm sorry, but you've dialled the wrong number,' she said coldly.

'Wait, wait! Please, don't hang up. I've got the correct line. You are... you *are* Martha, aren't you? Martha Verviers?'

'Yes, that's me,' she said.

'Don't you recognize me, Martha? Don't you?'

'No, I don't recognize your voice, which is fortunate for you, whoever you are. If this is your idea of a good joke, forget it. I don't find it funny. Who are you anyway, and what exactly do you want?'

'But... but you *must* recognize me, Martha. It's me, Paul, your husband.'

'Listen, funny guy, if it is of any interest to you, Paul is sitting in the next room here, reading the newspaper. So will you please go play your jokes on someone else?'

Click!

He kept on staring at the telephone, listening to the no-connection signal. Then he dialled the number, and again, and again. But no one picked up the receiver at the other end of the line.

He waited two full days before he dared phone again. By that time, he couldn't hold onto himself any longer. He hadn't stopped thinking about Martha during those two days and two sleepless nights. He could remember her eyes, her figure with the small waist and the strong breasts, and the way her hair kept on falling before her eyes, half hiding them. He could even recall the ringing sound of her laughter, and he remembered many other small things from their life together, things seemingly unimportant which had given full meaning to their married life. Their walks together through autumn parks, with the brown and golden leaves falling around them, and their voyages to Switzerland during the winter sports season, where he had once broken a leg when he had tried to ski. He relived their two weeks in Spain with the sun burning on their browned bodies, and their summer nights full of passionate love and the hope for the child that never came. And then, near the end, there was the white wall in the back of his mind, cutting the shards of memories from another earlier world, before he had been put here. The wall was there every time he tried to think of her death and burial. How did she die? Where was she buried? Or wasn't she really dead, and was it something which they had invented to keep him still so he wouldn't keep on asking for her? How else would he be able to speak to her now on the telephone?

But the white wall stayed in his brain, hiding part of it from him, impenetrable no matter what he tried.

Slowly he dialled the number, enjoying the burring tone.

'Hello?' he said himself, speaking first now.

'*You* again,' she said. 'Listen, Mr. Nobody, this nonsense has to stop. I don't like these anonymous calls, and neither will Paul.'

'But I am Paul; *I am Paul!*'

'If these insane calls don't stop, I shall complain to the police. So you are warned, Mr. Nobody. Stop calling me.'

Her voice, which had been swirling through his mind during those two days and two nights of nightmarish sleepless thinking, like a leaf caught in a stormwind. How desperately he wanted to see her again, to really speak to her. She couldn't stop that, she couldn't.

'Hello? Are you still there?'

'Martha... I love you.'

Click.

Six hours later, after the evening meal, he called again. While his fingers automatically turned the dial, he looked at the small window, into the starlit night, with the full moon a white eye in the black sky. The moon was deadly white, as white as the walls of his room, as white as the wall in his mind.

Connection.

'Martha, my dear, it's me. I love you.'

'*Who's there?*' a hard cruel voice barked. That voice, he recognized *that* voice also. He recognized and he knew, *he knew.* The voice came from behind the white wall, there were cracks in the wall, now tears, and pieces started falling downwards in his tortured mind, and there were holes now, big black holes, like empty eye sockets, and through the holes he could look into his own mind and back in time. The receiver slipped from his grip and fell on the table.

'No,' he shrieked, '*stop him. Stop me. I... I... we are going to kill her!*'

That week with Martha in their new apartment, when the

mysterious phone calls started coming, he remembered it all now, in all its ugliness, her shyness, her evading answers whenever he asked who had called, and then the suspicion growing in him, brooding, forming ugly patterns in his mind every time the telephone rang. He remembered the coldness of the receiver, that evening when he had taken up the telephone himself, and the man's voice, strangely familiar, who said, 'Martha, my dear, it's me. I love you.'

The white wall broke apart, opening the back of his mind completely, and he saw himself and the telephone, and the knife which he took from the kitchen, and the blood on the walls and the table and the telephone.

'*I'm going to kill her*,' he shrieked into the gasping abyss which opened its jaws before him, '*I killed her. I killed her.*'

He thought he heard her screaming through the receiver, just before he brought his feet down upon it, smashing it into a pulp of broken plastic shards, but it could have been his own shrieks that came to him from all the white walls around him and inside him. Then the white coated men came and took him, and brought him to the rubber padded room, as they had to do every night of the full moon during the four years since he had cut his wife to pieces.

Later one of the men came back and swept up the jagged bits of the smashed toy telephone.

SOMETHING SMALL, SOMETHING HUNGRY

THROUGH THE OBSCURING clouds of a grey fog, consciousness returned, and with it the frozen panic-feeling of falling, the
echoing outcry of the crowd, and the crushing pain came back.
Dimly, shadow figures moved above her, but they refused to come
into focus, their outlines kept on shifting and fading, as if they were
seen through the misty distorting lens of a cheap camera. There was a
sudden pain somewhere in her body, a sharp thrust which managed
somehow to break through the cloak of dumb constant pain which
was soaking into her mind. Her eyesight cleared abruptly, as if a veil
was taken from before her face, and hands and faces materialized on
the ghostly figures above her. Enormous fingers were reaching down
for her from unimaginable heights. She saw Frank, her husband, but
though she noticed that his hands were touching her, she couldn't
feel them, almost as if she hadn't a real body at all, and though his lips
were moving frantically, there was only the empty, waiting silence
around her, uninterrupted by any sounds. Frank still wore his fur
coat, and at his shoulders she saw Maghil, the three-armed clown
with the crying face and his eyes, red from too much cheap cognac.
Beyond them was Zigotti, the magician in his grey star-sparkling
evening dress, and Mr. Morbani, the director, who was talking to a
stranger, his white gloved hands tracing bizarre drawings in the
empty air.

There were also two men in white coats, staring down on her, and
one of them held a syringe in his hands. The injection needle was
empty, she saw, and the stranger was looking at her with medical
coolness. Their movements were strangely fluid, as if they were moving through a slowed-down movie fragment or dream sequence.
Above their heads, she could see the wooden ceiling of her caravan,
painted in dark blue, with the silver stars she had once painted there
in one of her crazy moods. Frank was speaking to her, but she
couldn't hear him though she tried hard, she could only see, notice
and absorb every detail of what happened around her with an

astounding clarity through the swelling pain. There was a weird feeling of isolation, of a complete detachment from these people and this place. In vain she tried to break through that barrier. She remembered the trapeze, and herself, high above the crowd, and then the long scream as she fell and fell. She knew that she had to say something to these people, something very important and very urgent, and she had to say it quickly, because her whole aching body told her that there was almost no time left. She opened her mouth to speak, and a sudden immense feeling of weakness and sickness spread through her. Her tongue moved like a piece of raw bleeding flesh against her palate. She didn't know if they even heard or understood her, but they had to know. She had to warn them, before the something was hungry again.

'It wasn't me...' she gasped, her voice a dry rattling croak, 'I didn't miss... my grip... something made me... close... my hands...'

A sickening sweet taste came in her mouth, as she vomited blood. The pain became all absorbing now, running in hot burning gulps through her veins, and red layers of wet mist began to move before her eyes, distorting what was left of her vision.

Then she knew she would never be able to tell them, but somehow, before she died, they had to know because otherwise others would follow. And suddenly, as her mind began flowing backwards, through the mists of time, she was a little girl again, alone in the big empty house, reading in her father's old yellowed books. She remembered one of the books in particular, a heavy volume which had frightened her after she had read it, and suddenly she saw the parallel and remembered the one word which mattered, the one word which could save them... if they understood it correctly.

'Vampire,' was the last word Elairie said to an uncomprehending audience of artists and doctors before she died.

Boro had heard the outcries from the big tent, and he had seen the ambulance and the police car arrive soon afterwards. He didn't go to find out what had happened—it didn't interest him very much. He continued his game with the two great dolls with the heavily painted faces and the false eyelashes, the dolls which could cry and say, "Mama", when he put them down. No one came knocking on the door of Boro's caravan to tell him what had happened. No one ever bothered to tell Boro anything at all, he'd find out himself in due time. And if he never found out, well, it didn't matter very much in Boro's world.

There was much noise and people talking around the circus, and Boro frowned, upset. Couldn't they go and make their noise somewhere else, so that they didn't disturb his playing? He drew the curtains, which stopped some of the noise, but not all. People were running around like crazy, always gibbering like a bunch of escaped monkeys.

Then Boro heard Elairie's name, and his head jerked up, the game forgotten. He straightened, carefully laid down the dolls in their two little beds, drew the greasy sheets over them, said goodnight to them and went outside to find out, after all.

The cool air mingled with the strong smells of the circus and the nearby small town. A few moments later Boro knew. Elairie was dead.

Something small had taken her.

The late afternoon sun was still burning hot through the windows of the office, and sweat was irritatingly itching Hank Dorwin's neck and his armpits. He desperately wanted to scratch himself, and he couldn't for the moment, which made him even more furious than he already was.

'What do you mean "an accident"?' he barked at the two inspectors, who were standing before his desk like two school boys caught with a girl by the headmaster. 'An accident? I have spoken to that director from the circus, Morbani, and he clearly said that the girl was the most able and qualified trapezist he ever had in his group. She can't have missed her grip. You've read the tape transcript of her last words?'

'Uh, yes sir, yes, we did,' Gary Vador replied for the two of them. 'We did read it, and it doesn't make much sense. Doesn't give any clues either to what happened.'

'The girl said that someone made her miss her grip.'

'If you'll excuse me, sir, but she said that something made her close her hands, which is something entirely different. Now when it happened, she was up there, sixteen metres above the earth, and there was nobody with her. Lon and I think that she simply missed her jump and tried to cover up her mistake.'

'Cover up a mistake? From a dying woman? Come on, you don't believe that yourself, do you?'

'Well, I don't know, sir. These circus people, they're a special breed. We seem to forget that they themselves consider their work as an art, and they have a special kind of pride in that. So I really think that it might be possible that...'

'Well, I do *not* think it possible, and unfortunately for you, neither do my superiors. Listen, I had to withdraw you both from the Berkeley Street case, because besides very reasonable minds, you both have a grain of imagination. The Berkeley Street case is a routine job, I have given it to Ted, he can deal with it. But this thing we have on our hands here has proved itself rather bizarre, to say the least of it. So you better start concentrating on it right now, as yet we're not absolutely sure even that it *is* something for Homicide after all. Have they mentioned the other cases to you?'

'No, frankly, we didn't know that there *were* others.'

'Oh, but there are, Gary, probably more than we know of. So far we have the files on two definite ones, but I have here also notes on five others which could very well have the same origin, wherever that may be. Look here.'

He grabbed a set of files and began spreading them over the desk like a deck of cards.

'But sir,' Gary objected, 'those are not our files. They're from Suicide and Accidents Department.'

'Sure they are, Gary, sure they are. Only it seems someone thinks they belong to us now. After the third strange case, someone in the Accidents Department became suspicious, he started digging in their back files and discovered six other similarities. So he transferred the whole bundle to Homicide. And here we are, stuck with them, if we like it or not.'

'But I don't see how they can...'

'Oh, you'll see soon enough, Gary, but it won't be much of a help. Here, let's take this one first, an accident on High Square, a few months ago. An important businessman, on his way to an urgent meeting. Suddenly without the slightest inclination, in the midst of traffic, he throws the steering wheel around and crashes straight into a truck coming from the opposite direction. No defects on the car, no skidding of the wheels, not even the smallest private reason for a regular suicide. The man came to on his way to the hospital, and an orderly heard him whisper, "The wheel, I must stop the wheel, someone is turning the wheel". A few seconds later he was dead.'

'Doesn't say much. There can be a million reasons for a suicide, and now that he's dead we'll never know the real one. His car was completely smashed up, I suppose?'

'Sure, but both Accidents Department and inspectors from both insurance companies in the deal checked the wreck completely. No faults anywhere. So they closed the case as an accident, or, if you wish, an unproven suicide. Next case, and I'm sure you'll remember this one, the suicide of Barrow Street's roof walker.'

'Oh, you mean the jewel robbery, where Bennie the Kick jumped from the roof of a six floor apartment? But he jumped himself, we've read those reports.'

'Do you think so? Let me tell you how it happened. Two of our men had cornered Bennie on the roof; he had already had to leave the jewels behind. There was no fire ladder, so no escape possible. So Bennie gave up, after all, what did he risk? A few months or at the most a year of prison, there was still nothing else we could prove against him. He came to the officers, and then, when he was only a few metres from them, he started to shriek, "Stop it, in heaven's name, stop it, stop pushing". He took two stumbling steps sideways and threw himself to his death, six floors below. But no one was pushing him.'

'So what? A captured thief, with quite a record already in our books, panics and takes the shortest, and deadliest, way out. Just a case of panic.'

'Could be, but it also could be something else. One such case is an accident, two are strange, but we have seven such cases here. I have only mentioned the first two, because they are the only ones in which we have definite statements about the last words of the victims. The circus girl is the third definite one, and the eighth in line. In the other cases, it's only a matter of guesswork as to what really happened. But someone "Up There" thinks they are connected in some absurd way or other.'

'So what are we supposed to do with that? There's nothing tangible in these things, nothing even to look for!'

Hank Dorwin felt an unreasonable anger welling up in him. The itching was intolerable now, and he hated having to explain the obvious to these two. Obvious? No, that wasn't the correct word—it was more like a hunch, but he couldn't spare the time to follow it up himself. They'd have to do that.

'There are just too many similarities in these cases,' he repeated, 'What it means? Why ask *me*? I'm asking *you* to find out what this whole mess is about. I haven't the slightest idea, but Accidents and Suicide have dumped the mess in our hands, so we have to see where it leads to. I'll be leaving in half an hour for another inquiry in the Marco murder, so I haven't the time for this thing. Here are all the files, go to the circus, go digging in the other cases, question anyone you like to, but try to get some results. Personally, I don't especially care *what* results. I'll even be satisfied if you can definitively state that they *were* just simple accidents, no more than that. But I have a weird hunch that it won't turn out so easy. So better get started.'

With these words, he let them go. When the door had closed after them, Hank sat down, took the files on the Marco murder, and then, happily, scratched himself.

At first, Boro didn't want to believe it. He heard what they said, 'Elairie is dead,' and he pictured it in tall red-flashing letters like the posters for the evening performances on the fences surrounding the circus grounds. The words didn't make any sense, they just stood there glaring at him, so he put them aside, swept them out of his mind. It wasn't true, of course it wasn't true, Elairie was alive and well, and soon now she'd come out of the artists' changing tent. She'd say a few words to Boro, and the afternoon sun would shine upon her gold webbed hair, and late summer would sparkle in her eyes.

Then someone else said it, and then again, and again, until the words began to burn in Boro's head. It couldn't be, could it? Or...

Boro remembered how the something small had felt, the aching hunger, then the triumph, the satisfaction, the feeding.

Then he knew that Elairie was dead.

A coldness crept over the sun, its chill fingers dripping down on Boro's upturned face like spiders' threads. He felt something he hadn't felt for many years, something that he had even forgotten existed.

Boro felt hurt.

It wasn't the angry but easy pain he had felt when hitting his thumb with a hammer, and it wasn't the nagging sickening hurt he had once felt after he had eaten something poisonous, but this was a horrible feeling deep inside, which began crawling all over him like a wet slug, an emotion which was like a dark empty hole which began sucking on his insides. He found himself thinking of Elairie, of the softness of her hands and the wiry wealth of her hair he had once touched. He saw her laughing when she left the tent after another successful performance, and he heard again the silver bells in her rich voice. He hadn't always understood Elairie when she talked to him, but then nobody else had ever bothered to speak to Boro at all, except for Elairie, beautiful friendly soft Elairie who was now dead and cold, and whose mouth was full of frozen blood.

Boro had stopped caring for people long ago, because to care for someone is being liable to be hurt. Only now, as he began feeling the empty dumb pain, Boro realized that he had cared for someone after all. And was hurt again.

Boro didn't like the feel of hurt.

'This place's rather hot,' Lon observed, dabbing his forehead. Director Morbani smiled without any real mirth, a polite drawing up of the corners of his lips, which didn't seem able to express a genuine, friendly smile.

'I like a hot, dry temperature in my living quarters,' he said, 'I come from a warm sunny country, and after all these years of travelling all over the world I still haven't gotten used to your moist climate here.'

He had invited the two policemen into his caravan, which was a luxurious miniature bungalow inside. Heavy curtains of warm sparkling colours hung before the big windows, his wooden desk was handmade and inlaid with mythological characters and scenes. That bulky thing alone must have cost a small fortune, Lon thought.

There were two paintings decorating the walls amidst a set of posters, and though Lon hadn't the slightest expertise on painting, even he could see that these were no cheap reproductions, but the real thing. The whole room breathed wealth, yet also held an impression of good taste and soberness. Morbani was a tall and slender man, and his posture fitted the room, as if it had been built around him.

'Now, gentlemen,' he said with his slight accent; 'I don't see exactly how I can be of any help to you. We all regret the loss of Madame Cauber, of course, but after all it *was* an accident. Accidents are expected in our profession, and though fortunately they are scarce, now and then they *do* indeed happen.'

'Yes, we know. That is in fact exactly what we're wondering about... was it an accident? We also know the last words she said before dying... She said that something made her close her hands.' Lon said.

Morbani made an impatient gesture with his aristocratic white hands, with the perfectly manicured fingers. 'Gentlemen, you know all the facts as well as I do. What else could it be but an accident? Elairie must have been delirious when she came to, those words you say, they are sheer nonsense. She was all alone up there—we had about seven hundred people watching the performance when she fell. There was no one with her.'

'So suppose she really did miss her grip, she didn't also have to die. Why was there no safety net?'

'The public, gentlemen, the public. It is always hungry for sensation, and the nets take away the possibility of danger. They make it all seem so easy, so safe. Besides, Elairie never wanted the nets, she didn't need them. And though we regret her loss, we won't restart using them now.'

'The accident didn't surprise you very much?' Gary asked.

'Oh, but you are wrong there, very wrong. I could have accepted and understood a simple accident, but not Elairie. She was one of our best and most experienced artists. I do absolutely *not* understand how she failed.'

'She couldn't have been under the influence of...'

'No drugs, gentlemen,' Morbani interrupted, 'you won't find any such stuff in my circus.'

'Let's keep this on an informal level, Mr. Morbani,' Gary said. 'My colleague and I are from Homicide, not from the Narcotics Department. We are only, and exclusively, trying to find out if what happened was really an accident, and if it turns out to be no more than that, we're satisfied and our job's done. What we ask is, could there be a possibility that she had taken... let's say, some medicine with a narcotic influence? Like sleeping pills or something like that, just enough so that her reactions would be a bit slowed down?'

'No, I do not consider this likely, not with Elairie. She was a perfectly healthy young woman, who hadn't the slightest need of any artificial help.'

'But you don't see any other reason for her failure either?'

'None at all. As you say, it is... strange. But that's all I can say about it. I'm sorry if I haven't been very helpful, gentlemen, but there's really nothing else I could add. What are you doing to do now?'

'If you don't mind,' Lon said, 'we'd like to question some of your people also.'

'Fine, fine. I'll bring them here. Who do you want?'

'No, please don't bother, we don't want any sensational cross-examinations. We'll just walk around a bit, and ask a few questions here and there, and see if someone has any special theories.'

Morbani smiled again, and Gary discovered that it was definitely an ugly smile. 'Well, you'll hear theories enough, I imagine,' Morbani said sarcastically, 'if they want to talk about them. Usually they don't like strangers, but go ahead, and if necessary say that I have ordered them to answer all your questions. Good luck with your inquiry.'

They stood up to leave, but in the doorway, Gary suddenly remembered something. 'There was something else,' he remarked, 'that last word the girl said... Do you know what it means?'

'Last word? *What* last word?'

'The girl said *vampire*.'

Was it some trick of the extra light coming in through the open door, or did Morbani really pale a bit?

'Vampire, she said? Yes, I know what a vampire is. I suppose you know also, so why ask me?'

'Let's stop this game of word chess. Of course we checked what a vampire is. Some kind of an undead person, who changes into a bat or wolf, and who preys on the blood of living human beings to sustain his unearthly existence. Sleeps in a coffin and things like that.'

'Yes, all that and some things more, a vampire is. But everything else I could tell you, you'll find with much more detail in any serious study of the occult, though intermingled with lots of superstitious nonsense. So Elairie said that, you say? I can't imagine what she wanted to express. If you don't mind, however, do you know if some of my people also heard this word?'

'Yes, her husband knows, and some others might have caught it. Why?'

'Many of my people are... as you would call it... illiterate. The only things they know are their jobs here in my circus. But they also have an inborn stubborn conviction about certain things... one of them being the supernatural. To say it frankly, you could call them a superstitious lot. That's why I'd rather you wouldn't mention it to them.'

'I don't see the connection between...'

'No? Just ask them about Yvana, and you'll see their reaction soon enough, and understand why I'm careful when dealing with superstitions with them.'

'Yvana? Who's Yvana?' Lon asked.

'She's our witch. Oh, a harmless old woman, who lays some cards, forecasts the future and does some pseudo-magical tricks. But most of my people really believe in her dark powers and in her protective magic. And they also believe in her evil eye, and though they won't say it outright, most are scared of her. Once, just after she had joined our company, a few bad things happened, small nuisances only, but annoying nevertheless. They immediately laid the blame on her, saying that she had thrown the evil eye on the circus and brought us bad luck. They gave me a lot of trouble then, so far even that I had to interfere personally twice to prevent their use of violence to get rid of the witch. I don't want to see these superstitious fears get started again among them. Some of them may never have heard of vampires, but those who have would tell the others soon enough. I'd rather evade those troubles.'

Boro saw the man come walking up to him. He was standing on a small patch of grass in front of his caravan, working on a wooden box the magician had asked him to make. It was a hot day, and Boro's throat felt very dry. His tongue was raw against his slightly cracked lips. He would have liked something to drink, but the magician had asked him to make the box quickly, so Boro had to do this first.

Boro knew the stranger was coming to him, he knew it from the way the man walked and stared, looking everywhere except at Boro. But Boro wasn't yet interested in the stranger, he could as well have been one of the many other circus people, always walking around and seeming to be very busy. Boro always saw everyone, but immediately placed them in a forgotten corner of his mind, not stopping to think about them. He collected them there like so many unreal shadow figures.

Then the man spoke, and came out of Boro's shadow country into the sun and almost stood on Boro's toes. Boro looked up and let the saw rest in his hands. 'Huh?' he asked.

'Something really weird you're making there,' the man repeated his question. 'What's it for?'

The man's face was young but strong, clean washed and shaven. He wore fine clothes too, nothing very expensive, but clean and fitting well to his lean muscular body, the kind of costume Boro never could wear and never would want to anyway. The man was smiling, a sparkle of white teeth with a few yellow spots, but his mouth was lying, his eyes were cold and inquiring. Boro knew that the man wasn't really interested in what he was doing with the box, so he decided not to answer him. He knew the stranger had been around already, asking funny questions of everyone in the circus. Boro wasn't interested in answering silly questions. Maybe if he ignored the man, he would turn his back and go away. So Boro took back the saw and restarted working.

'Man, it *is* hot here!' the stranger said.

Boro looked up again, slightly angered. So the stranger wanted to talk in any case. No use working further then, Boro never did two things at the same time. He once had tried talking while working, and his one leg still bore the scar where a slipping knife had jabbed him.

'It's a coffin,' he said, ignoring the later superfluous remark. 'I'm making it for the magician.'

'A coffin? Not to bury him with, I hope?'

Which was another silly statement. The stranger and he knew that the magician was still alive, so why should he be making a coffin to bury him? Strangers always made silly remarks which made no sense in Boro's world. He didn't answer the question, but kept on staring at the stranger and waiting for his next question.

'Maybe to bury the girl?' the stranger said. He never knew how near he had been to death himself in the space of half a second. Boro checked his hand just in time, before the sharp toothed saw came up like the open jaws of a hungry animal. No muscle moved in Boro's face, except for the baring of his teeth in what the stranger must have thought to be a very unpleasant smile.

'Elairie is dead,' Boro grunted. 'They bury her in nice coffin, nice warm soft coffin. Not in a cheap trick box for magician.'

'You knew the girl?'

Turmoil reigned in Boro's mind. Everyone knew Elairie, the stranger was again asking absurd questions. What did he want to know from Boro? There was nothing Boro could tell him, nothing Boro *wanted* to tell him. He couldn't speak of the searing pain in his insides, the emptiness of Boro's sunlight and how he had lain awake through the night, painting Elairie's shadow face on the dark walls surrounding him with their silence.

'We all knew Elairie. She was a good woman. A nice woman. She's dead. They'll bury her in a nice warm coffin.'

'You know how she died?'

'Something small took her,' Boro said. For once he had answered too soon, he saw it in the mild surprise, reflecting on the face of the stranger. Of course the stranger didn't know about the something small, no one knew but Boro and the animals and maybe Yvana.

'Something what took her?'

Boro looked at the man, then decided to put him back in the shadow world. Just for a second he had thought that maybe the man also would have known about the something small, but that had been silly of Boro. He lost his interest in the man, so he took up the saw and put it on the wood. 'I must make the coffin,' he grunted, 'for the magician,' and started sawing.

The stranger kept on looking at him for a few minutes, maybe thinking that he would say something else. Boro expected to hear a few other silly questions, but soon he forgot the man standing before him. He didn't even notice as the stranger left. All his attention was back on the burning teeth of the saw, eating monotonously through the stubborn wood.

Gary left the circus grounds and slowly walked back to his car. He hadn't learned much. These people could so easily be divided into three classes. The first group just looked at him as if he was something from another world with which they didn't want anything to do; and pretended not to understand him, or just answered with grunts which could as well mean "yes" or "no" or "go to hell".

The second group answered his questions but kept him at a distance with barely concealed hostility. Polite or not, they always regarded him as an enemy. The third group talked too much about things that did not interest him at all. Only on one thing did they all agree: they didn't understand how Elairie could have fallen. He had talked with her husband, a bulky arrogant man who looked pale, but otherwise seemed more untouched by the tragedy than the simplest of the working people. Morbani had been right about them being a superstitious lot, however—some of them mentioned the "vampire" straight to him, asking if he knew anything about it. Two of the men he had talked to openly said that someone had thrown the evil eye on Elairie, sending her to her doom. And then there had been that strange coffin-sawing fellow who just remarked that something small had taken her.

Gary saw no clear way to handle the case; the whole thing was no more than a stupid accident, no matter what the others all saw in it. But he supposed that Hank Dorwin thought the same about it, and had only dumped the thing in their laps to get rid of it himself.

Unseen but not unnoticed, a spectral cloud drifted through the circus. It started at two points at the same time, from the tent of an animal trainer, and from the mouth of the three-armed clown, both of whom had heard Elairie's last words before she died. The cloud changed shape and colour, as it passed from whisper to whisper, growing bigger and taller and darker as it advanced from mouth to ear, changing its form, each time a bit more horrible, a bit more frightening.

The fearful shadow wore a name, and with the name came dark thoughts which made some of the more rational people smile inside, but which left most of the others shuddering because they were simple people with many weird backgrounds and inbred, inherited fears. Some of them still remembered the old fires and singing and dancings, and the whispered stories, and also the old ways with things that were not quite human. The spreading word left impressions of bloodshot eyes and bared teeth and stale breath, it called to mind the noiseless flight of the bat and the whimpering of dark shadow-things in the night winds.

The word was "vampire", and it stalked through the circus, leaving a trail of hidden terror behind it. The fear wasn't spoken out loud, but, much more dangerously, it stayed just below the surface like a waiting animal, always sticking its head up in whispered conversations. And with the hiding of the fear, the tension mounted, a constant nervous strain, resulting in sudden harsh words at trivial incidents, in abrupt glances over shoulders at things that weren't there, in locked doors and hung garlands of garlic, and in softly spoken evening prayers to several kinds of gods for protection.

Gary met Lon already waiting at his car. He had taken off his jacket and was sweating heavily, wiping his forehead and eyebrows with a handkerchief. The sun beat mercilessly down, and they had to open all doors of the police car and wait a few minutes till most of the assembled heat had left from what felt like a furnace. While smoking a cigarette, they exchanged opinions on what they had tried to unearth amidst the circus people. Results were practically negative as they had expected. Nobody had seen anything unusual, nobody had remarked upon anything.

But they also both shared a feeling which hung like a cloak over the circus, an aura of suspicion, not merely because they were policemen asking questions, but a feeling which was hard to define, an almost expectant feeling of menace, something on which one couldn't place a finger but which was always just hiding in the shadows.

'I can't place it,' Lon said, 'they give you a creepy feeling, as if they suspect something is watching them all the time, waiting for them to turn their backs to attack them.'

'Suspicious fools, all of them,' Gary said, 'you've heard yourself what the director said about the vampire thing. Useless of course, they all knew.'

'You too? Seems something like this spreads rapidly. Still I wouldn't say they are all suspicious fools. I talked to a few quite educated people. They're not stupid, Gary, they just attach much more importance to such supernatural things as vampires than we care for.'

'Come on, don't fool yourself. What do you want us to do, open every grave in search for some bloodthirsty count, lying asleep in one of them, waiting for the next night to come? We're in no horror film studio, you know. If we're looking for something—and that's what we're supposed to be doing, and what we're paid for—it will be something quite human.'

'You don't believe we'll find something yourself, do you, Gary? You know as well as I that the whole thing stinks. It's a routine accident. I wonder why Hank has given us this one, he's smart enough to know for himself that there's nothing in it.'

'You don't think he's got it in for you?'

'I can't help getting that impression, Gary. Ever since I asked for a transfer to the administrative department, Hank has done his damnedest to give me all the lousiest cases. Well, he won't have the chance for much longer. My transfer is due next month. I'm splitting up with Homicide.'

'I can't see you getting used to such an inactive service as Administration. Classification of files in alphabetical and number order, filing reports, writing letters. Ugh, not for me, Lon!'

'Oh, I won't mind that so much. Besides Liliane definitely wants it. At first I thought it was only one of her whims, you know how pregnant women are. But she's made up her mind, and you know, maybe she's right, for her as well as for me, now with the child coming soon. I've waited some time before deciding to have a child, and in that time I've seen more than my share of the action and of Homicide. I don't think it's good for her in her condition; she knows I have the habit of getting into the dangerous parts of the business every time. Administration will be quite a restful change. But that's no reason for old Hank to start picking on me. He knows, after all, I'm not transferring for some personal dislike or something.'

'That's what made me wonder.'

'Well, maybe Accidents have put him in the same position he's put us in now. But well, an assignment is an assignment. And it isn't a hard one... We'll look around a bit and next week we'll make our report for "accidental death". And that'll be that.'

So they thought.

Boro looked up at the night. The darkness stretched out from the black star-holed sky, a shadow-fog over the world and the circus tents and caravans, in only a few of which small lights still burned. The magician was still up, Boro saw, and he heard the slight scratching sound of his metal saw. Probably working again on one of his trick boxes, sawing a bit here, painting a bit there, the hard wooden boxes with the sparkles of gold and silver, which turned into mirrored magic under the cold spotlights. There was a stifled mumbling roar from the animal cages, as one of the lions turned sleepless in his confinement. At two places Boro saw other shadows standing before their caravans, unable to sleep, yet also unable to define what made them sleepless.

Boro knew. He felt the tension, the uneasiness crawling through the night like some unseen slimy creature. He felt it in the feather touch of the night wind on his hot face, he tasted it in the smells that reached his nostrils through the stale air. Boro knew the animals were restless because they were as he was, they lived to live and didn't care for very much else besides their primitive needs. All their primary senses were designed for just that—they smelled the danger as Boro had felt it the very first evening. Just as he did, they knew the thing was somewhere near, waiting. Something small, they knew, and something very hungry. It had fed, it would feed again, and it wouldn't wait so long this time. That first show, Boro had sensed it but hadn't cared, as it hadn't been hungry. It had just been something which was there, which he had acknowledged as a presence and then discarded in the back of his head as something unimportant.

Then it had struck. It had fed.

And it had liked the food.

It was very primitive, it had no intelligence and it didn't reason, but it had the cunning of the wild animal. And it was hungry, more hungry every day, but it didn't feed every day. Like a gourmet, it waited, letting the hunger and the strain build up to a semi-sexual desire, until it couldn't restrain itself any longer. Then, and only then, it struck.

The other circus people felt it also, Boro knew, but not as he did. They felt uneasy, nervous, without being able to tell why. Boro could have told them, but no one asked him. No one ever asked Boro anything, except "do this, do that, and hurry up a bit", and that was sufficient. Boro did this and did that, and he hurried and was content.

But now it had taken Elairie and had hurt Boro. He began to hate the small hungry thing for that. It was long since he had tasted hurt; he had gotten used to it, absorbed it when he was young, and after Boro had grown up nothing could hurt him, nothing could sting deep enough to hurt Boro, because he didn't care for anything or anyone. Except Elairie.

'I'm home, Lil,' Lon called, closing the front door behind him. As he entered the living room, his wife Liliane rose from the couch, wiping the sleep out of her swollen eyes.

'Oh, already. I'm sorry, Lon, I must have fallen asleep.'

'Did you enjoy the TV show?'

'Show? Oh, I must have seen parts of it, but I can't remember much of it, you know how they put these things together. Must have been awfully boring for me to fall asleep while watching it! Give me your coat, I'll have dinner ready immediately.'

'Oh, don't bother. I can easily fix something in a hurry myself. You just lie down and rest.'

She laughed, as she came over to him and kissed him. 'Come on now, Lon, I'm not sick or anything, and I don't need *that* much rest. I'm already glad to be able to do something once in a while. You'll see, there'll be something to eat in a minute.'

'It's just that you seem awfully tired lately.'

'Well, it's not only tired, I'm mainly bored, sitting here alone with you out till late at night.'

'You were asleep yesterday also when I got home.'

'No wonder, with those stupid shows they've been showing on TV lately, and you know I can't concentrate on reading. Books bore me after the tenth page. So what else do I have left?'

'Well, it'll be better soon now, honey. My replacement comes in next week, and next month I'll be transferred off to inactive service. Then it'll be finish at six o'clock in the evening, like an ordinary office worker.'

'I'm glad for you, honey.'

'And for yourself also, no doubt!'

Yvana, the witch, was sitting before her caravan, her veiled eyes watching the movement of things she alone could see in the darkness, as the circus director Morbani came up behind her. She didn't move when his gloved hand touched her shoulder, though she couldn't have seen or heard him approach.

'So it's you, Mr. Morbani,' she hissed softly. 'Quoi de nouveau? Why do you come here to the old insane woman, when you should be at the performance which is now going on?'

'There is talk, Yvana,' Morbani answered, keeping his voice low. He lit one of his long cigarettes, watching the little clouds of smoke wriggle up to the sky as ragged spiderwebs.

'I know,' Yvana said, 'the people are afraid. They cross themselves and they look at me with hostility though it isn't me they fear. They are scared of the vampire.'

'I guessed you already knew. My people are alert, very alert and nervous. I don't like that, it isn't good for the circus.'

'There isn't much we can do about that.'

'Nervous strain is dangerous, Yvana, it causes accidents. And we've had enough of them. What is behind it?'

'Who knows? Maybe only talk, maybe something else. There are things in the space of empty air between you and me now, things we can't see or smell or touch or hear with our senses, but they are there nevertheless. There are worlds besides ours, some are bright and some are dark. I know some of these worlds and can control them, and I also know the others and fear them. Ce ne sont pas nos mondes,

Mr. Morbani, it is better to leave them alone.'

'Maybe, and maybe not. What do *you* think about the... vampire?'

She looked sidewards up at the tall dark shrouded figure behind her. His face was a black spot against the darker night sky, and the tip of his cigarette seemed a red burning star, a crimson evil looking eye.

'What should I think, Mr. Morbani? I have looked in my crystal, and there was no answer. I have cast the bones, and they spelled danger. Sometimes I imagine I can smell that danger, and it is here, something which does not really belong, something which has come into existence and which is very old and very evil, an evil which is not quite human. I can feel its evil and its hunger in the air all around us now, dripping its anticipation and horror all over us. But there my power ends. I do not know what it is or where it lies waiting. I can't fight it.'

She silently stroked Tana's black crawling fur. The cat had crept up beside her and was purring very softly now, a sweet penetrating humming in the brooding air.

'Can't you do something to calm them down a bit?'

'You know they fear and yet respect me, Mr. Morbani. But I can't do anything, because they won't accept anything from my hands. They are afraid of something of the dark world, and I too am of the dark side of things. So whatever I try to do will only cause more unrest, and will only bring their fears out of hiding. We can only sit back and wait.'

'Wait for what? Until they openly refuse to perform? Until their suspicions and fears erupt into a panic? There must be a way, Yvana. What goes around is only a whisper. There is not the slightest proof of anything unearthly causing Elairie's death?'

Yvana smiled a near toothless grin. Like a snake's her tongue licked her small cruel lips. 'The dark world consists of whispers,' she murmured to herself, the cat and the night sounds of the circus, 'the dark world is full of whispering things... They don't *want* proof.'

'I don't care for your dark world, Yvana. My people need reassurance. There's only that cursed word "vampire" the dying girl spoke. But there is no vampire, damn it. She just plainly fell through her own stupid fault. Nobody came near her to drink her blood, no bat visited her at night.'

'Do *all* vampires drink *blood*, Morbani? Did she really mean a blood-sucker, or was it just a hint she wanted to give us, to something which she had no time left to describe.'

Morbani stood glaring angrily at the old woman for a long time. Then when the blaring trumpets sounded from the great performance tent, he turned on his heel and walked away.

Tana kept on purring as Yvana's old brown fingers silently stroked her back.

Small shards of early sunlight crept inside and touched Boro's open eyes. The twilight shades were disappearing, but the nightly dark-ness in his head didn't go away, and neither did the sickening empty pain in his mind. The whole night through he had been speaking to Elairie's ghost face, which had drifted through his caravan; she had been speaking to him as if she was still alive and not buried under two metres of heavy earth and withering flowers, and the mirth of her silver laughter still rang in his ears. Reluctantly Boro got up and went outside, in the meantime taking a few bites from a dry loaf of bread he had still lying around from two days ago. He washed it down with a drink from a rusty bucket of rainwater which stood outside his caravan. The water was soiled and mud had formed a moving silt in the bucket, but such things didn't bother Boro. When he looked up, he saw Frank walking by, and an unreasonable anger welled up in Boro. He had never liked Frank, with his un-deformed, strong and healthy body, his so semi-intelligent way of talking and bragging and his luck with women. Damn Frank with his handsome masculine face and his skill on the trapeze, damn Frank who had been Elairie's husband, slept with her and made love with her, and who hadn't even shed a tear when she died. Then Frank disappeared from sight behind a tent, and Boro cut him out of his mind as he passed out of sight. But the pain inside still wouldn't go away, and that too angered Boro.

Then he saw the stranger coming again to talk to him.

The darkness was soothing, as it slept. It rested, curled up, its small body slowly moving as it breathed. It was well fed, even bloated for the time being. Outside things were stirring, it felt instinctively in its sleep; a mounting of strain which it appreciated very much, but didn't react to for the moment.

It had no memories of a beginning of its existence, it just felt that it was. There was no sense of the passing of time, only the impulsive realization that now, it wasn't hungry. Its only estimate of time was between each feeding, and somehow it knew that these intervals were getting shorter and shorter. It needed more and more food. It would have to feed soon now...

Gary looked at the bulky man whom he was approaching, and he couldn't hide the disapproval out of his face. That guy really stank, probably he hadn't washed in weeks. But there was nothing else to do except dismiss his revulsion and follow the only small clue he had, no matter how boring that would prove to be. Something which this man Boro had said yesterday kept on returning to his mind. He had discounted it as nonsense at first, but somehow it kept on haunting Gary, so he had decided to pay another visit to the campgrounds of the circus after all.

'So here we are again,' he said brightly, 'beautiful day, isn't it?'

The man just stood there, staring at him with those open uninterested eyes, an unmoving wax example of a typical moron. He didn't even bother to answer Gary or to acknowledge his presence, and Gary felt very much like giving him up entirely. There wasn't anything this moron could tell him which would help the quest. But then, there was no other lead and his inborn stubbornness prompted Gary to continue.

'You don't mind me talking to you, do you?'

'Just what do you want from Boro?' the other grunted. His teeth were as bad and as dirty as his hands and clothes. Like time-yellowed tombstones they stood in the ruined graveyard of his mouth.

'You said something yesterday which I remembered and it doesn't make much sense to me. So I decided to come back for a chat and ask you. What did you mean when you said "something small took her"?'

There was no other response but the drawing up of the lids over his blood-shot eyes, cold and staring as those of a fish. Boro didn't move, he stood there, statue like, waiting.

'You *did* say it, you remember?'

'I said that something small took her. That's all, there's nothing else to add.'

'But what something? Why did it take Elairie? How did it take her, and for what purpose?'

'Boro doesn't know. Boro feels the something small, it is in the air, it makes people restless. It has been here since we arrived. You must feel it too. That is all.'

'But why did it take Elairie?'

Boro kept on looking at the policeman, his eyes small red slits against the glaring sun. Somehow he wanted to tell this man because he was trying to find the cause of Elairie's death and maybe would avenge her. But he couldn't because one had to feel the something small, and therefore one had to be *like* Boro. It couldn't be explained in simple words, and Boro didn't know any others. So he lost interest, turned his back on the policeman and walked away.

Gary stood there, feeling like a damn fool. Then he cursed and went to buy himself a good drink on office time.

Yvana was sitting on her big shawl, carelessly thrown on the ground. With her shrunken legs crossed under her thick multi-coloured dress, her one earring burning brightly in the afternoon sun, she was idly playing games with her fortune cards. Boro walked up to her and sat down before her. She acknowledged his presence by looking up at him with one eye, before going on with her cards. Tana, the black cat, came gliding out of the shadows under the witch's caravan, evaded Boro, and sat down beside her mistress. She looked intently at Boro with her unblinking split eyes.

The silence and the heat beat down upon them, smothering them in languor. Even Yvana's hands were slower than usual as they made a love dance over the glittering cards like two brown scorpions in the mating season. Like the shards of a thousand imaginary lives, the little coloured cards, which spoke of life and love and death and immense fortunes no one ever reaped, glittered over the brown grey earth and the dry, once green grass.

'What is it, Boro?' Yvana asked suddenly, her voice a shrill wincing sound. 'Tu veux savoir le futur? Oui?' It was a rhetorical question and the witch knew it, as did Boro.

'Keep your lying futures for yourself and the fools who believe in them,' Boro grunted. He took a small pebble and tossed it lightly at the cat, very careful not to hit it. The beast made a retreating motion and bared its fangs in a short angry hiss, fury sparkling out of its flaring eyes like green fire.

'Tu ne doit pas faire ca, Boro,' Yvana rebuked. 'Don't do that. Tana doesn't like those kinds of games. She won't like you for them either.'

Boro laughed, a barking sound somewhere deep in his muscled throat, without any real mirth. 'Tana never liked me,' he said, 'and she knows I won't really hit her. Besides, Tana hates everyone.'

'Pas moi,' Yvana remarked shortly.

'No,' Boro said, 'not you.'

Yvana gathered the cards and began re-dealing them. 'So you don't want my futures,' she said, 'though there is truth in them, very much truth, for those who want to hear it. Well, no matter. Then what *do* you want from the witch, Boro?'

'Why should I tell you what you already know, Yvana?'

Yvana didn't answer; all her attention was fixed on the cards. Then she shoved them angrily away into a heap of coloured lifeless paper. She took her rune sticks and threw them. They fell upon each other in insane, boned patterns. Her nicotine brown fingers with the long, dirty and broken fingernails began to follow the pattern, creating other images in the empty air above the sticks.

Suddenly she looked up at Boro and pointed at something above his head. He looked and saw a lonely sparrow sitting near its destroyed nest, not far away in one of the trees.

'This morning,' Yvana said, 'Tana took her early walk into that tree. When she came back there was blood on her jaws and small feathers. The bird is alone now, it is aching inside. Nothing can change that hurt, nothing can stop the pain, because it is inside. So don't ask me, Boro.'

They sat looking at each other for a long time, their eyes fixed on Yvana's fingers, which were scurrying over the sticks like empty-bellied leathery spiders. Boro stood up, but as he started to walk away, Yvana said, 'Attendez!'

Slowly he turned around and faced her, and doing so he felt the emptiness and the pain that devoured his insides reaching out to her through his eyes.

'You don't like the pain, do you, Boro?' Yvana asked. He didn't care to answer her, and she smiled, her dry cruel lips drawing up above yellow broken teeth. 'But *it* does, Boro, *it* does. Remember that, remember Elairie and the pain *she* must have felt when she fell and died, then think of the hurt inside yourself and put them together into a mountain of pain, and then remember that *it* loves the pain.

She seemed incredibly old and evil, though Boro knew that she couldn't be as old as she seemed to be. He turned in disgust and walked away. Yvana stared grinning at his broad back, then turned again to her sticks.

Two days passed in heat and sunlight and shadow filled nights, and the lurking darkness slowly seemed to fade from the circus grounds as nothing out of the ordinary happened. Slowly the fear filtered out from strained nerves and a kind of peace settled down.

Morbani had just finished his dinner and sat down with a final glass of bitter wine when there was a knock on his door. Angrily he pushed his drink aside. The damn fools knew that he didn't like being disturbed at this hour of the day when he wanted his rest!

'Come in,' he called, and Boro came in, nervously wiping his clumsy sweating hands on his pants. Somehow his hands didn't really seem to belong to his body—he never knew what to do with them while talking.

'Well, I'll be... Master Boro! What can I do for you?' The sarcasm was completely lost on Boro, as Morbani had known it would be. This clown had no sense of humour or sarcasm. Sometimes Morbani had wondered if some of his people, including Boro, had any senses at all, if they even knew and cared that they lived, or if they went to their tasks and through the daily routines like so many puppets he controlled.

'May I... may I ask something, Mister Director?'

'Why, sure, Boro, anything to please you!' Morbani said, his voice sharp and cutting now. 'Doesn't the fool Boro know that his director dislikes being disturbed in the hour after noon?'

'Yes, yes I know, Director Mister Morbani. Should I come back later and ask?'

'Oh, to hell! Go ahead, Boro, what do you want?'

'I would like to do the trapeze number in the show.'

There had been only a few scarce times when Morbani hadn't immediately known what to say, and this turned out to be one of these times. It just went too high above his head, this unimaginative freak wanting to do a show only Frank and Elairie had been capable of. He couldn't be serious, could he?

Then Morbani laughed, all his accumulated nervous strain relaxing and exploding in a fit of high pitched shrieking laughter. Boro didn't react to this; he just kept on standing there. He didn't exactly appreciate the near hysterical howling sounds his director made because he had asked very seriously for something, and to Boro there was not the smallest reason for laughing at that. But then, neither did the humour hurt him, so he decided to wait for a clear and straight answer from Morbani.

'I have done the number before, Mr. Morbani,' he explained as an afterthought.

Morbani wiped his lips with an embroidered handkerchief, his initials in gothic scarlet letters on the white silk. 'Sure you have Boro, sure you have, but wasn't that a very long long time ago? And it wasn't a serious number either, was it? In fact I think I remember we cancelled it because the public wouldn't laugh at it anymore.'

'I can still do it. I would like to do it.'

'But you won't!' Morbani's temperament swung back on the fulcrum, changing in an instant from the shudder of mad laughter to the glowing of frustrated anger. 'Frank is very capable of doing the number alone until I find another able trapeze artist. I have already given him my instructions. Now get out, go clean the animal stables.'

Boro went out to clean the stables as he had been told. Morbani watched him leave with a disgusted expression on his face. He tried to recall the number Boro had once performed on the trapeze, which hadn't been so high in his time. Boro hadn't been bad at all, but when they had brought Frank and Elarie on the new trapeze, the public acclaim had been much greater. Two long poles were erected in the tent, each with a small platform on top and with a trapeze in between. The artist mounted to the first platform, and then began through his body and leg movements to move the pole, the platform, and himself forward and backward in the direction of the second pole. There were no hand holds anywhere, and when the moving pole and platform had reached their proper momentum, the artist jumped, his hands reaching for the trapeze and so on to the second platform. In fact it was quite a simple number, but as it was performed very high and with the necessary introductions and warnings about the danger involved, it was still a success.

Morbani turned his attention away and back to his glass of wine. The early evening sun broke through the window, sparkling in a colourful prismatic spectrum in the bloodlike red swirls of the fluid in his glass.

When Lon got home that evening, Liliane was sitting on her sofa, her face the deadly white of the surrounding clinical wallpaper. He dropped his jacket on the ground and ran over to her.

'What's the matter, honey? Are you all right?'

'Oh, it's nothing really, Lon, I'm fine. But I had a horrible fright this afternoon Haven't you heard it yet in the office?'

'I have been away on a routine assignment all day; it was so late that I came straight home without checking in first. What is the matter? What frightened you?'

'The thing that happened at the circus...'

'At the circus? When? What happened?'

'I was there late in the afternoon. I just felt so restless and alone inside these closed walls, so I decided to go for a short walk. I went to have a look myself at the circus, and when I got there I just wanted to see the animals on show. So I bought a ticket and looked around a bit, and then it was just feeding time, so I decided to stay and watch and... oh, Lon, it was a nightmare. They tore and ripped and ripped...'

She was sobbing against his chest now, and he clumsily patted her on the back. 'Easy now, honey, control yourself. What happened?'

'One of those circus men came to feed them. He went in... into the lion's cage with a bucket full of pieces of bloody flesh. There was a big crowd around, men and women and children watching. Then suddenly he dropped everything, stumbled shrieking to the lions and... and kicked them, kicked them in their faces with his boots.

They seemed stunned for a second, then they rose as one and went for him, and he went down with them all growling and snarling on top of him. Oh, I can still see it all before my eyes, the mass of yellow hair and manes and bared teeth, and the stink of the beasts and the blood, all the blood, and all the time he was shrieking and then screaming, screaming...'

'Please calm down, honey, this isn't good for you in your condition. You shouldn't have been there, you shouldn't have watched. I'll call a doctor...'

'Oh no, that isn't necessary, Lon. I'm calm now, but it was a horrible thing to see. And all those people just stood there at first, staring and gasping, almost as if they enjoyed the thing. There was a big man from the circus also, and he could have helped immediately, but he didn't, he just kept on standing there, looking.'

Something in her last words struck Lon. There was no precise reason for his question; he just grasped for the last thing she'd said— he would have asked anything to get her attention away from the incident itself. So he asked, 'That man, who was he? Can you describe him in detail? It might be important, you never can tell.'

Which she did, with the astounding almost photographic memory for detail he had always admired in his wife, and something did "click" in his mind. He remembered that description too well, from what Gary had told him. There could be only one man in the circus who fitted that picture so well.

The telephone rang.

'So there you are,' Gary said, looking up from his notebook as Lon entered and dropped his coat on a chair.

'I came here as soon as I received your telephone call,' Lon remarked, 'I was just home from that routine job they gave me this afternoon.'

'Yes, I know. We tried to reach you at your place before, but no one answered. Was Liliane out maybe?'

'Yes, unfortunately she was. She was there when it happened.'

'What? The new accident? Then you know already?'

'Yeah, Liliane told me everything, eye witness report. Gave her quite a shock, damn it. It couldn't have happened at a worse time.'

'Nothing bad for her I hope? Good that she's a strong woman, no nervous breakdowns or things like that. Well, I won't have to fill in many details then?'

'No, I don't think so, unless you know something new beyond what actually happened?'

'No, I don't think so. Another very illogical accident... animal feeder dropped all he carried and just jumped shrieking into the waiting jaws of a couple of very hungry lions. Seems he even kicked them. No sane man would behave like that! Neither would the animals react as violently as they did, seems they're usually quite tame, even when they haven't been fed yet. Yet they really tore him into pieces. Quite a butchery.'

'I've heard that from Liliane, besides something else which might interest you. That weird fellow you've talked to twice, the unresponsive one, he was there too.'

'That guy Boro? When it happened?' Gary asked.

'Yes, that one. Liliane said he just stood there without doing anything to help.'

'Well, it wouldn't surprise me from that guy.'

'I got a call from Morbani also.' Lon said. 'He's scared as hell, though he refused to admit it. Seems he's afraid his people will refuse to perform if something doesn't happen quickly. Talk's running wild in the circus and he's afraid his people will try something on their own.'

'What can they do?'

'Morbani fears panic or mob violence, against anyone they are likely to find suspicious. Well, we can't do much against that. I have sent a few cops over to the circus grounds, just to walk around and look important and watchful. I hope that'll put an end to any mob ideas they might have. But otherwise there's no fresh blood—no pun intended—in the case. I just wish we could drop the whole thing. I have sent two photographers to take a couple of pictures during the shows, a series of close-shots from the crowd and from the performances. Not that I think that will do any good, but it will give the impression that we're working hard on it. And you never know, maybe it'll bring up something which we've overlooked so far. Not that there is much to look at!'

***

The phantom of nameless fear, and the resulting anger at anything and anyone at all, began slowly to spread over the circus grounds like a parasitic slug. Nerves were brought to breaking point, resulting in small fights for silly reasons, in curses and bad work, and in many silent prayers to five different gods.

Yvana came to her caravan, her long multicoloured gown trailing behind her like an old peacock's tail. The general distrust, the up-building emotional turmoil of repressed horror and unvoiced terror were forming a darkening cloud around her. It was a dangerous kind of fear, because these were all grown up people who couldn't admit that they were frightened by something unknown, so they hid their fear. But something would cause it to erupt from its burying place, and then there would be no stopping it. They would become a blood thirsty mob, out for someone's blood, *anyone's* blood, if they thought him or her to be responsible for the impossible accidents.

She hoped that she wouldn't be the victim. Yvana knew herself to be the prime suspect of the circus people, as she had always been when something went badly wrong. Oh, they liked her all right, most of the time, and they used to come to her to hear their good fortunes and for small protections or curative charms, but she was still an outsider, sometimes respected, sometimes hated, but always shunned even by those she had helped. She was a part of the dark world, and they liked to touch that world now and then like a child touching the fire, but they didn't want personal friendship with someone who knew about the darkness and the night things.

She went inside.

And saw her cat.

Tana was hanging upside down on the wall, her feet wide spread in crucifixion. From the mouth, forever opened in a silent scream, and from the gaping cut throat, a dark stream of blood, long dried, had run down the wall in crazy scarlet patterns. A piece of paper, loosely torn from one of the circus posters, had been nailed under the cat's body, and though the blood had made dirty smears on it, the crudely lettered text was still readable. "KILL THE WITCH", it read.

The fools, Yvana thought after the first shock had worn off, bitter-ness rising in her like vomit, the bloody damned cursed fools! Did they really think that killing and mutilating her beloved Tana would help them, would stop the horror from striking again?

She couldn't help the impotent tears running down her cheeks, as she removed the body from its spider-like location on the wall. She had loved Tana, and the cat had liked her as much as a feline can care for a human being without giving up its proud independence. Yvana had to use a knife to get the body off the nails, and all the time an ice cold fury was rising in her,.

Afterwards, Yvana began to throw the bonesticks.

Boro was sulking in his caravan. So the fools didn't want him to do the trapeze, they thought he couldn't do it. But he could, Boro was dead certain of that, he still could do it better than any of them. Maybe not as good as Frank, but still better than anyone else. And he *had* to do it, for Elairie. If they would only let him.

The animals were restless again, the smells of fury and blood were still in their nostrils after their recent kill.

Something small was still hungry...

Grey-green smoke curled up from the copper bowl, placed upon a three-legged black stool. In fine shroud-like threads like ghostly fingers, the smoke moved slowly around the body of the black cat and the scarlet shawl upon which it rested. A candlestick with seven long black candles threw a flickering light over the proceedings, creating bulky shadows in the dark corners.

Yvana was handling the sticks, not the long wooden ones she used for simple fortune telling, but the small white ones with the knotty ends that made rattling noises as she threw them, intoning softly to herself in a changing pitch. Her room was covered with black and dark red. Tapestries woven with bizarre and frightening symbols and designs hung on the walls and over the windows.

Three times she threw the small bones, before she laid down the old parchment beside the dead cat. Then she turned the body on its back, in vain trying to push away the feet that were already rigid in rigor mortis. She took the rusty knife with the short delta-blade and the Aztec symbols, and cut open the body from the throat to the belly in one short snakelike stroke. Her fingers twisted something in the exposed insides. Then Yvana took the jar which she had prepared before and dripped a few drops of a pungent, colourless fluid in the open belly.

She didn't look up from her task when the door was softly opened behind her and closed again. She knew the door had been locked, and only one person had another key besides her.

'Mother!' a shocked voice said behind her, 'You once said you would *never* use the Mgai-ritual again, not together with the Eibor manuscripts.'

'Sit down and be silent,' she cursed. The smoke kept on coming in thick clouds now, obscuring the walls and the hideous grinning face of the copper statue , which lurked evilly down on the opened body of the dead animal. Yvana continued her chanting, making seven small cuts in the entrails of the cadaver. The knife made rasping sounds as it touched the exposed bones, while the nightly visitor turned his face away in disgust. Yvana wetted her fingertips in a bowl, filled with a dark slimy liquid. Then, murmuring insane words in an unknown tongue, she put her thumbs on the dead staring eyes of the cat and pressed, until they melted and ran away under her hands. Then she cleaned her fingers and the knife.

'I *had* to use the Mgai-ritual,' she said. 'You should know that by now, it's the only way to find out. Something is outside there, waiting, lurking, and striking. I have read the words from the Eibor manuscripts, and made the seven cuts of the spider. We *must* know.'

'But will we?'

She rose and covered the mutilated body with the soaked red shawl. The candles gave a flickering form of moving evil to her nearly mummified skin, her face seemed a wrinkled mask of age, her eyes unseeing dark holes into prehuman times.

'We have to wait,' she said, 'the ritual needs time to work. Tana has been filled with the evil of those who feared and hated and killed her. Now I have taken out that evil, and sent it out as a messenger through the night. He for whom it is meant will hear the message, and will come.'

'Well, let us hope.'

'Go back to sleep now, my son. You've troubles enough of your own.'

'Our troubles concern the same thing, Yvana. The same thing. Good night.'

The man went away, and Yvana blew out the seven candles, one by one, murmuring an incantation by every one.

And from under the caravan, where he had been lying and listening for some time, someone else crawled and hurried away.

It felt hungry again. Slowly it left its hiding place, something small, something hungry. It tasted the crowd, the many many waiting thoughts, the mounting expectation of something to happen, the inhuman hunger for the horrible, the sickening expectation of death. It let itself drift on the excitement like a swimmer mounting the surf of hot thoughts and feelings. The hunger was nagging now, almost pain, more overwhelming, more important each minute, but it was careful. It didn't reason things out, but it was cunning, and instinctively it let the tension mount, mount, higher and higher till it reached a breaking point.

Then it struck.

And fed.

That evening during the performance, another woman died. Calvin Louisan had never missed a throw in his whole career, and he handled his tools with the craftsman's certainty of many years experience, and—for show—with the lightheadedness of a clown. His number had been one of the highlights of circus Morbani for many years.

This evening his last knife ended up in the throat of his partner, burying itself deep through the flesh and her spine and piercing the circular wooden target underneath.

Calvin cried the whole night through that someone had stopped his hand when he threw the knife, until they gave him an injection which made him sleep.

The crowd gathered silently, the first ones, the nameless leaders coming out of their dark caravans like night shadows. Then others joined them, there was not much talk, only a few whispered words here and there. In small groups they came, until they were all before the unlit caravan.

Someone lit a torch, and then others followed his example. Their faces became hideously distorted into caricatures of the human race by the dancing light of the flames, the mob fury cutting lines in their features, the fear burning in their glassy eyes. Someone threw the first stone—there is always someone without a name who does. Glass splintered as the projectile struck one of the small covered windows. The door opened and Yvana looked out.

There was a short moment of petrified silence and movement, as if her appearance had put a stop to time during a shard of a second. Then she turned, and the mob yelled, 'Get the witch!' and moved with the quickness of a striking snake. Yvana tried to jump inside and throw the door shut behind her, but she wasn't quick enough. Hard, vicious hands clawed at her, feet blocked the door. The shrieking of the crowd dampened her protests as she was thrown in the middle of the circle of burning torches. Her shrieking and pleading for mercy, her proclaiming of her innocence, were all in vain.

The mass didn't want to hear her, didn't want her to be innocent. They needed a victim, and they had found one. Anonymous boots kicked her in the groin, stomach, and sides, fists were driven into her face. As they kicked and stomped her, someone was holding a glittering cross over her face. At first she tried to protect herself by rolling into a ball, but the pain left no place for logical reasoning. She tried to curse them, and then to scream, but screaming isn't so easy with a mouth full of blood and broken teeth. The kicking went on for a long time, till a burning torch was driven straight in her face. There was a long shriek which seemed to go on and on, and which stopped the mob. They stood staring down at the writhing, distorted creature at their feet, some wiped their hands on their clothes as if they didn't exactly know what to do next.

The torches were still burning around them as Morbani came bursting through the crowd. While he cursed like a lunatic, his long whip danced with snakelike strokes over their faces, leaving red stains where they were touched. They didn't defend themselves; their fury had burned itself out.

'You bunch of lunatic dumbheads, pigs, idiots,' Morbani shrieked at them. 'What did you think you were doing? Do all of you want the circus closed, half of you in jail and the rest on the streets without a

job? If the police find out about this, there'll be no more performances, no money, no food, but jail instead. Lynchings are out of time
and place, and so are witch hunts, you murderous bunch of pigs.
Who started this?'

There was no answer but the shuffling of feet and some murmured
protests. Then one of them spoke. 'She made bad magic. I heard it in
her caravan. She made black magic, and a woman died.'

There was a murmur of agreement from the crowd. Morbani
kneeled beside the groaning old woman and looked her over, while
whispering to her, 'Keep quiet, Mamma, your Marco will get you out
of this, but in heaven's name, keep quiet, let them think you're
unconscious.'

He straightened and yelled, 'You superstitious idiots. I should skin
you all alive, I should cut out your eyes and make you swallow them,
I should whip you all to death and I would, too, if it wasn't for the
performance. Go to your caravans and get yourself ready, I've seen all
your faces, and we'll talk about this later.'

The spokesman of the crowd stepped forward in the full light, a
black bulky figure, the burning torch still in his hand. 'She made bad
magic, Mr. Morbani,' he grunted, 'I heard it myself!'

Morbani's whip hung from his fingers, a long dark threatening
tentacle, full of waiting menace. The tip moved slowly like a tongue.
'So you have been spying around a bit, haven't you, Bunkel?' Morbani
hissed. 'I will tell you something, to you and all of you others. Yvana
has been making magic... *white magic* which I asked her to make. I
asked her to open the gates to the spirit world and talk to the dark
things, to find us a protection against the evil which is walking
among us. She has followed my orders, and what have you done? You
have nearly killed her, and wrecked her protection. You have acted
against my orders, you hulk of street dirt, you who have eaten the
food I have given you and lived on the money I paid you, you have
disobeyed *me!*'

There was a short dry crackling sound, as the long whip left the
ground and reached for Bunkel as if it were a grasping black finger,
and then there was a piercing shriek, followed by a sickening moaning.

Bunkel fell backward, then onto his knees, his hands over his face.

His mouth stayed open, issuing groaning sounds of pain, and blood began gulping between his spread fingers. Morbani extinguished the burning torch Bunkel had dropped, and his voice cut like ice through Bunkel's whining. 'I will deduct the price of a glass eye from your earnings at the end of the month, if you need one. But then, maybe you'll prefer a black patch—it will make you look more handsome. Be glad I don't give you up to the police, Bunkel. I could tell them many, many things about you which they'd be glad to learn.'

The bloodied tip of the whip began crawling over the earth in circling movements, like an animal searching for new prey. Then Morbani yelled, 'What on earth are you still standing here for, you bunch of lice? Get to your work, and take Bunkel to his caravan.' And almost as an afterthought, 'And get the old doctor and send him over here, if he isn't too drunk. He can see to Bunkel after Yvana.'

When they were gone and had taken Bunkel away, Morbani kneeled beside the old woman, glad that he hadn't needed the gun waiting in his pocket. Guns were noisy and a shot would have brought the police.

'I told you, Mamma,' he whispered, 'I heard the noise too late. But the doc will be here soon, and it'll be all right then.'

'No,' Yvana croaked, 'it won't. I'm not hurt so very much, the torch missed me but I made them think they'd hit me in the face. I screamed mostly to warn someone, but I'm hurting anyway. The fools kicked hard—I hope there's nothing broken except a few teeth. But they won't be all right, oh no, they won't. The message has reached, son, I could feel it when they were beating and kicking me, something small, something hungry... and it was feeding, feeding on me and on them, sucking and swelling and absorbing my pain and their hatred. It is still hungry...'

Lon was finishing a few reports—there was nothing else to do—when the envelope was delivered from the lab. He put his paperwork down and slit the envelope open. A set of pictures fell out, spreading like cards on his desk. He recognized the set of close-ups the photographers had taken during the circus performances. He sighed. What did Gary think they'd find in those?

Bored, he took them up and looked at them, one by one. Scenes from the performances—there was Morbani with his long whip and his horses, there Frank and his solo number on the trapeze, there the fat woman with the little dogs, then the magician with his mirror trick-boxes, and the clowns and animals and all the rest. Then he looked at the close-up shots of the crowd.

His heart stopped. He looked again and painfully started breathing again. He sat looking at one picture for a long time; then he dropped it in his pocket, took his coat and left a message for Gary. Then he ran out of the office.

Frank Cauber was cleaning a sparkling piece of pseudo-silver on his costume as Boro entered without knocking first. Frank looked up at the intruder, a frown on his forehead.

'What in hell do *you* want in my place?' he asked.

Boro hesitated; this was again one of those situations he didn't care to cope with. But he had made his decision, after all.

'I'd like to ask something,' Boro said.

'You... ask... something? From me?' There was a sarcastic sneer in Frank's voice which cut like a lancet knife through Boro's self confidence. The damn superiority of this man, who had a young strong body and a handsome face, and hands whose fingernails were never dirty or broken! Why did they all have to be so sarcastic because Boro wanted to ask something?

'Well, go ahead, ask. And then get the hell out of here, you're stinking again. Or should I say, as usual? Don't you ever wash, Boro? Or maybe you don't know what purposes water is used for, besides drinking? You know, water? The thing people use to clean themselves when they smell.'

Boro hated having to ask Frank. The begging itself didn't bother him very much—he was used to begging—but it was the fact that he had to beg from this cultured snob.

'I'd like to do the trapeze number this evening,' he said.

Frank's face froze for a moment in an unbelieving stare, then exploded in a thousand giggling fragments.

'You... on the trapeze? You're crazy, man, absolutely out of your silly mind! Boyohboyohboy, Boro, Our Man Boro on the trapeze, man, would they laugh, they would *howl!*' His voice, always on the edge of a shriek, cut painfully through Boro's ears. He didn't catch the humor of the situation; humor was something others understood and laughed about but which made no impression on Boro.

'You mean you don't want me to do the number?'

'I don't want you... Man, you must be drunk or high... but no, you're too stupid to take stuff... why even to dare coming here to ask me such an idiocy! I should throw you bodily out of my caravan for even daring to come in here without being asked, you worthless piece of shit. Why do you want to do my number, anyway?'

Frank had seated himself and the mirth was draining away from his face, which was slowly taking on a strange feverish look. Something was dawning in Frank's mind, a vague idea which he wanted to settle.

'Why *do* you want the number, Boro?' he asked again, his voice dangerously low now. He sat staring at Boro with hungry animal eyes, the spider in the top of her web, looking down at the twisting fly in its threads. 'Maybe... for Elairie?'

He had hit the bull's eye with that remark. He saw it in the sudden updrawing of Boro's eye muscles. So therefore the clown wanted the number as a kind of memorial act for Elairie. This was a game he liked to play, the kind of game he was used to. Frank liked to play with words and remarks; he greatly enjoyed using his knowledge of what made people tick inside their heads. Frank had always known the doglike loyalty—because he could hardly call it love—Boro felt for Elairie, and right now he decided he might as well have some fun out of the situation. Someone had once called Frank a psychological sadist, and maybe it was indeed the only correct term for the kind of person Frank was.

'And why for Elairie, Boro?' he smiled; 'maybe as a memorial to her grave, you know, kind of a symbolic monument? Her would-be lover who executes her task on the trapeze? Would you like that, Boro? I'm sure you would, else you wouldn't come asking.'

But Boro didn't react to the lurking cynicism, and the teasing went past his comprehension. He hated the insides of this man, with his smiling, sickening face, who had slept with Elairie and soiled her soft white body with his hands, who had kissed her and slept with her and been inside her, and who was now throwing mud in her dead face. But Boro's hate wasn't hot and burning, but very cold and cruel, something which had always been there and always would be, a constant hate against the whole world which despised Boro, and the world was now given a body and a voice in Frank. Even now, the hate wouldn't erupt if it hadn't been that Boro had come to ask something which he wanted, and Frank was refusing it. Boro had made up his mind, and what Boro definitely wanted he'd get. Frank's refusal left only one way out.

'Don't be afraid, Frank,' he said soothingly, 'it won't hurt very much.'

There was a sharp clicking sound as the switchblade flicked open.

Lon entered his house, still doubtful of what to do exactly. The picture felt like lead in his pocket, it glared at him through the fabric of his coat. Liliane welcomed him as usual, and he gave a tender little push against her swollen belly. Again he felt doubt stirring in his mind like a blind waiting animal. He shortly inquired how she felt and then ate in silence. His thoughts were running wild through his skull. He tried to tame them and bring them into logical order, but they refused to obey. All the while Liliane was looking at him with her bright grey eyes, so very clear and yet misty looking. She was more nervous than usual, he noticed, carelessly handling the cups and plates, but then no doubt her condition had something to do with that. Pregnant women are like that, one day in the heights of heaven, next day in the deepest depression and sulking for the most stupid of reasons.

When dinner was over, he settled down in his favorite chair and said, 'Liliane, come over here with me, will you?'

'In a minute, dear,' she called from the kitchen, 'as soon as I've finished these dishes.'

'I said, come here *now*,' he barked, and was surprised himself by the rudeness of his voice.

He had scared her too, because she came immediately and sat down.

'All right, Lon, you don't have to bite and bark, you know,' she said. 'What is it this time? You've been acting strange since you came in this evening. Is something wrong at the office? Or is it about your transfer.'

'No, it has nothing to do with that, Liliane,' he grunted. His fingers crawled stealthily over the picture in his pocket, as if he was doing something forbidden. 'Lil, we've never had secrets from each other, have we?'

'Of course not, Lon,' she laughed, 'Why should we?'

'All right then. Where were you last evening?'

Her eyes opened wide in surprise, then changed to mocking laughter. 'You aren't serious, are you Lon? Not the third degree! I was... but why should I tell you? I'm the suspect, I have the right to call my lawyer, right? How does it go, the warning you're supposed to read me, "Everything that you say or do from this moment on can be used against you", or something like that, correct?'

She was mocking him with her eyes, her fingers nestling in his hair like two wild birds beginning to build their nest on top of his head. He took her hands away and looked straight into her eyes.

'I'm asking you very seriously, Liliane. *Where were you?*'

'Why, I have been here the whole evening. You know that!'

'No, I don't. What did you do?'

'Do? When I'm alone? I washed the dishes, cleaned the house a bit, then watched TV.'

'What did you watch on TV?'

'I watched... I watched... "Heartbreak Show", and then an old comic film... I think...'

'No, you couldn't have. I checked the papers "Heartbreak Show" is every Tuesday only, and there was a horror film yesterday evening. You hate them, so you didn't watch that. And there wasn't a comic film on either channel. You did *not* watch TV.'

'Oh, but I did, I'm sure... only...'

A strange expression came over her face, as if she was staring through him, as if he wasn't really in the room and she was talking to someone else. When her voice came back, it was soft and strange and frightened. 'Lon... what did I watch? I... I can't remember. I remember turning on the TV set, and sitting down with a package of chips and a book, just in case it was a tiresome programme. Then the image came on and... and... I can't remember what it was. I can't!'

'Did you fall asleep?'

'Yes... yes, that must have been it. I must have tired myself too much, and I fell asleep before the programme started.

'And afterwards? When did you wake up?'

'I... I can't remember that either. I must have woken up, and gone to bed. Because you came home and I awoke, and I was fast asleep in bed.'

'But before, Liliane, *before*? Before you went to bed, where were you?'

Was she playing out a comedy sketch, he asked himself. He couldn't believe it, she seemed too sincere. She had never lied to him, but for everything there's a first time. But what if she really couldn't remember? But that sounded silly. He made his decision, and though knowing that he couldn't risk giving her a shock, neither could he really believe that she was sincere. He took the picture from his pocket and placed it before her on the table.

'This is where you were yesterday evening,' he said simply.

'Where I was? But Lon, this is silly. This is a picture from a crowd in... yes, in a circus.'

'This is one of a set of pictures taken yesterday evening in Circus Morbani during the performance. Almost everyone knows what happened, but it isn't in the papers yet; it'll be in tomorrow morning. There was another death yesterday evening. One of the elephants put his feet down on a girl lying under him. Crushed her into a mess of bloody pulp. They come closer now, at first with days in between, now two evenings in succession. Some of our people were there with cameras, taking shots of the audience, not really looking for something special. I saw the pictures an hour ago, and this is one of them. Look there, on the fifth row. *Look there, I tell you!*'

'But why... but... that's impossible. That's *me* there.'

'Yes, Liliane, you are sitting there in that crowd.'

'But that *can't be me*. It's insane! Lon, I wasn't there, I can't have been. It must be someone else who looks like me!'

She stared at him with panic filled eyes, the picture crumbling into a distorted paper sculpture in her twisting hands. She was looking through him.

'I wasn't there, it is someone else, I'd remember otherwise. I wasn't there, *I was not there... I... was ... not... there... I... must... say... I... was...*

not ... there... I was... not... there... was not... there... not... there...not... there... not... there...'

Her voice was raw, hoarse; like an animal cry it came gulping out of her throat. She wasn't seeing him any more, not even the room, but something else, beyond him, beyond the house.

He jumped up. 'Liliane,' he cried. 'Stop it!'

'I... WAS... NOT... THERE...'

Like a faltering record, stuck in the same groove, her voice droned on, endlessly repeating the same sentence, in short snarling words. He shook her, but her whole body was rigid. Then suddenly she slumped silently forward into his waiting arms.

After the doctor had left, Lon stared at his wife, lying on the sofa. The doctor had looked her over, but refused to give her anything. Instead he had handed a sedative to Lon and advised him to give it to his wife only if she really was in need of it. She was sound asleep now... her breathing labored but regular and the nervous crisis seemed to have passed completely. There was nothing to worry about, the doctor had said, she seemed perfectly all right. Pregnant women go from one small crisis to another, one just had to put up with their moods. As to the memory lapse, surely there was some explanation for that. Over-tiredness could cause some small lapses of memory. Anyway, the doctor would come back the day after tomorrow for a complete check up, if that was needed.

Lon was wondering. She really had seemed sincere, she *didn't* remember being at the circus. Then what was happening? Icy chills were running down his spine, as he felt the nagging presence of something which he couldn't put his finger on. Somehow Liliane was getting involved in the whole weird business... but how? And why? Could she have been drugged, or put under hypnosis? But by whom, and why? He remembered now meeting one of his wife's friends, a few days ago, who had asked him if Liliane had enjoyed the show at the circus, and his denial that she had been there. 'Such sensations aren't good for the baby,' he had mocked. But she *had* been there, though she refused to believe it. He was absolutely sure that she had been there that earlier time also, though she couldn't... or wouldn't... remember it.

Somebody didn't *want* her to remember going to the circus performances, somebody was using her in an inexplicable way for his purposes, using her as a focus... but for what? What reason could there be? Unless...

The thought came for the first time in its full hideous clarity. He had always thought exclusively about Liliane. Suppose there were others in the same situation? Some from the circus people, who had to be there every evening to do their numbers. And maybe some other people in the crowd, who went and afterwards couldn't remember it. There could only be one reason... a selection of victims. Almost all of the "accident" victims lately had been women.

What if Liliane was to be the next victim of an "accident"?

There had to be a clue somewhere. He remembered some of the stories he used to read, about folkloristic spells and such things as the pentacle in a werewolf's future victim's hand, or the Devil's Mark on witches. Such things didn't exist... *did they?*

The clue to the mystery must be somewhere in the circus. Hypnotism, mesmerism, black magic... they were all things used in circus numbers. Suppose the accidents and suicides that the Accidents Department had delved out of their files weren't really connected with *this* case? Gary as well as he himself had always had their doubts about those freak accidents. The case had really begun with the arrival of the circus... then the series of mysterious deaths had started with the fall of the girl, then that animal keeper, then the assistant of the knife-thrower, last the girl with the elephants. The deaths followed each other more and more quickly.

Well... this evening Circus Morbani held their final performance; they would leave tomorrow.

All the deaths would be classified as accidents, for there was no other solution. And maybe the horror would leave with the circus, leave this town and his wife alone.

He sincerely hoped so.

Something drew his attention to the floor, and he picked it up. It was the crumbled photograph. He stood looking at it for a long time, not unfolding it, not daring to look again at the face of his wife. Suppose... suppose it had really been his imagination, or someone who looked like his wife? It was possible, wasn't it? A picture could lie...

He brought out his lighter, and set fire to the picture. He threw it in an ash-tray, watching it burn with a small finger of curling smoke and a smell of burning celluloid. Then he disintegrated the remains into dust with his finger. He felt much better.

He went down to the refrigerator, took out a bottle of beer and settled down to watch TV and let his thoughts rest.

Boro had covered Frank's body very well; they wouldn't find it so easily. And, of course, as the hour of the performance drew nearer and nearer, Morbani got nervous, then frantic. And as the second part of the show began and Frank still didn't show up, and was not to be found in one of the cafes nearby, he reluctantly called for Boro, and announced to the crowd the new trapeze number with Boro.

Lon awoke with a blinding headache to the sound of his doorbell ringing. Dark moving clouds hung before his eyes, obscuring his vision of the TV set. The speaker on the show kept on making meaningless sounds, and the bell kept on ringing.

'All right, all right, I'm coming,' he murmured. 'Why don't you open it, Liliane? Liliane?'

He got up and almost sank to his knees and a needle of stinging red pain burned in his brain. He staggered to the door, his hands on his head. He turned the doorknob and let Gary in. Then, at the same time as he saw the terror spread over Gary's face, he noticed the red stains his hands had left on the doorknob.

'My god, Lon, your face! What happened?'

'My face? My face? I can't think, have a headache, a...'

Lon looked at his hands with the scarlet dripping from them. Gary walked over to the TV and shut it off, and Lon saw his face in the mirror with the dark shadow which ran from his temple into his collar, soaking his shirt.

'What happened, Lon? Who hit you? Where is Liliane?'

'Liliane? She's here. She's... *Liliane?*' The couch was empty. Liliane was gone. There was no time for explanation now. 'Do you have your car, Gary?'

'Sure, it's parked just around the block. Why...'

'Get going, quick. We must get to the circus.'

'The circus? But the show's started already. And where is...'
'I'll explain on the way. Let's go.'

Boro felt the first taste of the feelers of the something small as he climbed up the ladder to the platform. Tentative, searching, unsure still they touched his face inside his head and then withdrew temporarily. Higher and higher he mounted, and all the eyes stared up at him as the cold sweat lay on his back like chunks of broken ice. Then he was up, and the arena below settled down in comfortable darkness, absorbing the hungry eyes and faces and the open gasping mouths in a black shroud. There was now only the small platform, slowly balancing under the weight of his body as he stood up there, staring at the white burning eyes of the spotlights. They were all looking up at him now, and he felt the sensation begin to build up, gaining in momentum and mass, coming in like waves of a sea, waves that grew and grew, the suspense, the waiting for something to happen, and just below those waves was the thing the others called the "vampire".

He felt it quite definitely now, something very small and very hungry and very very deadly. But the thing was uncertain now, as if it sensed somehow that something wasn't as it should be.

It hesitated, hiding under the crest of the waves. Boro could almost smell the thing, so eager to feed and yet not daring to, and then Boro knew it wouldn't feed this night. It felt that he was different, it somehow felt that Boro knew of its presence, and maybe something in Boro's inner self frightened the creature.

At eye level, Boro saw the other platform; it seemed so infinitely small and distant, much farther away than when he had last done the number, but then that was long-ago. Boro was certain that he could reach the other platform. He began to move his legs and knees, spreading his legs till the tips of his toes almost reached the edge, then began the tumbling motion with his back, forward, backward. The darkness below came up and went down again together with the staring eyes of the spotlights.

While the car was roaring through the city like a bright-eyed phantom, Lon told Gary everything he knew and suspected. 'I must have fallen asleep while watching that damn TV show, and Liliane must have awoken and hit me with the ashtray so I wouldn't follow her. Or maybe she came to and hit me, without me hearing her behind me. Someone is controlling her, Gary, no matter how insane it may sound, someone is using her with some kind of hypnosis for his own purpose. Almost all the victims were women, and now she's there in the circus, I'm sure of that, and I'm afraid she's the next victim in line. Tomorrow the circus will be gone, so whoever wants her will strike tonight.'

'But who? And why?'

'Does it matter now at the moment? Maybe we'll never know. I only want Liliane safe from this thing. We've let ourselves be led on a dead end trail, hunting for a vampire. Whatever the thing is, it doesn't feed on blood. Maybe it feeds on death itself, who cares? Hurry up, we're almost there.'

Boro saw his shadow reflected at the top of the tent, a hideous caricature of a human being, a thing to be pitied, and suddenly he knew that it was like this that Elairie had seen him all those years, some lowly creature she knew, someone to say good morning and good night to, and maybe to laugh a bit with and pity him. He saw her face swimming up to him out of the dark and lonely places in his mind, those places he had securely locked up because they had made him cry when he looked into them. He remembered her through his years of loneliness, and he remembered how he had felt once when Frank had beaten her up, and how he, Boro, had dared to lift his hand and wipe the tears from her face, leaving a dirty streak of make-up and dirt from his hands on her cheeks, and then Boro knew that he loved Elairie, loved her as he had never imagined he could love another human being, something beyond his mind and body, loved her who was dead and buried under the heavy soil.

Forwards and backwards, his feet shifting over the platform, the trapeze and beyond that the other platform veered closer to him and then retreated again, following the motions of his distorted shadow on the tent sail. The helpless pain bubbled up in him, came up in shrieking wings out of the depths of his mind: she was dead dead dead, and she had never known his love for her and he had never known the silk of her body or even the knowledge of her sentiments, dead, her soft rounded golden haired body crumbling into dust and mummification among the crawling worms, in a suffocating coffin, her lips cold and forever closed in a frozen smile, her eyes unseeing, her heart no longer beating, and the pain, the cold cruel pitiless pain, soared up in cold waves, ran over his mind and body like screaming little creatures, and just below the screams he felt the excitement which came over the parasite, the almost sexual hunger which gulped in the lurking thing, somewhere down there in the waiting darkness, in hiding among the watching mass of nameless people. Forwards and backwards, the platform balanced, closer, farther, to and from the smiling face of Elairie whom he had loved and never possessed, and who was dead dead dead dead, and the pain was a spotlight burning red holes in his mind; he never felt the tears running down his distorted face of light and shadow.

Then he jumped.

The crowd was staring full of frightened fascination at the freakish clown figure, high up in the air, as Gary and Lon made their way through the audience, searching in the darkness for a well-known face.

'There she is,' Lon cried suddenly, at the instant as the man up in the air left the platform, his hands reaching forward into emptiness.

Boro flew through the emptiness towards the trapeze, his mind feeling the dizziness of flying. He knew he had succeeded when his fingers touched the trapeze, refused to close on it and he fell downward into the darkness. What happened didn't take a second, but it went on for an eternity for Boro. The vampire left his hiding place, jumped up to Boro in one grasping movement and was suddenly all over him, a hungry feeding crawling thing over his mind, sucking and absorbing all Boro had ever felt, the loneliness of his youth and the pain of the beatings he had taken, the emptiness and solitude of his life and the small joys he had felt for a job well done, the detached enjoyment he had felt cutting Frank into pieces and the pain and love he felt for Elairie.

As the body tumbled down, he grasped the thing crawling inside his head, grasped it with those things it fed on, smothering the parasite with a flood of emotions. Then he knew the real identity and nature of the vampire, and in a split moment of triumph he felt the shock and fear of the thing as it stopped its feeding and tried to leave him, but he held it, burying it under his own pain and dread, while the thing frantically tried to escape, but too late, too late, too late; the thing made a last panicking movement, as it and Boro both died when his body crashed on the ground.

The pregnant woman in the shrieking crowd was oblivious to the excitement and screaming all around her. Her wide open eyes staring into nothingness, Liliane grasped Lon's hand beside her and whispered, 'It kicked... the baby kicked...'

Then, in a strange far-away voice, 'it is quiet, now...'

MY FINGERS ARE EATING ME

"...with strange eons, even death may die."
(H. P. Lovecraft)

*T*HE MOUTHS BETWEEN *the worlds open and close,
following patterns which are still beyond our knowledge and
understanding. Through the centuries many groups have tried to
disclose the patterns, without much success. Now and then a
specially gifted individual managed a breakthrough, but mostly
didn't survive the results. If he survived what came out of the
Mouths, persecution and the burning stake were his destiny. The
smart ones went in hiding, writing down their knowledge and so
aiding those who came after them and continued their research.
Many of those books were destroyed or buried in closed cellars and
catacombs, but a few always survived as if in some way the beings
with whom the books dealt wanted them to survive, as if to confirm
their reality of existence. Even smarter authors disguised their
research as fiction or poetry, some even made a living of it. But
whether they were alchemist, magician, occult researcher, writer or
poet: they shared the knowledge that we are not alone on this world,
that this world isn't even ours. The Mouths have been active
millions of years, and most of the researchers imply that mankind
was the most recent offspring of some of the minor beings who came
through the Mouths.*

*During millions of years many times the Mouths, opening gates
between different worlds and realities, have spawned things on this
earth. The reports on those are varied and it's often impossible to
state what is possibly fact and what is straight myth. Were the Old
Ones really the first ones to come out of the abysses of darkness,
were the Shoggoths really the first life form they created on earth,
one thousand million years ago? What is the real story behind the*

war between the Old Ones and the race of Cthulhu, and his servants
of Dagon? As the Mouths opened and closed, other visitors followed:
the nameless cone-shaped beings, the abominable Blind Beings who
built their black basalt cities six hundred million years ago. Then
the Great Race came, and after them the Mi-Go. Many of these
beings are still worshipped as gods by small and secret cults, and it
may be the strength of that worship which keeps these gods alive,
though fortunately for mankind restrained by the Elder Signs. Some
of them shield their domains off from our reality, such as Cyäegha
and his Nagaäe, alive but hidden in Europa. Cthulhu dreams in the
sunken city of R'Lyeh somewhere in the Pacific Ocean, still
worshipped by the minions of Dagon and those who serve the
Waiting Dark. The gigantic library of the Great Race is said to be
somewhere under Australia. Most of these godlike beings brought
their own servants with them, and in due time they intermingled
with the others and even the human race, thus creating new strains
such as the Feeders.

(From the untitled book by Kazaj Heinz Vogel, as
rewritten as *Von denen Verdammten, oder: Eine Verhandlung
über die unheimlichen Kulten der Alten* [Of the Damned, or: A
Study of the Unholy Cults of the Ancients],
    by Edith Brendall, 1907).

IN THE APARTMENT OF GLEN CANMOOR, POLICE-
INSPECTOR (RETIRED):

Please, come in, make yourself comfortable. So you want to know all
about the nightmare, do you?

The nightmare started quite innocently. Don't they always? The
tenth of April, almost thirty years ago now. You were a small toddler
then, weren't you? No? Well, then you do look much younger than
you are. In my time a star reporter had to have quite a few years of
action behind his back before he got an assignment like this. But
then, let's be frank, you aren't a star reporter yet, are you? Yep, that's
what I thought. You think this interview is going to be your big
break? Who knows, it might be.

By the way, how did you trace me? It's been so many years, all I wanted is to keep quiet about the whole fucking business. Now you're here to start things up again. Yep, it's easy to see why: it's close to thirty years. The media like to remember things and happenings after decades: ten, twenty, thirty... who gives a shit. Oh, I just see the headlines: "Thirty years ago the horror began in the London subway", and so on. You really believe anyone will still care, after that time? It's all been buried and forgotten. But if you think you can make a hit out of it, go ahead. I'll even forget that you must have gotten my name and address by ways which certainly weren't legal. I did tell you on the phone that I do not want my name mentioned anywhere, remember! And I also made it clear that you don't gossip about my whereabouts or knowledge of all this stuff. I made an arrangement with you, and after this it's finished, I don't want any harassment afterwards.

Yes, do look around. Poor place to live in, isn't it? Not the kind of place you probably thought you'd find Glen Canmoor, retired police inspector, living. I hope the empty bottles of cheap whisky don't disturb you. Yes, I'm an alcoholic, have been since... then. I drink too much, more than is good for my health, more than I can afford with the bloody cut-price pension they have given me. But it helps me to sleep, without the constant nightmares. Which reminds me: you brought the money? Can I get it now? Thank you.

All right, it's what we agreed on. Not a fortune, but this will keep me in booze for some time. In exchange you get my story and copies of all the materials I could lay my hands on. And you will not reveal to anyone where you got this stuff, not even when the Yard is breathing down your neck. They always hated panic stuff. They managed to snuff this one before it got out to the great public. They covered it up nicely: "mad bombers in the Tube, we got them all". The public swallowed it all. Of course in the meantime they got some real Islamic bombers but they knew what they had on their hands then, no need for cover ups. They won't like it however if you start digging up what happened twenty-five years ago, especially not since some tabloids have started reporting on a few strange disappearances in the Underground.

You want to make the connection between those weird

happenings twenty-five years ago, and what is happening now. Go ahead, make the connections. It's time people hear the full truth, no matter how horrible that is. They shut me up very quickly then, just retired me out of the force. Cited mental health problems, and stuff like that. Well, at that point I didn't care very much. I had enough trouble coping with the nightmares. I was smart enough to add things up for myself. I was also smart enough to shut up when they told me to, before they put me in psychiatric care. As they did with some of my colleagues. What they had seen and heard, it got under their skin. In more ways than you can believe. They couldn't live with it, so they were... isolated.

Maybe I worry about nothing. Maybe it really ended there and then, and what is happening now are just isolated incidents which have no real bearing on what the tabloids are yapping about now. I don't know, and I don't care. Maybe you'll find out, I don't care either. I'll do my part, as promised, and the rest is up to you.

You want facts. Good, here is the first fact. A photograph. There weren't many photos taken then, we didn't have the time for that. I saw about four pictures, there must have been more, but they all disappeared into hush-up "top secret" files, which then got lost, you know what I mean. Those I've seen were bad enough, I have no need to remember the others. Always had a weak stomach when it comes to gore. This is the only one I could make a copy of with a cheap Polaroid. The colours are faded after those years, but there's enough left to see.

ITEM OF EVIDENCE 1: THE PHOTOGRAPH:

A young man is lying on his back on the ground. The ground consists of small stones and black earth. Behind him a wall of concrete is seen. To the left is a piece of metal which can be a rail track. The man has been dead for several days. He is lying on his back, his arms stretched out. The fingers are clasped. One leg is stretched under the body in an impossible way. The decomposition has started but the damage to the body is not only due to that. The head lies crooked, turned around, the neck broken. The eyes are gone, as are parts of the lips, exposing the jaw-bone. Through a hole in the left cheek the inside of the mouth can be seen. The neck is a second open wound. There is almost no blood, only the gasping rotting shards of flesh. From the neck down the body has been split open to the navel. The shirt is in pieces. It is clear that the wound has been made by dozens of cuts by one or several large and sharp instruments, used in a blood frenzy. The ribs are exposed, some broken but strangely enough sticking up, as if they have been broken from the inside. A spaghetti of some intestines is still left in the space where the stomach, liver and such were, but most of the entrails are gone.

GLEN CANMOOR (continued):
Not a pretty sight, is it? Some of the others I saw were much worse than this one, they were of women and children. This was one of the victims they found in the maintenance section of the Underground tunnels, at the start of the "clean up". Hey... use your handkerchief or whatever, but don't throw up on my floor, fuck you!

Good, keep it in. Some of what you're about to hear is worse than this photograph. You see, they used some just as food, as they did with this poor chap. Others they used... but I don't want to run ahead. Always keep your readers in suspense, eh? Frankly, I have my doubts whether your newspaper or tabloid or whatever, ever will publish all this, even with the evidence you're about to get. Freedom of press, my ass. But then, that's not my problem anymore.

Yep, I know, a photograph like this really gets under your skin. Other things do too, in quite another way, as you'll find out.

The first links were laid on that April tenth, but of course it had been going on for much longer. Months, years, I have no idea. Who misses a few tramps or homeless people? So many people disappear in London every year, as they do in every big city. There are so many people on this fucking planet, I suppose even God can't keep count of them.

When it started they began to put all reports on missing persons in London together and finally began to make the right connections. One of those reports was about a happening on the night of April sixth to seventh, which seemed to stand apart, but was the start of the real investigation. Of course I don't have the original report, but I do have a copy. Here it is.

* * *

ITEM OF EVIDENCE 2: THE REPORT OF
CONSTABLE PAUL MCKIRBY:

Marble Arch Police Station, London, April 7th, 8.15 am, made after I completed tour of duty.

While doing my regular rounds, I entered Marble Arch Station. A young man, who identified himself as Danny Vermeert, was acting very strangely. It was immediately clear to me that the young man had had a few drinks too many. He claimed to have been witness to a murder on one of the platforms. Though it was clear that he was intoxicated and his words were very confused and fantastic, I decided to humour him. We went down and explored the two platforms. Of course there was nothing to be seen. Though the murder he claimed to have seen had been extremely violent and bloody, there was not a trace of blood or any violence, except a trashed soft drinks machine, which of course is not unusual. Since at that time of night no more trains were coming, it seemed clear to me that the young (and drunk) man had fallen asleep on one of the benches, had had a vivid nightmare and then had run upstairs to report the horrible thing he (thought) he had seen. Since the young man was dressed civilly and for the rest acted as a gentleman, I made notes of his story. After that he calmed down and (while sobering up) began to realise that he must have dreamed it. I helped him hail a cab to get him to his hotel, the Bridgestone Private Hotel.

All identity details further in this report 3778/31.

GLEN CANMOOR (continued):

Things like this happen all the time, you know. You'd really be surprised about the stories some drunks come up with. If we'd have to rush a police force into action every time a drunk reports of bloody murder or some gory horror story, we'd have nothing else to do than chase wild gooses. Of course, this one time... it turned out to be the real thing. Which we realised a few days later.

April tenth, the next (and first official) link which started the investigation, and which is the one I was personally involved with. We got a call from a Mr. Charles Reever, owner of the Bridgestone Private Hotel in Gower Street. He asked for a constable to be present at the opening of hotel room number sixteen and a report on the contents of the room as the resident hadn't shown up for some days. Now of course we all know about disappearing hotel guests, leaving without paying the bill. Of course the owner could get in that room with his spare key, but an official report has to be made. Just in case the missing person resurfaces and claims all his luggage has been stolen from his room in the meantime. So we sent constable Lumrey to make the report.

Please bear in mind that we're talking about things more than twenty years ago. No mobile phones with cameras then, no MP3 or iPods. A portable tape recorder on batteries seems so silly now, but it was hi-tech then.

ITEM OF EVIDENCE 3: THE REPORT OF CONSTABLE RAMSEY J. LUMREY:

April 10th, at Bridgestone Private Hotel, Gower Street, London.

The missing person was entered in the hotel register of the Bridge-stone Private Hotel as "Danny Vermeert, Arteveldestraat 69, City of Gent, Belgium". He had reserved room 16 for the nights of the 5th to the 9th of April, bed & breakfast. Mr. Reever, the owner of the hotel described the missing person as male, young, not much older than thirty, dressed casual, jeans, small beard but nothing really striking in his appearance or dress code. He had said that he was a freelance reporter for some European magazine or tabloid and was planning a review of the lesser known aspects of London. As if there are any left, the owner remarked here. Vermeert always carried along a portable tape recorder on batteries, which Mr. Reever thought to be a very expensive and professional machine.

Mr. Reever last saw his guest on the morning of April 7th. He didn't show up afterwards and didn't spend the nights of April 7th and 8th in the hotel. As Mr. Reever needed the room at noon of April 9th for new guests, and it hadn't been evacuated (or vacated, and not paid for) he asked for our assistance. The guests for room 16 were temporarily put in a vacant room in another hotel close by. Mr. Reever has no idea where his guest has spent the last two nights. He doesn't really care either except for the bill of 75 pounds to be settled.

In room 16 I found: an open suitcase, various clothes, shaving stuff and other things usually left lying around by a tourist who is planning to come back to that room. Nothing abnormal except the absence of Mr. Vermeert himself. I wrote it down in my report 988/77, adding an E/3 with a detailed list of what obviously belonged to the missing person. A copy of the E/3 was given to Mr. Reever, after which I packed all what belonged to the missing in his suitcase and took it to the station.

GLEN CANMOOR (continued):
Nothing really impressive, is it? Of course at the station we went through everything with a microscope, you never knew with those guys from small European countries such as Belgium. We found stacks of documentation about London, his return tickets for boat and train (no one even dreamed of Eurostar then), his used entrance tickets. It's all on the E/3 but not worth checking, none of that was important. What was important was the handwritten pages in Vermeert's notebook.

Personally at that time I didn't think it was all of any importance. You know, young fellow alone in London, I remember thinking: he'll turn up when he's sober, probably without his wallet. But that would be his problem, he'd have to come to us to declare the loss of his papers, his eurocheques (yes, they still used them then) and so on, and then he'd have to go to the Belgian embassy to get papers to return to Belgium. I thought: that guy is sleeping it off in some strip club in Soho.

Until we read his notebook.

Police routine is slow, everywhere. That's why it's called routine: nobody worried because some guy has been missing for two days. But the written pages in his notebook got me worrying. This Danny Vermeert was either mentally seriously disturbed, or he was smoking or stuffing something up his nose which was doing bad things to his brain. Of course, if in those years we threw every foreign junkie in the slammer we'd have nothing else to do. So the first thought was that Vermeert had come here to get some of the stuff he wanted and that he was walking around London in some hallucinative condition. You don't tell the hotel owner you came here to buy some stuff for your nose. Anyway, we did contact the press agency whose address we found among his papers. Believe it or not but his original story was true: he had been sent here to write a report. But he hadn't turned up back in Belgium. The police in Belgium checked with some acquaintances known at the press agency, but all they knew was that Vermeert was in London working on something. We had an Identikit drawing made based on the description by Mr. Reever, and two officers checked some bars and places in Soho. No success. Nobody had seen Vermeert or knew him, which was exactly what he had expected.

Then a note was found in the post box of the Notting Hill Gate Police Station. It was written in pencil on a piece of newspaper. Here is a copy of that note:

ITEM OF EVIDENCE 3: THE NOTE:

"I found this tape near the locked gate of the Tube of... no, that doesn't matter. The tape was in a portable recorder which was still on 'RECORD'. I didn't steal it, I found it, and it's mine. The tape was fully recorded so I listened to it. I don't know what to do with it. You are assholes. The recorder is mine, but the tape... I don't know. I don't like you but I think you should hear what's on it. It's insane but maybe you'll understand it. Insane stuff for the insane. It scares me. So enjoy it, pigs."

GLEN CANMOOR (continued):

Pigs. Yep, that's what those who didn't like us called us back then. Quite dated now. Anyway, we got that note through the usual channels, together with the tape it mentioned. The recorder itself was never found, probably found its way to someone else on the stolen goods market. Now, we did get some crazy messages regularly. They were noted but nothing ever came out of them. This was different because of what was on the tape, and because we knew that Vermeert had been carrying his tape recorder. At first we thought it was some kind of radio play, something for a midnight horror show or something like that. But it seemed so damn real.

We didn't know it yet, but the nightmare had really started. Somewhere in the spiderweb of bureaucracy connections were made, links were found. Loose events were put together. The search for the missing Danny Vermeert had been a routine thing till then, and as I was involved with that I got a close up on all what followed.

The nightmare would take nine days. Nine days and nights of total secrecy and hush-hush. A nightmare which has never left me, though I only lived it second-hand. But you know how it is... once my curiosity was aroused, I found my way to the channels needed to get my information.

I must admit I never got a full insight in everything that took place in the Tube station but mainly in the maintenance tunnels, the miles and miles of darkness spreading under the city. Because it was there that most happened. Once the contents of the tape were known, the Yard suddenly took over. We were advised to sit back till they needed us. Everything became top secret, suddenly the whole place was swarming with politicians whose face you usually only see on the telly. And army guys! Yapping their asses off about terrorists. My ass! Terrorists had nothing to do with it but they made a nice explanation for the press and the general public afterwards.

Vermeert wasn't on drugs, he wasn't insane. What he wrote in his notebook, what he spoke on his tape recorder, weren't hallucinations. But of course none of this had been made public. Which is why I did ask a precise and rather high price for the documents I gave you. No matter what the tabloids wrote afterwards about the nightmare, they wrote what the government and the army wanted them to write. Told them to write! What Vermeert saw and recorded was the truth, and that's the horror: knowing what the nightmare really was, and knowing that nobody admitted it. Maybe these files are again under scrutiny now, with those strange disappearances all over London those last weeks. Politicians, army commanders, whatever, they didn't understand it then, how will they understand it now? How this could have been with us for so many years, unnoticed, living, spreading.

They did believe they'd eradicated the roots of the evil with their cleansing action. Oh, I'm sure they felt so secure and safe, the gentle-men in high positions who gave the orders but never went down into the tunnels themselves, armed with flashlights. They haven't seen what was found there, not even on photographs. Wouldn't want to disturb their stomachs. And the general public never knew any better, they accepted the terrorist story as it was.

We Londoners are so used to our metro, the subway, the Tube, that we have developed a kind of blind spot about it. You know, when last year real terrorists bombed the Tube, many commuters had to get a map of the city to get home without it. The Tube is a multi-layered underground city below London. An exhaustive spider's web of rails and stations and maintenance tunnels. To us it's perfectly normal, including the weird characters inside: the punkers, the musicians, the drifters, the drunks and junkies. We see but we don't really notice anymore. Maybe it needed the eye of a foreigner, an outsider, to see what was wrong. The strange and unnatural way it all comes together into a web. A coherent web, no matter how incoherent and absurd the individual parts are. If you mention a web, you automatically need a spider. Somewhere. The subway in London is over one hundred and eighty years old. A structure which has been changing, year after year. Time enough to get an identity, a personality of its own. Time enough to learn about humans, what they are, how they act, how they taste.

As I said, after the contents of the tape were revealed, all was taken out of our hands.

On April fourteenth a team of detectives went down. They started at Notting Hill Gate (which, I'm certain, is where the tape was found) and searched all the stations, within a radius. The stations themselves weren't that important, the tunnels were and the maintenance rooms inside the tunnels. On April fifteenth the entrances to seven stations were closed by the army. The official news was that they had found an old army bomb in some tunnel. After which they closed down five other stations. Lots of Londoners had to take a cab or the bus. Now who in his sane mind would not believe that an old World War Two bomb was responsible for such widespread action?

It created chaos, those trains which ended up at the wrong places. Queues for buses took more than an hour, all cabs did golden business. Then the official press releases came out: a bunch of terrorists had been hiding in the maintenance tunnels. What terrorists? IRA? Palestiniens? Arabs? A lot of crap, but the general public believed it. The newsmen said so, the tabloids said so, the politicians said so.

I saw the army troops going down, dressed in asbestos suits and armed with flame throwers! Whatever was down there, it wasn't terrorists or old Second World War bombs.

The "bombs" were found and deactivated, there was a shooting which left five army men dead, as well as all the terrorists. The identity of the terrorists was never revealed and no organisation ever claimed responsibility.

What really happened down there in the dark tunnels, those black mouths in the earth? The photograph I showed you is one example of what they found down there. There were many others. On April twenty-first all Tube stations were open again to the public. The cleaning had happened.

Really?

I don't know. I have my doubts when I listen to the tape of Danny Vermeert. Here you have a photocopy of the handwritten pages from his notebook, the one we found in his hotel room. Here is also a copy of the tape and a copy of what it said on it. The quality of the tape is not very good, but clear enough.

Whatever was down there in the tunnels was eradicated by fire, almost twenty-five years ago. Or was it? I have my doubts. I never use the subway anymore. Cabs are more expensive and busses are slower, but they're safe. They're outside.

So here are first the handwritten pages. Some of them seem quite funny now, such as the time needed on the boat, the remarks on the closing hours of pubs, the prices of the fares for a cab and such. Remember, this is a time trip to twenty-five years ago.

ITEM OF EVIDENCE 5: THE HANDWRITTEN NOTES OF DANNY VERMEERT:

April 5.

Finally arrived, thought I'd never get here. Close to four hours on that stupid ferry was boring enough, fortunately not too many passengers (that early in the morning) but the company of a bartender who was trying to catch up with the sleep he missed the night before. Then had to get on an all-station stop train at Dover. Don't know at how many stations he stopped... twenty, thirty? Lost count. Much too many before we finally got to Victoria Station.

Way past noon by that time. Bought a cheeseburger (or something which looked a bit like it) in a fast food joint in the station, including a horrible tasting sauce on it. Cab fare to the hotel was cheap at least, two pounds. The hotel is small but clean. No luxury, no TV or phone in the room, don't need them anyway, and what do you expect for twenty pounds a night. The owner is a nice chap who likes to chat. Gave me immediately the address of the Stockpot Restaurant near Piccadilly Circus, the cheapest in town (he said) and quite good for its price.

Hugo (my editor) had warned me: if you give me a piece on horrible hauntings at Tussaud's wax museum I'll kick you back over the channel. That's when I mentioned a piece about "The Unknown London". So now I'm in London and I don't quite know where to start. My head is spinning a bit. Bought a bottle of tax free whisky on the boat, and finished half of it out of boredom. Should have a good meal first.

Bought a couple of magazines at the station: *What's On* and *Time Out*. Everything you want to know about London. Agatha Christie's *The Mousetrap* is still playing, and there's a new Weber musical about Evita Peron. The guards at Buckingham Palace, market at Portobello Road Saturday morning, and all the other stuff I precisely don't want to see.

Writing it down to order my thoughts. Worked the same way two years ago when I did my "Dark Side of Paris" series. Always make notes in advance, then use the tape recorder when at locations.

Good. It's four o'clock now. First going to have a bite, then—just to cross Hugo—having a look at Tussaud's. Just to compare it to Paris.

Same day, evening. Tussaud's was fine, only the Chamber of Horrors proved a disappointment. Adolf Hitler in uniform at the entrance, a guillotine, an electric chair, some light and sound effects. Sure, John Christie, John Haigh, they're all there but there's no real mood. Even the small street representing Jack the Ripper's London, is hardly impressive. Most fun are the images of tourists. One sitting on a bench with a newspaper in his hand, the other on a railing looking down with a camera on his belly. You only notice that they are wax figures too when you pass them the second time and they haven't moved. A nice touch was a guy in security guard's uniform, watching an execution scene. So lifelike I touched his face and fuck, he bit my finger! No, I didn't scream out but it surely was a close shave, and the guard absolutely got fun out of the act. We got to talking and he said that for real gory horror I really should see the London Dungeon. Guess Tussaud's didn't pay him enough as he recommended another waxworks show.

Had dinner at the Stockpot (cheap but nice) and walked through Soho. Cabarets, peepshows, lots of video stores and sex shops, no hookers on the streets. Decided to take the subway, the Tube to get back. No lack of Tube stations in London. It's almost a world of its own: the many corridors and enormous stairways which seem to go on forever, the naked concrete platforms, the overflowing waste bins, crushed cigarette packages and crushed beer and soft drinks cans all over the floor. So casual and yet in a strange way alienating, because even at such a late hour, there are so many people around of all races and colours. And of course in every corridor there is some musician, with a cheap amplifier and a guitar or a Recorder, trying to earn some change, though everywhere there are posters forbidding exactly such activities.

The London subway system is a maze of its own: Central Line, Circle Line, Bakerloo Line, and so on, more than ten lines crisscrossing and intersecting. Takes some time to get used to it, but strangely enough it functions perfectly... for Londoners!

The trains themselves: announcing themselves by a hushed breath of air oozing out of the tunnels, then the dark holes of the tunnels spit out the trains as enormous silver worms or entrails. The doors opening, the monotonous tape recording of "Mind the gap!" as if some idiot would really fall down in the gap between the platform and the waiting train, doors closing, and gone again, in less than half a minute. Sometimes less than a minute between some trains. Rush, rush all the time, even if you have all the time in the world, as I did, you get caught up in the rush. Caught in the sheep pack there is a feeling of connection with those fast speeding people which makes you go faster out of your own will. The fastness catches you and starts to take you along with its own rhythm. Man is a pack animal.

"Keep to the right" on the escalators so that those in an even greater hurry can rush past you, up and down as so many frenzied ants. A fine of fifty pounds if you dare to push the red button and stop the stairs. It starts to give you the idea that you are a small cog wheel in this machinery, thousands of wheels locked together to keep this charade of humanity alive and functioning. The trains are the central parts, the steel worms with their lighted eyes and many opening and closing mouths to absorb or eject their contents on the platforms. The subway is like a Gestalt, a human created being which is now filling this city beneath the city, these thousands and thousands of miles into dark tunnels and maintenance places and stations. It feels as if I and the other passengers are only decorative pieces, ornamental stuff, with no real function in this city underground which feels like the real London.

The idea jumped fully born into my mind, so sudden that I stopped and a fat Englishman bumped into me. Under normal circumstances anyone in my country would have yelled "Watch out, asshole". This gentleman just took a step back and said "Excuse me, sir", then went on his way.

The idea: so simple yet so vast. The subway as an autonomic being. Not London at night, but the Subway, London's real and literal underground, the real heart of the city. This cold mechanical world of white neon lights, enormous platforms and the gaping toothless mouths of the dark tunnels, inhabited by the silver speed worms. Yes, that looked great. First thing to do tomorrow is get some complete maps of the subway, some books on when and how it was built, and more of the usual background stuff for such an essay. Or a series of features. Find out what makes some of the stations more interesting than others. Some of them look quite old. When was this all built? One hundred years ago, or older? Maybe there are stations now no longer used but with some creepy legends about them. Who does the maintenance? Must talk to some people who know. Maybe get a permit from the city council (or whoever is in charge) to visit some of the tunnels and maintenance workshops.

First of all: never forget the human interest factor! If I do, Hugo will skin me alive.

I continued my way, this time consciously focusing on single people and ignoring the faceless crowds. The subway musician with Rasta hair and an Arabic fez on his head, his jeans discoloured and torn, his feet naked in sandals, the old dirt under his fingers and toe-nails. The mindless look in his staring eyes as he played continuously the same moronic three note tune on his German flute, not looking at anyone who passed, just staring numbly into whatever nothingness his mind was hiding in.

The fat housewife, shoulders bowed under the weight of two large shopping bags she carried, the way her nose rose when she passed the flute player, as if she smelled something rotten. Two new-wavers dressed in worn black leather, the arms covered with studs, and studs in their noses and lips as well, one with Nazi symbols tattooed on his shaved skull. The smartly dressed African man with starched white collar, a disastrous tie. The pretty girl much too young for such a short skirt and the black fishnet stockings, which made her look like a cheapie pickup. The pale kid with the coat down to his knees, sticking his dirty fingers under everybody's nose mumbling "Spare some pennies for me please".

Everybody a single world of his own, but all together the breed of the underground, a crisscross of subway lines but also of individual worlds.

I started to notice more and more details which I had tended to overlook before. As if the idea I now was working on had cleared my mind of some kind of stupor or fog which had prevented me from seeing what I wanted to see, what I needed to see. As if my senses had been partly asleep or stunned and were now working overtime to catch up.

These were all small details, things one sees countless times every day, but now they seemed to have an importance of their own, as if they were screaming at my face: look at me, look at this, notice that, put it all together. The movie posters on the walls—some torn so that you had glimpses of two, three movies, none of which were playing any longer. The constant warnings "Beware of pickpockets", a crushed beer can on a step of the stairs down, its empty mouth gasping at me.

And specially the trains, the constant humming of the trains, sometimes an electrical short and the smell of ozone and oil, the quickness and grace with which the trains spilled out of the dark tunnel mouths. All these things fit together in my mind, created a mechanical painting which was at the same time revealing and confusing, because I hadn't made it out yet. These were just loose ideas spinning around in my mind which in due time would be turned into the canvas I needed.

At the moment they were as confusing as the map to the various stations on the various lines. Look and solve the puzzle, find "This station" somewhere up or down the line and then try to find out whether you have to take the platform left or right. The markings inside the wagons are even worse, just schematic. I trusted the map I had (and which unfortunately proved a couple of years out of date), got out at Charing Cross only to discover that this station was still marked as Strand on my map and "my" Charing Cross was now Embankment. Not to spoil my fun! I got to Euston Square Station only to find out that Goodge Street Station was much closer to my hotel.

Found a pub still open, though I got in just when the bell was rung announcing "Last orders, please!" and secured me two pints of Old Speckled Hen, one of the better bitters. Video games had made their entrance even in the sacred solitude of pubs, and the various "pwiet-pwiet" noises irritated me. Was just starting my second pint when the owner swung open the front doors, inviting everybody to get out now so that he could close up. When he started putting the chairs on the tables I finished my pint and left.

At the hotel. Read some pages of a novel I picked up from the free table at the reception where tourists can leave their discarded holiday material, just to clear my mind so that I can focus again on my work.

I imagined the subway very late, the people discarded, the platforms empty, overgrown by rubbish, old pages of newspapers fluttering as scattered crabs, crushed cans of beer and soft drinks, the round drinking holes staring up as empty eye sockets with a glint of wetness on them as shed tears. No more travellers, only the trains themselves plunging as fat worms through the silent dark tunnels, stopping at every station and opening their greedy mouths, but nothing coming in or coming out. It's a very weird and morbid idea, like a Bosch painting set in the 20th century. Really must find a way to incorporate that idea in the series.

April 6, noon.

This time took the subway at the rush hour, starting at seven this morning. It's as if the whole of London streams down into the Underground, being absorbed by the waiting entrances, a mass of shoulder pushing people, as lemmings. Bodies back to belly, shoulder to shoulder, pushing, agitated, working their way down into the stomach of the city. In the wagons you're pushed on all sides, smelling sweat and aftershave. No matter how nice the British queue for a bus, none of that discipline remains once they get inside the subway. Everybody wants to get on the bloody same fucking train.

Again tried to notice the things the usual traveller doesn't see. Intrigued by the mass of graffiti, some quite artfully done. But also disturbed by some of the weird symbols in the graffiti. I have always been a sucker for graphics and some of these signs had a bizarre way of really catching and holding my attention. Again that feeling that there was something there which just evaded my understanding, something in those signs which was more than just doodling or tagging. Once I had noticed that I began to recognise several tags repeatedly, until it was as if I was following a pattern created by those tags.

Spent the morning visiting the infamous London Dungeon at Tooley Street. Nice show, a true trip through gore and torture down the centuries, but really horror? Not quite. The dummies are just too artificial, the blood is just too red and the giant speaking devil is just too silly to even mention. Crossed Tower Bridge to get a look at the Tower itself. No ravens in sight. Sorry Poe, no "Nevermore" at this time of the day. Probably just took their lunch. And pubs still close afternoons.

Tried the subway system in all directions this time, and am getting used to reading the symbols as they should be read. From Ealing to Kenton, from Camden Town and the hippy market to Whitechapel, or rather what's left of the original district Jack the

Ripper used to explore in 1888. You can do Ripper walks and see all the places where he cut open his victims, but they're all new places, new buildings, just one pub, its walls covered with old newspapers, reminiscing the Ripper murders. The subway is in fact quite a cheap system to spend the day for the homeless and beggars: with a ticket of forty pence you can spend the whole day travelling around, as long as you don't get out at any station.

Got the information I needed in one of the antiquarian bookshops at Shaftsbury Avenue: one coffee table book about subways all over the world, and a slim volume about London's. Fascinating lecture: the building began over 140 years ago! The book has some really nasty incidents such a tunnel collapsing and those buried under it resorting to cannibalism before they were rescued. There are some other things which I must check out. Such as the story of several small skeletons found during the digging, and even mention of signs painted on the walls of grottos. As if a group of refugees had already been living underground years before the digging started. This brings me to some stories I heard about the homeless who spend their whole life inside the maintenance tunnels and only come out to beg.

Went to Carnaby Street after a lunch of hot soup and bread and bought a small gift for Hugo: a key holder with a male and female figure. When you push a button they start fucking. I know Hugo hates this kind of kitsch.

Night of April 6. No, early morning.

My second night in London and I'm sitting in my hotel room, sweating like a pig. Have to write things down now, to convince myself that I'm not stark raving mad, that I saw what... I saw. Hard, my fingers are shaking, ink is smearing what I try to write. Not a nightmare, I'm not drunk. Stupid. If I hadn't spent so much time in that pub, if I hadn't downed four pints and chased them with a Malt... yep, then my breath wouldn't have smelled so much and maybe the policeman would have believed me.

I'm scared. Scared to believe what I've seen.

All right, I do have a vivid imagination, and after my rather morbid ideas last night I did have a nightmare about the subway. But I'm not prone to hallucinations, and I don't take any stuff, LSD or whatever.

In a way I have been lucky. After he had taken down my state-ment, the policeman let me go, though he must have been convinced that I was stoned. Probably wanted to save himself the paperwork of confining me to a cell for the night to sober up. What he certainly didn't do, was believe me.

Can I believe it myself? Is what I think I saw possible, or did I really have a hallucination? A nightmare while being fully awake? No, I can't have been that drunk. I don't feel drunk now. Maybe all I think I saw wasn't exactly as I interpreted it, but then, I fail to grasp a more rational explanation.

In the evening I had obtained tickets for a musical. Had very cheap tickets for something new, called *Little Shop of Horrors* which proved to be very funny. Not part of my assignment, but I wanted to let the ideas I had about the subway submerge into my brain, where it always works itself out eventually. So when the show was finished I walked from Leicester Square to Tottenham Court Road where I found out to my dismay that the only pub in Oxford Street, the Tottenham, was so busy that I went in search of another one in the side streets. There I got a few drinks, got into a heated conversation at the bar with some football fans (seems all British are). Don't know shit about football but after a couple of pints I could talk about it with the best. Chased it all with a malt whiskey and was put out with the rest of the guys when the pub closed.

To keep it short, I was quite drunk when I stumbled out, remem-bered that I had forgotten to go to the toilet in the pub, and suddenly really had to go very urgently. Walked straight on to a public toilet, one of those booths where you have to put money in, except this one had a nice statement "Out of order". Really didn't want to do my thing between cars on the road (British fines are heavy for indecent exposure) so I went down the nearest Underground station, and relieved myself in an official toilet. Then... well, I took a ticket, wanting to go to the hotel, which was absolutely stupid as I was within walking distance, but somehow in my confused state of mind, I wanted to take the subway to Goodge Street Station, which was (as I had discovered before) closest to my hotel. Problem was I had trouble focusing on the displays, all coloured dots and letters swimming together. In short, after I had stopped a few times, I really didn't know where I was any more. No excuses, I was just drunk, and it just felt good to sit in the carriage, watching the dark tunnels and lit stations drift by. I felt very tired, my eyelids went down and suddenly I had that abrupt feeling of falling down into a bottomless pit which really tears you out of the twilight zone you have been drifting in. My head snapped up as if I had a jolt of electricity, my neck muscles were aching, and suddenly I was clear awake. The worst of the drunkenness was over. I think. How can I be certain now?

I must have been dozing for some time, because I remember sitting alone in that carriage, but now I had company. In the farthest corner a distinguished middle aged man was sitting. Sitting stiffly, his feet firmly on the ground, his hands on a small case on his knees. Small eyes looking straight ahead through horn-rimmed glasses.

My eyes drifted to the second passenger, sitting opposite my seat. An unwashed older man, dressed in a worn coat full of holes and whose original colour had long been drained. His long unkempt hair and beard were full of filth. He was sitting hunched forward, on the edge of his seat. I fully understood why the well dressed specimen of the species has chosen the farthest seat. If I had ever seen a more unappetising specimen of the human race, it was sitting in front of me.

The train arrived at another station, my eyes tried to focus but I couldn't read the name. The doors opened, then closed again. The old man in front of me coughed, a gurgling sound as if he was going to throw up his innards in a moment. In a second he's going to beg me for a quid for some booze, I thought, and the idea filled me with repulsion. Don't know why, I have seen drunks and tramps, but in some way this man filled me with a feeling of repulsion and disgust. Don't know exactly what caused it, he was dirty and he smelled bad, but I had seen worse. Can't explain the reaction I felt when looking at him, as if everything in my mind and body was repelled by this man.

What had woken me up? I hadn't drifted into consciousness normally. Now, thinking it over, it must have been something I saw or heard or felt while drunk asleep, something which pulled me back into reality, but what?

There was only this old hobo. I observed him unashamedly, or maybe I was just still a bit too drunk to care. He had bristly eyebrows hiding most of his eyes, above a beaked nose. His head was bent low, his mouth hanging open. I watched a drip of saliva forming on his under lip and then oozing down, descending on a silvery thread of slime. Unable to stop watching my eyes followed the descent of the drop to his hands.

The skin of his hands was moving.

Thinking back, maybe this was what caught my attention when he sat down, the item which pulled me back out of my dream. He had big hands, brown with dark spots of age. His hands were clasped one over the other, the fingers quite restful. It was the back of the hands which were in a constant flowing movement. Intriguing and disgusting. It looked as if constantly below the skin air bubbles were created which flowed then to the arms or the fingers and disappeared there. Fascinated I looked at the snakelike movements of his skin. Had to be some kind of muscle cramp, or a neurotic disease creating those weird movements.

Suddenly he lifted his head as if he felt I was watching him. Our eyes met and I quickly looked away and pretended to look outside. I didn't want to see those eyes a second time. White and swollen they were, with pupils so small they were just dots in the egg-like white. The flesh around the eyes was puffy and swollen, and just below those eyes I noticed the same strange muscle movements below the skin. A shiver ran along my spine and I suddenly felt very cold. My stomach kicked, I felt the sour taste rushing up in my throat and swallowed to keep it down. Probably had a 50 pound fine here also if you threw up in a train.

The train slowed down and I stood up. Wherever I was, I needed to get out, away from this weird old man. The doors slipped open and the train spat me out. I stumbled on the deserted platform and started walking towards the WAY OUT sign. My footsteps echoed along the deserted walls and stairs when I mounted them. What fucking time was it? Looked at my watch, and cursed. My watch was gone. The old metal strap always had the habit of opening. I stopped and tried to clear my thoughts. It was not an expensive watch but I hate losing things. I could only have lost it on the train while I was dozing, or it had dropped in my hurry to get off. The train was gone by now, but there was always a slight chance that it had fallen on the platform.

I looked at the notice on the wall. THIS STATION... MARBLE ARCH. Fuck, I was on the Central Line, of course in the wrong direction of where I had to go. Well, I had to return and get on the Northern Line anyway, so with a bit of luck I'd find my watch back on the platform.

I started the descent into the bowels of the subway, remembering that I had to take the other side to get on the Northern Line. Wanted to check on the watch first, so I stepped on the platform where I had descended from the train. My watch wasn't there, but something else was.

My two travelling companions had also alighted after me. The finely dressed gentleman was lying on his back, his body convulsing, his feet kicking in the air. His bag was lying a bit farther on the platform. The vagabond was sitting on his knees, bent down over the convulsing man.

For a moment I was confused about what was going on. Was the man having a heart attack or an epileptic seizure of some kind and was the vagrant trying to help him? Or had the he hit him and was trying to rob him? Whatever it was, in the first case the tramp could use some help, in the second case the traveller needed help and the vagrant, I felt certain, I could handle.

So I went over to them. The tramp didn't hear me, or didn't care. He was sitting on top of the fallen man, holding him down with both hands. This wasn't helping someone sick. The prostrate man's hands were tearing at the shoulders of his attacker, trying to push him off, but though the tramp was much smaller the efforts of his victim didn't do much good.

I saw the face of the man lying down. His eyes were bulging, his mouth wide open and gurgling as the tunnel of the subway ready to spit out a train.

The sleeves of the hobo's coat were pushed up and I saw his long abominably thin arms. His wrists and arms were crawling with the bizarre muscle movements below the skin, as if a thousand insects were running there. His hands were not just holding the man down, his fingers were INSIDE THE FACE OF THAT MAN!

Buried up to the palms of his hands inside the soft flesh of his victim and moving unceasingly under the skin. Fine streams of blood were running over the face of the victim as if forced up out of his pores and creating a red spider-webbed pattern. The thumbs of the assailant were locked just under the chin of his victim and as I watched they pushed the chin up till there was a dry click and a rush of blood spurted out of the man's mouth.

I felt stunned, caught in a scene beyond reality, everything was the white of the neon lights of the platform, and red as the blood spilling out of the victim's mouth. Then the pale arms of the tramp became red, a deep red starting at his hands and rising up his arms, strengthening the muscle movements, the arms thickening and vibrating as if his arms were sucking mouths.

I stumbled backwards, and the tramp looked up as if he had just now realised someone else was there. The small pupils in his eyes were enlarged now, two black pits taking over almost all the white, two eye sockets to hell, two gasping pits of darkness. His loose hanging lips closed and he grinned at me. With a plopping sound he withdrew his long, dripping fingers out of the face of his victim. Blood spurted freely from eight circular wounds, turning the writhing face into a red mask, drowning the gurgling sounds from his open mouth.

I turned and ran, all ideas of helping the unfortunate man forgotten, driven only by the sense of self preservation. God, I'm no coward but this creature was not something I dared to confront. My shoes clicked on the stairs up, the echoes sounding as if he was already behind me, catching up in pursuit. Blood was rushing and humming in my ears. My heart was pounding and whatever my brain did, it wasn't thinking, just feeling the urgent need to get out of here! Before "it" got to me too.

I fell, crashing my face against the kiosk of the ticket seller, screaming that there had been a bloody murder. I clapped my hands against the glass, not realising that I was screaming at the top of my lungs in Flemish. Now I realise why he looked at me as he did. I think I blacked out right there and then but somehow I didn't fall down.

Some time must have passed but I was totally unaware of that. I stood with both hands against the ticket booth, blood running from my broken nails as if I had tried to dig them into the metal, and there was a Bobby next to me. You know them, the phlegmatic British cop, complete with his big helmet (looking straight out of a tourist post-card) and the stern look in his eyes as he quietly and civilly asked me what the matter was. In the UK you don't have to carry ID on your person but I had my passport and showed it to him, probably yapping and yelling all the time as he took his time examining it while I was begging him to come down with me and help that unfortunate man who was bleeding to death on the platform. I noticed the constable's nose wrinkling as he smelled my breath, but then he returned my ID and we went down together, his hand all the time resting on his truncheon.

So we came on the platform. The cop looked at me, questioning. 'The other platform,' I yelled, 'he's on the other side.' So there we went. And there was nobody there, not the old bloodsucker, not his bleeding victim. Nothing, not a single drop of blood.

'He took the body on the train,' I said, 'the train which has come and gone while you were fucking looking at my fucking papers! There must have been at least two trains in the time you took before we went down.'

The Bobby looked at his watch and shook his head. 'Sorry, sir,' he said, 'there have been no trains since then, not at this time of the night.'

Bloody cops. Always think they know better.

I shook my head. I was being stubborn or stupid, pick your choice. 'I saw it all,' I said. 'There must be something as proof, his bag, blood somewhere, on the rails...'

We walked the platforms, all two of them. There was nothing there. The Bobby was starting to look angry.

'Then he took the body in the tunnel,' I said stubbornly. 'He must've taken it somewhere. I'm not mad. You have to inform people, lock up the tunnels. He can't have gotten far with a body to carry.'

'Listen sir,' the constable said, 'that's quite enough of a spectacle now. You see there's nothing there. Nothing happened here except what you think you've seen. And frankly, sir, you've drunk quite enough, I suppose. Dozed off, bad dream. Why don't you go back to your hotel now? I'm certain you'll feel better in the morning.'

I stuck to my story. I knew that I was no longer drunk but could I convince this asshole without ending up in a cell for drunks? If they closed down the subway right now, there was no way that murdering hobo could escape. But did they? No way.

I had to follow him to the police station where he took half an hour to take note of my story, then started typing his report out using only two bloody fingers and repeating every sentence once he had managed to finish it. I just sat there, knowing that it was all useless. No search would turn up anything now. I just signed his report of my "fantastic story", just wanted to get out of this place. For a moment I thought he was going to make me spend the night right there, but he even waved down a cab to take me back to my hotel and wished me a good night and a pleasant further stay in London!

That's it. That's what happened, what I've seen. But what have I really seen? A murder for robbery? No way, this was something much more personal and horrible. I still see those slender fingers of that attacker, sinking down in the weak flesh of his victim's face. Were his nails that sharp, or did he use something, small razor blades or something similar attached to his fingers? But then what about what followed? The rippling under the skin, the dark red colour rising up from his hands and wrists into his arms. As if he was absorbing the blood of his victim into his own body, draining the man.

I must be nuts. I'm speaking of vampires here. Dracula, old Vlad, where are you? This isn't fucking Transylvania.

No, I'm quite sober now and sane in mind and body. I have no explanation but I know what I've seen.

But who will believe me?

April 7, early noon.

Only had about two hours of real sleep, waking up every ten minutes, bathed in sweat and seeing those staring eyes of that murderous creature in front of me. I have to rationalise my fear and disgust. I'm a reporter, so let's start thinking as a professional. I've seen a much darker piece of London than I expected and it shocked me. But it also wetted my curiosity.

Now at daylight things look different. Even could laugh at my horror fantasies when I read what I had written down last night. I must really have been quite drunk to believe such a distortion of reality. Yes, I am certain that I have witnessed a murder and robbery. But I've done my duty, reporting what I saw—or rather what I thought I'd seen—to the police, and if they preferred not to believe me, that's not my fault. Can't really blame them to discredit such a weird story. But that man, whoever he is, is dead and will be missed one of these days. They'll probably remember my story then, but there won't be much I can add to it. I gave them a quite accurate description of the murdering tramp, but what have I imagined there? Was he really as old and feeble as I remember him? I don't think so, an old man could never have gotten on top of the middle aged man he attacked. The muscular distortions I imagined could have been the work of the weapons he used, whatever they were. Small blades attached to his fingers, maybe with hidden springs opening and closing them? Strike quickly, open the artery, and the victim is yours. After all, that's where his thumbs were placed, keeping the arteries open and gushing blood. Just keep the victim down, not for very long, just long enough till he's weakened. Then disappear with the victim in the tunnels if you know your way around there. Time enough lost before the cop went down with me, time enough to clear up the blood and discard the body.

Spent the whole morning in the subway, as if unconsciously I'm searching for something, a clue, a memory. More and more this London Underground is getting to me, the atmosphere down here, the ceilings and walls pushing down on me. It's almost claustrophobic but I have never suffered from that affliction. It's like a smell which isn't, a feeling of being inside some gigantic animal of stone and steel and electricity. The platforms, the tunnels, they're all like the innards of some enormous being and the humans are as parasites inside. Even without the humans the subway would go on, some surrealist nightmare of empty trains coming and going, mechanical voices intoning "Mind the gap". As if the subway is a Gestalt, an entity whose only contact with the real world are the stairs to the streets outside. The subway is like a gigantic underground creature, living its weird primary life. A creature with its own rules. Its own language, its own secret code. Strange, sometimes the notices to the various platforms and lines start to look like something I should remember, as if they reach down deep inside my mind and touch something hidden there, but it won't come out in the open. The bizarre graffiti, especially some of those which clearly aren't tags, try to tell me something which I feel I ought to know. But then they become distorted, run out of focus in my eyes, they evade my sight and become gibberish to me, as if something is distorting them into something else. As if inside the belly of the beast I now begin to see more than I should see, and the primal beast isn't happy with that recognition.

People are constantly rushing past, pushing me, they don't look at the indicators, know them by heart and maybe that's why they don't notice, why their minds don't absorb what is behind those markings and signs. Or maybe I'm just crazy, but the idea surfaces every time again. Markings, signs and codes. Codes not meant to be seen or even noticed by an ordinary human. Intelligence has many forms. Think of the subway as a very primary animal with a basic intelligence. Why not?

Every animal has parasites...

Parasites. That is the clue, only I don't know yet where that clue leads me. My thoughts are drifting, rambling. That's the way my mind works. Loose thoughts, crazy ideas and suddenly they all blend together.

At first I thought of normal humans as parasites in the belly of the beast. But most of them are unharmed. London has, as every big city, more than the usual quota of hobos, drunks, robbers, pickpockets, drug dealers, scum... parasites on society. Feeding on normal people's lives. What if a new breed of parasite wanted more?

What if that vagrant is such a creature?

Hold on, I'm going back into fantasy realm. Was just getting convinced that my imagination transformed an armed robbery into a gothic horror story, and now my mind's going back to that routine.

I know I'll have to find out the truth. I don't feel any fear, it's broad daylight, the sun is shining (believe it or not, even in London that happens sometimes) and I know that I can stand up against an old tramp, even if he's not as feeble as his body suggested.

The dark side of London could indeed turn out to be much darker than I ever imagined. Must buy a camera, see that I get some photographs. Mostly mood pics: the platforms late at night, deserted under the cold lights. The rubbish between the rails. The rails themselves as metal fingers creeping out of the tunnels. And the tunnels, those black gasping mouths. And the signboards, pointing to where?

GLEN CANMOOR (continued):

Here ends the written notes, and the final story begins. He sounds quite absurd, that Danny Vermeert, doesn't he? Well, wait till you read the transcript of his final tape. As I said, he used a small portable recorder with a very sensitive inbuilt microphone. Must have had it hanging around his neck most of the time. There are many sub noises and white noise, some passages are so hard to understand that they were left out of the transcript. But nowhere was anything added. This is what Danny Vermeert met in the subway, deep down there...

ITEM OF EVIDENCE 6: TRANSCRIPT OF THE CASSETTE OF DANNY VERMEERT.

I found him again. The murderous old tramp. He's sitting in the carriage next to mine in the subway train. We just left South Kensington Station on the District Line, going west. I can see him through the small window in the door between the carriages. I've been following him for the last hour. He never leaves the subway. I suddenly spotted him on the platform of Cannon Street Station, and since then we've been on about every line. What does he want? Where is he going? He can't live down here in the subways... or can he? Does he have a normal place to go?

I take care not to be seen by him, he must be able to recognise me as the man who saw what he did last night. I could have warned a policeman, but for what? They didn't believe my story. So now I'm on his trail on my own.

Sometimes he stays on a platform for a long time, letting several trains pass. He's always looking around, observing... what or who? The other travellers? Blindly looking for another victim, or hunting for somebody specific? I'm keeping my distance but I don't let him out of my sight.

Much later. And already very late. Not many people around now, some of the platforms we walk are almost deserted. Haven't let him get out of my sight. Always try to keep one wagon between us. Even in the stations when he's switching lines I always keep out of his direct line of sight. Maybe I should try to find a cop but that's risking his disappearance. Can't do that. Wish I had brought a camera, with a sensitive film I would've been able to get his photograph without a flash warning him. My stomach isn't quite right, the after effects of the beers last night. Also haven't eaten anything this evening, no time, can't risk losing him again. Many of the stations we are passing through are desolate, at many there are construction works going on, except now nobody's working.

No idea what time it is since I lost my watch. Late, that's certain though it's been hours since I saw daylight... or evening light. We're staying underground. Not many people around now, and the trains are less frequent also. Gets harder following him without him noticing me. But I'm very careful, and he never looks behind. I have seen what he can do but I feel confident, and he's smaller than me.

The train stops and I see that he gets up. He holds tight to the hanging straps and through the small window I see his hands, again that wavelike movement of the muscles under his skin. His fingers are long and slender, his fingernails long and dirty, but I see no knives or anything like that. Maybe he's not hunting tonight?

He gets off the train, I follow him. About five people on the platform. Big posters apologising for the debris because of construction works going on. Some walls are partly broken down, stacks of stones and sacks of concrete everywhere. No workers around right now.

The train doors drift shut, the train leaves in a silent hush of air. Why is everybody standing still on the platform? Only a young woman is moving, walking towards the stairs leading to the exit. The vagrant is closing in on her.

He trips her from behind. She goes down. Her face smacks onto the stones, her handbag goes flying. He is on her back in an instant, moving so very quickly. I can't believe my eyes. There are four people standing around them, why don't they do something?

I start running. The woman is screaming. She is blond... was blond, her hair is turning red. I clasp the tramp by his shoulder and tear him away from the woman, throw him aside. His stretched fingers are red and dripping, his mouth open, slime on his chin, glittering between his yellow-brown teeth. The woman pushes up, trying to get up, turns over. Blood is spurting from deep cuts in her neck and throat. She throws her head back and forth, oozing blood on the platform in deep red gulps.

Do something! The others are standing around us, as frozen statues, just staring. Witnesses, now I have witnesses!

Then he's getting up. I see his eyes... I see their eyes, all their eyes. Staring white globes with minuscule dark pupils, swollen eyelids. I understand.

Parasites. Not one, but a group, a pack of predators. They're not hiding in the tunnels as I thought, they're all around us by day, walking the platforms, riding the trains, unnoticed by the crowds of people acting out their boring everyday lives, looking at the signs hidden from normal travellers, looking for the right victims, waiting for the right time. As here, and now.

The tramp is standing in front of me, his body is shaking and wriggling as if he's having cramps, but it's those muscles working all over his body, making it twitch in the after-frenzy of the bloodlust, or whatever possesses him. He's looking at me, but does he really see me? There is no intent, no focus, his eyes look like blank cameras, observing, filing for future reference. There is no emotion.

The woman's body is between us on the concrete platform. She's making gurgling sounds, breaking her fingernails as they claw on the concrete. Her mouth is open, blood is running from her lips mixed with saliva, but most is just pumping out of the wounds of her throat. It's making a wet corona around her head, a dying queen with a red silk crown. She lifts her shoulders, manages to get her upper body up from the ground, stretching one supplicating hand at me, then she loses her strength and falls down on her back. Her legs kick once, twice, then she lies still, life drifting away in a pool of her blood. Appealing fresh warm blood, its sickeningly smell rises into my nostrils.

The others get closer, they start to crowd us. They stretch their arms, their fingers twitching as small tentacles. They reach for the blood.

The train... when is the next train? A train with passengers, maybe with some kind of security agent... No train is coming. I am pushed aside, the pack crushes down on her body, they cover it with hands and fingers, heads and mouths. Wingless vultures. The horror of it is that they make no sounds. No slobbering, no smacking of lips, no sucking noises. They are feeding utterly silently, as vampiric ghosts.

Only the tramp remains standing, he has had his first taste of her. His arms, free from the sleeves of his jacket, are thick and pulsing with movement, the veins, or whatever they are, dark red, his long fingers are wriggling in all directions, not as fingers can move, they wriggle like tentacles or snakes. Then he comes at me. His face shows only the drained emotion I have learned to know, but I know he recognises me.

Before me the pack is feeding on the now dead woman, their backs are shivering, they are writhing as if they're having a sexual encounter, backsides and legs shaking, feet thrashing against the concrete.

The exit is behind me. I know I can make it, as the thing advances on me, his hands and fingers waving at me as if he is smelling me. But strangely enough I don't feel fear, only revulsion, and anger. Anger at this being and his mates. These things, what are they, what right do they have to prey on my species? I take a few stumbling steps back, looking around for a weapon, anything. The construction site, the stones, and a shovel. I bend and grab it, and as he comes at me I swing the shovel. It is sharp and my aim is perfect.

His hand is cut off at the wrist and thrown with a wet smacking sound against the wall of the platform, then falls down on the concrete. A neat cut, a red star on the wall. He doesn't react, just stares at the blood spurting stump where his hand was.

The hand on the floor... moves. The fingers move, crawl, a sickening spider leaving a red slimy trail.

He stares at it and then bends down to pick the horrible thing up with his left hand. I lift the shovel and strike again. And again. Don't dare to think about what I'm doing, just want to hit him, hit it! I hear the sound of his skull cracking, hot wetness spitting on my face and hands, and then he's up, his left hand grabbing me, I scream, his nails bite through my wrist, hurt, it hurts, his face a split melon oozing grey red mass, these are not brains, a crawling red mass of things. He lifts himself on my arm, his open mouth comes at me, the teeth thin and long and sharp, deadly needles coming at my face, god, this thing should be dead, should be dead... kick it strongly... loosens its grip for a second long enough tear my hand free blood on my wrist lift the shovel down down... fountain of red things as if his skull is spitting them out red hole where head was head hanging loose mouth still moves needle teeth clash hit again again split it open in the chest and it goes down.

It goes down finally, and I'm still standing, the shovel in my hands. I hear crackling sounds as ribs splintering, opening up, I see what is inside not innards god what is this partly smashed, partly rotting red but not that green blue between those ribs is something else all connected as threads an unearthly system of nerves and muscles or whatever but it's all alive. Alive crawling things, things too small to see what they are bugs or roaches or spiders too many of them all connected thousands of them filling his body being his body spilling out of the holes I made and then regrouping as soldiers as an army getting back inside.

That caused the muscle movements that was what needed the blood inside him keeping him alive keeping IT alive even when I killed it keeping every part of IT alive and reforming it.

It gets up. The crawling insides are oozing out but it still gets up. The right arm is gone, a stump hanging uselessly, the head is hanging by a few muscles on the neck but the lips are moving, the teeth are grinding, the open oozing innards are pulsating not by a heartbeat but by the thousands or millions of small things inside it.

I'm bleeding from tens of small cuts and bites on my hands and arms, my palms are wet with my blood and the ooze he spat on me. As the thing shambles towards me I hit it again and again, have to finish this thing, have to stop this nightmare. Smash the shovel into the moving innards, kill hundreds or thousands of those things crash his body against the wall, and it still comes back. The innards ooze over the wall, across the floor and come back to the body, crawl back inside, leave no trace of blood or anything on the wall or the concrete, probably even take their dead back inside the host body. It keeps on living, keeps on moving.

A sudden sharp pain in my leg, look down, the solitary right hand claws into my leg, nails through my trouser legs into my flesh burn like acid cut on it with the shovel, cut it in two, keeps moving, fingers stuck onto my flesh, grasp them loose and throw them away.

The others are rising from their feast. Two of them are taking the emptied body of the woman, dragging it towards the waiting mouth of the tunnel. Not a spot of blood on the concrete, they licked it clean. When the next train arrives, there will be nothing left, no traces of what happened here. The others are turning toward me, shouldering with their crushed yet still living friend. Their faces are dead, just lifeless masks, their eyes biological cameras, alive only their bodies, their stretched arms, the reaching hands and fingers with long nails.

They are slow. Logic. Think. Any moment a train must come in. But what if on that train are only more of them? This time of night, what if only the predators travel? These zombies, these undead things possessed by an alien life.

They approach. They don't try to keep up the human appearance of movement, no longer necessary here and now. All parts of their body seem to act and move on their own, shaking, wriggling, stumbling... sickening, unnatural, but moving and approaching. I still have the shovel, but... the tramp with his hanging head, two, four others. They've come back from the tunnel where they hid the body, and there's more of them now, more than those who got off the train. Maybe by day when they are riding the trains, they in some way control their body movements, making them appear as normal people. Normal, but in a big city, who cares. Now they act as what they are: vessels for something else, something inside them, using their bodies as cover, as clothing, living them. Their bodies must have been human once but now they're just marionettes, puppets, and the thousands or million puppet masters are inside, controlling them, using them.

No way they will stop me. I feel strong, righteous. These monsters will not stop me. I feel high, never took any drugs but this is what it must feel like. I can take them on, all of them. I attack first, get three

264

of them with one stroke of my shovel, smash one head with the blade, throw two aside, one on the rails. Second move, cut midways with the blade, Jezus, their bodies are soft, cut one in half, spilling all its insides on the platform, oozing moving mass immediately crawling together, two parts fall and jerk on the platform, then red things out of them, clasping together, pulling the body together again, fixing it.

Turn, run away, exit, up the stairs, nothing I can do down here. Up the stairs, exit notices, where? Another stairway, splits, what side to take? No time to read the signs, WAY OUT, get up, get out.

Stop, have to catch my breath, my hand hurts, burns. Fingers burn, can hardly move them.

No sounds behind me. Maybe they have left. Hiding in the tunnels with the dead drained bodies of their victims. How many people disappear in London every year? Tramps, drunks, drifters, runaways, people no one will miss. They hunt their victims, search for them. No idle choices, there's a pattern here. How many tourists never go back? Who knows where they've gone? Missing, sure, but where?

Another stair, these fucking subway stairs. Ah, the kiosk of the ticket collector. Nobody there! Chuckle, wouldn't know where I put my ticket to give him. Last stairs up.

Scream, yell. Iron bars, the exit is closed with an iron gate! Past the hour of the last train, the exit is closed. Can't GET OUT CAN'T GET OUT!

The lights are dimming. Can't be! But they do. They are cutting off circuits somewhere down there. Darkness closing in. Looking through the gate, no way I can open this. Don't even know in which station I'm in, see street lights to the left, that's it. Grasp the bars, prison bars, chains, a strong lock. Start screaming, this is a street, someone must hear me!

Stop after some time. Seconds, minutes, useless. No human on the streets, what time is it, no idea, in what part of London am I, no idea. The bars are wet, not rain, warm wet with blood from the many cuts in my hands. The blood is black in the scarce light from outside.

Sounds. I hear them. They are still there, coming up, slowly, surely. They are many, they feel strong yet they fear me. Let them come, I still have the shovel. Back against the iron gates, I can beat them off, even till daylight, someone will come to open the gate in the morning. I hope. I think. I must believe.

Cut them into a thousand pieces of whatever they are, I will, won't get me, no way, no fucking way, don't want to die here, down here, no, will not die here, bled to death by those things, those insects, those parasites, to feed them, to give them my body to wear as a coat to find new victims.

Sit back, relax for a moment, they don't come closer yet. That's what they do, use the blood, feed on the innards and then take the bodies, the skin, the clothes, dress up in them, wear them and look like a human, maybe smell a bit but useful to get along, to ride the trains.

They are coming up the stairway. See the first shadows, the one without the head is among them. Head now loose, cut from his body, has it under his left arm as a trophy. Eyes stare at me, the mouth still moves.

I'm going to put this recorder beyond the gates, so they won't get it. Strange, don't know what will happen to me, will they get me, will I get out, but I don't feel afraid. No, don't lie, I'm afraid, but most of all I'm angry at those things. Recorder outside, hope the batteries will hold long enough to keep on recording whatever happens. You whoever finds it, bring it to the police, let them hear what's on it. Let them know what's down here in the subways.

So, that's it. Come on now, you! Someone will learn what happens here. Come on, creeps, taste my shovel, what are you waiting for? Need any more severed hands, any more crushed heads?

Fuck, I sound as if I'm drunk. I feel strange. As if I can take on the whole world. Think. Logic. I feel insane. I think insane. This is not me. Should be shitting my pants but I'm just waiting for them to make their move. Ready to get them. Oh yes, gonna get them. Feel strong, feel powerful.

There they are. Coming up, so slowly, so careful. God, those things oozing in their open bellies, their gasping mouths. Losing every aspect of humanity now. They fill the stairway but they don't come closer. They just wait. They can get all over me, what chance do I have with this stupid shovel against a dozen of them?

I feel sick, have to throw up, suddenly, baagghh, all over my pants and shoes. All exhalation suddenly gone, as if the fear burst open, filling me as a deadly flower. Suddenly scared, so scared, what have I done to deserve this, what have I been thinking these last hours? Don't want to die like this, not here, with my back against those locked gates, eaten alive by those bloodsucking things.

Something wet running down my legs, warm and stinking, pissing myself. Don't want to die here in the darkness.

What are they waiting for? They are so many, why don't they just attack, right now, finish it off? The only sound is my own breathing, those things don't make a sound.

Then... a sound! A car. Sudden flash of lights across wet stones. I put my hand outside the gates, I scream, and then the car is gone in a flash. Has the driver seen me? Not a chance. The entrance with the gate to the subway is in the dark. If he saw anything, what? A drunk inside the subway, putting his arm out?

I sit up, my fingers burn, they lose their grip on the shovel. It goes down the stairs, clattering on the steps. My stomach is burning too, I have cramps. My head bends forwards, I throw up again, not much left however to vomit. Bitter taste in my mouth, emptiness in my head. Brains feel like a big empty place, full of white light and nothing else. Except the signs, the patterns, rushing along the walls inside my skull, flashing black and red, don't know what they mean, what they're trying to tell me. Going insane at last. Took me a long time. Funny, haha.

Feel sick, very sick, cramps tearing my stomach apart, then racing along my spine, my back hits the gate, back of my head hurts. Legs give out on me, fall down on my knees on the stairs, my head above the darkness down there, see them there, staring up at me, waiting, for what?

No, won't get me, you creeps, see the shovel, stair just below me, stretch my fingers, but they don't obey, can't grasp the shovel. Another cramp, fall sideways, curling up, pain is awful, scream, scream, pain doesn't stop, then turns back into sickness, all over my body. Lie on my left side, curled up as a baby, knees against my stomach, feet sticking out, crazy, elbows sticking into my stomach, hands stretched out. Have to ward them off, that's what I'm doing, isn't that what I'm doing?

Cramps in my spine, stretching my head back, hard against the gates, hurts, all muscles of my body move and contract, shakes, hot and cold alternate through my veins, burn and shiver, ice and hot desert roll over me, crush me, bury my mind.

See my hands, in front of me, skin moving, veins growing and throbbing with a life of their own, skin shifting, skin drifting, flesh loose and giving away.

To what?

The wounds, the bites in my hands and arms, and legs. That's why they wait. They infected me! Whatever is inside them, they put it inside me, it runs through my blood now, infects my body, changes it.

No, no, NO! Don't want to become like them, don't want to be one of them. Crush my teeth, bite on my tongue, taste my own blood in my mouth. Not one of them! This is my body, I own it, I will command it.

Order the muscles in my hands to move, they obey, stretch my fingers, move them, one nail bites into concrete and breaks, no pain, strange, no pain, no nail.

My fingers move, I order them to move but they go in another direction. Come closer, then the broken nails clasp my arms, bite into my flesh, crawl up, stop them, can't stop them! Help me, somebody help me, stop them, stop them! Try with all my will but inside my brain is only an empty space filled with weird symbols I can't understand but my body understands them, reacts to them, interprets them.

Hands clasp my arms, rip through flesh straight to the bone, blood runs wet, but as snails they glide upwards. Closer to my face, two white things streaked with blood, gliding up my blood, want to shake them off, my brain is screaming, ordering them to back off, body doesn't respond, frozen, a bag of flesh and innards, waiting, waiting there for them. Coldness all over, all inside, stomach of ice, lungs screaming for air, muscles frozen, except those hands, up at my face now. In front of my eyes, rising up as red soaked spiders, fingers spreading open as flower stalks, see finger tops opening under the nails, under the nails flesh opens, flowers of flesh opening and showing me mouths, many small mouths with many small teeth, every finger a nail as a dagger ready to open the waiting flesh and below a greedy mouth with teeth, coming down, all coming down into my eyes and my cheeks and lips and oh god—

My fingers are eating me!

GLEN CANMOOR (continued):
The rest of the tape consists only of sounds. Slurping, sucking, smacking sounds. And the screaming. No use putting that on paper, so you're spared them. I heard the original tape, tried to get a copy for you but that didn't work out, so you're spared that. You don't look so good, if you don't mind me saying so. Frankly, after reliving this stuff again, I can use a drink. I have a very nice malt here. Yep, I suspected you could use one too. So here goes. Cheers, up yours!

Well, that's better. Danny Vermeert was not recovered. Or maybe, parts of him. Some things they found in the tunnels were... never to be identified as belonging to someone specific. DNA research wasn't used at that time. You see, maybe they just wanted him for food and for his skin, but then they would have taken him themselves. He had only the shovel, and there were many of them. But they let him eat himself. So I think they found him good enough to let him become one of them. With his obsession for hidden signs, he knew far more about them than they did themselves, only he hadn't realised it. It's a personal opinion but I think he became one of them, maybe one of those who were destroyed by the flame throwers they used down there, or maybe one of those that got away.

Did we get them all? Well, the public announcements and the big chiefs said we did. Of course we didn't, how could we, at that time we had no idea what they were. At that time we all had our own ideas of what these creatures were, and where they had come from. Some thought they had come from space, millions of years ago, and had been hiding in the bowels of the earth, till something liberated them, maybe even the excavation for the Underground, 170 years ago. At that time there had already been weird accidents and killings, tales of cannibalistic drifters in the hidden tunnels. Maybe they were alien but they surely adapted to this world. Nature and evolution never stop, maybe even our hi-tech world now is only a further step on the ladder, to whatever lies at the end for humanity. Or for them. But dear me, I'm rambling on. Just had to keep you occupied for a bit longer.

What's the matter? Itch in your fingers, your neck? Don't worry. It'll pass. Can't move your arms, your legs? Yes, I know. The drug is tak-ing effect. Don't worry, it won't hurt you. Just make you relax.

See, take humans and cancer. A dead end, a wild growth of cells, intent on the stupid idea of destroying its own host. Typical earth style, kill the host and you die yourself. Cancer is not intelligent, it's a very stupid mechanism, but it kills nevertheless. Now imagine a non-organic being developing some kind of cancer, a wild growth of its own cells. But not to destroy but to grow, get more, get smarter. Absorbing others, strengthening its own entity. Not killing but changing the cells, making every newly absorbed cell part of the one big entity. Every life form needs growth. Normal cancer grows and then destroys itself. This one doesn't. Development, procreation, survival of the fittest. Everywhere in the universe, even in those spaces and on those alien worlds beyond the Mouths which brought them forth.

Surviving has always been a big thing on this planet. Some don't, the dodo and the dinosaur didn't, the chicken did, as did the human being in several stages of evolution.

They who came here, spread over millions of years, knew this very well, though at first it must have been very primal. They came down before man walked the earth, beings which had very little organic matter. They were patterns, beings of alien energy using what matter they needed to give them some sort of bodies, some shapes. They mingled with the air and the sea and the earth, were given names in myths and legends, Wendigo, Cthulhu, Nyarlathotep, Cyäegha, and all the others. They don't mingle much, though lately they are communicating through their servants as they're getting more powerful, obtaining an insight in what they are and what they want. They still hate each other, but they don't interfere. They came down on this world and somehow this little intelligence of the humans is useful, every bit helps. Every new disciple becomes part of the whole but retains a bit of his own identity. The Feeders are part of such an entity, a bodiless being, a gigantic mathematical pattern. As the children of Dagon serve Cthulhu, so the Feeders are its servants. Vermeert began to see beyond the symbols, but he was wrong when he thought of them just as ciphers. They are all parts of the whole being, the whole subways with its many layers and levels, is one gigantic secret code, one entity: a balled fist against the Elder Ones, wherever these cursed ones went. It has no name, it needs no name, we just think of it as That Which Is, or: We. We feel the whole, but realise we are only a small part of it, small fragments of one of those things you would call Gods. You have given them names, even places where they rest and wait, like R'lyeh.

That hardly matters to us, we cannot fully grasp (and don't dare to) the totality of That Which Is. We are only the pawns, the foot soldiers. A simple rule is: every human dies, accidents, old age, sickness, war. Every human wants to survive. They believe in heaven but no one can prove it exists. Give a terminal cancer patient a choice: dying of the disease or living on in some kind of form, what do you think he'll take? No matter what gods you pray to, every living thing wants to survive. Go beyond death and see what's there.

Every form of life had to learn if it wants to survive. Life itself is a continuous struggle, adapting to new circumstances and conditions, and in the meantime getting a constant flow of new information which builds the intelligence, and makes the entity itself stronger, more conscious of what it is, what it can do, what it wants. That is what it wants from us: growth, strength.

I was down with my fellows in the tunnels during the cleaning and at the time I thought I knew it all, we'd kill and burn those murdering bastards, whatever they were, wherever they had crawled from.

Then they took the case out of my hands. Rather a disappointment. My life had been my job at the police force. I never married, my work was my life, and then they took it all away from me, orders of some big shots, and I was kindly asked to retire early.

Of course now I know much more of it, know how they manipulate everybody, how they cover it all up. But at that time in my life, suddenly I was alone. Loneliness is a kind of cancer too, it grows in your mind and will destroy you if you let it go on.

Then you go in search for the answers they've taken away from you. You go in search for others who think like you, feel like you. In fact you need a new world, one you can still be part of. I knew parts of the real story, but when and how it got me, I never knew. Maybe someone touched me in a crowd, maybe I touched an object which was already infested. It doesn't really matter. Vermeert ate himself because he got bitten and cut by the others, but it doesn't have to be that way. The total being is only part organic, and that part is us, the once-humans, the servants, the Feeders. It spreads other ways too, like how it started getting to Vermeert but not strong enough: by signs, tokens, symbols. Its ways have changed since Vermeert. That Which Is got me and it took me some time to accept what had happened... but then, I had no choice left. I began to understand, I began to see, for the first time I began to SEE what reality was. How I could fit in. And I did, as so many others before me have done. There's no choice, but once you accept it for what it is, you blossom open, you see, you know, you feel, you ARE. Part of the whole, part of the enormous godlike being. You become part of We. You'll live forever, you know you're only a pawn in this play, a microscopic part of its being, but you also remain yourself. You're just different, discover other worlds, and other needs. Accept and adapt, that's all it needs. You see me at this moment with those two stupid organic cameras you call your eyes, I see you, I feel you, I taste you with every cell of my body. I even see you with the ten mouths in my fingers.

Don't worry. The door is locked. Nobody knows you're here except me. The drug I have given you isn't very heavy, you can scream if you want to, but it won't be much use. Nobody in the apartment except us.

You don't have to be afraid. In fact, I'm certain you'll be grateful to me.

I'm part of the entity, but as a part I still have my own small needs.

Just want to touch you now. Right under your eyes. See, it doesn't hurt, just let my fingers glide in.

NOTES ON THE STORIES

Composed Of Cobwebs is based on real incidents, the feeling of isolation and loneliness. Everything happened except for the murder. Originally written in English 1971 as 'Walking on the Edge of Night', based on real events and the poem 'In Ruins' by G. E. Symonds. Published in the Netherlands, and in Belgium as a special illustrated folio, and in France. In English published in *Return From The Grave*, UK (1976) and USA (1977), in *Murder Most Foul (1984)*. Parts of it were made into a short movie *Make-Up in Blood* in 1976.

Ten. Students and teachers, the arrogance of some, the vengeful hatred of others, turned out this tale. Originally written as 'When You'll Be Ten' in Dutch in 1985, winner of an award for original crime stories in Belgium. Published in Belgium and the Netherlands. Rewritten and updated in English in *Cemetery Dance*, USA (2005).

A Taste of Rain and Darkness. I have a horror of violence, which is why it so often graphically turns up in my work, to show how ugly it is. Here I wondered how Hell would be for an undead murderer. Originally written in 1962 in Dutch as 'To Walk the Night', rewritten in English in 1969. Published four times in Dutch and French as 'Out of a Curtain of Rain and Darkness'. Published in English in *Weird Window* 1, UK (June 1970) and in *Bizarre Fantasy Tales* 1, USA (Fall 1970).

I Wonder What He Wanted. I wanted a very stylish and classic supernatural story but all told between the lines. Originally written in Dutch in 1964 as 'Metempsychosis', rewritten in English as 'A House with a Garden' in 1970, rewritten as 'I Wonder What He Wanted' in 1970. Published in the Netherlands, Germany and Spain. In English in *The Year's Best Horror Stories 1*, UK (1971), *The Year's Best Horror Stories Series 1*, USA (1972 and 1975), and as 'A House With a Garden' in *Weirdbook 5*, USA (1972).

A Whisper of Leathery Wings. Everybody likes a good monster now and then, trying to get you. Originally written in English in 1973

273

as 'Demon Mask'. Published in the Netherlands, in Spain and France. In English in *Fantasy Crossroads 9*, USA (1976). Just for fun I also turned it into an erotic horror novel 'The Carnal Desires of the Witch' in 1977 for a cheap men's magazine in Belgium. It paid more than the literary publications!

The Taste of Your Love. Inspiration here were a few visits to discotheques in Italy, many years ago. Originally written in English as 'A Drink of Dark Wine' in 1969, rewritten as a straight horror version 'The Taste of Your Love' in 1969, published together as a two-parter 'The Twisting Ways Of Love' in Dutch. Separate publications in the Netherlands, France and Japan. In English in *The Year's Best Horror Stories III*, USA (1975), *The First Orbit Book Of Horror Stories*, UK (1976), *The Best Horror Stories*, UK (1977, 1984, 1985). Just for fun: for those last three I never was paid, I bought them all second hand without knowing they had been published.

The Whispering Horror. The whispering horror was my first professional sale, based on my childhood nightmares. Originally written in Dutch in 1964 as 'In the Cellar', rewritten in English in 1966 as 'Whisper of Terror', then twice rewritten as 'The Whispering Horror' and 'Let Me Whisper To You' in 1967. Published in the Netherlands and France. In English in *The Ninth Pan Book of Horror Stories*, as 'The Whispering Thing' in *Weird Terror Tales* 1, USA (1969/1970) and as 'Let Me Whisper To You' *in Shadow Fantasy Literature Review* 3, UK (1969).

 The Man Who Collected Eyes was based on an episode when I was eight or nine years old, my mother had an accident with her motorbike and was over a year in a hospital. During that time I lived with a protestant preacher. Every morning when I woke up and opened my eyes, I saw that poster on the wall with the triangle and the watching eye of God. Originally written in Dutch as 'Eyes' and 'The Most Beautiful Thing in the World' in 1963, rewritten in English in 1969. Published in the Netherlands, Austria and France, became a radio-play in Belgium. In English in *Shadow Fantasy Literature Review 6*, UK (1969) and *Starling Mystery Stories 16*, USA (1970)

Belinda's Coming Home! Originally written in English as 'The Night Lucy Came Home' in 1982 for one of my own magazines, I just wanted to write a real nasty story. Rewritten and greatly expanded under new title in Dutch and in English in 1984 as 'The Night After Belinda Came Home', 'Belinda's Homecoming' and the final title. Published in Belgium and the Netherlands. In English in *Dunwich Dreams 2* (1982), *Alone On The Darkside*, USA (2006).

Like Two White Spiders. Don't tell me you never had the idea your hands were doing things on their own? Originally written in Dutch as 'Hands' in 1962, rewritten in English in 1971. Published under various titles 'As Two Big White Spiders', 'Like Two White Spiders', 'Two White Spiders', in the Netherlands and Germany. In English in *The Year's Best Horror Stories 3*, UK (1973), *The Year's Best Horror Stories Series 2*, USA (1974), *The Century's Best Horror Fiction Vol. 2*, USA (2011).

Dunwich Dreams, Dunwich Screams. The plain house I live in is called Dunwich House, because of my admiration for Lovecraft and his story 'The Dunwich Horror'. Only later I learned about the real Dunwich in England, the history of which I turned into a novel for younger readers 'The Ghost of Dunwich'. The theme was a bit too adult, so finally I rewrote it and turned it into a mythos story. This story is based on my own visit to Dunwich, and my research there. It continues my "European' cycle" of Mythos stories, begun with 'Darkness, My Name Is' and others. I always wanted to write a story about the real Dunwich, England, incorporating its weird history into the Mythos. Mainly because 'The Dunwich Horror' was the story which really got me hooked on Lovecraft, when I was much younger, and I always wondered why Lovecraft, with his enormous knowledge of British history, had never used the real Dun'ich. Well, I did it now, as my tribute to HPL. I have taken some literary liberties setting the first great destruction of Dunwich in 1537 because the political and religious upheavals in the 16th century were better suited for a good story, and made a better link with the Mythos. But most of what you've read here is factual. As a Mythos reader, the choice is up to you to what is fact... and what is fiction. Originally written in Dutch 1993-1994 as a YA novel 'The Banshee of Dunwich' published as 'The Ghost of Dunwich' in 1995; adult rewrite in English and expansion 1997-1998. In English in *The Black Book* (on internet), UK; *Tales Out Of*

Dunwich, USA (2005).

Behind The White Wall. Originally written in horror and science fiction versions in Dutch as 'Dialogue with Nowhere' in 1964, the horror version rewritten in English in 1970. Published in Belgium, the Netherlands and Germany. Was made into a very nice short horror film *Flash-Black* in 1975. In English in *Weirdbook 12*, USA (1977).

Something Small, Something Hungry was written after I had read an overdose of Theodore Sturgeon stories, and really wanted to write something as good as he did. I don't think I managed but still like it. Originally written in 1970, a bit of a tribute to the works of Sturgeon. Published in the Netherlands and France in an abridged version. In English in *Weirdbook 13*, USA (1978). Special anecdote: in 1976 it was rejected because it was just too long by... my dear David Sutton! I'm so glad he's now using the long version.

My Fingers Are Eating Me. Originally written 1983 in Dutch, published as 'Under your skin' (1984), turned into a Young Adult novel 'Metro of fear' (1992), turned into a radio play 'Underground' (1996). For some years a Dutch movie was planned by a young and gifted director, but lack of financial backing caused him to drop it. This mythos version was written in 2005 for a cancelled anthology, unpublished until now. This story was originally inspired by my first visit to London in 1970 or 1971, and the way I was impressed by the huge Tube system which at some time I began to see (as does Vermeert in the story) as an enormous semi-mechanical and psychic being with an identity of its own. One late evening, getting out on a deserted station platform, I went up the staircase... and found out that the exit was locked off by a steel gate. Of course I just went down again and took the next train to the next station where I got out, but it was an unsettling moment. Back in Belgium I wrote a four page synopsis with notes, but (as I had lots of other commissioned writings to do in that time) only got back to the story in April 1983, when I wrote a much shorter version in Dutch, under its present title. The story was written for a literary contest for original SF & fantasy stories in the Netherlands, but alas, the jury hated gory horror. It went out to various publishers (including the Dutch version of *Playboy*) and they all hated it. In 1984 I expanded it and retitled it 'Onderhuids' (Under Your Skin) for an original horror anthology I was editing for a Belgian publisher. The deal fell through but that version finally saw print in *Ragnarok*, a Dutch original anthology in 1993. In 1991 I turned the main theme into a YA horror novel 'Metro van de Angst' (Subway of Fear) which was published in the Netherlands in 1992, got into several reprints and four separate editions (including a full length reading by my daughter Brenda as an audiobook), and still is one of my best selling books. I adapted it into a 16 minute radio play *Ondergronds* (Underground) in 1995, which went out on Dutch radio in January 1996. I started an English translation but then in 1997 Guilermo del Toro's *Mimic* movie came out. Reading the first reviews, I thought "Hell, that's my story!": it had a subway and insects masquerading as humans to hunt their victims. Of course, del Toro couldn't have read one of my originals and the movie (based on Donald Wollheim's story) proved sufficiently different, but I lost interest in the translation. Those pages somewhere got lost in my files as I pursued other stories and markets. Though those earlier versions lacked direct references to the Cthulhu Mythos, it has always been a claustrophobic Lovecraftian story to me, so it was a pleasure to adapt it once again and now into my European version of the Mythos, making links to 'Darkness, My Name Is', 'The Waiting Dark', and others. This final version (again under its very first title) has been totally rewritten, updated and expanded to the present form, in September-November 2005.

Also available from
Shadow Publishing

Phantoms of Venice
Selected by David A. Sutton
ISBN 0-9539032-1-4

The Satyr's Head: Tales of Terror
Selected by David A. Sutton
ISBN 978-0-9539032-3-8

The Female of the Species And Other Terror Tales
By Richard Davis
ISBN 978-0-9539032-4-5

Frightfully Cosy And Mild Stories For Nervous Types
By Johnny Mains
ISBN 978-0-9539032-5-2

Horror! Under the Tombstone Stories from the Deathly Realm
Selected by David A. Sutton
ISBN 978-0-9539032-6-9

www.ingramcontent.com/pod-product-compliance
Lightning Source LLC
Chambersburg PA
CBHW031102260626
47172CB00001B/189